WINDFALL

WINDFALL

Michael D. Hartley

Library of Congress Control Number: 2017903903
ISBN: Hardcover   978-1-5245-9181-6
                Softcover   978-1-5245-9182-3
                eBook   978-1-5245-9183-0

Print information available on the last page.

Rev. date: 03/31/2017

To order additional copies of this book, contact:
Xlibris
1-888-795-4274
www.Xlibris.com
Orders@Xlibris.com
748575

For Rosemary Large

CHAPTER 1

THE LIFE OF THE TEACHER of economics at the State University of Zanzibar ended when he stopped after work for a beer at the seafront Mbuyuni pub on Mizingani Road. At the bar's entrance, Jomo Willow climbed out of his chauffeur-driven Mercedes and hurried through brass-studded wooden Arab doors to an enclosed courtyard. The evening air had a dense smell of sun-bleached fish carcasses beached in stagnant tidal pools beside sand traced with the crawl lines of crabs.

Inside the pub's thick walls, Jomo removed his sunglasses and broad-brimmed hat. He sat on a barstool and used a handkerchief to mop sweat off the top of his clean-shaven head. He ordered a Serengeti lager from a tall bartender with skin as coarse and wrinkled as a tortoise's neck. Jomo took a long pull on his beer and stretched out his muscular legs, a broad grin on his face. The professor had reason to celebrate. The manuscript of his new book *The Root Causes of Africa's Economic Stagnation* had arrived on his New York publisher's desk. Adding to his sense of wellbeing, his life at home was a timeless vision. Jomo and his wife Renée had two small children. Along with a one-eyed cat, he lived in a colonial style mansion. Water snakes frequented his garden's ornamental pool and dined on frogs.

Even though window fans sucked out stale air, the pub reeked of cigarette smoke and sweat. At a corner table, neon Tusker beer signs reflected off the shiny faces of two muscular men. They had pronounced facial scars and hair in dreadlocks. Coarsened by the sun and the wind, the faces of the two men combined the mixed features of African tribal brutality and the cruelty of Arab slavers.

Jomo suspected they were criminals from the mainland. He lit a cheroot and breathed out smoke through his nose. He felt the skin on his face shrink and grow hot as the two men nodded at him in a familiar way. Jomo gulped down the remains of his beer. He used the back of his hand to wipe froth off his upper lip. His thirst quenched, he headed for the exit.

Outside the pub, a sea breeze rattled banana leaves, and the sound of a ship's horn wafted in from the bay. When he saw no sign of his Mercedes, Jomo tapped the tips of his tasseled loafers on the pavement. While he waited, he watched two boys kick a soccer ball on the beach. When the men from the bar strolled up behind him, Jomo sensed two sets of narrow obsidian eyes bore into the back of his head.

Almost unnoticed, a thin European entered the square, his gaze fixed on Jomo and the two men. He wore a wrinkled cream tropical suit and a polished pair of crocodile skin boots. The freckles on his face and hands reminded Jomo of the speckles on a fish's belly. His stare appeared innocuous, but to Jomo he seemed oddly menacing. Wrapped in his left hand's tapered fingers, the man pulled out of the folds of his jacket a Glock equipped with a silencer.

Jomo scrambled behind a wall of shattered masonry. He pressed his chest, stomach, and knees into the sharp pieces of brick. He watched the shooter's muffled shot kill one of the men from the bar, a bullet through his heart. His companion withdrew a handgun from his pocket. The shooter proved too quick for him. He fired two shots into his shoulder. His victim dropped his weapon and clutched at the bullet holes, blood flowing through his fingers. On his knees, he pleaded for his life like a squealing warthog stuck on a spike in a trap.

Jomo heard another shot that ended man's cries. It was quiet in the square except for the low moan of the wind. Jomo's throat went dry when he heard the crunch of the shooter's boots on loose gravel. When the shooter stood over him, Jomo glanced up at his sunken cheeks and reddish pencil-thin moustache. His intensely cruel milk-blue eyes made a cold vapor wrap around his heart.

The shooter raised the Glock and pointed the weapon at Jomo. He grinned before firing two bullets into the top of professor's head.

CHAPTER 2

R YAN MOAR NEEDED TIME TO think what he should say to Joanne about going to East Africa. On a narrow path, his wife's terrier trotted beside him. The dog barked when Joanne came out on the deck of the couple's cedar home in North Fargo. The evening sun coated Joanne's blond hair. Her advanced pregnancy gave her face a healthy glow.

"I recognize that special look," Joanne said when he climbed the steps to join her.

She could see determination in Ryan's face. Ryan reached to touch Joanne's hand on the deck's railing.

She frowned. "I need you with me when the baby's born."

Ryan turned to the turbulent river. "I will be back in time."

"I'm surprised Renée could afford you. I don't imagine Jomo's university paycheck amounted to much."

"Renée didn't object when I mentioned my fee." Ryan leaned on the railing and shifted his feet. "Apparently, she lives in a big house with plenty of domestic help."

She leaned down to scratch her terrier's crown. "I'm due in six weeks."

"I'll have things wrapped up long before then."

"You never know how long a murder investigation takes." Joanne's hand clenched on his arm. "Besides, you know nothing about the island's crime situation or its politics." Joanne paused to watch a cabin cruiser on the river, her hair blowing in the breeze. "According to *Planet Travel*, Zanzibar is a dodgy place."

"Renée assured me that the locals are friendly."

"If it's such a congenial island, why did someone murder a harmless academic?"

Ryan massaged Joanne's shoulder; her well-toned muscles felt as taut as cable wire.

"I'll be honest, I don't want you to go," Joanne said. "Apart from tropical heat, think about tsetse flies, yellow fever, malaria, and sleeping sickness." She turned to face him, her face flushed. "Think about our child without a dad."

"I've had all the shots."

"There's been a series of Al-Shabaab terrorist attacks along the Kenya coast."

"I'll take every precaution."

"The East African seashore is prone to cyclones." Joanne wrapped her arms around her chest. "You've always had this phobia of storms."

Slivers of light cut through the poplars and sparkled like fireflies on the river's surface. Ryan bit down on his lower lip, his face rigid.

""You've made up your mind, haven't you?" Joanne said. "You are a selfish bastard."

The Kenya Airways 737 broke through a layer of cumulus on a circuit downwind. Seated by the window, Ryan spotted the steel skeleton of the Zanzibar airport terminal off the starboard wing. When the airliner banked, Ryan saw beaches of white sand on the port side. In the ocean, he recognized the graceful curve of a dhow's lantern sail that rotates to harness wind from any direction.

During the landing, Ryan remained absorbed in the pilot's maneuvers until the aircraft's wheels bumped along the concrete runway and taxied until the crew cut the jet engines.

Ryan stepped out of the air-conditioned cabin onto the ramp's blast furnace heat. Inside the terminal, he hauled his luggage off a carousel. He looked for Renée. The last time he saw his sister-in-law was over a decade ago. Renée had attended a memorial service for her sister Kathy, Ryan's first wife. At the funeral home, Renée had worn her hair as short as wheat stubble. Her slim build and tiny hands gave her the appearance of being younger than a woman in her early twenties. During the service, her expression had remained flat, her eyes empty, as if she had no feelings for her dead sister's passing.

At the terminal's exit, Ryan's cell phone chimed. When he answered, he heard Renée's hoarse voice. "Ryan, thank goodness you're here."

"Why aren't you at the airport?" She remained silent. He could feel a muscle spasm build inside him. "Renée, what's going on?"

"Early this morning, three men broke into our house."

"Are you okay?"

"We're still in shock. Apart from a few bruises, the kids and I are okay. We're staying at the Al Mutlaq Hotel."

"Are you in any immediate danger?"

"We're safe. The hotel is guarded."

"I'll catch a cab and come immediately."

In the background, he heard piping children's voices plead Renée for attention.

"I'm strung out tighter than a kite string," Renée said. "I have to look after the children. They're exhausted and traumatized." Her voice turned to a timorous whisper. "See you in the morning at the Al Mutlaq."

After she disconnected the line, Ryan lined up for a taxi. At the cab stand, a boy with thick veins in his arms caught his eye and half raised his hand in a salute. He had curly hair and the wispy beginnings of a beard. He wore scuffed tennis shoes and a belt high on his hips that held up his khaki cargo pants.

"Want a taxi, sir?" he asked.

Without waiting for a response, he grabbed the handle of Ryan's rolling luggage.

"Do I have a choice?" Ryan said, following the boy and his suitcases.

The boy's broad smile displayed well-formed white teeth. "Bari Khan at your service."

Bari released his grip on the luggage so he could swing his arms in a wide gesture, culminating in a clasp of hands, followed by the holding of thumbs and a second handshake. Bari's shoulder muscles flexed under a yellow T-shirt emblazoned with the Tanzanian flag. He stuck two fingers in his mouth and whistled. A rusty Renault drove ahead of the lineup of cabs and slid in beside Ryan. Bari loaded the luggage in the trunk, and he opened the back door. Ryan climbed inside and sat in a seat that smelled of goats.

"Where to?" Bari asked, climbing into the seat beside the driver.

"The Serena Inn."

The taxi's exhaust ejected clouds of black smoke and pulled away from the airport. Proceeding on the left side of the road, the driver honked at a donkey cart and swung around an overloaded bus. When the taxi driver clamped hard on the brake to avoid a rooster, the abrupt halt threw Ryan out of his seat. The beads hanging on the rear-view mirror performed a wild dance.

Bari gripped the dashboard, as Ryan lurched back to his seat.

"Don't worry, Maulvi is a first class driver," Bari said. "He knows shortcuts to keep the fare low."

In a stretch of road beside coconut and clove plantations, the taxi picked up speed. Maulvi slowed down when the car came to a row of banana stalls and booths of animal hardwood carvings on reed mats. The driver then entered in a maze of coral-stone houses with balconies made of filigree woodwork. A fishnet of telephone and power lines stretched across the streets and clung to walls like cobwebs.

"Who taught you English, Bari?" Ryan shouted above an ululating torch singer coming from a ghetto blaster beside the driver.

"Tourists," Bari said, his hair shiny with perspiration.

Maulvi turned a sharp corner and the narrow street gave way to the whitewashed walls of Ryan's hotel. The three-story building had red tiles, barred windows, and mahogany double doors. When the taxi stopped beside clay pots of hibiscus, Bari handed Ryan's luggage to a slight young man in a braided suit.

"Do you know the Al Mutlaq?" Ryan asked Bari when he climbed out of the taxi.

"That hotel is no good. No Wi-Fi, no TVs in rooms, no air-conditioning."

"Will you show me how to get to this hotel tomorrow morning?"

"Okay." Bari turned his face away and pushed at one eye with the heel of his hand. "I know Zanzibar very well."

"Meet me in the lobby at ten." Ryan turned his eyes on Bari. "I want more than a guide, I need a sidekick."

Bari looked puzzled. "What is a sidekick?"

"Someone to keep me out of trouble." Ryan hesitated. "The work I do is sometimes dangerous."

Bari crossed his arms and shrugged. "I'm not afraid."

"What about your parents? Would they worry?"

"They're under the earth."

"Who looks after you?"

His face seemed full of play. "My sister, but I take care of her." Bari glanced at the red glow of the sun on the horizon. "I have to go now."

He gave Ryan a V-sign before he ran down a back lane to the shore littered with beached dhows.

After Ryan checked in and went to his room, he lost none of his paranoia picked up from working under contract for the Central Intelligence Agency. In his hotel suite, he dismantled and reassembled the phone, unscrewed light bulbs, looked under the bed, and opened drawers and clothes closets.

When he didn't find anything suspicious, he strolled outside on the balcony. The lights of yachts and fishing boats reflected off the calm surface of the bay. The moon was white hot in the night sky and humidity hung like a soggy blanket on his shoulders. He went back inside the air-conditioned room and turned on the TV. The lead story on the ten o'clock BBC news covered the failure of an international team of investigators to find suspects in a bomb attack at the Norfolk Hotel in Nairobi. A spokesman from Scotland Yard said no organization had claimed responsibility for the blast. Ryan suspected the bombing was the work of a copycat terrorist, imitating similar attacks on luxury hotels in Jakarta and Mumbai.

He turned off the set, undressed, untied the mosquito net, slipped between crisp cotton sheets, and slept until sunrise.

In the lobby the next morning, Ryan recognized Javed, the hotel receptionist who had carried his luggage to his room. Javed shouted in a shrill voice and waved his arms at Bari, who had just entered the lobby.

"Hang on, he works for me," Ryan said.

Javed stopped yelling at Bari, his face cautionary, his narrow chest rising and falling. He had black slicked down hair and facial skin as smooth as tallow. He made a sucking sound, his dark eyes fluttering as though in a situation beyond his control.

"Beach boys not allowed in this hotel," Javed said, his face becoming a mask of suppressed irritation.

"We connecting here?" Ryan said.

Javed handed Ryan a set of car keys. "Your rental Volvo is parked at the front of the hotel, sir."

Ryan took the keys, and he stalked out of the lobby with Bari. In the parking lot, the salty air hinted of rain. Out of habit, Ryan crouched down to search for any evidence of explosives underneath the Volvo. Satisfied that the vehicle was clear of bombs, he climbed behind the wheel and switched on the ignition. Bari directed him to drive north on the ocean-front Mizingani Road. He drove by the Old British Consulate, the Arab Fort, and a sprawling banyan tree, home to a family of monkeys.

Bari told Ryan to make a right turn on Malindi Road. He then drove down a narrow street until he reached the Al Mutlaq Hotel's weather-beaten sign in front of twin wrought iron gates. The hotel overlooked the sea. A row of satellite dishes on the roof broke the mood of someone's vision of a Moorish palace complete with miniature minarets, balustrades, and wide concrete balconies. The Al Mutlaq dominated a small settlement of shops and ramshackle houses that clung on either side of the hotel like bookends covered in brown fungus.

Ryan parked in a lot inhabited by a flock of crows. On the beach, surf rolled in on white sand. Further out to sea, waves crashed on a distant reef. He walked down a pathway of shell fragments to double doors covered in brass knobs as large as pineapples. When the doors opened, a slim woman in a sari came out to greet him.

"Welcome to the Al Mutlaq," she said in a thick European accent. "I'm Audrey Bradt, the hotel manager. I hope you are coming to stay with us."

"I don't want to disappoint you; I'm here to visit one of your guests, Renée Willow."

Persian carpets covered the lobby's marble floors and inlaid pink seashells decorated the walls. Arabesque arches hung over a mahogany reception desk.

"Renée has taken the children for a walk on the beach," Audrey said. "I'll send a gardener to let her know you have arrived."

Audrey invited him to an outdoor café where fireball lilies in brass pots gave off an intoxicating smell.

"I'm still in shock when I first saw Renée's bruises," Audrey said, seated opposite Ryan.

"She told me about last night's attack," Ryan said.

Audrey curled one tanned leg under the other. "Around two in the morning, Renée and the children arrived at the hotel in a taxi."

"Did Renée describe to you what happened?" Ryan asked, his gaze focused on other diners and servers weaving between wicker tables and chairs.

"She didn't." Audrey raised plucked eyebrows. "When Renée checked in, I'll never forget the raw panic in her children's eyes." Ryan's forehead felt moist in the heat. "She mumbled something about being beaten up by intruders."

"Did she say if she had reported the home invasion to the police?"

"On this island, it wouldn't do much good—the police are often in on these robberies." She leaned forward, her eyes examined him, her breath moved across his face. "The policemen on the beat in Zanzibar are paid so little, they often resort to stealing to supplement their wages."

Ryan examined her eyes, the color of hot chocolate. He suspected that behind the gleam were secrets he needed to know about.

"Why did Renée choose this hotel?"

"The Al Mutlaq belonged to her late husband."

Ryan was surprised Jomo could afford to buy the place on his university teaching salary.

"You mean he owned the Al Mutlaq?" he said, leaning forward.

Audrey nodded, and she used a napkin to dab the corners of her bloodshot eyes. "It's so tragic, Jomo being gunned down in the prime of his life."

"Did you attend his funeral?" Ryan asked, putting on sunglasses to shield his eyes from the glare off the sand.

"I did. His funeral service in the Anglican cathedral attracted many mourners."

"Who came?"

"The university crowd, a smattering of civil servants, students, and European permanent residents on the island."

11

For a moment, the sunlight caught the sheen in Audrey's black hair that she wore piled high on her head like a fur cap.

"After the service, Renée told me she had hired a private investigator from North Dakota to look into the circumstances surrounding her husband's death." Audrey hitched up her red silk tank top and straightened the sari that reached to her ankles. "Judging by your accent, I presume you're the PI." Ryan nodded. "From what I've learned from detective novels, your next question is something innocuous like what was my relationship to the deceased?"

He leaned forward, his brow knitted. "That's a good place to start."

Ryan examined small wrinkles around the skin of her eyes and the delicate shape of her nose that contrasted with the size of her long fingers wrapped around a napkin ring.

"Were you and Jomo good friends?" he asked.

Before Audrey could answer, Ryan heard the soft pad of sandaled feet. A muscular server placed a teapot and two English china cups beside Audrey and left.

"We had a business relationship." Audrey poured the tea and used a strainer to catch the leaves. "Six months ago, Jomo hired me to manage this place."

"Why did he pick you?" Ryan said, glancing at the beach where Bari was talking to a skinny blonde in a bikini.

"I presume he regarded me as the best candidate," she said.

Ryan rubbed stubble on his chin. "Where are you from?"

"I was born in Amsterdam. When I was going to school, my parents moved to London."

"What brought you to Africa?"

Audrey fiddled with a dangling gold earring made from an intricate weave of crescent moons. "Three years ago, my ex-husband and I spent our honeymoon at the Twisted Pines Resort on the island's west coast. Zanzibar's charm captivated us. We, however, saw none of its dark underbelly of poverty and corruption. When we returned to London, James twisted his spine in an industrial accident and received a generous disability pension. We then decided we could afford to live well in Stone Town. You wouldn't believe how far British pounds stretch in this part of the world."

Below a sky filled by a patchwork of puffy clouds, Ryan spotted Bari race to the surf and swim to where the blonde treaded water beyond the breakers.

"We began our new life living in a restored Arab villa," Audrey wetted her lips before she continued. "In six months, our love affair with Zanzibar mutated into the biblical whore of Babylon. We tried to smile at the island's lack of sanitation, ignorance, and backward thinking. As well as the insularity of its Afro-Arab culture that breeds hatred and dissention." She blew out her breath, as though releasing frustration trapped inside her slim frame. "James became enamored with Johnnie Walker and the charms of a local woman who cleaned and cooked for us. Eventually, he became homesick and went back to London to live with his mother. I stayed. After he left, I worked as a recreation director at the Serena until one of my girlfriends told me that Jomo needed a manager to run this hotel."

"Did you mix socially with the boss?" Ryan asked, stretching and interlacing his fingers above his head.

Audrey stared at flapping bedsheets on a clothesline, her face shaded by thick shadow lines from sunlight filtered through venetian blinds. "Naturally, we met at cocktail parties and club socials. Our relationship remained a business one."

Ryan regarded her over the rim of the cup. "When was the last time you saw Jomo alive?"

"He came at his usual time to the hotel on the day he died, about four in the afternoon. He worked out in the gym for half an hour before meeting me in my office."

"What did you two talk about?"

She lowered her long eyelashes, her face colored. "We discussed routine matters: number of guests, payroll, bar sales, garden and beach maintenance."

A fat tortoiseshell cat ambled in from nearby shrubs, arched its back, and rubbed against Audrey's ankles. She leaned over to pinch the cat's spine with her red fingernails.

"When you last met Jomo, did he appear preoccupied or depressed?" Ryan said.

She glanced at him sideways. "Come to think of it, he did mention that he had received some nasty emails."

"Do you know anyone who might want to harm him?"

Audrey shaded her eyes to watch a pleasure craft speed to open water, leaving behind a wide wake of foam. "I can't think of a soul."

A gardener in a stained T-shirt started to sweep sand from a paved path to the beach.

"Did you ever hear any gossip about a university colleague having a grudge against Jomo, or some professor who clashed with him over ideology?" Ryan asked.

Audrey twirled the sunglasses in her hand. "I've never heard his name linked to any university squabbles or backstabbing. As in most academic circles, competition for scarce funding is cutthroat."

"Did you meet any of his colleagues?"

"He sometimes invited professors and students to the hotel for a drink or a meal. Dr. Burton Chilongola was a frequent guest."

"How did Burton and Jomo get along?"

"Not well. I often heard them bicker about economics and politics."

At Ryan's feet, a red-mouthed agama lizard scurried across the pavement.

"Outside of the university, did Jomo have any close friends?" Ryan asked.

Audrey searched for crumbs and brushed them off the table. "He often visited an English widow, Zoe Singh, in her dilapidated villas."

"Is it possible Jomo and Zoe were more than just good friends?"

Audrey threw her head back, her piled hair shaking. Her laughter had a hollow sound like a hoot. "Good heavens, no. She's woman in her nineties."

"Can you think of anyone who profited from Jomo's death?"

Audrey shrugged. "I certainly did. In his will, Jomo left this hotel to me."

CHAPTER 3

When Renée returned from her walk, Ryan pulled his chair closer to her chaise lounge beside the hotel's crescent moon shaped pool. Renée had a cut in the middle of her upper lip and a bruise above her right eye. Her skin had a weathered look from long exposure to the sun. Whenever Ryan caught her eye, her smile flickered on, as if controlled by a light switch. She wore dark horn-rimmed glasses and a white cotton robe over a form-fitting orange swimsuit.

When Ryan's eyes fastened on Renée's angular face, a sudden wave of bitterness haunted him. At his first wife Kathy's funeral, Renée hadn't bothered to say goodbye to her sister at the cemetery. After she had left the reception, she sashayed out on the arm of one of his police colleagues. Renée removed her glasses to expose the full extent of purple bruises around her eyes.

"Who did this to you?" Ryan said.

"A gang of off-duty policemen," she said, glancing at the pool where her two children played in the shallow end.

"How did you know they were cops?"

"I recognized one of them when he removed his mask." Despite the look of pain and enameled grief, her manner turned razor-sharp. "After Jomo's funeral, I found five puff adders slithering on my kitchen floor." She knitted her fingers together between her thighs. "After the gardener used a *panga* to behead these poisonous snakes, I tried to call the police, but someone had cut the telephone line. During the night—after the children and I barricaded ourselves in my bedroom—thugs ransacked Jomo's study. Eventually, the gang broke down the bedroom door." A blotch of color formed at her throat. "The leader threatened to rape me in front of the children. Finally, they let us leave. On our way out to a waiting taxi, my son Daniel discovered our tabby nailed to the front door."

"Why kill the cat?"

"In the nineteen fifties, the Mau Mau in Kenya crucified cats on doors to frighten whites into abandoning their farms."

Ryan removed his aviator glasses. "Why do you think these cops terrorized you?"

"After Jomo's murder, they must've thought that without a man to protect me, I'd be an easy." Renée let loose a long breath. "The state pays policemen a pittance, hardly a living wage. As a result, they periodically raid houses and steal what they can to supplement their wages. But all they took was Jomo's laptop and the contents of his filing cabinet. They ignored appliances, televisions, and Jomo's prize collection of Arab knives."

"Any idea what they wanted from Jomo's files?"

"I haven't a clue."

Ryan clasped his hands around the back of his head, leaned back, and stared at circling gulls.

"What do I know about Jomo's actual murder?" he said.

"Reports are sketchy. No official announcement has been published." Renée's eyes flashed with intensity. "Staff Sergeant Lipumba wouldn't tell me anything. Yet, this morning on the radio, he said the police have a prime suspect. The killer apparently murdered my husband for his wallet and watch." She studied the wedding rings on her finger. "This doesn't hang together. When my maid went shopping this morning at the Creek Road market, she found out from a mango seller that Jomo and two other men were gunned down outside the Mbuyuni pub by a *mzungu*, a European. According to Aidah, when the killer left the murder scene, he whistled a tune before he disappeared into a warren of narrow streets."

"Did Aidah find out the identities of the two other murdered men?"

"She described them as *washamba*, the Swahili name for thugs or hooligans."

Ryan straighten up, and he caught her eyes when she looked up. "Wouldn't the murder of a university professor make news?"

"The local government controls the media. They're unlikely to publicize his murder. News of his death would discourage tourists coming to the island. Stone Town's only independent newspaper, *Dira*, shut down months ago."

Ryan tipped his chair back against a low partition. "Before Jomo went to Africa, he struck me as a man in a hurry, determined to introduce a new economic model to Africa and to fulfill a dream to convert the continent into an industrial giant."

"I think his ambitions may have contributed to his death. I am sure his ideas enraged socialist politicians and alienated some of his colleagues."

"Are you suggesting a politician or a university professor could've hired a contract killer to shoot him?" he said, setting his chair upright.

"It's possible."

The reflection of sunlight shining through red and green stained glass on shrub leaves looked like butterflies inside a giant bowl.

Renée leaned over and fished around in a shopping bag beside her chair. She handed him a wooden box, which she unlocked. "I did manage to save Jomo's special keepsake box."

Ryan opened the box, spilled the contents on the table. He sifted through a pile of tarnished medals and ribbons.

"Jomo won those awards in marathons," she said.

In an envelope, Ryan found family photographs of Jomo's parents in front of a circular mud hut. In another photo of Jomo, he had a mischievous smile on his broad face. His thickset arms were around Renée's waist. Next, he found a stack of letters held together by a rubber band.

"Do you know anything about these letters?" Ryan asked.

"Not a thing."

Ryan noticed that the letters had the Al Mutlaq Hotel letterhead. He planned to read the letters later. In the pool, Renée's son and daughter splashed each other.

"What possible interest could the police have in the academic papers of a university professor?" Ryan said.

"The authorities may have considered them controversial and inflammatory. Some of the papers I'm sure were connected to his new book." Her voice ended in a whisper. "He was such a gentle giant. I never imagined anyone would want to shoot him."

"There's someone out there who went to a lot of trouble to have him gunned down."

Renée sat straight in her chair, her cheeks stiff and unnatural with the effort of trying to maintain her composure.

"Do you think the shooter killed him by mistake and the two other men were the real targets?" Ryan said.

"That's possible." She smoothed down her hair as shiny and oily as paint. "I'll give you a retainer now."

She handed him a Barclay's Bank cashier's check for twenty-five thousand dollars.

Ryan wondered how she could afford his first class airline ticket as well as this large check? He knew Jomo's murder wasn't as simple as the professor being shot by a thief or gunned down at the wrong place at the wrong time. So little about events surrounding his assassination appeared to be known. T island had no media freedom to allow investigative reporters to cover the case or a cooperative police force willing to share information.

Ryan glanced at his watch. "Renée, I have an appointment to see Staff Sergeant Lipumba."

Renée had an undisguised look of sadness as she stared beyond him to the children who were making monkey noises. The skin high on her cheeks crinkled and seemed about to vibrate.

She didn't look at him when she spoke. "If I were you, I would have serious reservations about talking to Patrice Lipumba. You'll find out soon enough that he's nothing more than a crooked tyrant in an Armani suit."

CHAPTER 4

AFTER RYAN TOLD BARI THAT it was time to go, the boy
released the girl's hand and he strolled away from the beach,
an inscrutable look on his face. When Bari turned to wave to the
girl, she blew him a kiss.

"Maybe you'll see her again," Ryan said as they drove away
from the hotel.

Bari's eyes stared at the surf sliding up on the sand.

"I hope so," he said without much conviction in his voice. "But
she has a *msalaba* mother."

"What does that word mean?"

"Cross."

Ryan parked on a narrow street near the police station, a drab
building made of weathered coral stone. Despite Renée's misgivings
about Lipumba, he decided there could be no harm in making a
courtesy call to the officer in charge of Jomo's murder investigation.
In a reception room, a gaggle of women grouped around a tall
police officer. The women pleaded with him in Swahili. When Ryan
interrupted to ask him for directions to Lipumba's office, the cop's
mouth squeezed into a button. He folded his arms and towered over

Ryan. He told him in a booming voice to go down a corridor to the second office on the left. Ryan knocked on the staff sergeant's door, and a loud voice ordered him to enter.

Lipumba stood up from behind his desk to shake Ryan's hand in a cautious manner, as though he was feeling his muscles. The staff sergeant wore a double-breasted herringbone suit and a matching striped tie. Above him, a ceiling fan stirred hot air. He released Ryan's hand and patted him on the shoulder.

"I already know who you are, Mr. Moar," the police officer said, "where you are staying, and the purpose of your visit to this island."

Without waiting for Ryan to reply, he pressed a buzzer, and a young woman in a tight khaki blouse entered with two mugs on a tray. She gave Ryan a hard stare before she handed him coffee. He thanked her, and he sat down on a chair opposite the staff sergeant.

"Your first time in Zanzibar?" Lipumba said.

"Yes," Ryan murmured.

The smile faded from Lipumba's broad face. "You are here to investigate Dr. Jomo Willow's murder on behalf of his widow."

Ryan wiped a slick of sweat from his forehead. "Yes, sir."

"What do you think of our heat?" Lipumba asked, stroking his neatly trimmed beard.

"It's all right if you're within arm's reach of a beer cooler."

Lipumba laughed, a dry sound like sand swept down a narrow street by a hot wind. The police officer didn't sweat despite the humidity inside his office. Ryan felt a trickle of sweat go down his spine.

"Do you have a business card?" Lipumba asked.

When Ryan opened his wallet, he felt uncertain. Did handing his card to Lipumba mean an invitation to offer him a bribe? Unsure of the protocol, he decided against giving him any money, although he knew kickbacks in Africa were a common practice to smooth and cement relationships. Instead, Ryan decided to wait until they could meet in a more informal setting over a beer in the Serena's Uhuru bar.

He handed him his card and buttoned his wallet back into his hip pocket. When staff sergeant examined the card, Ryan noticed a flicker of disappointment flash across Lipumba's face.

"I understand you have in custody a prime suspect," Ryan said, taking in the measure of Lipumba's cropped gray hair, sloping girth, and wide, cruel mouth.

"We do have a suspect and that's all I will tell you at this time," he said.

For the next few minutes, Lipumba gave Ryan a dry account of how Jomo died: time and cause of death, type and caliber of weapon, and location of the shooting outside the Mbuyuni pub.

"The handgun that fires a twenty-two with a suppressor makes this homicide look like a contract hit," Ryan said.

Lipumba smiled broadly. "Why do you think that?"

"Pros like to use small caliber rounds that bounce around inside the skull. This guy kept it neat and tidy. You mentioned you didn't find empty shells at the site. These murders are the work of a hired assassin."

Lipumba crossed and uncrossed his legs, the size of tree trunks. "Before we go any further, I must warn you, I can only discuss a few aspects of this case."

"All right by me. Do you have witnesses?"

"The street was empty," Lipumba said, his face impassive, his voice betraying irritation.

Ryan found the lack of witnesses hard to believe, considering how the narrow streets of Stone Town were crowded during the day.

"Are you aware of any threats against Dr. Willow?" Ryan asked.

"No one has reported that to me."

"Can you tell me anything about your suspect?"

"He is a criminal well known to the police. We caught him when he tried to pawn Dr. Willow's watch."

"Has he confessed to the crime?" Ryan asked, his face drenched in sweat.

"Not yet. But this piece of shit will confess." The staff sergeant's Adam's apple jerked as he swallowed drained the last of his coffee.

"What do you know about the two other men killed alongside Dr. Willow?" Ryan asked.

Muffled sounds seeped into the office through the open transom. Ryan heard a staccato cry that combined laughter and a sob. To Ryan, the noise resembled the residue of prisoners past and present who had the misfortune of passing through this place.

"Those men's death had nothing to do with Dr. Willow's murder." Lipumba glanced at his Rolex. "I'm late for a meeting."

"One more question," Ryan said, getting up. "Dr. Willow was critical of East Africa's current crop of politicians and the region's business practices. Is it possible he could've been killed by someone opposed to his views?"

Lipumba lips twisted in a grimace. "I know nothing about Dr. Willow's politics."

He banged a swagger stick on the desk that caused dust to rise from a worn leather blotter.

"Your time is up." He knotted his tie tighter. "Take as long as you like with your investigation, Mr. Moar." He held up his hand. "But, I must warn you, do not interfere with the work of my police officers. I don't appreciate an outsider poking his nose in my business." He stood up and tucked his stick under his arm. "Do I make myself clear?" He leaned his knuckles on the desk. "Let me remind you, Mr. Moar, you are a guest in Zanzibar." Lipumba straightened and stuck two fingers in his collar to stretch it. "We do not tolerate people who abuse our hospitality."

The staff sergeant swung his baton in the direction of the door. "Goodbye, Mr. Moar. I wish you luck with your inquiries."

Like hell you do, Ryan thought as he headed for the office door.

Beyond the Kizimkazi Mosque, the city's stone buildings fragmented into ramshackle houses surrounded by ripening maize plots. Ryan drove east along Malawi Road and then slowed down when he passed palm trees and scrubland packed full of school children in scarlet and gray uniforms.

To reach Jomo's house, Bari told Ryan to turn left down a wide avenue of eucalyptus trees. He parked in front of a villa surrounded by a high whitewashed wall half hidden behind bougainvillea.

Wrought iron gates guarded well tended flowerbeds and green lawns. The veranda's intricate fascia boards and carvings had a coat of fresh paint. Sunlight reflected off a still pool, a sheet of rippled gray silk. On the front steps, a green snake startled him before it slithered into a clump of mimosa bushes. He fiddled with Renée's key chain until he found the right key to open the lock in the door's stout beams. In the hallway, transparent geckos clung to the walls like ornaments.

Decorating the living room's wall were curved daggers and Arab brass plates. An answering machine's red flasher lit the darkened room in an eerie glow. He listened to a message from the editor of the *Journal of African Economies*. He asked Jomo to arrange a lunch meeting at the New Africa Hotel in Dar es Salaam for two visiting American economists from Yale University.

After Ryan turned off the machine, he heard cockroaches skitter across the hardwood floor. In Jomo's study, intruders had opened two metal filing cabinets and scattered papers on the floor. To reach the second level, he climbed a narrow, spiral flight of stairs in an enclosed stairwell. In the master bedroom, he found a small, squat safe underneath a nightstand, a dial and lever in the front.

He rested his pocket flashlight on top of the safe, crouched on a Persian carpet, and pressed an ear against the door. Ryan tweaked the dial for a few minutes, his face puckered and eyes closed in concentration, while sweat blossomed on his forehead.

Finally, the last tumbler fell into place and the door creaked open. He chuckled and planted a kiss on the metal surface. He swept the contents of the safe on the floor. He sifted through envelopes full of dollars, euros, and Tanzanian shillings. When he returned the money to the safe, he wondered how Jomo had acquired so much cash.

Before relocking the safe, Ryan spotted a small framed photo he had overlooked. It was a picture of a woman in front of the Al Mutlaq. She wore heavy black eyeliner that seemed to accent a look of surprise, as if the photographer had taken the picture when she least expected it. He removed the photo from the frame. Scrawled on the back in pencil was a curt message: "Forever A."

He pocketed the photo and scratched his head, bemused. Somehow, Audrey didn't seem the type to murder her lover to inherit his hotel. Yet most murder victims were killed for a lot less.

Ryan went downstairs and locked the front door. He stood on the steps and looked up at the grand old house haunted by the specters of the island's history of traders in slaves and ivory, Omani sultans and British administrators, and more recently, a crucified cat.

When he climbed into the Volvo, Bari assured Ryan that they had time to visit the university and be back at the Serena before dark.

Ryan drove south through small villages of thatched roofed houses made of mud and wattle. Patches of blue sky appeared above the banana trees. In the west, heavy clouds pressed down on the city like a huge garbage can lid.

On the way to the university, Ryan and Bari stopped at a roadside restaurant named the Karibu Chakula, Good Appetite. After ordering the special of the day, they sat on reed mats and used their fingers to eat goat curry, dried strips of coconut, chopped mangoes, and rice.

While seated, Ryan noticed a thin column of smoke rise in the distance, a swirling black line against a backdrop of rain clouds. He expected the smoke would bring fire engines. When he asked Bari about the fire, the boy said it was common to let out-of-town buildings burn to the ground rather than dispatch scarce engines and firefighters from Stone Town to put out the blaze. Bari stared hard at the pillar of smoke through the restaurant's propped open window made of wattle and palm fronds.

"That smoke comes from the university," he said.

"Come on," Ryan said, standing up from his cross-legged position on the floor mat in one fluid motion. "It's time to go."

Ryan drove on a paved highway for half a mile and then turned left down a narrow gravel road. Ahead of him, the intensity of the smoke appeared to fade. At the university's front gate, a security guard carrying an assault rifle on his shoulder stopped the car. He escorted them to a parking lot beside a squat, narrow building overlooking the ocean. Distant waves broke on a reef and turned the crests the color of ivory.

Ryan left Bari to guard the Volvo. He approached a student wearing a charred T-shirt. Ash in his hair made him look old. Ryan asked for directions to Dr. Burton Chilongola's office. The student told Ryan to follow him. The acrid smell of smoke assaulted Ryan's nostrils. A small building beside a Nissan hut was a smoldering ruin. The charred upright beams reminded Ryan of a zebra's ribs picked bare by vultures.

"Did you help to put out the fire?" Ryan asked the student.

The young man nodded. "I was part of a bucket chain the students organized."

Ryan dipped his toe into the smoldering debris. "What is this building?"

"An office and a computer storage room."

Behind him, students prowled over the charred ruin. Ryan crouched down to sniff the air close to the piles of ash. "Whoever started this blaze used an accelerant."

The student didn't answer, instead he used a stick to probe the remains of a blackened laptop.

"Did the office belong to Dr. Jomo Willow?" Ryan asked.
"Yes."

Ryan crunched through the remnants of the office that had been flattened by the collapsed roof. He brushed debris off a filing cabinet and opened a drawer packed full of sheets of blackened paper turned to ash.

Ryan dusted off his hands. The student crossed a narrow courtyard to a narrow building. At the end of a corridor, he pointed to a book lined office. Behind a hardwood desk, a fat man was talking on cell phone. He wore a long white robe and a skull cap. His forehead was as shiny as an apple under the light of a table lamp. Ryan turned to thank the student, but he had scurried out of sight.

Dr. Chilongola's ringed fingers covered the mouthpiece to acknowledge Ryan with a wave. He shouted into the mouthpiece before he disconnected the phone.

"I presume you're Mr. Moar," he said, his hands splayed on the desktop, the backs as ridged as starfish. "As you have probably noticed, one of our university buildings has burned down. I have to deal with this disaster, so can't give you much of my time."

"That fire is the work of an arsonist," Ryan said.

"How can you be so sure?"

"Whoever started it doused the building in gasoline."

"We'll find the culprits. Our security guards are searching the campus right now." His lidless brown eyes watched Ryan, his mouth a tight seam. "On the phone, you mentioned you are investigating Dr. Willow's death." Any warmth in his voice evaporated like ice in the midday sun on Stone Town's corrugated iron roofs. "Aren't such matters best left to the authorities?"

"Staff Sergeant Lipumba is a busy policeman."

His eyes narrowed to slits. "Why the bloody hell do you Americans think you can do a better job at policing than anyone else?"

Surprised by his sudden anger, Ryan softened his tone. "I want to offer my sympathy for the death of your faculty member, Dr. Willow." Ryan paused to keep his eyes fastened on the professor. "Don't you find it an odd coincident that so soon after Jomo's death, someone deliberately set fire to his office and burns his papers?"

The professor turned to stare at him in stony silence, his narrow, fierce-looking eyes glaring at him through the lenses of his tortoiseshell frames.

When Chilongola remained silent, Ryan continued, "His widow's home was invaded by a gang off duty police officers who removed selective files from his home. What possible interest would the police have in stealing an academic's papers."

"I don't know."

"The police officers beat up Renée and traumatized her two children. The family has been forced to seek refuge in a hotel."

The professor raised bushy eyebrows flecked with gray.

"I am naturally shocked by this attack on Dr. Willow's wife and her children," he said.

Ryan looked out the window at sheet lightning rippling across the clouds. "Could Dr. Willow's death and the subsequent fire be somehow connected to his work at the university?"

"Possibly." Chilongola made a tent out of his fingers and raised them to the rolls of his double chin. "You see, his reputation is under suspicion."

"What sort of academic impropriety is he accused of?"

Chilongola chuckled as though Ryan had said something amusing. "Plagiarism."

"Who accused him of stealing?"

"I did."

Ryan glanced at the professor's bookshelf topped by a bust of the country's first president Julius Nyerere.

"Why would he steal from you? You are an obvious follower of Nyerere. You are in the socialist camp; Dr. Willow advocated free enterprise."

The professor regarded Ryan as though he'd affronted a sacred object. "To us, Nyerere will always be *mwalmu*, teacher. We revere his memory. He once told me he became a schoolmaster by choice and a politician by accident."

Ryan leaned forward. "His village collectivization experiments ended in failure."

"That remains to be seen." Chilongola removed his glasses, his eyes jittery and bloodshot. He used circular motions to clean his spectacle lenses on his robe. "I am now the acting head of economics." A clock tower chimed the hour and Chilongola sprung to his feet, as if he was responding to an alarm clock. "I have to attend an emergency meeting. Not, however, about the fire. We are faced by an even greater threat. We have to protect our property in case Akilah hits us. A cyclone named Akilah is moving west toward the island."

"When is Akilah expected to land?"

"In a day or two." The professor got up and jingled money in his pockets. "You have to leave now."

"Before I go, did Dr. Willow keep any papers anywhere else on campus other than in his office?"

For an instant, the professor raised his eyebrows, as if the question surprised him.

"I'm afraid all his papers were lost in the fire," he said.

"Who do you suspect did it?'

"Hoodlums, or what you Americans call Halloween pranksters."

Ryan tried not to smile. "Don't you see someone's gone to a lot of trouble to single out his academic research for burning?"

The professor's gaze swept up and down Ryan, as if he were about to admonish a student for an infraction. He swung around to stare at the dark clouds gathering over Stone Town. His eyes smoldered, and his head tilted to one side, while a thread of sweat trickled down his round cheeks.

"I have to agree with our president, Dr. Mironko, who has described the fire as an unfortunate coincidence," the professor said. "He told me to remember that the history of Zanzibar is a tragic one. Despite the melding of the islands to the mainland, there are forces bringing political instability and economic uncertainty that threaten our survival. Memories are long. The revolution still haunts us—the overthrow of the sultan, the massacre of Arabs and East Indians by gangs of killers, and the forceful takeover of businesses and private property. His advice to us is to remain calm, lick our wounds, and don't provoke the beast that lives among us."

CHAPTER 5

B Y THE TIME RYAN ARRIVED back at the rental car, the heat had plastered strands of sweat-soaked hair to his forehead. The fiery heat of the wind had picked up and swept across the parking lot with the intensity of a dragon's breath. In the shade of bamboo, he spotted Bari surrounded by students.

After Bari saw Ryan, he shook hands with the students and headed for the Volvo. Ryan turned on the ignition and the air-conditioning. When Bari climbed into the car, Ryan asked, "Did your friends have anything to say about the fire in Dr. Willow's office?"

"It was a big shock," Bari said. "The students liked the professor. He helped grads get jobs at the local hotels, instead of having to leave and look for work in Dar es Salaam."

"Did they have any suspicions about who started the fire in Dr. Willow's office?"

"They said two boys broke into his office to set it on fire. Guards have arrested them."

At the guardhouse, they waited for the barrier to be lifted.

"I want you to find out where these two fire starters live," Ryan said.

When the barrier went up, wind battered the side of the car and the sky let out a downpour. Heavy drops of rain on the road's baked surface condensed into steam.

"Watch out for cattle," Bari said.

"What happens if I hit one?" Ryan said.

"If the owner catches you, he will slit your throat."

The next morning, rain had scrubbed the sky clear, and the scent of the sea filled the air. After laps in the pool and a champagne breakfast buffet, Ryan left the hotel and walked south along the beach. He felt comfortable and cool in shorts and sandals. A group of small boys raced ahead of him. In between two anchored dhows, the boys dived into the waves, their heads bobbed like buoys.

Beside a stone breakwater, Ryan followed the directions inland that Audrey Bradt had given him to Zoe Singh's villa. When he stopped for a moment at Maendenelo Street, Ryan recalled Jomo's box that Renée had given him. Last night, he had read a series of Audrey's love letters to the professor. In the notes, Audrey wrote of how her love for Jomo had hit her hard and deep. Her passion for him had begun to wear her down, to erode any defenses she had to combat her obsession for him. She wrote that she had reached the stage of exhaustion, past caring.

When he arrived at Zoe's iron gates, he saw dead creepers encrust the walls and entwine the shuttered windows. Ryan pushed open the gate and entered a courtyard covered by mist. Out to sea, the low moan of a ship's horn emanated from the sleek lines of a yacht. The vessel's bow cut a swathe of foam through the calm surface of the sea. On board, Ryan spotted uniformed crew members on the bridge and partygoers jammed the aft deck. The yacht's horn made another hoot before the vessel swung around the point to enter the harbor.

A rat scurried down the path that led Ryan to an ancient door riddled with holes where brass ornaments had been ripped out of the wood. In a garage, Ryan spotted the aerodynamic fins of a pale blue Cadillac. He pulled on the metal handle of a doorbell and waited. No one answered, so he used the flat of his hand to bang on the door. As if in response to the banging, a dog barked and a rooster crowed. Through an iron grill, a shutter opened, and a wizened man's questioning eyes fixed on him.

"Here to see Zoe Singh," Ryan called out.

The stooped man unbolted the door and opened it a crack. After he let Ryan inside, he wiped his hands on his white T-shirt. Ryan followed him down a dark corridor that connected to a sitting room decorated with potted plants, Persian carpets, and stuffed Victorian couches. When he entered, an ancient woman put down a black fan on a table inlaid with ivory. She pushed up on a cane to stand and stretched out a hand, twisted into an eagle's talon.

"How do you do, Mr. Moar, I'm Zoe Singh," she said in a deep voice, a smile creasing her sunken cheeks.

"Please call me Ryan," he said, shaking her hand.

Curled in a ball at her sandaled feet, a border collie remained asleep. Zoe adjusted a choker of enormous pearls around her neck and sat down on a sofa. The makeup around her eyes and powdered nose gave her a ghostly appearance. Zoe ushered him a seat on the sofa, allowing them to sit facing each other. Against the wall, a glass case displayed the dried wings of butterflies, long since collapsed, leaving behind multicolored smudges, beside an open Steinway grand with missing keys like gaps in a boxer's mouth.

"I don't get many visitors, particularly good-looking young men," Zoe said.

"Thank you for agreeing to see me and help me investigate Jomo's murder by answering some questions," Ryan said.

She adjusted the folds in her white silk gown, long enough to touch the marble floor. "First, I'll ask one of my own. How is Renée taking her husband's death?"

"She's still in shock after his death and the brutal raid on her house."

"She told me all about the attack. Terrible." Zoe stroked the fox fur's shrunken head she had draped around her shoulders. "Have you met Audrey Bradt, the new owner of the Al Mutlaq?"

"Yes, I've already interviewed her. Audrey's devastated."

"Why? After inheriting his hotel, she's fallen into a pot of lard." Zoe covered her mouth with her hand and chuckled. "To show her faked grief at Jomo's funeral, she sniffled louder than the grieving widow."

"I've since learned they were very close."

"That's putting it mildly. They were lovers."

To Ryan, Zoe appeared as fragile as a pressed flower, yet underneath, he detected she had a shrewd, enduring quality as strong as steel.

"A mystery to me is what Renée is going to live on," Zoe continued. "I don't expect the university had much in the way of a pension plan." She shook her head. "And how in the devil did Jomo manage to buy the hotel on a teacher's salary?"

"That's something I'd like to know."

"The only possible way for him to acquire a windfall in so short a time is by fraudulent means. Knowing Jomo, he chose his illegal activities carefully to avoid any possible police entanglements. Otherwise, Patrice Lipumba would have demanded a large cut of any mendacious arrangements he could have made."

"What kind of legal or illegal activities do you suspect he delved into to make himself rich?"

"Hard to say. There're plenty of local hoods he could've hooked up with, but the serious money is made on the mainland. Isn't follow the money the approach private investigators use to track down culprits?"

He nodded. "That's a common practice in my trade."

Zoe dabbed her forehead with a lace handkerchief. "I suspect finding my friend's killer isn't going to be easy."

When he told her about Lipumba's veiled threats and Burton Chilongola's commitment to socialism, Zoe said she wasn't a bit surprised that the staff sergeant and the professor were both reluctant to cooperate.

"Apart from being good friends, Audrey told me you were Jomo's confidant," Ryan said.

Zoe raised her fingers to her lips in an attempt to suppress a girlish giggle. "Good friend, certainly, but I'm hardly his muse."

"Did Jomo tell you anything about his new book?" Ryan asked.

"He didn't show me a draft. I suspect his book focused on African economies and politics. He passionately opposed African one-party or one-man rule. He also objected to any form of government interference in the private sector." The collie asleep at her feet stirred. Zoe leaned down and scratched the crown of the dog's head. "He thought the only way to improve African living standards is to scrap large-scale projects and put money into grassroots family enterprises."

"Can you think of anyone who might want to kill him?"

Ryan's eyes suddenly locked on a velvet cushion beside her. Printed on the cover was a grotesque caricature of Jomo. He had blue teeth and his skin as bleached and mottled as a blowfish.

"Some civil servants and politicians in Dar es Salaam and Dodoma believe in the socialist ethos and would oppose his free enterprise ideas," Zoe said. "There are government hotheads capable of ganging up on him, but unlikely to mastermind his assassination. On the other hand, Chilongola is quite capable of hiring a local assassin."

"It would take a man of influence and financial power to engage an outside professional killer to gun him down."

She inched her hand forward and touched his fingertips. "This island has always been crowded with violent, unsavory characters, but I can't help you sort through the current crop." Zoe made a clicking sound with her tongue. "So, you came halfway around the world to solve a murder in a place time has forgotten and God has abandoned."

Ryan glanced for a moment at the circling wooden fan above his head in a ceiling dotted with mold mounds.

"Do you know anyone who could help me in a professional way to find Jomo's assassin?" Ryan asked.

She studied him for a moment. "I knew at one time many people who could help you. Unfortunately, they have either left the island or have passed on." She lifted her chin in defiance. "Some good people do come back. One of them is Amari Hussein—he runs Zanzibar's only private investigation business."

Ryan leaned forward. So far he had been confronted by the stark reality of carrying out his inquiries on his own in a secretive, hostile, and confrontational community.

"Can you tell me anything about Amari?" he asked.

"When the sultan still ruled, Amari's father sent his son to be educated at an English public school. Upon graduation, he joined the Metropolitan Police Force in London. After a few years on the beat, he decided to return home."

Zoe paused to ring a little brass bell. Khaled entered holding a tray in his shaking hands. He placed a brass Omani coffee pot in front of Zoe.

"I promise to provide you with Amari's contact information before you go," she said. She poured Ryan a cup through a spout that resembled a toucan's beak.

"What brought you to Africa, Zoe?" he asked.

She put her cup down on a mahogany trunk adorned with inlaid shells. Focused on the sea, her eyes went small with memory, for a moment, distant.

Zoe told Ryan that she was born in Grimsby, a grimy seaport on the Haven River in Northeast Lincolnshire. Her father owned a brick factory. When war broke out, her parents wanted to keep her safe from the German bombs, so they dispatched her to East Africa to stay with an aunt in Nairobi. She lived in Kenya's capital until she was in her late teens. While visiting Mombasa, she met a dashing young Indian merchant from Zanzibar. Despite fierce opposition from her parents and aunt, after a brief courtship, she married Debrendra Singh.

"At the time, mixed marriages were considered taboo among the British settlers," Zoe said. "My husband brought me here to live in this house. You wouldn't believe it now. This ruin was once a palace where I entertained Sultan Sir Khalifa Il bin Harub Al-Said and some of his wives and many of his charming children. The British governor and his wife, Sir Charles and Lady Eastwick, came for tea. Ernest and Mary Hemingway stayed here. The writer had so much fun marlin fishing in Debrendra's cabin cruiser." Behind her rimless glasses, Zoe's right eye twitched. "It was a few days before Ernest's awful air crash."

Zoe put a trembling hand on her painted mouth.

"Ava Gardner and her husband Frank Sinatra spent a rather inebriated evening with us," she continued. "Ava was making the film *Mogambo* at the time for MGM. I never understood why such a spirited beauty would even look twice at Frank, a scrawny crooner." She laughed. "Ava could have had her co-star Clark Gable."

Coming from the street, Ryan heard a sudden strangled scream that vanished as soon as it appeared.

Zoe told Ryan that Debrendra owned clove plantations and spice factories. Among the expensive gifts he gave her was the Cadillac in the garage that Ryan had seen earlier.

She waved her ringed fingers around the room. "My husband and I and our two children lived in absolute splendor until the revolution."

Zoe sat in silence giving Ryan time to examine her sad gray eyes and her oval face. He suspected that in her youth she had been an exceptional beauty. She traced her fingers along tiny jagged scars on the bottom of her jawline.

"During those terrible days between January 18 and 20, 1964, a chimera rampaged across the island in the form of a ragtag army of Marxist and Maoist revolutionaries led by a Ugandan named John Okello," she said. "His mob began by carrying out mass killings of Omani Arabs."

During the revolt, Zoe heard the endless sound of human fury as the mob sacked Stone Town and murdered its inhabitants. While she listened to the screams of the dying, the drains ran red from the blood of victims.

Zoe pulled her fox fur around her shrunken shoulders, as though she were in a draft. "Before the sultan and his family escaped in his yacht, he warned Debrendra to leave. My husband stubbornly ignored his advice. He naively believed that the uprising was against Arab domination."

Zoe's watery eyes searched the room, as if looking for ghosts. To avoid the layers of heat mushrooming against the ceiling, Ryan strained to catch the slight breeze coming from the open window.

"My husband was under the illusion that the revolutionary hatred of Omanis wouldn't swell into the ranks of the East Asians and the few remaining Europeans," Zoe said.

When the shouts of drunken rage from the hordes came closer, trucks piled high with corpses drove past Zoe's gates. Debrendra persisted that he had always treated his workers fairly and they would be spared. The revolutionaries soon looted East Indian shops. During the night, as Zoe and her family waited in terror, rumors circulated that Royal Navy Marines would land to rescue them. British destroyers remained on the horizon and rescue forces never came ashore.

Early in the morning, a rowdy crowd surrounded Zoe's villa. From upstairs, she watched the rabble slaughter her menagerie of peacocks and monkeys, and then the mob roasted her pets on a spit over a fire. The hordes then welded axes and *pangas* to attack the doors. When the mob broke in, she remembered Debrendra's face contorted in horror and surprise at the ferocity of the attackers. The rabble welded knives to slice her husband's esophagus, almost decapitating him. The mob then executed Shahid, her teenage son. Then the mob rammed the heads of Debrendra and Shahid on stakes and paraded these hideous trophies in the streets.

"The murdering horde then fell upon my daughter," Zoe said. "They dragged Karena into a corner and for hours queued up to rape her, while forcing me to watch."

The room went quiet, the only sound a low growl from the collie when he moved his head to rest on Zoe's embroidered slippers.

The pack of angry men took great pleasure in beating Zoe unconscious. Tired of tormenting her, the mob dumped her body in the garden. When Khaled found Zoe alive, her servant buried her under rags, loaded her in a cart, and pushed her to the nearby British club. Inside the clubhouse, Europeans who had lived through the rampage let her in. The survivors used a massive bookcase against a door to keep the mob at bay.

Zoe gave him a weary rise and fall of her thin eyebrows. "I hope I'm not depressing you."

"Please continue with your story, Zoe."

In the countryside, predators of every stripe massacred whole villages, and bodies decomposed in the sun. The gagging smell of rotting bodies enveloped the land. Vultures and marabou storks grew fat on the dead and dying. The scavenger birds stripped the bones of victims clean. As if tired of the slaughter, the revolutionaries forced surviving women and children into fishing boats. They anchored the ships in the harbor and left them to die of dehydration and heat exhaustion. The combined heat and humidity made the smell of the dead inside the houses almost unbearable. To celebrate the orgy of killing, rioters commandeered Zoe's Cadillac for a wild parade.

"They drove my American car up and down Mizingani Road." She took a deep breath. "They even draped testicles over the Caddie's hood ornament."

Zanzibar's long night of the soul ended when Tanganyika's president Julius Nyerere sent troops to intervene. In the meantime, the revolutionary council had seized Zoe's husband's plantations and factories. They left his widow a wing of her former villa.

"The council turned parts of my house into crowded tenements for squatters," Zoe said.

"Did you ever think of leaving?" Ryan asked.

Zoe shook her head. "My parents had long since disinherited me. I manage to live on a small stipend from my husband's investments in London." Zoe crumpled a handkerchief into a ball. "Most of my dear friends have left, relocated to California and to British Columbia. Even, if I could, I've never thought of going anywhere else to live." She raised her bent shoulders in a shrug. "I like to stay close to the graves of my husband and my children. They are buried in the small British cemetery. Like everything else, weeds have overgrown the headstones. I keep my family's graves shipshape. There's an empty plot beside Debrendra reserved for me."

Ryan sipped the strong coffee and stared through the open window at the sea. "Are you bitter?"

"Not really. At my age, I even like being alive. One morning, I came face-to-face at the fish market with one of my tormentors. I thought I would be terrified, but instead I felt calm, almost serene." She gave him a wry smile. "The main thing to remember is that we are all in the same dust cart at the end of the walk."

CHAPTER 6

SHARK LEANED ON THE POLISHED brass railing of his yacht anchored in Stone Town harbor. He wore slacks and suspenders, a long-sleeved white shirt, a green tie, and a matching emerald pin. His smooth cheeks radiated the freshness of the morning. He gazed at the undulating contours of Prison Island. His lips twisted in a crooked smile as his thoughts drifted to the giant tortoises, inhabitants of the island. In another lifetime, Shark wanted to be a tortoise. Despite being encumbered by a heavy shell, male tortoises copulated most of the time. As a tortoise, he thought how simple and pleasurable life would be, if in his next life, he emerged as one of these Prison Island denizens.

He strolled along the deck, he felt buoyant but also disconnected. His guests had gone ashore. He missed chatter, music, and the noise of ice tinkling against glass. The only sound was waves slapping against the yacht's bow. For an instant, Shark caught his reflection in the glass of a porthole. His portly image made him wince. Before a plastic surgeon rearranged his features, Shark had once been handsome. Once the scars healed, Shark couldn't recognize his face, except for his deep-set eyes.

"Good morning, Papa," a steward called out to him on his way to the kitchen.

Shark nodded and smiled. He had come a long way from growing up on one of East Dublin's mean streets. He had his Irish mother's high cheek bones and thick hair. From his Kenyan butcher father, he had inherited broad shoulders and strong hands. So far in his life, he followed his dad's work ethic of first taking care of himself and then his family. In his early teens, Shark had gained the reputation of a young man who always smiled. Even after a street brawl, he learned how to swallow his blood and smile so others wouldn't know he was hurt.

After school, Shark worked as a delivery driver, until a part-time hustler connected him to the city's underbelly of rackets, loan sharks, and ties with pimps in Dublin's flourishing call girl business. Shark soon parlayed his earnings into a chain of flower shops, pornographic film studios, and high-class brothels. A decade later, he had transformed his Dublin-based businesses into a worldwide enterprise. Shark—whose real name was Darcy O'Connell—earned the Shark moniker from his business colleagues for his knack of snuffing out competitors. Whenever he took control of a rival's business. he made it a habit of smiling as he drank a glass of Irish apple brandy.

He took a sharp intake of breath at the brief sight of a shark's fin—curved in the shape of a miniature dhow's sail—slice through the waves. His eyes took on a duller light when his thoughts turned to his former mistress, Thelma Draffon, an aristocratic English woman. Behind him, he picked up a jigger of tequila from a cart and drank it all. Three weeks ago, Shark had found out that Thelma—instead of shopping in Stone Town—had visited a discrete hotel accompanied by his Spanish chief petty officer, Marco Mindosa.

After discovering her affair, Shark had disposed of his former mistress far out in the Mozambique Channel. Determined to show her no mercy, he had ignored her pleas for forgiveness. On the starboard deck, he signaled to a guard to press the barrel of a handgun into Marco's spine. If her lover refused to slash both of Thelma's ankles and throw her into the sea, Shark ordered his guard to shoot his chief petty officer.

Marco's hands shook when he cut deep into Thelma's shapely ankles. She cried out in terror when he picked her up and threw her into the choppy sea. As the yacht drifted, breakers on a reef drowned out the sound of Thelma's screams. Her blood in the water soon attracted predators. Looking through powerful binoculars, Shark had stood on the bridge to watch the giant tails of hammerheads roil the water, turning the sea red as the sharks shred her body into fish chum.

An hour after the yacht returned to Stone Town, Shark had arranged to have Thelma's lover killed in a back alley. Two hired assassins gagged and tied up Marco. After they tortured him with sharp sticks, the killers shot him in the head and dumped his body in a trench beside an ancient burial ground behind a ruined mosque.

Even the satisfaction of vengeance didn't erase the weight of Thelma's betrayal that formed like knives around Shark's heart.

Shark ignored the salute of an armed guard when he went below deck to his office. Using fingerprint identification, he unlocked the reinforced steel door. He sat at his desk and logged on to his computer to check the financial markets and the latest world news from BBC and Al Jazeera.

As a fallout of the worldwide financial meltdown, he grinned at pictures of growing unemployment lines in Dublin. Shark grinded his teeth at the next news report from Nairobi. At a guest house in Kampala, Ugandan police had arrested his friend and colleague Idelphonse Nizeyimana. UN officials had accused Idelphonse of being a major player in the Ruanda genocide. The former Hutu intelligence officer bragged that he had been instrumental in massacring an average of eight thousand Tutsis every 24 hours for 100 days. During the slaughter, Idelphonse had fattened his investment holdings in the Isle of Man and the Cayman Islands by confiscating dead Tutsi properties and bank accounts. Idelphonse had once reminded Shark that great fortunes are made in the chaos during the fall or rise of nations.

Shark relocked his office and walked down a corridor to his stateroom. He flung opened the double doors. In his circular bed, a naked young woman lay asleep, her lush red hair fanned out on the pillow. She had the rose complexion of English royalty. The sight of one of her exposed breasts above the pink silk sheets made desire stir in his loins.

Shark had met Aisling Quinn a week ago at the height of the Cannes Film Festival in the chic Chicka-Dee nightclub on the Boulevard de la Croisette. Inside the club, a skinny boy metal band from Sweden belted out a rock beat. Above him, the overhead lights reflected off Shark's shiny dark suit and made the diamonds embedded in his gold tie pin sparkle. On the packed dance floor, Shark's small eyes soon spotted Aisling's red hair piled high in a chignon.

Shark weaved his way to Aisling's side. She wore purple pants and a glittering green blouse. When he offered to buy her a cocktail, she eyed him with suspicion, until added that he was a producer of feature films. The striking young redhead turned out to be an Irish thespian anxious to work in Hollywood rather than performing in cheap domestic dramas for Irish TV. After five margaritas, Aisling smiled often to expose her even white teeth. Shark leaned forward to offer her a role in his next feature film. Aisling accepted. She appeared overeager when he suggested that he give her a lift in his Bentley to the Carlton bar to talk terms. Instead of taking Aisling to the hotel, Shark told his chauffeur in French to go to the Jettée Albert-Edouard in the old harbor. Aisling's hands had raced to her red lips at the sight of the sleek, floodlit lines of his 90-foot yacht.

During the time it took to sail from the French Riviera to East Africa, Aisling had become more than another ornament in Thelma's Dior gowns and Cartier diamonds. To his surprise, Shark had grown fond of her. Aisling had qualities the string of other mistresses—who drifted in and out of his world—did not.

Even though she remained a mystery to him, she had street-smart instincts and global stock market savvy. She understood the root causes of the world's economic doldrums, and she had intimate knowledge of the inner workings of Wall Street, Hong Kong, Zurich, Frankfurt, and London stock exchanges.

Shark could feel the blood tingle in the back of his neck. Clever women made him nervous. A vision of beauty, Aisling's catalogue of sexual adventurism and a brilliant mind heightened both his satisfaction and his unease. Shark wiped sweat from his brow on his sleeve. To cool down, he decided to go back on deck to feel the sea breeze on his face. Shark chose the bow, facing Stone Town harbor. Outrigger fishing boats selling trinkets ringed a cruise ship like a giant whale surrounded by a school of minnows.

He speculated if it was possible that Aisling could have betrayed him. Although she tried to mask her interest in the operations of his global business in frivolous chatter, she had an inquisitive mind—a dangerous quality in Shark's secretive world. At a cocktail party, he overheard Aisling spill out details of his real estate manipulations to an Irish colleague. Her intimate knowledge of the time he had chosen to unload his holdings before the crash could only have come from his computer files.

He could feel his breathing quicken. How the devil did Aisling hack into his laptop? High-priced security technicians had assured him his computers were hacker proof. The knowledge she may have obtained could be highly inflammatory in the hands of the authorities. Damn her, it could ruin him.

Despite his growing attachment to Aisling, Shark knew he had to make sure she never left the island alive.

CHAPTER 7

A T NOON, THE SAME DAY, sunlight filtered through a haze of low clouds on the balcony of the Splendide View Restaurant where Ryan and Bari sat back and relaxed over coffee to admire a dozen yachts in the harbor.

After lunch, Ryan drove to Amari Hussein's address on New Mkunazini Road. He parked beside high walls topped by pieces of broken glass embedded into concrete. Before entering the PI's house, Ryan squinted at menacing storm clouds. The superheated air made him feel as if he faced the blast from a smelter.

The distant single spire of the Anglican cathedral towered above Amari's corrugated iron roof. Sudden heavy rain forced Ryan to dart for shelter below a scrolled cast-iron gate built into the wall. A pregnant woman answered the doorbell. She smiled at him through a thin black veil. She beckoned him to follow her across a courtyard where scrawny chickens scratched and pecked at the damp ground. She unlocked the front door, and he followed her down a narrow corridor to a flight of stone stairs to the second floor. The rain abruptly stopped and pools on the concrete floor glistened in the harsh sunlight. On the landing, Ryan could see the bay, bright blue except for pockets of water as dark and silken as velvet.

A faded canopy shaded folding chairs, carpets, and potted plants that converted the space into a sitting room. Hibiscus hung from supporting beams and swayed in the wind. Amari sat in a chair drinking coffee out of a little cup, an open file on his lap. He wore small, rimless glasses, cream-colored slacks and a checked shirt. He shook Ryan's hand.

"Join me," he said, pouring him a cup of coffee from a brass jug. "Drink it slowly; my brew packs a punch."

As thick as syrup, the bittersweet coffee burned Ryan's throat. Amari removed his cap, his shiny head bald except for a monkish gray fringe. Amari's eyes squinted from the smoke of a cigarette smoldering in an ashtray. His red lips were in sharp contrast to the dark color of his pockmarked face, discolored as if his skin had been smoked on a fire.

"Where did you park?" Amari asked.

"Beside your house," Ryan said.

"By now, your hubcaps are stolen and someone has walked away with your tires."

"I hired a lad to watch out for thieves."

"Where did you find him?"

"When I arrived at the airport, this young guy secured me a cab. Bari Khan now acts as my guide."

"Take my advice: when you're with this boy, keep an eye on your wallet and watch. We call beach boys like him *pasasi*, ticks." Amari leaned hard on his chair's armrests. "Many of these touts are connected to the drug trade. Most of them are users and they steal to support addictions. While you are on this island, Ryan, trust no one, including the staff at your hotel. The police often employ them as informants."

Ryan stared at water dripping off the canopy and the wind sweeping through the broad banana tree leaves in the yard below him. The sky was filled with thunder and lightning. Gradually, the storm signs faded into the ether.

"Is there enough work on the island to keep you busy?" Ryan asked, trying to dismiss images of the threatening cyclone sucking the bay into its maw.

"It may surprise you, but plenty of people want my services. In a conservative Muslim island, errant husbands and cheating wives are relatively rare, however, I do find missing children, locate stolen cars and fishing boats, and I even uncover lost treasures. These waters contain wrecks and illegal diving has become a cottage industry." He wiped sweat off his shiny forehead on his sleeve. "How did you find me?"

"Zoe Singh gave me your name. I also checked your website."

"My son Asante is a techie; he put the page together. Even in this primitive backwater, my website is where I get most new clients."

Ryan stood up to look over the iron railing at rainwater inside a stone house's collapsed thatched roof.

"Why did you quit the London police force?" Ryan asked.

"So, you have researched me. After ten years in the Metropolitan Crime Division, I thought it was time to return to Zanzibar and start my own agency." He stretched out his sandaled feet. "You could say I traded blue serge for a *dishdashah*."

Ryan heard the soft clack of thongs behind him. The veiled woman he had seen earlier laid a plate of sliced mangoes and pineapples on the table. Amari thanked her and she left.

"Is she your wife?" Ryan said.

"She is my current *wife du jour*. I have adopted the Swahili custom of having as many wives as I can afford. She is my favorite. The other two wives are jealous because neither of them has produced a child."

Ryan slapped a mosquito and studied the bloody mark among the hairs on his arm.

"My friend, you appear restless, preoccupied," Amaris said.

"I've a feeling I'm being watched," Ryan said, reluctant to admit his fear of storms.

Amari smiled darkly. "When you arrived, your passport must have attracted the attention of the local security services. I suspect you have had a tail on you ever since you left the airport." Amari pointed at the street below, where a bearded man in a striped shirt held an open umbrella above his head. "I happen to know that man is employed by TISS, the Tanzania Intelligence and Security Service." He gave Ryan a disarming smile. "If they wanted to deport you, you would already be gone." Amari cleared an obstruction in his throat. "Next time we meet, I suggest a restaurant on the beach at high tide; it will be difficult to hear what we're saying, our voices scrambled by the surf."

"Why is TISS taking such an interest in me, an American tourist here to explore Zanzibar's delights?"

Amari stared at Ryan with an intense gaze. "It must be something in your past that has put you on a list."

"At one time, I worked for the CIA."

Amari puffed hard on his cigarette. "That'll do it."

Ryan sniffed the salty odor coming from the bay. Apart from the squall's dense, dark clouds, there was no hint of the arrival from the west of a churning white vortex of wind and water. Ryan had seen on satellite images of Akilah grinding its way to the Zanzibar coast. As the cyclone could make it difficult to contact the PI, Ryan decided to secure Amari's services before the storm hit Stone Town.

"I need your expertise to find who killed Dr. Willow," he said. "Interested?"

Amari smiled. "If you want to hire me, my fee is one hundred United States dollars per day, plus expenses."

"Consider yourself hired."

Amari stood up to spit over the rail.

"I never met Jomo Willow. I only knew him by reputation. In some circles, he wasn't particularly liked. He could be abrasive. He had a habit of rubbing important people the wrong way." Amari sat down and made a tent out of his fingers. "Dr. Willow wanted to change the way Africa does business."

"Did his drive to reform the economic system make him enemies?"

"He often criticized the government's bloated bureaucracy and mismanagement. His public statements have annoyed civil servants in high places. I am sure these government employees have raised more than one glass to celebrate the news of his death. But his anti-socialist leanings are unlikely to have caused enough hatred to have the authorities plot to have him shot."

"Apart from economic policy differences, why do you think anyone would want to kill the professor?"

"After examining the circumstances surrounding his death, it could have been an accidental shooting. Dr. Willow left the Mbuyuni pub at the wrong time. The real targets were Atish Azzabi, a local crime lord, and his bodyguard. The assassin must've thought Jomo was another of Azzabi's colleagues. As far as trying to find any clues at the site, they have long been washed away by rain."

Amari's third wife's wrists jangled with gold bracelets as she picked up the empty cups before she disappeared through a beaded screen.

"Why haven't the local cops made any public statements to acknowledge the shooting of Azzabi and his bodyguard?" Ryan asked, sitting down again.

"In their usual fashion, the police are being tight-lipped."

"When I talked to Lipumba, I had the impression that he was trying to pin the blame for Jomo's death on a thief, who had in his possession the professor's wallet and watch."

Amari pushed his glasses further up his hooked nose. "Ryan, this is Zanzibar. You'll be disappointed if you presume that the police will be looking into this case to steer it through the system and ultimately lead to an arrest of the real criminal. It's a lot easier to take into custody a man trying to sell stolen goods so he can have enough cash to feed his family and send his kids to school in new uniforms."

Amari stubbed out his cigarette and leaned forward. "Did you grease Lipumba's palm?" Ryan shook his head. "Big mistake, my friend."

The strength of the wind picked up and Ryan imagined the storm rushing toward the island, a massive black swirling hump, gaining momentum and size.

"Did the police do an autopsy on Jomo's body?" Ryan asked.

He shook his head. "Before the police arrived, Jomo's corpse had been stripped naked by street people. The police then tossed his body into a holding shed without adequate refrigeration. As for gathering any clues, there isn't much. After a day in this heat, Jomo would have swelled up like the Michelin man. His widow had difficulty finding a coffin big enough to contain him. They had to hack off his legs to fit him inside the box." Amari stood up and leaned the full weight of his big arm across Ryan's shoulder. "The murder of Dr. Willow remains for the police an open case, but they're not going to follow up on other suspects unless their superiors lean on them, and that's unlikely."

"Wouldn't the American ambassador have anything to say to the government? After all, Jomo and his wife are US citizens."

"If your ambassador follows the usual pattern of diplomats, officials in Dar es Salaam won't pay much attention to the death of a Tanzanian-born American married to a US citizen." Amari sat down again and rested his elbows on the table. "You and I are probably the only ones who have any interest in finding out who murdered Dr. Willow."

"Any witnesses?"

Amari consulted a notebook. "Two boys saw the assassin shoot two bullets in the back of Dr. Willow's head."

"Did they describe the shooter?"

"They said he was white."

"Age range?"

"In his late thirties."

"Any distinguishing features?"

51

"He had a crew cut." Amari stroked the salt-and-pepper stubble on his chin. "He had to be a professional hit man." He examined the back of his hand, knotted with thick veins. "When I questioned the boys, they said his weapon made a sound like a whoosh of air, a muted pop. So, he used a silencer. When I removed one of the bullets from a wall, it was soft-tipped and largely deformed, so it would impossible to trace."

The man suspected of following him folded his umbrella and talked on a cell phone. On the other side of the street, a woman in skin-tight shorts and spiked heels scurried into a waiting car parked in a narrow shaft of sunlight.

"Are you familiar with the local crime bosses?" Ryan asked.

"If I truly value staying healthy in this town, any knowledge I have of these individuals I keep to myself. I am sure you understand my need for secrecy. We have criminals involved in the lucrative drug trade, who spend a lot of money to protect territory and privacy." Amari lit another cigarette and blew smoke out of the corner of his mouth. "Tread carefully, Ryan. These guys don't want anyone—particularly an outsider—snooping around in their turf. What I can tell you is that there's a new, more ruthless organization muscling in on the drug scene. It's run on the same lines of a tightly controlled terrorist organization, demanding absolute loyalty to the leader."

Ryan fluttered his damp shirt against his chest. "Is this new guy on the block connected to Islamic extremists?"

"Depends on what you mean by extremists." Amari ran a comb through the hair on his chin. "Before these terrorists became corrupted by power and cruelty, most extremists started out as strict religious fundamentalists." Amari stared at the dark clouds. "What's at stake is a clash of values. They don't particularly like American values. An organized society like yours exists around amoral appetites for material possessions and individual choices."

"It isn't all about material possessions. What about personal freedom?"

"Islam views people as more than the sum of their desires and appetites. People have moral values and responsibilities to the community. Whereas America imposes on others its values by force, if necessary, a soulless allegiance to free markets and personal choice. The force used by Islamic fundamentalist groups is an act of spiritual, cultural, and social resistance. As a result, the progress of the United States and its allies to settle the conflicts in the Middle East is in decline, while the advancement of Islamists is revived and on the ascendance."

"How can you explain the extreme prejudices and cruelty of Hamas and Hizbullah? Surely, you can't gloss over the beheadings, crucifixions, rapes, suicide bombing of civilians, and notorious anti-Semitic propaganda."

Amari said nothing in rebuttal, and Ryan remained silent.

Ryan's thoughts drifted to home. It would be early in the morning in North Fargo. Joanne would be on the treadmill or doing yoga exercises before preparing breakfast for Charlene and Gary.

Was he a complete fool for trading his blended family for a discussion on the merits of Islam versus the secular values of the west in a strange and exotic island that had become an increasingly hostile place? He knew these thoughts to be self-defeating, and he had better move on.

"What else can you tell me about this new crime organization that's forced its way into your island?" Ryan asked.

Amari laughed without humor. "You want a real mystery, Ryan? On the surface, Zanzibar appears peaceful enough, attempting to reinvent itself as a sanitized tourist destination. Unfortunately, this secretive new organization has set up shop in Zanzibar to take advantage of our pliable police force and easy-to-bribe judiciary."

Ryan stared down at a boy asleep, one arm over his eyes on a flattened cardboard carton in the cab of a truck peppered by rust pockmarks.

"This new criminal organization has tentacles that reach into every shady corner of the island's murky world of money, drugs, murder, and vice." Amari stood up to stretch. "Believe me, despite its violent history, Zanzibar is far from becoming another Somalia—a failed, lawless state controlled by extremists." He paused, his sad, bloodshot eyes widened as he stared at Ryan. "What is more ominous is that in the last few months, this criminal organization has established their headquarters in a luxurious walled villa on a remote beach on our west coast where they operate in relative obscurity. Their objective has nothing to do with religion. They want to acquire more wealth and power to expand their influence and deadly commerce in this region." Amari glanced at his watch. "Ryan, I'm running out of time. I'll email you in a day or so to set up our next meeting. Meanwhile, there's a nasty storm Akilah threatens the island. If this cyclone maintains its category three strength and hits Stone Town head on, it could do severe damage."

Ryan stood up and glanced at storm clouds on the horizon. As if sensing danger, all the yachts in the bay except one had headed out to sea. The sun behind clouds above Prison Island gave the harbor an overall pallor of gray, a hint of something growing dark in the depths, massing.

CHAPTER 8

THE EVENING SKY HAD TURNED purple and the wind smelled of salt spray. Weather forecasters predicted that the storm would veer south of the island and make landfall near Lorenzo Marques on the Mozambique coast. While seated in the Serena's Baharia restaurant, the deck lights of the yacht *Sundancer* winked at Ryan. He wondered why the only luxury vessel still anchored in the bay had not sailed to some safe harbor.

While savoring an ancient Bordeaux wine, Ryan suddenly put down the glass and stared out at the choppy sea. Joanne had phoned him this afternoon, and her call had disturbed him. She mentioned that her son had started to take a more than step brotherly interest in his daughter, Charlene. Gary had taken her for a drive, and they didn't return home until well after eleven. When Joanne confronted Gary, he denied anything going on between them. It was Charlene who had persuaded him to stay out later than the ten o'clock curfew. Gary claimed that they had spent the evening at Starbucks, where they drank coffee and talked. Knowing her son, Joanne didn't believe for a moment that he hadn't made advances to Ryan's attractive teenage daughter.

Ryan knew that Charlene was at an age when she could be influenced by a wild young stud like Gary. Ryan picked at his plate of giant shrimps, porterhouse steak, and asparagus in Hollandaise sauce. These clouds of worry over his daughter's apparent interest in Gary had dulled his appetite. Charlene was everything a father could want in a daughter—exceptional grades, poise, striking good looks, and common sense—except for one thing; she was attracted to his stepson.

Ryan gazed at the last sparks of the sun. Beside him, an overweight man in a white suit ordered a scotch and soda. He watched the waiter pour a triple of the golden liquid into a glass filled with ice. The man took several large gulps of Johnny Walker and smacked his lips. Ryan imagined the burning taste of whiskey slide down his throat, lighting places inside him that only he knew about.

He recalled how a hit-and-run driver had knocked down his first wife, Kathy. The man then raped her while she was unconscious. The driver had then dumped her into the Red River, where she drowned. Her killer was never found. For several months after her death, he had sought refuge in the bottom of empty shot glasses in bars beside running water.

Ryan massaged the back of his neck, his fingers kneading deep into the tendons. A great emptiness swelled in his chest, compulsions he hadn't felt for years gripped him. His heart raced, and sweat beaded on his forehead at the thought of scotch going down his throat like gasoline poured on a burning match.

He pushed away his untouched plate, signaled the waiter, and signed his meal check. When Ryan stood up, he sent his chair crashing to the floor. Offering apologies to the waiter, he left the restaurant and headed for the beach. Ryan removed his sandals and buried them under dried seaweed. Walking barefoot on the white sand, he listened to the sound of waves crashing on the shore. He watched the light of dhow's hurricane lamp in the stern glided past him like a star in a silent night.

Beside a row of beached dhows, Ryan imagined Joanne whispering love thoughts in his ear. The thought of facing the storm alone in his suite extinguished the romantic image of his wife. The prospect of waking up the next morning after a night of drinking with the foul taste of alcohol in his mouth—as putrid as a rotten parrotfish—made him want to puke.

Lining the shore, the night disguised the rot and decay of weathered stone mansions. The dark blotted out the cracked walls, peeling paint, and broken shutters. The overlay of darkness gave the buildings the unreal appearance of false fronted movie set pieces.

He watched the dhow's lateen sail billow in a sudden gust of wind like the inflated skin of jellyfish. Known on the island as the Portuguese man-o'-war, the jellyfish's tentacles had a poisonous sting. When the dhow's lamp became a pinprick, he wasn't surprised to see the yacht *Sundancer* speed out to sea, her streamlined hull buffeted by waves.

The air felt cool on his cheeks as the heat and humidity was swept away by fierce gusts of wind. He shivered. Did dark clouds coming from the east mean the big storm had changed its predicted southern course and was closing in on the island?

Ryan returned to the stretch of beach in front of the Serena, where the wind whipped up sand particles. Shielding his eyes, Ryan spotted what looked like a white sheet on the bay's choppy surface. When a flash of lightning over Prison Island lit up the sea, the white object appeared for an instant like a giant seabird with a broken wing. He waded into the surf. As he swam closer, he saw a woman floundering in the waves.

He swam with sure, swift strokes toward her. When he reached her, she lay sprawled face down in the water, her red hair fanned out like exotic seaweed. Treading water beside her, he spun her on her back, hooked his arm around her head, and blew air into her mouth.

Maintaining a firm grip around the woman's chin, Ryan used his other arm in a sidestroke motion to swim to shore. As soon as his toes touched sand, he carried her in his arms to the shore.

He laid her on her back and twisted her head sideways to scoop seawater out of her mouth with his fingers. Her wet hair streamed down the front of her body, reminding him of Venus in Botticelli's classic painting.

Ryan placed one hand under her neck and tilted her head back and pinched her nostrils. He then blew air hard into her mouth. He paused to feel a nonexistent pulse in her neck. Ryan turned her on her side and slapped her several times between her shoulder blades. After he continued mouth-to-mouth for a few more minutes, he became aware of a ring of silent, wide-eyed children gathered around him.

As air started to move in a regular rhythm into her chest, he felt relief, followed by rising panic. There was still no pulse in her neck's carotid artery. For twenty minutes, he switched back to compressing her chest. Still no sign of a pulse. He sat back on his heels to take a breather. The children watching him began to chatter. He looked down at her chest rising. Relief swept over him as she started to breathe on her own. He used his shirt to wipe her wet face, he listened to her sigh, and he watched air puff up the smooth skin of her tanned cheeks.

He wondered if she was a pampered passenger on board the yacht *Sundancer*. Did she drink too much champagne and tumble over the railing into the sea? He leaned over her when he saw her eyelids flutter.

"Where am I?" she whispered, her green eyes wide and fearful.

"You're okay, you're doing fine," he said.

Ryan stood up, took both her arms at the elbows, and pulled her to her feet. Her body convulsed, followed by sobs. Ryan folded her in his arms, and she stopped crying. She clung to him, her nails biting into his spine. While he stroked her back, she turned her frightened eyes to the children.

"Take me away from here," she whispered.

When Ryan picked her up, she nestled in his arms. She cringed at the sound of thunder. The roiling clouds produced a network of lightning that lit up the beach. He carried her through the hotel's back door and into an empty games room. He climbed the fire escape stairs to the second floor and used his guest card to unlock the door. Once inside his suite, he eased her down on the bed. She closed her eyes and snuggled in among the sheets.

"You must get out of your wet clothes," he said, shaking her shoulders.

Her eyes opened and she stumbled to the bathroom. After he heard taps running, she returned in a terry cloth hotel robe, a towel tied in a turban around her head. She climbed into bed and curled into a tight ball.

"Were you on board that yacht in the harbor?" he asked.

She rolled over on her side to face him.

"Yes," she whispered, shielding her face with her hands.

He poured a miniature bottle of scotch from the minibar into a glass. She sat up, dropped both legs on the floor, and drained the drink in a couple of gulps. The alcohol calmed her.

"Why were you trying to swim ashore?" Ryan asked.

She remained silent and removed the towel from her head. A few strands of hair fell down in front of her face. She lay down again, and Ryan listened to the uneven rhythm of her breathing. He pulled the sheet over her and untied the mosquito netting.

He poured himself a miniature bottle of Cutty Sark from the minibar. Despite misgivings, he drank the contents.

"Sweet dreams, whoever you are," he said.

He stripped off his wet pants and put on a muscle shirt and boxer shorts. He stretched out on the couch, listening to the wind roar and rain pelt against the windows. He got up to go to the window, where he saw lights around the pool illuminating waving palm trees and wind fanning rain in sheets off the tiled roof. The shutters banged against the wall like jackhammers. The noise brought back his old boyhood fear of storms. The sounds and fury caused a cold vapor of fear to wrap around his heart.

Shivering, he crawled into bed beside her. She turned to face him and stretched out her arms to pull him to her.

"Hold me, darling," she said.

She arched her shoulders to loosen the robe, and she pulled the gown down around her ankles. Ryan held her, and the closeness of her naked body excited him. She helped him strip off his shirt and shorts.

"I don't think we've been properly introduced," he said in a hoarse whisper.

"Aisling Quinn," she replied in a voice Ryan detected had a faint Irish lilt in an otherwise upper-class English accent.

"I'm Ryan."

Ryan tried to block out his primal fear of storms by kissing her lips with an animal like hunger. The overhead lights dimmed and then went out, but the rain suddenly stopped; a strange stillness crept into the room. Loud knocks on the door forced them apart.

As the bangs grew louder and more urgent, Aisling whispered, "Don't let them in, they'll kill me."

"Who?"

"Papa's men."

Ryan climbed out of bed, pulled on his shorts, and went to the closet, where he removed the Bolo Mauser Amari had lent him from its holster. Aiming the handgun at the door, his other hand reached out for the handle.

CHAPTER 9

AFTER RYAN OPENED THE HOTEL suite's door a crack, he pushed it further so he could see the hotel corridor was empty.

"Who's there?" he called out. "I'm armed. Show yourself and put your hands up."

No one answered, so he flung the door open. Adopting a firing position, he scanned the corridor in a wide arc.

Ryan discovered Bari crouched behind the door.

"Man, what the hell are you doing here?" he said, lowering the handgun.

Bari stared wide-eyed at the weapon in Ryan's hand.

"I saw you pull that woman out of the water," he said.

"What were you doing on the beach?"

Bari looked sheepish. "I keep an eye on your back."

Ryan stared at brief flashes of lightning; the fury of the storm had paused for the moment.

"Don't pull that stunt on me again." Ryan ruffled his damp hair. "I don't want anything bad to happen to you."

Bari's rigid composure cracked just for an instant. "After you carried that woman inside the hotel, two men talked to kids on the beach and asked question about where the *mwanamke kijana* had gone." He paused. "The kids pointed to the hotel."

"Did you recognize them?"

"No."

Ryan tried to sift through this new information, get a grip on what it all meant. He beckoned Bari to come inside the suite. When they entered, Aisling was seated on the bed and she had put the robe back on.

"Who's he?" she said in a voice so thick it sounded as if she found it hard to swallow.

"Bari Khan," Ryan said.

Bari glanced at Aisling and then turned to Ryan. "I have found the younger brother, who burned down the university office."

"That's great, good work," Ryan said. "Why isn't he in police custody?"

"His older brother is in the youth detention center. The police let the younger guy go home."

"Do you have his address?"

"Yes. It is close by."

Ryan looked out of the window's venetian blinds at light rainfall. "We may as well question this young fire starter before the big storm hits the island."

"Please don't leave me," Aisling said.

"I'm not going to be away long," he said, pulling on his runners. "You'll be safe as long as you don't open the door to anyone except me."

Ryan strapped the handgun under a windbreaker and closed the door. They headed for the fire exit that led to a narrow back lane.

"His name is Ali Hassam Khanga," Bari said as they jogged toward the old Portuguese fort. "Ali lives on Balnara Road off Hurumzi Street."

After leaving the string of hotels on the shoreline, the road became pitted and uneven, and the buildings were shabby and rundown. The narrow streets closed in around them, made more confined by the angry clouds boiling above them. A woman squatted on her haunches in a doorway glared at Ryan. In a street littered with broken masonry, Bari paused.

"This is his place," he said, pointing to the wooden door of a shack.

Oppressive heat pressed on Ryan's shoulders. Bari knocked on the cracked door and waited. Behind the door, Ryan heard a woman speak in Swahili, soon to be overshadowed by a young male voice.

"What did they say?" he asked, turning to Bari.

"Come in, the door is open."

Ryan entered a cramped room with a mud floor. A twig-thin boy confronted him. He sported a mullet and wore a pair of new Nikes and acid-stained cutaway jeans.

"I'm looking for Ali," Ryan said, glancing around the room. A gleaming new mountain bike was propped against the wall beside framed photos of bearded imams and quotes from the Qur'an. He heard a rattle of pots from a woman, bent over a sink in a tiny kitchen.

"I'm Ali," the boy said.

"I want to ask you some questions about a fire at the university," Ryan said.

"Why should I talk to a *muzungu* when I've already told the police everything?"

Bari explained to Ali in rapid Swahili that Ryan was a private investigator.

"I don't care who you are," Ali continued in English. "My home isn't a place for a fucking tourist. This is where Swahili people live. Go back to your hotel and leave us alone."

"He wants to talk now," Bari said.

"Talking to him gets me in trouble. I don't want to end up in a youth detention *boma* like my brother."

The wind outside picked up and rattled a loose shutter. The woman entered the room to close the windows. Through the glass,

Ryan could see clouds in ominous formations that resembled a rolling seascape seen from below.

"If you tell me what I need to know, I won't bother you again," Ryan said.

The old woman spoke to Ari in Swahili, and Bari translated. "She's telling him to say nothing. The family is in enough trouble."

"The police will never know I've spoken to you," Ryan said.

The boy held his gaze for a moment, the only sound the whistling wind in a wall crack.

"Okay, I'll talk if you give me one hundred American dollars," Ali said.

"Will you tell me the truth about why you and your brother set fire to Dr. Willow's office?" Ryan said.

"We did it for kicks," Ali said.

"I don't believe you."

Ryan stared at Ali's wide dark eyes set far back in their sockets. The intensity of the coming storm sucked the room dry of air. A clap of thunder shook the house and made Ali jump. His mother shouted in Swahili, and the boy signaled to her with an upright hand to keep quiet.

"You're wasting your time, white man," Ari said. "Go away, enjoy yourself like other *muzungus* and drink whiskey and chase naked whores around the pool."

Ryan grabbed the boy by the front of his Real Madrid T-shirt and twisted it to apply pressure on his throat. "Why go all the way to the university to get your kicks when you could've easily burned down a house in Stone Town?"

The boy remained silent, so Ryan tightened his grip. Ali struggled, kicking Ryan's shins with his trainers. Rain pounded on the corrugated iron roof, and Ryan could hear the *whoosh* of water cascade down the narrow street. He squeezed Ali's windpipe and at the same time hoisted him off the ground. The woman picked up a hand whisk and beat Ryan's back. Bari stepped between her and Ryan.

"Go easy on him, Ryan," Bari said.

Ryan relaxed his grip and released Ali. The boy bent over to cough and clutch his throat.

Bari continued, "You have a Raleigh bike and new Nikes. Man, you like nice things. Take his money and you'll buy more cool stuff."

Ali rocked his arms from the shoulders down to the finger tips. Outside, Ryan heard a cry that sounded like a demented seabird. Lightning illuminated the room and cast a white light over their faces as though they were covered in white powder. Rainwater from the street seeped under the door.

Ryan didn't particularly like what he was about to do.

"I could always tell the police that you lied to them about the fire being lit on a dare," he said. "If they know the truth that someone gave you money to torch Dr. Willow's office and destroy evidence needed to find his killer, the cops will be mad as hell."

The woman could see the anguish in Ali's face. She tugged on his arm, as if she wanted him to tell her what was going on.

"Your brother is now in a juvenile detention center where he is housed with boys his own age," Ryan continued. "What do you think the police are going do when they hear that he lied to them? He is going to be transferred to an adult facility, and his sentence will be doubled. He's going to be in the same cell block as murderers and rapists. These inmates are nothing compared to guards. always on the prowl for fresh meat. Some of them are infected with HIV. If you try to squeal on them, they'll accuse your brother of being a queer. Under your penal code, this means he's sentenced to life imprisonment."

"You are a filthy piece of white shit," the boy shouted above the roar of the rain. "Okay, this is how it went down. We were playing soccer on the beach. These two big dudes offered us five hundred dollars each to burn down an office at the U. They gave us cans of petrol and showed us how to make wicks out of old rags."

"What did these men look like?" Ryan asked.

Ari licked his top lip. "One of them had rings in his ears, while the other had brown skin and arms covered in tattoos of naked

65

women from his wrists to his armpits." When he glanced around the room, his eyes resembled pinballs. "They said if we told anyone what they wanted us to do, they would always know where to find us." His fingers started at his groin and moved up to his neck. "If we squealed on them, they would open us like a fish from here to here."

Ryan and Bari stood in the deep alcove of the door to avoid getting wet from holes in the roof.

"From Ali's description of these two men, I think they could be the same as the two I saw on the beach who wanted to find the woman you rescued," Bari whispered in Ryan's ear.

"If they are the same guys, then we have to figure out the connection between the redhead in my room and the reason for burning Dr. Willow's office," Ryan said in low voice. "The man named Papa who owns the yacht from which she escaped may be the link we are looking for."

When Ryan and Bari left Ali's home, they stepped into the fury of the storm. The wind pinned them against a wall. Ryan gripped Bari's elbow, and they struggled forward, heads down. The rain came down in sheets, striking them with the force of a fire hose.

"You are coming back to the hotel with me," Ryan shouted, his voice almost lost.

They moved blindly, using their arms to protect their faces. A beam supporting an outdoor stall snapped. A piece of wood passed over Ryan's head so close that he felt it stroke his hair. When they turned a corner, the gale battered them.

Bari slipped in the water up to his knees. Ryan hauled him up on his feet. He could hear a terrible roar coming from the ocean, where waves crashed against seawalls and breakwaters. Without power, houses were dark except for the occasional flicker of candle flames and hurricane lamps. Ryan spotted the hotel's entrance and plunged forward. Locking arms, Ryan and Bari stumbled inside the Serena's double doors.

CHAPTER 10

ACK IN THE HOTEL SUITE, Aisling was asleep. Ryan tried to
shield his fear of the storm from Bari. He made a bed for the
boy on the couch. As soon as Bari was settled, Ryan climbed in
beside Aisling, who melted in his arms.

Ryan blocked out the cyclone's rage in a frenzy of lovemaking.
Aisling proved to be an experienced sexual aficionada. For Ryan,
repeated sexual encounters released tension, but an ugly blot forming
in his conscience eclipsed any real pleasure he gained from the sex acts.

How could he betray Joanne with such casual ease? His
infidelity left behind a seamy sense of shame like an oil slick on the
surface of a pristine lake.

In the twilight, Ryan opened his eyes to blink at flashes of
sheet lightning. Beside him in bed, he listened to Aisling's heavy
breathing. He sat on the edge of the bed, his arms clenched across
his chest. He had a metallic taste like blood in his mouth. Bari's
couch was empty. Ryan stood up and opened the double doors to the
balcony. The heat swelled around him. Huge waves had beached the
skeletal remains of shattered dhows and narrow outrigger fishing
boats. On the sand, the high tide had left a residue ring of branches

and seaweed. In the courtyard, the wind had stripped bare palm trees of fronds and hibiscus and hydrangea leaves blanketed the surface of the swimming pool. Across the courtyard, ripped red tiles left gaping black holes in the hotel's roof.

Ryan closed the balcony doors and went back into the room. Among the tangled sheets, Aisling still slept, a contented smile on her velvet smooth skin. After he dressed, he turned on his flashlight and went downstairs to the dining room.

Two sober British tourists sat at a table in shocked silence, staring at shattered plates and scattered cutlery left behind by looters. Ryan found a sole member of the kitchen staff who made him some tomato sandwiches. After he left the kitchen, he overheard an American couple fret about finding a way to leave the island. The hotel's doors swung back and forth in the wind. In the parking lot, the beam of his flashlight bounced off the fractured glass of smashed car windshields. Thieves had ripped stereos from dashboards and stolen tires left vehicles lopsided.

Ryan climbed the stairs two steps at a time to return to his suite. After he unlocked the door, the beam of his flashlight shone on the girl's bare backside as she scrambled into bed. She sat up against the headboard and stared at him wide-eyed through the mosquito netting, as if she were a child caught raiding the cookie jar. Her guilty look soon evaporated, replaced by cockiness. She pulled back strands of long hair that had tumbled over face. Ryan noticed someone had moved his laptop.

"Good morning," Ryan said. "I've brought you breakfast."

He handed her a sandwich, and she nibbled a part of it. Ryan opened the Venetian blinds. Pools full of debris left over from the tidal surge covered the tiled patio floor. A naked man with crisscross cuts on his back and buttocks lay facedown in a puddle.

"The storm has eased," Ryan said, turning to face her.

"Thank the Lord," she said, tucking her knees beneath her chin. "What time is it?"

"Ten after ten," he said, straightening the laptop on the desk.

"Where's the young man you brought in here last night?" she asked.

"I expect he's gone to make sure his family is safe."

She blinked at puffy clouds through the open Venetian blinds.

"Two men tracking you knows you are here," Ryan said, sitting on the edge of the bed.

Aisling pouted, a look of fear darkening her face.

"Our little encounter on the beach attracted the interest of these two men, who questioned kids on the beach to find out where you went," Ryan continued.

Her eyes darted around the suite. "Where can I go? I don't have money or clothes to wear."

"Before I help you, perhaps you could begin by telling me who you are and where you came from?"

She cocked her head and lapsed into silence. Then she placed the flats of her palms on her knees. "My word, Ryan Moar, last night you were a real swordsman."

"Never mind about last night. How did you know my last name?"

She bit her bottom lip and remained silent.

He glanced at his laptop. "Did you hack into my computer, ready my mail?"

She stretched out her arms. "Give me a kiss before I tell you a bit about meself."

During the Cannes Film Festival, Aisling told Ryan, she had met a man in a nightclub who claimed to be a film producer. A party atmosphere reigned in the club where the clientele was *trés chic*.

"The place crawled with journalists and celebrities," Aisling said. "Angelina Jolie and Brad Pitt made a brief appearance." She dropped her eyes to stare at her long painted nails. "I accepted this man's invitation to come on board his yacht to talk terms and sign a contract. He took me to the harbor in the backseat of a silver

Bentley. On board, I was soon ensconced in a room furnished with French antique chairs and Monet landscapes."

The next morning, Aisling had a pounding headache. She lay sprawled in between pink silk sheets in a circular bed the size of a small swimming pool. She had never experienced such luxury, and she relished the lavish attention poured on her by her host. By the time the yacht sailed around the Horn of Africa, her film producer boyfriend had vowed to rename his yacht *Irish Eyes*.

A hard gust of wind blew into the room through a shattered glass window. Aisling pulled the sheets over her head like a nun's wimple before she continued. "I've always wanted to act in films rather than make cosmetic commercials for ITE." She removed the sheet from her head and a look of resentment flooded her face. "He promised me he would make me a star, but as soon as we anchored in Zanzibar, he ignored me." She appeared empty now, her cheeks hollow. "Does this sound like the plot of a Daniele Steele novel?"

"What's his name?" Ryan said, sitting beside her on the bed.

"The crew called him Papa."

"Apart from movies, what exactly is Papa's business?"

She laughed, a harsh, bitter sound. "Film production is a portion of his empire, and most of the movies he makes are for the pornographic market." She rested her hands on her lap, staring straight ahead, trying to disguise her vexation. "He heads a cartel of sorts. Big in the Irish drug trade and real estate. During his stay in Zanzibar, he met some partners in a villa outside of Stone Town." She grimaced, her face bathed in a white glow from the morning light. "When he returned from the meeting, I smelled whiskey on his breath and another woman's perfume clung to his suit."

Ryan stood up to stretch. Aisling wound a sheet around her naked body, climbed out of bed, walked behind him, wrapped her arms around his waist, and pressed her loins against his thighs. When Ryan disentangled her arms, she went to the dresser and swept his hairbrush through her long hair in drawn out strokes.

"What propelled you to risk your life to swim to shore from his yacht?" Ryan said.

The skin on Aisling's cheeks flushed. "Yesterday morning, when I came on deck for breakfast, Papa ignored me, his face dark and hostile. Then I overheard him whisper into his cell phone in Arabic that I'd become a liability and he wanted me eliminated."

"Pleasant chap." Ryan leaned over her. "You speak Arabic?"

Aisling put down the brush on the dresser and glanced at her face in the mirror. "For a while, I worked in the Middle East Division of the Anglo Irish Bank."

"Why did he want to kill you?"

"After too many drinks at a cocktail party, I blabbered to one of Papa's Irish associates details about his real estate manipulations." Beams of sunlight lit up the room for a moment to highlight the contours of the pained expression on her face. "The man I spoke to made a killing in Dublin real estate. Papa advised him to unload his property holdings days before the market tanked."

"How did you uncover this confidential information about his business manipulations?" Ryan said, resting his hands on her shoulders.

Aisling swept back her hair in a jerky motion. "By hacking Papa's computer."

"When you hacked into mine, what did you find out?"

Aisling seemed to teeter before answering him, her eyes charged with light. She looked out through the window at the stripped down palms and the waves sweeping up on the beach. When she turned to face him, he tried to read her expression, a combination of apprehension and fear. Ryan took his hands off her shoulders, picked up his laptop and weighed the computer in his hands.

"If you managed to get through his firewall, you must be pretty good, huh?" he said. "In comparison, I bet my computer was child's play."

She applied hotel cream to her hands, arms, and elbows.

"Aisling, don't try to lie to me. While I was out with Bari, you had plenty of time to peak at my files."

She paused to wipe cream off her face with her fingers. "Apart from finding out your last name, you're a Yank."

Ryan stared into Aisling's eyes. "Is that all you found out about me from my laptop?"

Aisling hesitated before answering. "You're married. Your wife is expecting."

The drumbeat of the rain on the roof slackened, and weak sunlight filtered into the room. He could smell the hotel soap on her skin, he took in the fullness of her breasts and the thickness of her hair that she had tied with rubber bands into a ponytail that reminded him of the way his first wife used to wear her red hair.

"What am I going to do with you?" he said.

"I want to go home to Dublin," Aisling said, getting up and thrusting herself into his arms.

"You won't go far in a Muslim country without something to wear."

"There's always this sheet," she said, pulling it in front of her face in a mock veil.

Ryan heard her take a deep breath, and Aisling returned to the bed to finish eating the sandwich.

"Apart from being a playboy movie maker and real estate mogul, what do you know about Papa's personal life? Habits?" Ryan asked.

"I know he's married, but his wife and children aren't a part of his life. He has many women, and I've worn their clothes and jewelry."

The lights flickered on and then went out.

In the sunlight that penetrated the clouds, her cheeks had taken on a deeper color, and her lips were full and glossy without lipstick. She turned toward him, her thighs spread apart, her eyes roved over his face.

"Does Papa have any identifiable scars or tattoos?" Ryan continued, breathing in the air that smelled of heated, crushed vegetation.

"I noticed from tiny scars on his face that his features have been altered by plastic surgery," Aisling said.

"How can you be so sure?"

"During the night, while we sailed past the Somalia coast, Shark couldn't sleep. When I saw him go to his sitting room, I was curious to find out what he was doing, so I followed. Through a crack in the door, I saw him standing in front of a hand mirror. He held a large photo beside his face in the glass to compare the images."

"What did the old Papa look like?"

"Jesus, he was a handsome devil. Think of Omah Sharif, when he was younger—large bedroom eyes, thick hair." She paused to eat another mouthful of the tomato sandwich. "Papa is ugly now. He cuts his hair short in a military style. He has sunken cheeks and a wide forehead. His eyes are narrow slits, and his nose is stubby like a pig's."

"A prince turned into a frog." Ryan paced in front of her. "He obviously mourns the loss of his former self. Where did he have the face job done?"

"I don't know."

"Besides you and Papa, who else is on board *Sundancer*?"

"He had a full complement of crew members: bodyguards, chefs, waiters, maids, and deckhands."

"Are his guards armed?"

"To the teeth."

"What kind of weapons?"

"Uzis, AK-47s, and for side arms, they carry Colt Mustangs .380."

Ryan cocked his head to the left. "You know your ordnance."

"My father was an arms dealer and I read his catalogues."

"Did your dad have the IRA on his client list?"

She stretched like a contented cat. "He always denied it, but I suspected he supplied arms to the boys in the north."

"Is he still in the trade?"

Aisling lowered her eyes. "Last year, an assassin killed him in the Dublin International Airport's shopping loop. A man crept up behind him and wrapped a cloth drench in some kind of poison. He died five minutes later. Even after an extensive investigation, the police never found his killer." A sense of loss flooded her face. "My dad wasn't a violent man. He was a fussy, meek-mannered guy. He was a natty dresser, a wearer of ascots and morning coats. He tested the weapons he sold at his private range. My mother expected he would be gunned down one day, but instead he died from nerve agent poison outside the airport's fish-and-chips shop."

Gusts of wind pounded the walls, and the room quivered for an instant. The lights came back and stayed on.

Aisling sat up and tucked her hands under her chin. "How am I going to get home?"

"It won't be easy. If Papa thinks you are a threat to him, he will have people watching the island's airport and ferry terminals."

Ryan shivered in spite of the heat. To find Aisling a safe passage to the Irish embassy in Dar es Salaam, he would need Amari's help.

Aisling stood and wrapped her arms around his waist. "I never imagined I'd come ashore on a hostile and dangerous island to find myself rescued by a handsome hulk."

"You have both Irish luck and emerald eyes."

"That's not exactly an original pickup line." She unlaced her fingers and brushed a strand of loose hair from her cheek. "Your brown eyes have a kind quality about them, but they also have a hint of cruelty."

"Really?"

The lights dimmed and plunged the room back into semidarkness. Without air conditioning, the heat hung over them like damp cotton. When Ryan leaned forward and gazed into Aisling's eyes, he noticed they had flecks of gold.

"The big question forward is how to keep you alive." he said.

CHAPTER 11

B Y EARLY AFTERNOON, THE CYCLONE had moved south to the Mozambique coast. Ryan went downstairs to the lobby, empty except for Javed, who had a bored, insolent look on his clean-shaven face. Ryan caught his eye as he tried to stifle a yawn. Ryan picked up a copy of the *Daily News*. Banner headlines highlighted the extensive damage of the storm to Stone Town's buildings and seawalls.

"Where's everybody?" Ryan asked.

"Some guests have left the Serena for safaris around Mount Kilimanjaro and in the Serengeti Game Park."

"Any casualties?"

"Not in this hotel."

"When will phone service be resumed?"

"I don't know. That's not up to us."

Ryan left the hotel compound and walked down Shangai road. The hot wind ruffled his hair, and dark storm clouds massed on the horizon. Gulls circled the beach before seeking shelter inland.

Ryan strolled by an apartment, where looters had broken in and robbed tenants. Small discarded appliances and clothes littered the street. Canned food and cabbages lay half submerged in puddles outside the shattered door of a grocery store. The tidal surge had washed in dead fish and seaweed to clog the drains.

He found an open pharmacy with iron-barred windows sandwiched in between two buildings carved into tenements. Behind the Sunny Side drugstore, wind had peeled corrugated iron roofs off houses like open sardine cans. Torrential rain had swept away stalls in an outdoor market, and waves had stranded chickens and goats on pockets of high ground.

A bell tinkled as he entered the shop, and an Indian woman's broad smile greeted him. To disguise Aisling's appearance, he bought a box of black L'Oreal hair color, a makeup kit, and a tube of InstaTan. His next stop was a clothing boutique, where he purchased a brown cotton *jilbab*, a paisley shoulder shawl, a black *hijab* to cover Aisling's head, a pair of flip-flops, and a variety of panties and bras.

On his way back to the Serena, he jogged around the weather walls of the Arab Fort to the Jamituri Gardens. Along the beach, men pulled undamaged dhows off the sand and hauled them into the surf. The tops of bare palm trees were dented by the wind, and spiky cones from casuarinas littered the path. Boys played football on a dry part of the lawn, and the wind carried their voices across the park.

While Ryan shopped, Aisling listened to the roar of the sea. When she opened the window, a dense haze blurred her vision of the bay. She returned to the bed, stretched out, and closed her eyes. She had the sensation of everything around her being severed from reality. The near drowning experience and the storm's fearful roar had left her nerves wafer thin. During her futile attempt to swim ashore, when saltwater had filled her lungs, she had never encountered such a frightening experience

Aisling sat up and tried not to think about her narrow escape from Shark, but memories of being on board the yacht haunted her. She shivered at the rumors she had heard of passengers on his yacht being thrown overboard and eaten by sharks. She pictured a shark's teeth rip her well toned body into shreds in a wild feeding frenzy.

The near drowning in the bay had shaken her self-confidence. If she managed to escape to Dublin, would Shark's men be waiting in the city to kill her?

Her mind wandered back to her work at the Anglo Irish bank. She had never thought of banking as a real job, but it was secure, unlike the way she felt now, drifting to an uncertain future. Aisling's bank salary had paid for her expensive tastes, and her desire to gravitate to higher social circles. She soon found ways to please rich men, including her bank boss.

Aisling's relationship to Papa had been more complex than being the mistress to a senior bank vice-president. In the end, the connection between her and Papa had become a complicated pastime of trying to amuse him—almost like solving riddles, something she was good at.

Aisling spotted Ryan's laptop on the desk. She decided again to hack into his computer. She turned on the machine and her fingers flashed across the keys. She had learned hacking techniques from a boyfriend at the bank. As soon as she found her way in, she continued reading his emails. Aisling discovered that Ryan worked as both a security specialist and a private investigator, and his spouse, Joanne, was pregnant.

On the island, he was investigating the death of a university professor, Dr. Jomo Willow. His client had recently transferred twenty-five thousand dollars from a branch of Barclay's Bank to his Citibank account.

When Aisling heard voices outside the hotel room, she switched off the laptop, jumped into bed, and lay down. She relaxed when the sounds disappeared. She fantasized about changing her life. She wanted to leave the fast lane and to get away from her jet set lifestyle. She wanted to settle far from Dublin. She imagined living in an ivy-covered cottage in an Irish village on the rugged west coast, overlooking Dingle Bay.

Aisling imagined having morning tea and toast on a terrace beside a rose garden. A man who resembled Ryan in jodhpurs came over to kiss her cheek. He then joined her for a ride along the beach. In her mind, she metamorphosed into an Irish Miss Marple. She helped the handsome private investigator solve crimes. The two them would poke around for clues in country estates, rural pubs, and smelly bogs. The loud noise of a shutter slamming against the wall shattered her bucolic make-believe world.

When she heard more thunder, she shivered, even though the room was stifling. Despite a sudden warning voice, she wanted to possess Ryan and longed for his warm embrace. Something in his eyes was so inviting; he seemed so right for her. After she went back to sleep, she awoke when Ryan shook her shoulder. In the semidarkness, she recognized the outline of his unshaven face and hairy chest matted with sweat.

"Get dressed in these clothes now," he said.

He pointed to the outfit at the foot of the bed.

"I can't wear those things," she blurted out.

"Yes, you can, if you want to stay alive." He handed her scissors and the bottle of hair color lotion. "Dye your hair black and cut it short. I've found a place, where you'll be safe for a few days."

"Why can't I stay here?"

"Those two men—who I suspect work for Papa—will soon come for you. You'll stay at Zoe Singh's house until I can arrange a dhow to take you to the mainland."

"Who is Zoe?"

"She is an Englishwoman." Aisling pulled her face into a distorted shape. "Don't hold that against her."

"I don't care for the English."

"At least, her last name is Singh not Cromwell."

She strolled toward him. "Please hold me."

He shook his head. "No time for that."

"All right, there's no need to get snarky."

She sneaked a glance at Ryan's sullen face in the daylight. The African sun had tanned his skin, shoulders, and torso a golden brown. She longed to run her fingers through his unkempt black hair. His eyes were a deep brown, flecked by pinpricks of yellow like the shimmer of sunlight on the Indian Ocean.

"That boy on the couch, what does he do for you?" she called out from the bathroom, where she rinsed color into her hair.

"He's my assistant."

She smiled when she thought of the African boy as a young Watson to Ryan's Sherlock Holmes.

She came out of the bathroom, leaned closer to him, her warm breath on his face. He pushed her away.

"Get into your disguise," he said.

She cut off her curls and put on the Swahili clothes that smelled of mildew.

When she emerged in the new clothes, Ryan said, "That's better. All you need is InstaTan to transform you into a local."

She ran her fingers through her short black hair and then adjusted her headscarf. Ryan stood behind her as she stared in the mirror at her transformation. She then glanced at his sensual lips that made her wonder if he had Spanish blood in his lineage.

"Now that you've changed me into a native, why don't you tell me about your pedigree?" she asked.

Ryan laughed. "I'm actually American-East Indian. My dad is originally from Bengal, and Mother's parents came to North Dakota via the Hebrides."

"Scottish and East Indian bloodlines have made a gorgeous combination."

"Oh yeah. What about you? Has your family always lived in Ireland?"

"We're from Drogheda. Did you know Pierce Brosnan came from Drogheda?"

"Did he now? As soon as you put the fake tan on your face, it's time to go."

On the way to Zoe's house, Ryan checked and double checked to make sure they weren't being tailed. In a narrow alley, a running man collided into Aisling and sent her sprawling onto the rain slicked pavement. A puddle soaked her ankle-length *jilbab*. Ryan picked her up. Aisling moaned as blood flowed from a scalp wound, and he tore his shirt to make a bandage.

"I feel too faint to walk," Aisling said, leaning against his shoulder.

He held Aisling, pulled her arm around his neck, and half carried her along the waterlogged streets. Her limp body swayed like a drunk in a headwind and blood from her head wound seeped into his makeshift bandage.

When they arrived at the villa's iron gate, Aisling's eyes remained closed, and she mumbled some garbled words as though she was in a semiconscious state. Ryan felt a paralyzing fear that Aisling's head injury was serious. Even though, anxious to be rid of her, he wanted to see her safely to her embassy in Dar es Salaam. As they waited at the gate for Khaled to let them in, he felt enormous relief when Aisling opened her eyes and stood on one foot. Khaled spotted them from a second-story window, and he scurried down the outside stairs to unlock the gate.

The interior of the villa was lit by the golden light of hurricane lamps. In the living room, Zoe offered tea and scones. The house was quiet except for the sound of drips from ceiling leaks that were collected in cast-iron buckets. Zoe brought out a first aid kit, and she cleaned and bandaged Aisling's head wound. Aisling's teeth chattered as if she had a chill, her skin pale under her bottle tan.

Even though he had taken every precaution, Ryan had a nagging feeling that they had been followed to the villa. Sensing his unease, Zoe handed Ryan a scotch and soda. He thanked her, and he felt the whiskey's sharp bite in his throat and the accompanying warmth in his stomach. He leaned on the mantelpiece, head bowed. His thoughts were of Joanne and the baby growing inside her, but, after last night's fling, he couldn't lose a feeling of shame.

"I have to go," Ryan said, draining his scotch.

Seated on an ottoman, Aisling stood up to clutch his hand; her eagerness hinted of intimacy. He noticed Zoe watch her stroke and kiss his hand, a quizzical expression on her lined face. Despite being shut off from the world, he knew Zoe had a keen sense of worldly ways. He had told her of Joanne's pregnancy. For a moment, he daren't pull his hand away from Aisling's caresses to prevent drawing attention to an awkward situation.

"Please, don't leave me," Aisling whispered, choking back tears.

"You'll be safe here," he murmured, easing his hand from her grasp.

"What am I to do while you're gone?"

"The rules are simple. For your own safety, don't go near any hotels, bars, ferry terminals, or the airport. Papa's men are probably on the lookout for you in these places. Wear the Swahili clothes at all times, keep dying your hair. Also, apply the fake suntan lotion on your face to alter your appearance." He pulled on his rain jacket. "I'll be back as soon as I've arranged to hire a dhow to take you to Dar es Salaam. Your embassy will issue you a new passport so you can go home."

Aisling gave him a wan smile, before he headed for the door. "Don't be long, darling."

CHAPTER 12

AT THE FAR END OF the Serena Inn's reception desk, pool chairs, folding tables, and bar stools were stacked in haphazard piles. Behind the desk, Javed's head was buried in a pornographic magazine. When Ryan approached the desk, his youthful face flushed as he tucked the magazine under the counter.

"There's a message for you, sir," he sputtered.

He handed Ryan a slip of paper with a note for him to phone Joanne.

As Javed slid Ryan's rental car keys across the counter, he said, "The bar is open, but the restaurant is closed."

Ryan pocketed the keys and glanced around the empty lobby.

Javed cleared his throat. "Will you be accepting additional room charges for your guests last night?"

"Mr. Hussein stayed in my room for one night. Add the charge to my room."

"Yes, sir." Before Ryan turned to leave, Javed added, "Apart from the storm, how has your stay been at the Serena?"

"Wonderful."

Javed looked down at his cracked fingernails. "How did the young lady enjoy our hospitality?"

"What do you mean?"

"I have seen you carry this *muzungu* woman from the beach to the hotel."

Ryan leaned over the counter and grabbed the front of his collar. "Don't mention to anyone that this lady stayed in my room, understand?"

"I'm afraid I can't do that."

"Are you threatening me? If so, I will inform your manager that while on duty I caught you reading a filthy magazine. He'll probably fire you."

Ryan released his hold on Javed's shirt, and the receptionist clutched his throat and gasped for air.

"Breathe a word of her being here, and I'll rip your God damned throat out," Ryan said.

"Do you want to see the hotel's security tape?" Javed said, squinting through his rimless glasses down the corridor. "If the police make inquiries about this woman, it would be my duty to hand the tapes over to them."

Ryan wanted to vault over the counter and wrap his hands around Javed's windpipe. "Give me those tapes."

"There is a surcharge for this service," Javed spluttered.

"How much?"

"Five hundred dollars," Javed paused to let the amount sink in. "I only accept cash."

"Don't insult me, Javed."

"You're in no position to refuse my offer. One phone call to the police and they will confiscate the tapes. And when they find that your woman entered this island illegally, they will arrest her."

Ryan's rage started to build.

Javed leaned back, trying to get some distance. "Two men last night asked me about this woman. They are not the police. I told them nothing, but they said they would be back."

Javed stiffened and braced for Ryan's next outburst.

Ryan stepped closer, his eyes level and cold. He leaned on the counter. "Give me the tapes."

Javed gave Ryan a lopsided grin. "You pay or I talk about the redhead in your bed."

Ryan counted the money and fanned the bills on the counter. "If anyone comes to the hotel asking about this woman, I want you to tell them she never stayed here, she never existed."

Javed licked his thin lips. "I swear to everything I hold sacred that I will not tell anyone."

His hands passed over the money, and the notes disappeared below the counter.

Javed handed him the security tape. "You can count on me to be discreet, sir."

As Ryan headed for the stairs, he thought of how Javed was about as trustworthy as a starving hyena. In the dim red emergency lighting, Ryan fumbled for his room key. A nauseating odor penetrated his nostrils, reminding him of the putrid flesh of an unearthed corpse. When his runners slid on the marble floor, he bent down to feel a sticky, thick liquid. Nailed to the door, the beam of his pocket flashlight reflected off the eyes of a cat. The light caught the saliva in the cat's open mouth. The cat's intestines oozed out of gashes in the feline's furry stomach.

Ryan shuddered at the thought of staying another night at the Serena. His mind raced. This grotesque calling card meant one thing; those who nailed the dead cat to the door would be back. He had better pack and find a secure place to stay.

The storm had ripped off the Hotel Kaponga's shutters and shattered windowpanes of the boutique hotel. At midnight, when Ryan entered the Kaponga's carved wooden door, a slender woman in a flowery sarong welcomed him by extending a hand to be shaken.

"The name's Georgina Cavendish," she said in a distinct Southern drawl.

After Ryan inquired about a room, Georgina accepted his cash for a week's stay and his false name without question. She didn't even ask to see his passport. When she handed Ryan his key, she wished him a pleasant stay.

Beyond the lobby, Ryan crossed a covered central courtyard, where empty flower pots and metal tables were embedded in concrete. He climbed a flight of stone stairs and opened the door of a spacious room, overlooking the Old Customs House on Mizingani Road. He paused to breathe in gulps of humid and moist air. Only a few pedestrians walked the streets, heads down to avoid the wind. Leaves stripped from the trees and shrubs plastered the slicked roads and on the surfaces of pools of floodwater.

Ryan stripped off his clothes, climbed on the bed, leaned against the headboard, and punched Joanne's cell phone numbers on his mobile.

"It's me, sweetheart," he said when she answered the phone.

"What's that racket? I can hardly hear you," Joanne said.

"That's the sound of a dying cyclone."

"How did you survive this storm last night without me to comfort you?"

Guilt roared back at him in waves. "I did all right solo, but missed you."

"How did you overcome your fear of storms?"

"Deep breathing." His answer sounded contrived and phony. At the thought of his pregnant wife, Ryan started to sweat and feel the sting in his eyes from the salt. "How are you and junior doing?"

"Dr. Henderson is keeping a close eye on me. He's told me to ease up on my teaching schedule."

"That's good." He rubbed the stubble on his chin. "I've had to change hotels."

"Why?"

It was times like this that he hated having to fudge the truth. He could never tell her about Aisling. His betrayal of Joanne

85

during the night of the storm caused an ache to grip him around his stomach, as if he had taken a large dose of self-loathing.

"You're awfully quiet, Ryan, you okay?" Joanne asked.

"I'm fine."

"What's the reason for moving from the Serena?"

"If I'm to continue my investigation, I have to keep a low profile and avoid the police."

"Are the police discouraging you from investigating Jomo's murder?"

"That's the message I'm getting, but I think I can wrap this case up soon."

"I've a better idea. Catch the next plane for Nairobi tomorrow morning."

"The airport's shut down."

He heard her sigh. "I want you to leave this island and its depressing history of violence and human misery before it swallows you up, and you lose your way in Stone Town's labyrinth of narrow streets."

Without air-conditioning, Ryan felt overheated as gusts of wind battered the windows. There was a painful silence that led Ryan to a moment of clarity.

"I'm meeting a local PI for lunch today," he said.

"To put you on the right track?"

"I expect so, but I have to work *poli, poli*—Swahili for slowly, slowly."

"That doesn't suit your temperament." She laughed, a hollow, brittle sound. "I know you so well. Despite *poli poli* progress, I think you've fastened on to this case of finding those responsible for Jomo's murder as tight as a barnacle. You can't let go any more than you can your own marrow."

"This case has turned me into two people. One of them knows a gifted economist—a man who wanted to make a real difference in Africa—has been gunned down, and justice needs to be served. In the other's shoes, I'm beginning to have a gut feeling that it's time to go home. Why should I solve Jomo's murder? The police are determined to pin the shooting on an innocent man."

"Stay or leave? Which person is the real you?" When Ryan remained silent, Joanne added, "I've never known you to give up on a case despite enormous opposition. It's not in your nature."

Ryan rubbed his unshaven jaw. "I'm beginning to feel ashamed for even thinking about quitting."

"Your dilemma reminds me of something my mother said when I was growing up. 'Face what you fear, and seek out the truth of things you don't understand.'" She paused for a moment. "I think this case is designed to test your mettle, but I'm afraid it is going to kill you in the process, and you will leave behind a fatherless baby boy."

"I'd never do that to any son of mine." Ryan stared at the mosquito netting surrounding him. He tried to imagine her blue eyes looking deep into his. "Give me a few days more to get to the bottom of this mystery. I miss you so much—more than you can imagine."

"Remember last fall how well we worked together in the Black Hills?"

His eyes were moist for a moment. "You were magnificent, but I never want to put the lives of you and our children in such terrible danger again."

"No one controls the winds of fate," she whispered. "They blow as they please." He heard her cough that sounded more like a sob. "I still don't understand how Renée is able to pay you. Jomo must have received a huge windfall to buy a hotel and own a palatial home." He heard her sigh. "A mystery that I wish I was there to help you solve."

"I wish you were here."

"Be careful, my precious barnacle."

"No one could ask for a better life partner. I love you," he whispered.

"I love you, too," Joanne said. "I feel dizzy. I'll have to say goodbye or in your case goodnight."

She disconnected the line.

Ryan stretched out on the bed and studied the patterns on the wallpaper made by the shadows of blowing palms. He listened to the wind's shriek; the heavy black sky threatened to unleash more misery.

CHAPTER 13

AT NOON THE NEXT DAY, Ryan parked his rental Range Rover on a side street. Beside him, Bari looked bleary eyed, his face empty, as though he had just come from a funeral. A swarm of gnats hovered around his springy hair, and his hands swept around his head to chase the insects away.

"What's happened to you, man? You look terrible," Ryan climbed into the vehicle. "Is your sister all right? Did the storm damage your house?"

"She is okay and our house isn't flooded."

"I'm glad to hear you were both safe and dry." Ryan noticed Bari's sullen expression. "What is bothering you?"

"It's dangerous being around you, *bwana*."

"I know, but we ain't done yet, partner."

The streets started drying up in a sudden burst of fierce heat as the heavy clouds parted.

"For you, this island is no longer a safe place," Bari said.

"It usually is that way when I'm getting closer to finding the killer."

Bari remained silent, his gaze drifting from the windshield to where birds freckled the sky in haphazard circles, as if looking for somewhere to land.

"I need to know what's wrong," Ryan said, turning on the ignition.

Once in the street, Ryan swerved around clumps of broken tree limbs, and he spun the wheel to avoid hitting a snapped telephone pole. On the other side of the road, a man stripped to his waist tried to tape cracks on his store's cracked front window.

Bari remained silent as he stared at muddy pools churned by car wheels on the side of the road.

"What's up?" Ryan asked.

"Nothing."

Ryan parked in front of a rooftop restaurant. "Wait here."

Ryan climbed two flights of narrow exterior stairs to the café, where a waiter was sweeping leaves and twigs off the damp floor. He went to a counter and bought coffee and a plate of omelet-filled chapatti. He carried the takeout meal in a paper bag to the Land Rover.

"After all you went through in the storm, you need a good breakfast," Ryan said, grinning.

Bari sniffed the bag. "Smells good," he said, rubbing his flat belly. He started wolfing down the steaming chapatti.

"I need you now more than ever to help me," Ryan said. He paused. "What do you say if I double your salary?"

Bari's face brightened. "You mean that, *bwana*?"

"I sure do. And from now on, call me Ryan."

"Okay, Ryan," he said before stuffing down the rest of the chapatti and licking his fingers. "That's a deal."

"Feeling better?"

"You can believe," he replied, his cheeks bulging with food.

Ryan left Bari to mind the car, and he returned to the rooftop restaurant to meet Amari. He sat at a table overlooking the harbor. The wind had snapped trees and blown branches into the streets.

Debris clogged the drains and floated on the surface of pools in the narrow alleys. Puddles made it difficult for pedestrians to wade through brown water and floating trash. In the street below, a young woman came out of a carved doorway in a bright *kanga* head scarf. As she stepped into the street, she lifted her skirts to reveal a pair of knee-high rubber boots. Denuded of branches and bark, A splintered baobab tree denuded of branches and bark, appeared on the horizon like gnarled fingers pointed in anger at the sky. Despite the storm, sellers of African carvings had set up booths of rows of giraffe and impala hardwood statues in the hope of attracting tourists brave enough to leave the hotels.

When Amari arrived, he was breathing hard, as if he had run all the way to the restaurant. Ryan ordered coffees and samosas from a waiter, who served them immediately and left.

"The streets are turned into rivers this morning, Ryan," Amari said, surveying the panorama of destruction. "Many people have been injured in the storm, but only a few people are dead. A man drowned after he wandered out on the beach and a wave swept him out to sea." Amari leaned forward and touched Ryan's hand for a moment. "He's not the only casualty or potential one we have to worry about."

"What do you mean?"

"If I may be blunt, I think the time has come for you to pack up and leave the island," he said.

"You're the third person in the last twenty-four hours to give me the same advice. I'm beginning to feel I'm a pariah in Zanzibar."

Amari rubbed the heavy scars on his left hand. "You're a dreamer, Ryan, if you think you can carry out a high-profile murder investigation without treading on toes."

"But I've gone out of my way not to antagonize anyone."

"I don't agree. The police are furious at what they perceive as flagrant inference."

"They have accused the wrong man."

"That may be the case, but your continued presence is beginning to make them lose face."

"There has been a miscarriage of justice."

"For God's sake, this is Africa." Amari sipped his coffee out of a tiny cup. Below them, an ambulance with revolving red lights picked up a sheet covered body carried on a stretcher. "I'm not disputing your evaluation of who killed Jomo, but the police claim they have found the murder weapon in the accused man's hovel."

"Where does a street vendor get hold of a sophisticated handgun?"

Amari started drumming his fingers on his knees in an effort to get a hold on what he was saying. "This evidence could've been easily planted in Mezengo Muhogo's shack by the police to make their case airtight." He leaned back in his chair. "Once you're in the security of North Dakota and in the bosom of your family, does it matter if an unknown street vendor is hung in a faraway island for a crime he didn't commit?"

Ryan shrugged as brown water streamed down a drainpipe to the street below him.

His voice became hoarse, irritated. "If I know Mezengo is innocent, why wouldn't I try to prevent him from being convicted? I wouldn't want that on my conscience. What's going to happen to his family?"

Out in the bay, a loud horn sounded as a container ship entered the harbor.

"I told you from the beginning this was going to be a difficult case," Amari said, gazing at the ship's red bow cutting through the choppy waters. He didn't speak again until the vessel had passed their line of view. "It is always complex when you carry out an investigation and politics gets in the way. Dr. Willow was killed a few weeks before your country was to sign a multimillion dollar aid and food program with the Tanzanian government. Believe me, after Jomo was shot, there were a lot of civil servants having sleepless nights in Dodoma, including President Jakeya Kikwete."

"That explains why Lipumba is so anxious to discourage me from sniffing around in his sandbox."

"Don't be too harsh to judge Lipumba. From the beginning, he's been under enormous pressure to get a speedy conviction."

Ryan didn't reply, pausing to take in the view of the docks, where a lone dhow glided out to sea, its lateen sail billowing like a crescent moon.

"In the future, don't you think some honest cop will take another look at this man's case file?" Ryan said.

Amari pursed his lips and then shook his head, as though the words meant nothing to him. "In a case of this kind, if the police follow their usual procedure, Lipumba will see to it that the file goes missing."

"You think it's easy for him to consign this case to the garbage dump? Lipumba must know he's let someone get away with murder."

Amari laughed, a dry, empty sound devoid of humor. "Believe me, Ryan, Lipumba will be well compensated. In a month, he'll be given a promotion, his name splashed all over government-controlled newspapers. The president is sure to give him a citation. Forget the whole episode, Ryan, there's really no point in clinging to this hopeless case."

"When you attempt to cover up the past, it has been my experience that something always goes wrong." There was a crunch of pebbles, footsteps on the wet gravel, as the waiter came to refill coffee cups. "I'm not giving up."

"Bravo, Ryan," he said, leaning forward to take a sip from his cup. "You've spoken like a copper true to his profession." A long silence followed, broken by the blare of a car horn. Amari continued, "Well, this is indeed a surprise. I thought you'd cave in and take the easy route back to your state of North Dakota, but instead you insist on finding out the truth." Amari cracked his knuckles that sounded like burning wood. "In doing so, I hope your bones don't end up in an unmarked grave."

Ryan could feel sweat spring from his pores. "On another matter, Amari," he added, leaning forward. "I need to find a dhow skipper willing to take a woman—with no questions asked—across the channel to Dar."

Amari threw up his hands. "Don't tell me you have become entangled with a woman? Is she escaping from a jealous husband?"

Ryan told Amari how he had rescued a playboy's mistress, Aisling Quinn, from drowning in the bay.

"If you have a fat bank account, I can give you the name of a dhow skipper who is discreet," Amari said. "He's a smuggler, so after he's completed the voyage, he won't go blabbering about this trip to the police."

"Where can I find him?"

"Go early in the morning to the Old Dhow Harbor at the end of Mizingani Road, opposite the Clove Distillery. Ask for Freeman Mkapa. The name of his dhow is *Makunduchi*. Tell him I sent you. He's reliable, if you pay him well."

"I'll give him any fee he wants."

"So, after your mystery woman is out of harm's way, you'll devote your energies to solving Jomo's murder?"

"That's the game plan."

"I am curious. Can you tell me something about the circumstances surrounding this woman's escape?"

Ryan glanced at a green lizard on the wall basking in the sunshine. "I believe the man she's running away from could be the crime lord you mentioned who is trying to take over the local drug trade."

"What's the name of her lover's yacht?"

"*Sundancer*."

"What did she say was the owner of the yacht's name?"

"Everyone on board called him Papa."

"Why does he want her silenced?"

"Aisling found out about his criminal cartel by hacking into his computer. As a result, he threatened to throw her overboard and feed her to the sharks." Amari looked at Ryan quizzically. "That's what she told me."

"After you rescued her, did she sleep in your hotel room?" Ryan squirmed in his chair. "It was rude of me to ask that question. It's none of my business to find out whomever you slept with. However, I must warn you that if any of the hotel staff are aware of her being with you, word could leak back to Papa. Many five-star hotel employees are unofficial spies for the police or on the payroll of the drug lords. Did anyone see this woman in your bed?"

Ryan told him about the arrangement he'd made with Javed to give him the security tape of him carrying her through the hotel's beach entrance.

"When you moved from the Serena to your new hotel, I hope you didn't leave a forwarding address," Amari said.

"I told no one. When I checked into the Kaponda, I paid in cash and used an alias."

"That's good. Don't use a credit card. That's one way the police or Shark's men can track you down. Does anyone know about your new digs?"

"I've told Bari."

"That's not a smart move. You put far too much trust in that boy."

Ryan told him about the cat nailed to his bedroom door.

Amari scratched his ear. "I have hunch this cat mutilation has everything to do with Papa. He's the new boy on the island. He's muscling his way into the local crime scene. His operations are so secret, no one really knows what he's doing." Amari stroked his beard and remained quiet for a moment. "Let's work from what we know as fact. Nailing that dead cat to your bedroom door is the same tactic they used to terrify Renée. It could be the common denominator in the case of Jomo's assassination."

"What kind of maniac would resort to tactics that border on black magic, voodoo?"

"Whoever is behind this mutilation expects you to flee the island."

"I'm not quitting."

"Who are you doing this for? For Jomo's wife and kids? For God perhaps? Or for some old-fashioned obsession to see justice done?" Amari's forehead was seamed with furrows, his eyes an indistinct brown, as though the sun had leeched most of the color out of them. "Have you really thought things through? I don't think you are fully aware of the odds stacking up against you."

Ryan got to his feet and went to the rail. In the distance, he could see the black walls of the Arab fort. "I'm tired of chasing smoke."

Amari furrowed his hawkish brows. "I suspect Papa's intelligent, comfortable in his role as head of a rogue crime cartel." He inclined his head. "Before we talk further about him, join me for lunch after the ten thirty morning service at the Anglican Cathedral. By that time, I'll have something concrete for you."

Ryan stared at him, his mouth agape. "The Anglican Cathedral?"

"Surprised?"

"I thought we'd meet after prayers at the mosque."

Amari stood up and clapped him on the shoulder. "Can't do that, old chap. You see, I'm a Christian."

CHAPTER 14

EARLY SUNDAY MORNING, RYAN WALKED from the Hotel Kaponga to the cathedral on the eastern side of Stone Town near the corner of Mkunazini and Creek Roads. At the nearby docks, whitecaps beat against the prow of a cruise liner, while tourists flocked around curio and souvenir stands on the quay.

The church's single clock tower acted as a beacon for Ryan to follow as he strolled through the maze of narrow streets. Having a few minutes to spare before the ten o'clock service, Ryan explored the grounds of the church built of a mixture of concrete and crusted coral stone. Ryan thought the gothic architecture would make the cathedral equally at home in Zanzibar or Sussex.

A sculpture of a man and a woman standing beside three slaves chained together by the neck stood inside a stone pit half full of brown water. According to a plaque, Anglican missionaries had built the cathedral on the site of the old slave market. The church's altar stood on the spot of the whipping tree, where slaves were tied and beaten to display to potential buyers their strength and endurance.

When the bells began to ring, Ryan strolled through the cathedral's arched doorway and entered the cavernous interior. He paused as his eyes adjusted to the dim light, while his nose absorbed a faint musky odor of incense. In the nave, a white-haired woman handed him a prayer book. He wandered down the aisle and sat in a wooden pew, resting his feet on an embroidered prayer cushion.

Ryan hadn't been inside a church for some time, and the sensation made him feel like meeting a friend he had neglected to see for many years. The cathedral's stained glass windows reminded him of the older, traditional architecture of churches in Fargo's inner city. Apart from a smattering of sunburned tourists, local parishioners filled the pews. Standing next to the gold leaf altar of a haloed Christ on a crucifix, he spotted Amari in a white surplice beside a thickset vicar wearing a gold-trimmed chasuble.

The red-faced cleric led the hymn, singing in a spirited voice that echoed in the high-vaulted ceiling. During his sermon, Ryan felt his head droop. Lulled by his sonorous voice, he fought off sleep. He came awake when a murmur rippled through the congregation.

A squat, muscular man wearing a yellow baseball cap pulled down low over his eyes stood crouched in the aisle close to the altar. He held a handgun with a silencer in his outstretched arms. Two rounds burst into Amari's chest. Blood soaked his white vestments, fanning out from the wounds like the opening of a red hibiscus's flower. Amari staggered for a moment, clutching his chest, before he collapsed on the polished marble floor.

Ryan vaulted over the pew in front of him. The shooter turned and leveled his gun at Ryan. He crouched down, while bullets slammed into the pews, splintering the wood and raining chips on the congregation. When the shooter ran down the aisle to the exit, Ryan scrambled to his feet and raced after him. Outside the church, the assassin mounted a motorbike and roared around the traffic island in front of the cathedral.

Ryan knew it wouldn't take long for him to disappear into the labyrinth of narrow alleys. Across the street, he spotted a young man on an idling motorcycle, a cigarette dangling in the corner of his lips.

"I need to borrow your bike," Ryan shouted, fanning a handful of dollars in his face.

The young man looked startled and didn't understand him. He yelled at Ryan in Swahili to stop pestering him.

"Oh, what the hell," Ryan said, throwing the notes on the biker's lap. "Take the money."

Ryan pushed him hard off the saddle, climbed on, and revved the engine. He sped off in the direction the assassin had taken down a narrow street toward the Old Dhow Harbor. Ryan twisted the throttle, and the bike shot forward, engine screaming. He followed the roar of the bike ahead of him. In a narrow alley, his wheel skidded in a puddle and the bike's wheel struck a vendor's stall. The frail structure collapsed and scattered mangoes on the street.

Ryan righted the bike and followed the assassin down steps that led to a fish market. He spotted the killer weave around the stalls. For a moment, he raced parallel to the him in an adjacent row of stalls. This was the first time he got a good look at the bearded man dressed in a long-sleeved white shirt and tight jeans. The assassin almost spun out of control when his bike nicked a stand and his wheels slithered on scattered zebra fish.

Quick to recover, the killer swung to a dirt road, and his bike disappeared around a corner, reappearing in a park. His motorcycle veered close around boys playing soccer in a rain soaked field. He then accelerated down a gravel path lined by tall palms. From there, Ryan followed the biker, heading for the tangled streets of Stone Town.

Ryan lost sight of the killer for a moment when he turned right on Funguni Road. When he caught up to him, the distance to between them narrowed. The assassin glanced over his shoulder so he could take a shot at him with his handgun.

The sound of the motorbikes drowned out the shots. One of the bullets shattered Ryan's windshield, and his bike bucked from the impact. Ryan's hand slipped off the throttle. He struggled to get his hand back to rev the engine to make up for lost ground. The shooter threaded his way around buses and donkey carts to cross the busy Main Road toward the docks, knifing close around the bumpers of honking cars.

Ryan followed him, ignoring the blare of horns and the curses from drivers. For an instant, a man pushing a cart of coconuts slowed down the killer. The shooter then headed for Malindi Road, enabling Ryan to close the gap. He hung close on his tail, while the shooter searched for a way to escape. Amari's shooter opened the throttle full as he speeded by a row of souvenir shops, before entering the chaos of an open-air market.

The assassin made a sudden bank left and raced for Creek Road. Ryan followed him south on the busy artery at the edge of Stone Town, darting in and out of heavy traffic. To avoid hitting a cyclist, Ryan braked to send the bike into a power slide. After pulling the motorbike out of the skid, Ryan entered a grove of banana trees. The track shifted sharply to the left. As the killer's bike hurled around the corner, he lost control, bucked, and fishtailed, before being thrown into a violent roll into a ditch and over an embankment.

Ryan found the shooter trapped beneath his wheels-up Harley-Davidson. His legs were twisted out of shape and blood fanned out from a chest wound. His eyes flickered, and his right hand tried to reach the semiautomatic strapped to his chest, but his fingers were too shattered to obey his command.

Ryan searched the injured man's pockets until he found his wallet. His billfold contained no identification of any kind, not even a driver's license.

"You are a fool to try and outrace me," Ryan said, leaning over him.

The assassin opened his eyelids, blackened by bruises. He managed to whisper something that sounded like a ghost's breath that floated across a graveyard.

"Tell me who you work for," Ryan said.

Half-closed eyes stared back at him, a look of defiance on his mud stained face.

Ryan took his cell phone out of his pocket. "I'm calling an ambulance."

After he punched in the emergency number, he explained to a receptionist the nature of the accident. When the killer's blood-coated lips parted, Ryan leaned closer.

"Rasul, Rasul, Rasul," he whispered.

"Who is Rasul?"

Ryan heard the killer's cell phone ring. He probed inside the man's jacket until he found his blood slicked phone. He brought it to his ear.

"Habari," Ryan said.

"Who's this . . . Paul?" a harsh voice replied.

"He's here but unable to speak."

The other end of phone was silent for a minute.

Ryan said, "If you're Rasul, I know you hired Paul to kill a man in the cathedral."

Silence. Then a voice said, "Where is Paul?"

"He's alive under the twisted metal of a beat-up Harley. He needs medical attention. I've called an ambulance. He is five miles southwest of Stone Town, near a sign advertising the Mbweni Ruins. Look for a crowd. He has a broken leg."

The phone went dead.

CHAPTER 15

WHEN RYAN RETURNED TO THE Kiponda, he had a shower to wash away the mud and grit. He had returned the borrowed Raleigh motorbike to a spot near the cathedral. Feeling clean and refreshed, he phoned Renée. She picked up immediately.

"Hello Renée," he said.

"Your voice sounds hollow, are you okay?" she said.

"Not exactly, Amari's dead."

"Oh, no."

Ryan told her how the gunman had murdered Amari in front of the altar and the subsequent motorbike chase.

"Now that Amari's dead, who is there to help you?" Renée took a sharp intake of breath. "This case is becoming complicated and dangerous. The motorbike chase isn't likely to endear you to the locals."

"I haven't heard from Lipumba, so maybe he appreciates me for apprehending Amari's killer."

"On the other hand, I'm surprised he hasn't put you in prison for stealing the motorcycle and reckless driving."

He paused to listen to the faint thump of music coming through the open window of the Bottom's Up Bar. "I have an important lead that will point me in the right direction to finding Jomo's killer."

"That's great." Renée's voice developed a tremor. "Ryan, I'm worried about you."

"Give me time to nail it down."

When Ryan hung up, the next phone call from an old flame. She threatened him from different angle, closer to home.

At noon the next day, Sylvia Bannerman sat in a corner of the Serena Inn's Terrace Restaurant at a table covered in a white tablecloth. Crystal glasses glinted in the shrouded haze, a smudge of paint across the sky. Sylvia wore a white Chanel suit and her short auburn hair hung in curls to her athletic shoulders. She sat opposite Ryan, looking out at the ocean, still restless after the storm. For lunch, the hotel had set up a buffet of silver chafing dishes beside iced shrimp in glass bowls and fruit arranged in pyramids.

Despite the heat, Sylvia looked cool and composed, her hands on her lap. She closed her eyes for a moment to feel the sun on her smooth cheeks and to smell the buffet's enticing aroma of coffee and kebabs. When she stood up to refill her plate for more lobster, caviar, and oysters, she glanced back at Ryan to study his chiseled face in profile and his muscular build accented by his formfitting sports shirt.

The last time Sylvia had seen Ryan was in Washington five years ago. She had told him that his appearance had changed little—his face remained unlined and his snub nose as cute as ever. Returning to the table, Sylvia reminded herself it was time to end the chummy, idle chitchat and get down to business. But first, she dug out a piece of lobster leg from the shell and dipped it in a tiny bowl of hot butter sprinkled with bay leaves.

"Before coming here, I delved into your file," she said, using a napkin to dab the corners of her mouth.

"Since when have I been of interest to the state department?" Ryan asked.

"After several years of exemplary service with the West Fargo Police Department—marred by some disciplinary issues—you went into private practice. This venture turned out to be rather a disaster, depending on whomever you talked to. After that, you ended up working for the CIA in Langley. You were then posted to London, Belfast, and the Middle East, ending your service in some hot spots in the Balkans. You cut short a promising career as a spy to return to security and private investigation work, which you have found lucrative. You even had time to marry Joanne Sutter, a college drama instructor."

"You've done your homework, Sylvia." His eyes drifted to her ring finger. "I see you're not married."

"Tried it once, to an actor."

"I take it he wasn't a keeper."

"His ego was larger than his talent." She let her breath out slowly. "I always call that dramatic stage of my life the downside of *An Unfunny Thing Happened to Me on the Way to the Altar.*"

"So, it wasn't a long run."

She avoided his eyes to dab a napkin on her buttery red lips. "He didn't turn out to be a man for all reasons."

She removed a strand of hair from her eyebrow and looked him in the face, her eyes going small with memory.

"Anything wrong?" he asked.

Sylvia took a sip from her champagne flute, before she offered to refill his glass from the bottle in a bucket of melted ice.

Ryan shook his head. "What were you thinking about just now, us?"

She turned to stare at a tanker that appeared as if by trick of light, an indistinct stick of gum stretched out on the horizon, ethereal and gray.

"You taught me a thing or two, Ryan," she said, her voice sounding small and distant. "After a while, you have no choice but to carry on and deal with it."

104

"You like all the petty politics you have to stickhandle your way through in Washington." He grinned. "What about our time together, when we were off the clock?"

"Most of the time, you were only half there. You had someone else living inside you named Kathy."

Ryan got up from the table and wandered over to the railing that overlooked the beach. The sand had a high watermark of debris tossed up by the storm. Smoke from a barbecue pit smelled of roasted chicken, and a ray of sunlight glittered like yellow diamonds off the bay.

Sylvia followed him and tapped him on the shoulder.

"Come back to the table, Ryan, please," she said.

When they sat down again, Sylvia said, "That was clumsy of me. Will you accept my apology?" Ryan remained silent, staring at dhows crowding the harbor; the sails reminded him of shark fins. "When we were together, you were the only one. I want you to remember that for as long as you live."

"You mean the only one in bed with you at the time?"

Ryan leaned back in his wrought iron chair and laced his fingers around the back of his head. "What was this pressing matter you wanted to see me about?"

Sylvia looked at him from under her brow. "I hope you're not thinking about an extended stay on the island." She nibbled on a caviar-covered cracker. "Ambassador Hugh Dowling has been informed by Dohoma that you are becoming a nuisance to local authorities."

"What's the Tanzanian government's beef?"

"There are charges pending against you."

"Sometimes things go pear-shaped when you're in the middle of a murder investigation."

"It has also come to the government's attention that while you have been on the island, you have caused considerable mayhem."

"What are they talking about?"

"There was a shooting in the cathedral followed by a motorbike chase in the streets. While driving a stolen bike, you terrorized locals."

"After I witnessed the shooting in the church, I did my civic duty to track down the killer." Ryan's eyes moved slowly over her face. "I've reimbursed the motorbike owner, compensated the mango seller for damage to her stall, and apprehended a killer."

Her eyes widened, her anger growing. "I don't care if you think you can buy yourself out of trouble. To put it bluntly, Ryan, you are becoming an embarrassment to the American government."

She looked over at the cocktail bar's empty stools, and she straightened her shoulders. He pretended to look out at the bay, but she was aware he half stared at her with more than curiosity.

"You're not going to give me one of your lectures are you, Sylvia?" he said.

"Frankly, your investigation into Dr. Willow's death has caused an uproar in local government circles," she said. After a brief silence, she added, "If you refuse to leave Zanzibar by the end of the week, senior officials are prepared to launch a formal complaint against you."

"You came all this way from Dar to tell me this?"

"The only reason Dodoma is holding back on arresting you is that Tanzania is about to sign an aid-and-trade package with our government, and they don't want to embarrass us by deporting or incarcerating an American citizen."

"No one seems to be too concerned about an American citizen being gunned down in a street in Stone Town. Following his shooting, his wife and two children being severely traumatized by thugs, his widow suspects were off-duty cops. Since then, the family has been forced to flee their home and seek refuge in a hotel."

Sylvia drained her champagne glass. "The police already have a prime suspect in custody in the Jomo Willow case, awaiting trial."

"You mean the impoverished coconut vendor who robbed Dr. Willow's corpse for his watch and wallet. He pawned them for cash to feed his wife and five undernourished kids."

"As far as the authorities are concerned, it's a straightforward case of a thief shooting his victim."

"How did this man obtain a sophisticated weapon equipped with a suppressant? Before he killed Dr. Willow, he shot two drug dealers in quick succession."

"That's just hearsay."

"The shooting had to be a professional hit."

"The police are treating these killings as two separate incidents, the first two related to gang turf wars. In the case of Dr. Willow's death, the suspect used the bedlam that followed to kill and rob the professor."

Ryan threw up his hands. "One shooter assassinated all three men."

"The police backed by the attorney general's office are sticking by their story." She turned to the bay, sniffed the salt, and then watched a dhow glide by the patio close enough, so she could hear the wind rustling the canvas sail and the chatter of the boatmen. "That's why the ambassador sent me to try to extricate you out of this explosive situation that you've created for yourself."

"I don't believe what I'm hearing. The whole of the law enforcement's case smacks of conspiracy."

There was an uncomfortable silence, long enough for Sylvia to inch backward and scrape the metal chair legs on the tiles as though preparing to leave.

Ryan groaned. "Why did the embassy send you?"

"I'm well qualified."

"What qualifications? Your consular skills are PR and media relations." There was a sudden edge to his voice, as razor-sharp as a machete blade. "Why don't you tell me the real reason they sent you rather than some other diplomatic flunky?"

They fell silent as the waiter cleared away plates and offered them Black Forest cake with mango drizzle, which they refused.

"To be honest with you, Ryan, Hugh thought that as I've known you in another life, I would be well positioned to persuade you to pack your bags and catch the next available flight to Nairobi."

"I can't do that. I'm closing in on the bastard who gave the assignment to the hired assassin."

A moment elapsed before Sylvia spoke again.

"From now on, Dr. Willow's murder is to be left entirely in the hands of Zanzibar's law enforcement," she said, a note of finality in her voice.

"You mean Staff Sergeant Lipumba's version of what happened is the truth, no matter what other compelling evidence is on the table."

Feeling frustrated, Sylvia scanned the patio, marveling at the speed the staff had taken to clean up after the storm. Any sign of debris on the patio had been swept away, the tiles polished to a high gloss, and translucent blue water filled the pool. The only reminder of storm damage was a few naked palm stumps and hibiscus and azalea bushes stripped of leaves.

"The island police's force amounts to no more than organized intimidation, bribery, and shakedowns sanctioned by the government," Ryan said. "There's something you probably don't know about the Zanzibar police force. A reliable source told me that the government follows an old British colonial policy of hiring police officers from the mainland to keep locals in line. They're almost always non-Muslims and have little empathy for the island's inhabitants. As a result, there is an acute animosity between the inhabitants and the police."

Sylvia could feel sweat clinging to the back of her blouse like a wet sheet. The sun had made its way into her blue eyes, so she put on dark Safari glasses.

"I must warn you that there's not much we can do if the police clap you in irons." Sylvia said. "Don't expect anything like our country club minimum-security facilities. Zanzibar's prisons have a reputation for being filthy and disease ridden."

"I'm staying put."

"Now you've decided not to go, you obviously can't stay at the Serena."

"I've moved."

She hunched the solid shoulders of a competitive tennis player. "We could still have you forcefully removed."

"You mean to send in the FBI? Gray serge is a little heavy for the tropics."

Sylvia hardened her eyes. "Ryan, you're being unreasonable."

"Well, I'm sorry you diplomats feel that way, but an American professor has been murdered and I'm determined to find his killer."

"Oh, come off it, Ryan. You're not the noble private detective you think you are. Either Dr. Willow's widow is paying you a bundle to solve her husband's murder, or you've been affected by too much African sun or too many Zanzibar daiquiris." She paused for moment. A motorized dhow cut across the placid water and disturbed the silence. She glanced at the boat before turning her gaze back to Ryan. Her eyes flickered about his chest, as though she were looking for some place to insert a dagger.

"If you insist on remaining, you're on your own," she said, her voice dripping acid. "There's nothing we can do to ensure your survival."

CHAPTER 16

AISLING SAT ON A THREADBARE ottoman in Zoe's crumbling former palace, trying to catch a breath of air. Through cracks in the window shutters, she could see the balcony's rusty railings and sunlight reflecting off the blue ocean. She wanted to step out into the light, but Zoe had warned her not to go on the balcony.

She felt that the heat inside of her *hijab* had turned into a sauna. She hated this gloomy house. She couldn't believe that the musty old place had once been a palace. Thin to the point of emaciation, Zoe reminded her of photos of inmates in the Buchenwald concentration camp, nothing but bones and cartilage. The elderly woman's cheeks appeared to have collapsed, and her claw like hands were pitted with age acne. Her small dark eyes set far back in their sockets seemed to be forever watching her.

Despite the warnings, Aisling drifted out on the balcony. She hoped a sea breeze would cool her heated face. Inside the garden walls, she watched Khaled sweep fallen palm fronds from the pathway. Gripping the balustrade, she thought of how she hated being cloistered in this crumbling ruin.

Ever since Ryan had taken control of her life, she had developed more than a crush on him. She had fallen in love with his movie actor good looks and muscular physique. Last night, Ryan had come to life in her dreams. This morning, instead of wizened Khaled, she had imagined that it was Ryan who had brought her coffee, mango slices, and soda bread apple scones for breakfast.

When she heard the muezzin's call for prayer, she went back inside and put her hands on her ears to block out his amplified voice.

Zoe entered the room. "Can't stand the noise?" Zoe's eyes seemed to penetrate her mind. "You are a soulless creature."

"What's he yelling about anyway?" she murmured, lowering her hands from her ears to her lap.

"God is most great. I testify that there is no god but God. I testify that Muhammad is the prophet of God. Come to prayer. Come to success. God is most great. There is no god but God."

After sunset, Zanzibar's streets drained of people. Driving down the dank, narrow alleys, Ryan kept checking in the rear-view mirror to make sure he wasn't being tailed. On the way to Zoe's villa, he fretted about whether his plan to reach the mainland would succeed without being intercepted by the police or Papa's armed men.

Above him, a woman let loose a scream that rode up Ryan's spine like a bullet. He saw a woman lean over a balcony. She screamed again, and when he looked back, she had bit her mouth, her lower lip covered in blood.

By the time he parked outside Zoe's villa, the night sky opened up, alive with stars. The heat had caused sweat to soak the back of his shirt. He rang the bell, and Khaled let him in. Despite his age, the ancient retainer climbed the stone steps to the living room as agile as a much younger man.

Ryan found Aisling coiled on top of an ottoman, her feet tucked under her buttocks, an ashtray of cigarette butts on her lap. After seeing Aisling again, he felt a sudden prick of shame. Did Aisling's uncanny likeness in appearance to Kathy combined with his fear of storms weaken his resolve to resist her? Did he really think being trapped in his hotel during the cyclone gave him a readymade excuse for infidelity?

While he ruminated about his cheating on Joanne, Aisling removed her head scarf to reveal her short hair.

"You're dressed okay," he said, standing beside her.

"These clothes make me look ridiculous," she said, putting on the face of a spoiled child.

Ryan opened the shutter for a moment to look out at Stone Town in the moonlight. In the street below, the wind had picked up, and gusts whipped stray plastic bags in the air.

"Have you come to take me away from this awful place?" she asked.

"What?"

Aisling crushed a half-smoked cigarette into the sand-filled ashtray. "You don't know what it's like having that old hag watching me all the time and finding any excuse to criticize me."

Ryan stared at her with an open palm of resignation. "I've done everything possible to keep you safe—"

"I don't care, I'm sick to death of this house," she interrupted. "Zoe hates me, she calls me a bloody Irish bitch."

He raised his hand to dismiss her objections. "Oh, come on now, Aisling, she's not that bad."

Her eyes darted around the room, and her body quivered. "I'm so afraid she will betray me to Papa at the drop of her hat."

He grabbed her arm. "When we leave here, you must always wear your head scarf and never speak to anyone."

The sound of a cry carried on the wind from a passing dhow startled her. Aisling reached for him, wide-eyed in terror. He held her for a moment until the cry grew fainter, no louder than water drip in a pail.

"What was that?" she said.

"It's nothing," he said, his mouth close to her ear. She held him tighter, her arms around him, one hand behind his neck, bending him toward her, kissing his face in a kind of frenzy, her body quivering.

He untangled her arms around him. "Relax, you'll soon be off the island."

Her nails bit into his arm. "If I stay much longer, Zoe and her creepy servants will drive me mad." She closed her eyes and then sighed, a sound not much louder than a faint breeze in the palm fronds. "You rescued me from a terrible death; I will always love you."

"You must understand, we can never—"

"Did our lovemaking mean nothing more than ships passing in the night?" she interrupted. "It may be over for you, but my feelings for you will never diminish."

As they faced each other, her arm pulling him closer, Ryan could feel her breath on his neck. Behind him, Ryan heard the soft footfall of Zoe's embroidered slippers. He wrenched Aisling's hand from around his neck and pushed her away. Zoe's cold gray eyes fixed on him. How long had she stood at the doorway to listen to them bicker?

"Time to leave," Ryan said, glancing at his watch.

"What if they're waiting for me outside?" Aisling said.

"We'll go out the back door." Ryan lowered his voice. "Trust me. Once we set sail, you'll be in Dar by morning."

She paced, her hands folded under her armpits. "If there's a showdown with the harbor police, what's to stop the dhow's crew from throwing me overboard to save their skins?"

He opened his jacket for her to see the handgun Amari had loaned him, sticking out of the back of his pants.

"Even though you have a Mauser Bolo, I'm still afraid. I can't trust—"

"How can you say that?" he interrupted.

"I'm sorry, Ryan, it's my nerves talking," she interrupted. She flung herself at him, her head falling against his neck so he could feel her breath. Zoe frowned at her outburst.

"For God's sake, get a grip of yourself," she snapped.

"Honest, I didn't mean to be—" Aisling whispered, tipping her head back.

"We have to go," Ryan said, disentangling her arms around him.

"A word," Zoe whispered to Ryan on the landing leading to the back stairs.

Ryan stepped back into the living room and closed the door.

"Ditch this Irish strumpet as soon as you can," Zoe said. "She'll bring you nothing but grief."

Clouds hid the moon and darkened the city's Old Dhow Harbor, and a light rain had left a thin layer of mist over the harbor, turning the dock into a surreal place of intrigue and menace. For centuries, this harbor was used by Arab traders to unload slaves from the mainland—survivors of a perilous journey in cramped ships. For Ryan, the harbor still retained an oppressive atmosphere, as though the dead from the slave ships haunted the dhows, which were packed close together in the cove. In his mind, he heard the screams of the slaves being unloaded and the sound of whips splitting shiny flesh. Slavers had made a practice of covering their prisoners in oil to make them look healthier and fetch a higher price in the nearby market.

As Ryan cruised by rows of dhows, Aisling lay her head on his shoulder, while she whistled the tune to *The Gypsy Rover*. After he parked the rented Range Rover, he handed the keys to a young man from AVIS waiting on the dock. After the rental company employee drove away, Ryan led Aisling to a dhow named *Makunduchi*. In front of boat's rolled up sail, he spotted a grizzled man, who squatted on the deck, gutting fish. The man tossed a mullet's innards into a bucket and stood up to greet Ryan.

"Freeman Mkapa," the skipper said. "You are Ryan Moar."

"Yeah," Ryan replied.

Freeman was a giant, over six feet in height. He worked his face and mouth as he chomped on a cheroot.

"We sail soon," he said.

"That's good," Ryan said.

"Is this the woman?" Freeman said with a skin-crawling smile on his narrow face, pointing at Aisling, who clung to Ryan's arm.

Ryan nodded.

Freeman leaned down to look closer at her eyes. "They are green."

He then pulled back and wiped his hands on the seat of his tattered pants.

"She has the evil eye," Freeman muttered, turning away and heading for the stern.

"Having second thoughts about taking her, Freeman?" Ryan said.

"She puts me and my crew in danger."

"From what? That superstitious stuff is nothing but mumbo jumbo."

"She puts a curse on this dhow."

"If you don't take her, the deal's off."

When Freeman smiled, Ryan felt a hot gust of wind brush his back and crawl down his spine.

"If I take her, I double the risk of losing my dhow, everything I own, even my life." Freeman glared at Aisling huddled against the dhow's side.

"Are you going to double the amount you pay me?" Freeman said.

"That's outrageous, you goddamn pirate."

"You don't have much choice," Freeman said, moistening his lips with his tongue. He glanced at the dock. "You no longer have your car. Walking back to your hotel is dangerous at night. You could be robbed or murdered." Freeman paused to listen to the wind. "If you want me to take you and the girl tonight to Dar, you pay a thousand

115

dollars cash." He grinned and displayed his stained teeth. "To catch the tide, we have to sail now."

Ryan handed him the money. Freeman counted the bill before stuffing the wad of notes in a wallet connected to a chain that he wore around his scrawny neck.

"If the police patrol boat stops me, what do I tell them?" the skipper asked.

"I hired you to take me night fishing, and the girl is a local. She is going to visit her sick mother. She is unable to speak."

Seemingly satisfied, Freeman nodded. Ryan waved to Bari as he climbed on board the dhow. Bari shook hands with Pengo, the other member of the crew, a wiry youth who sported dreadlocks.

As the skipper steered the dhow across the harbor's sheltered, calm surface, it occurred to Ryan that some things in the port never changed—the muffled sound of oars, money exchanging hands, a woman spirited away in secret, and a snap of canvass billowing in a night breeze.

Freeman pointed the dhow's narrow bow to the open sea. The vessel tacked to where waves started to swell. When the dhow entered the Mozambique Channel, Ryan spotted a few shafts of yellow light from hurricane lamps on distant fishing boats. Freeman set a course that passed a few scattered islands before he steered the vessel southwest.

If the dhow capsized in the channel, Ryan knew they could never survive the shark-infested waters. He dismissed this sudden fear from his mind. Clear skies and a steady breeze were good for sailing, and they should reach the coast by morning. Beside him, Aisling leaned over the side to look at the dark, swirling ocean.

"For you, I hope Dar es Salaam lives up to its Swahili name, haven of peace," he said.

"I'm terrified of the sea," she said, clutching his arm.

Ryan felt her closeness, something intimate. Once Aisling had landed safely on the Tanzanian coast, he would be relieved to be rid of her. He felt confident that Joanne would never know of her existence. The night together during the storm would remain forever hidden, to become in time a distant memory.

From the dhow's deck, the Zanzibar shore glowed, strung out like Christmas tree lights. The wind stirred and brought with it the fresh scent of the sea.

Aisling's stomach heaved, and she leaned over the dhow's side and retched. The waves slapped against the bow and made the dhow rock in an uneven lurch. When she sat down again, Aisling recalled how much she hated sailing in her family's sloop along the Irish east coast. Even while on school outings at the beach, she had never wanted to wade in the ocean.

The dhow heaved in a swell, and the sudden motion made Aisling queasy again. Her throat felt parched, her lips dry, and her tongue thick and swollen. All she wanted to do was gulp tepid water in a flask. The end result of drinking so much, forced her to get up often to piss seated on a toilet seat suspended over the side. Whenever she had to urinate, Pengo, Freeman's deckhand, watched her, a wide grin on his shiny face.

Back on the deck, the dhow's pungent smells of kerosene, rotten fish, moldy blankets, and unwashed men's bodies caused her stomach to heave again. Aisling wiped her mouth on the hem of her *hijab* as she felt the rough timber side dig into her back. Closing her eyes, Aisling tried to mask her misery by visualising Ryan making love to her. When violent waves rocked the dhow, the image of Ryan blurred. After the storm, he became distant. It was obvious to Aisling that all Ryan wanted was to be rid of her for good.

In dealing with Ryan, she had a trump card. She knew the location of the terminal where she had transmitted Papa's files that contained the identity of Dr. Jomo Willow's assassin, as well as the reason why the professor had to die.

She sat up and hunched her shoulders forward to take another sip of water. She watched Freeman and Pengo tug on a rope to adjust the sail. The wind had picked up. Ryan lay curled like a cat on a blanket in the stern. She envied his ability to sleep. She took comfort in knowing that as soon as she arrived inside the embassy compound, consular staff would issue her a new passport and arrange for her to fly to Nairobi and then to an uncertain future in Dublin.

Her mind reverted back to Papa. He may have sailed back to the Mediterranean, but he would return soon to his headquarters in the capital city. Her former lover would want her dead, wherever she ended up. The files contained the secrets of his criminal organization and in the hands of Interpol could ruin him. She knew she could never escape his net even if she lived in another country. Aisling could barely concentrate on what lay ahead. As far as Ryan was concerned, he had removed her for the moment from the threat of Papa's killer squad. Instead of fretting further about Papa, she tilted her defiant face toward the faint outline of the Tanzanian coast.

In the east, the dawn smudged the sky the color of tea, and for Ryan, the distant shoreline south of Dar es Salaam came into sharper focus, where fog clung to a lagoon like wet strips of gray canvas. Ryan made out coconut palms silhouetted against the brightening sky.

While Freeman tacked the sail, Ryan came and stood beside him.

"You did a good job, skipper," he said.

"I hope I never make another voyage like that again," Aisling said, joining them. "I feel as though I puked my guts out."

Ryan handed her water, and she drained the bottle in a series of gulps.

"Where are we?" she asked, wiping her lips on her sleeve.

"Minandi Beach, about ten miles south of Dar," Freeman said.

She peered over the side of the dhow at the shoreline bathed in a light pink by the rising sun. Freeman lowered the sail, and the dhow's keel glided toward shore.

"Is this where we get off this leaky tub?" Aisling asked.

"You're going ashore," Ryan said, lowering his voice. "I'm going back on the *Makunduchi*. To help you disembark, Freeman will steer the dhow closer to the beach."

She clutched his hand. "Ryan, I'm shaky after being seasick, completely drained. I'm too ill to make it to the embassy on my own."

"That wasn't part of the deal."

She busied herself wringing the seawater out of the hem of her robe. She leaned over to rummage inside the woven reed *kikapu* that Zoe had given her to keep clean underwear and toiletries.

"Please take me," Aisling whispered.

Ryan rubbed stubble on his cheek. "From now on, you're on your own."

She shot him a hard look as she ran her fingers through her short hair.

"What if Papa's goons catch up to me in Dar?"

"Do you really think they'll find you in your disguise in a city with a population of over two million?"

"All they have to do is park near the Irish embassy, and then grab me."

"That isn't going to happen."

She pushed back her head scarf, her face was contorted, her skin roughened by the wind.

"It feels like his terror squad is closing in, choking me," she said, clutching her throat.

The dhow entered the quiet waters of the lagoon, and the air of desertion hung over the collapsed *makuti* roof of mud brick and wattle houses. Freeman and Pengo whispered to each other, and then they burst into a fit of giggles as Ryan and Aisling argued like an old married couple.

Pengo dropped a rope ladder over the side.

"The water's shallow on this sandbar," Ryan said. "Once you're on the beach, all you do is walk to a main road and catch a *dolodala* bus to take you to the city." Aisling looked petulant and sullen. "It's no different than catching a double-decker on Grafton Street."

Aisling remained sullen and silent.

"Quit stalling, Aisling," Ryan said. "I've given you more than enough shillings to get a taxi to take you to the embassy."

Her gaze was riveted on him. "What if—?"

"There's nothing daunting about catching a bus in rural Tanzania, hailing a cab, and then giving the driver an address in the suburbs," he interrupted. He herded her to the side. "I'll help you climb down the ladder. The water isn't deep. You can see the sandy bottom."

Her eyes swept around the edge of the palm-fringed shoreline. "Papa will stop at nothing to kill me."

Ryan heard a faint splash of a fish and the roar of surf breaking up on the distant reef. The sun hung over the ocean having slipped out from behind a bank of clouds. The hot wind's breath stirred clumps of palms on the edge of the white sand.

"You exaggerate your importance to him," Ryan said. "By now, he's forgotten all about you."

Ryan could see by the set of her jaw that she was about to reveal something important. He turned his gaze to the blackened coral rocks glazed with water and seaweed, jutting out of the chain of small islands.

"I have to tell you something," she whispered.

"What in hell do we have left to say to each other?" Ryan said.

"It has to do with Papa's files."

"What about them?"

"I transmitted all of them from his yacht to a terminal in Dublin."

He gripped her arms, forcing her to face him. "Why didn't you tell me this before?"

Aisling remained silent. Ryan noticed she no longer looked frightened, on the run, alone.

The sky turned the color and texture of rose petals, and the banana trees and patches of bamboo throbbed to the tune of bird chirps. The red orb of the sun behind thin clouds hung like a metal shield.

120

"Papa wants me dead." Her voice adopted an Irish lilt. "Those files have enough to put the flamin' devil in the clink."

Ryan felt a wad of trepidation slide down his windpipe. He listened to the wind in the palms and heard a fish flop to the surface of the calm water, and he could smell the heavy odor of dried seaweed. Ryan could see the uncertainty in her face, like a woman about to light a match in a kitchen that smells of natural gas.

"His organization is so secretive," she whispered. "It doesn't have a name or a corporate identity, but his headquarters are in Dublin."

Ryan sounded matter-of-fact; he had jammed his anger back inside. "You led me to believe that Papa is a playboy intent on muscling his way into illicit drug trade in East Africa. You said he is active in Irish real estate manipulation, owns a big yacht, collects expensive art and beautiful women. What is his real business?"

"He and his associates are much more. The operate a host of criminal enterprises: illegal arms sales, people smuggling, kidnapping, and political assassinations."

Ryan spotted a fishing boat putting out to sea. Otherwise, the lagoon was quiet, a backwater. A bell rang and broke the silence to summon children to school.

Ryan took a deep breath of the cool, salty air. "Could these files have the name of the man who murdered Jomo Willow?"

"I am sure they do. Take me to the embassy, and I promise I will give you access to those files in Dublin." Aisling wrapped her arms around his neck. "You will take me?"

Ryan pulled back. "All right, but first, what is Papa's real name?'

"*Papa* means Shark in Swahili. His birth name is Darcy O'Connell. Within his inner circle, he is known as Shark, only Shark."

"You told me a skin doctor did surgery on his face."

"It was done by a plastic surgeon in Dar es Salaam. I don't know the doctor's name."

Ryan thought there wouldn't be much of a demand for plastic surgeons in Dar es Salaam, so the doctor's identity would be easy to track down. Ryan loosened her arms around him, but she hung on like a limpet. He heard footsteps behind him, and when he turned, Pengo grinned at him, his mouth wide, displaying his perfect set of matching teeth.

"We touch sand soon," he said. "Do you want to go back with us?"

"I'm leaving with *memsab*," Ryan said.

The dhow shuddered as the keel hit bottom.

Ryan swung over the side and jumped into the waist-high water. Aisling climbed down the rope ladder, and fell into his open arms. Ryan plopped her down on the white sand.

CHAPTER 17

AFTER THE TAXI DROPPED AISLING off at the Irish embassy on Toure Drive, Ryan told the cabdriver to take him to the only plastic surgeon in the city, Dr. Gabby Kimoro, who had an office on Samora Avenue. Aisling had told him that Papa—whom he now knew as Shark—had his features altered by a Dar es Salaam plastic surgeon. Twenty minutes later, the taxi pulled up in front of a glass and steel building, on the third floor of which was the doctor's office, near the New Africa Hotel. Ryan paid the cabdriver's fare and phoned Dr. Kimoro's receptionist, Gala Ngoma, to make an appointment for the following day.

At a nearby internet café, Ryan printed a photo of Dr. Kimoro from his website. The surgeon's webpage had a gallery of before-and-after, head-and-shoulder photos of patients, who provided glowing testimonials of his skills in making them look young. He then bought a reusable computer disc in anticipation of hacking into the doctor's computer to download Shark's medical file.

Ryan left the internet cafe and ordered a coffee and simosa at a bistro beside the entrance to Dr. Kimoro's office. While he waited, he picked up a copy of the *Daily News*. He lowered his paper to glance at a container ship entering the harbor. He could smell the sea salt and the warm odor of wet sand. On the horizon, there was a distant hint of rain, and electricity filled the clouds. He was struck by the port's new buildings, bustling markets, and clean streets. The faces of well-dressed Africans had a distinct sense of purposed compared to the moribund mood of Stone Town's narrow streets.

As a semitrailer went through an intersection, Ryan spotted the surgeon emerge from the building. From his webpage, he recognized the doctor's chiseled features and perfect skin. Dr. Kimoro went to a newsstand to buy a newspaper, tucked it under his arm, and pushed his hands into his pockets. He was a slender man with athletic shoulders and a distinctive feminine walk that accentuated his loose, flapping wrists.

Ryan thought the doctor would be more at home in a salon, teasing hair, than using rock-steady hands to make precise incisions to rearrange facial features. At a crosswalk, Dr. Kimoro paused and placed his hands on his hips, as if to take stock of the weather. When a thin man approached him, Ryan suspected he was trying to sell him *bangi*, the name the locals gave to marijuana. He raised his open hand as though he wanted to slap the man. A savage stare on the doctor's face made the man cringe, and he soon disappeared among the throng on the crowded sidewalk.

Ryan followed Dr. Kimoro along Sikonine Drive. The doctor passed the ferry docks and St. Joseph's Cathedral. He ducked into a side street and moved past mounds of mangoes, paw-paws, and custard apples on vegetable stands beside an open-air market. Satisfied that the doctor was on his way home, Ryan doubled back. When he got back to Kimoro's office, he mixed in with office workers streaming out of the building. Inside the lobby, a security guard didn't stop him from taking the elevator to the third floor.

On the landing, he peered up and down the empty corridor. He spotted Dr. Kimoro's name in large gold type on a frosted glass door. He froze when he heard voices and ducked into an emergency stairwell. When the chatter disappeared, Ryan picked Dr. Kimoro's office lock. As soon as the door swung open, Ryan took the precaution to wrap a scarf around his head until only a slit remained uncovered around his eyes in case the plastic surgeon's office had hidden cameras. At Gala Ngoma's desk, he sat down and turned on an old Dell computer.

After the welcome screen came up, the machine's access prompt demanded a password. He tried a few combinations involving Kimoro, the clinic's name, SkinBeautiful, and Gala Ngoma. After blending them without success, he ransacked Gala's desk drawers to see if he could find a notebook or other reference to her password. He found nothing. Gala had potted African violets on her desk. One of the pots had a piece of adhesive tape stuck to it. He picked up the pot and spun it around. Printed on a slip of paper were some Swahili words he soon recognized. He punched the keys for *habarigalakwaheri*, hellogalagoodbye.

The aging machine wheezed, purred, and clicked. Ryan stared at a list of Dr. Kimoro's case files. He scrolled down the patient list in search of Darcy O'Connell, Shark's real name. He copied Shark's file on his new computer disc. As soon as he was finished, he pocketed the disc and headed out of the office. He took the elevator to the reception desk, nodded to the security guard, and exited into the street.

Feeling famished, he strolled in the twilight to the New Africa Hotel. Ryan entered the hotel's lobby and went to the Bandari Grill, a long narrow room smelling of fresh flowers and furnished with wicker chairs and matching tables. After being seated at the far end of the restaurant, Ryan spotted Dr. Kimoro reach over to stroke the cheek of the fresh-faced woman seated opposite him. Ryan wondered whether he touched her out of affection or was he checking the quality of his handiwork.

Ryan imagined the plastic surgeon would notice the next the telltale signs of a break-in at his office. After a quick search, he would be relieved when he found nothing valuable missing. Dr.

Kimoro would then contact the police, who wouldn't find any clues and recommend the plastic surgeon upgrade his security system.

Near the window, Ryan glanced through a gap in the curtains at an airliner's safety lights winking at him as the Boeing 737 flew across the night sky. While examining the menu, Ryan couldn't suppress a grin. Not having to worry about Aisling—now under her government's protection—made him hungry. From the waiter, he selected a bottle of Drappier Brut Grande Sendrée. To accompany the champagne, he ordered a medium rare porterhouse steak and mushrooms.

Ryan breathed in hard and let air out in a long sigh. He felt completely relaxed for the first time in weeks. Inside the restaurant, he had found a place free from danger like the protective dome of a giant conch shell.

The waiter placed a hand on Ryan's shoulder. "Sir, you look remarkably happy. Tell me, did you have an outstanding day?"

"Not even close," Ryan replied.

"How are you planning to celebrate the rest of the evening?"

Ryan frowned. "Take the ferry back to Zanzibar.

At dawn the next day, Ryan went for walk on the beach. In the bay, small boats rocked in the outgoing tide. Ryan inhaled the cool morning air and watched the fishing fleet of dhows sailing out of sea. Last night in his room, Ryan had opened Dr. Kimoro's file on Shark. The plastic surgeon had altered the Darcy O'Connell's nose, cheeks, chin, and brow. The file contained before and after surgery photographs. The new face had no comparison to the former. He listed his place of permanent residency as the Clarence Hotel, Wellington Quay, Dublin, Ireland. His date of birth, September 14, 1976. Ryan had then booked an evening flight to Nairobi and tickets connecting him to London and Dublin. By now, Ryan expected Aisling had arrived at Nairobi's Jomo Kenyatta terminal and boarded a British Airways flight to Heathrow. London.

At the hotel entrance, he noticed a wizened East Indian man reading a newspaper. The block-type headlines sent his mind into a tailspin.

He devoured every word: "AIR TANZANIA JET BLASTED OUT OF THE SKY KILLS ALL PASSENGERS." He got up, grabbed the newspaper from the startled man. The subheading seemed to shout at him for attention: "FOREIGN TOURISTS AMONG THE DEAD ON FLIGHT BOUND FOR NAIROBI." The headline of a sidebar read: "INVESTIGATORS EYE POSSIBLE TERRORIST CONNECTION TO AIRLINER EXPLOSION." The news hit him hard, as if the round knob of an African club had slammed into his stomach. Aisling cold have been on the doomed flight.

If Shark's men had sabotaged the Air Tanzania jet to eliminate Aisling, his hit squad had the skills and resources to breach security at Julius Nyerere Airport and place a bomb on board airliner. It wouldn't take long to track him to the Kaponga. He needed to leave the island.

On his way to find a taxi, Ryan zigzagged around potholes and morning traffic on Mizingani Road to hail a cab that took him to the Al Mutlaq. At the hotel, he joined Renée at café table, where she was drinking tea.

"You look tired," Renée said.

"I've been busy," Ryan said.

He showed her the newspaper's front page. She leaned forward to read the headlines. On the patio, guests glued to the morning news coverage of the airline disaster.

Renée said, "Does this crash have any connection to Jomo's murder?"

Ryan nodded and gave her a summary of a woman, who may have been on the doomed flight, transmitted files Dublin.

These files contain the name of Jomo assassin," he said. "I leave for Dublin tonight."

"You're closing in on those responsible for his death." Renée sat with her back stiff. "I'm determined to see this assassin brought to justice." She jammed her tiny hands into the hip pockets of her slacks. "You'll probably need more money. I'll arrange for another twenty-five thou transferred to your account."

Ryan paused to take in the wide sweep of the beach at low tide. For as long as he had known her, she had always been a penny pincher. How could Renée afford to pay his fees so easily? He leaned back in his chair to get some distance. When he took on the case, he expected not to be paid, as Jomo probably lived from paycheck to paycheck. How did this impoverished academic manage to house his family in a mansion, buy a hotel, and have a sizeable bank account? Could the answer as to how he had acquired this sudden windfall be found in the Irish capital?

"Are you all right, Ryan? You have an unusual expression," she said.

"I'm okay," he mumbled. "How did Jomo get to be so rich?"

She put down the teacup on the saucer with a clatter. "I honestly don't know."

"A few year ago, you left Fargo carrying not much more than two plane tickets and two nickels to rub together. Yet, in a short timeframe, Jomo has plenty of money in the bank."

A hard light flashed in Renée's eyes. "My husband was a good man."

"There's no mistake about that. But before he left the states, Jomo told me his salary barely cover your expenses and his books never made a dime."

She slammed her hand on the table. "Are you questioning Jomo's integrity? So what, if he made money on the side? After all, he was an economist."

Suddenly, Renée stood up and knocked over a teapot. A stain of dark chai spread across the table cloth. She glared down at him. "Look what you made me do."

At that moment, Ryan didn't feel sorry about leaving Zanzibar, but he knew the island's stunning beauty and harsh reality would always haunt him.

CHAPTER 18

WHILE RYAN TOOK A TAXI back to his hotel to pack, Staff Sergeant Lipumba glanced at his gold-plated Rolex. He estimated he had another twenty minutes to claw his way through the piles of paper on his desk, a bureaucratic jungle that threatened to engulf him. If he didn't get away soon, he wouldn't have time to drive to the Zanzibar pearl shell co-op to buy a pair of earrings for his second wife Habeeba. She had hankered after a beautiful set of amethyst stones in gold he had promised her on her birthday.

Twenty years younger than him, Habeeba was tall and athletic, in contrast to his first wife, Taabu, who had a bent back from working in his fields. After multiple pregnancies, Taabu now had withered skin like an overripe mango and breasts that looked as flat and leathery as cuttlefish. After Taabu found out about the earrings, she became jealous of Habeeb. Apart from being insanely envious of his younger wife, she kept nagging him about their three children's need for new school books and uniforms.

Thinking about the price tag of the earrings made him queasy, but he didn't want to disappoint her. He opened the first file on top of several others in his in tray. It was a report on the increased use of cocaine and heroin over the most common drugs of choice, including alcohol, cannabis, and *khat*. Why bother sending him information he already knew from whenever his men did spot checks on the nearest street corner? He was suddenly distracted by noise from the adjacent dispatch room. It seemed all the phones were ringing at once and going unanswered. His own phone added to the cacophony.

He picked up the receiver and grunted his name into the mouthpiece. The caller's voice seemed familiar, but he couldn't put his finger on his identity. He addressed Lipumba in English as police chief and that pleased him.

"Whoever you are, I'm busy," Lipumba said in a curt, official voice.

"If you want your cash flow problems to disappear, you'll find yourself un-busy," a man's smooth voice said.

"Who are you?"

His familiar voice sounded quite pleasant, but the tone had an undertow of menace. "If you do me a favor, you'll be well compensated."

Lipumba tried to curtail any eagerness creeping into his voice. "What is it you want me to do?"

"Arrest an American named Ryan Moar. You had better act quickly. He is planning on leaving the island this evening."

"What do you want me to do with this private investigator?"

"After you have him in custody, hand him over to me."

Bari crept down the Hotel Kaponga's dark corridor. He mulled over his situation for a bit while he listened to tortuous tunes of a big-time pop star ricochet around his skull on his Walkman. He knew Ryan to be resourceful, but he didn't think he could escape from an ambush about to unfold.

Before leaving for Ryan's hotel, he had smoked some *bange* to bolster his courage. He needed to think about his own survival, find a way to get out alive. He stopped outside Ryan's room, removed his earphones, and pressed his ear to the door. He detected no sounds. He banged on the door four times in quick succession. Waiting in the dank, airless corridor sent acid flowing into his stomach. He banged on the door again. Had Ryan left after he saw the two police cruisers parked in the shadows behind the hotel?

Bari heard Ryan's voice telling him to enter. He opened the door and paused on the threshold. The room was dark except for a wedge of light from dim wall lamps. Ryan stood by the window, and he turned around to slip the ammo clip into his Mauser Bolo. In the gloom, Bari inched forward until his shin collided with an unseen coffee table.

"Hi Bari," Ryan said. "Did you arrange for the taxi?"

"Maulvi is waiting at the kitchen back door," Bari said.

Ryan dug into the pocket of his windbreaker and fanned out airline tickets. "I'm leaving Zanzibar. I have to continue my investigation in Europe." He glanced at his watch. "I don't have much time to catch the six o'clock flight to Nairobi."

"There are police vans parked behind the hotel."

"Damn." Ryan raced to the door. "We'll take the fire escape."

At the bottom of the stairs, Ryan heard the sound of boots pounding on the pavement. When Bari hesitated, looking for a way out, Ryan grabbed his arm and pulled him across the courtyard to a narrow passageway. Bari cried out when two police *askaris* pointed rifles at them. Ryan and Bari raced in the opposite direction. The *askaris* fired warning shots over their heads. Ryan dropped to the ground, landing on piles of rotten vegetables. The next rounds slammed into the wall inches above his head, showering him with a fine white powder. Bari ducked down, but a bullet grazed his leg. Ryan snaked over to where he sat clutching his calf, blood seeping through his fingers.

Ryan grunted and draped Bari over his shoulder. Ryan crept along a winding alley. He heard more shots behind him, but the firing soon receded. As they neared the mouth of the alley, Ryan didn't see any *askaris*. In the distance, he heard whistles and saw the beams of flashlights probed the gloom behind him.

Ryan staggered across the street to a small café. When he threw open the door, patrons stared, eyes wide in shock at Bari's blood-streaked leg. Renewed gunfire sent diners scurrying under tables. Ryan helped Bari through a door leading to a kitchen.

Behind them, *askaris* warned customers to get out of the way. Ryan weaved around two startled cooks, who were stirring steaming pots on a stove. Ryan kicked open the back door, and he stared into the barrel of Staff Sergeant Lipumba's handgun.

CHAPTER 19

RYAN LAY NAKED ON THE damp mud floor, his body aching from cuts and bruises. He was struck by the foul stench of stale sweat and fresh human waste. The round room was dark except for a patch of sun under the bottom of the door, a glimmer of light the color of yellow sodium that came from a hurricane lamp. The duct tape wrapped around his wrists and ankles made even the slightest movement difficult. He heard no sounds except for occasional voices and snatches of African music from a radio. It was as if the island had grown quiet, slipping back into its own primitive past.

He had no idea how long he had been inside the hut. After his arrested, a police officer handcuffed him and handed him over to four men in military fatigues. They pinned him down on the pavement, and pummelled him with fists and short sticks. To protect his body from the beating, Ryan had pulled his knees up to his chin in a tight ball. After he saw flashing lights and heard ringing in his ears, he lost consciousness.

Without netting, mosquitoes bit him to distraction. The stifling heat had the intensity of a steam bath. During the night, he felt a sharp pain in his big toe. He kicked something furry. An animal scurried across the floor. He tried to pull his feet in closer to protect them, but gave up because of the tape around his legs and ankles. He decided to stay awake in case any rats tried again to gnaw on his toes.

By morning, the stink around him made him want to vomit, but he couldn't bring anything up. His swollen tongue probed painful bruises in his mouth, where his captors had punched his face. He squeezed his eyes shut in a bid to block pain from a blow to the back of his skull. Every time he breathed the stale air, he felt further agony that he suspected he had a cracked or broken rib.

Toward dawn, Ryan heard a key turn in the lock, and the door creaked open. The silhouette of a tall man with a pronounced belly floated out of the dim light.

The man spoke in a dry and precise voice. "Good morning, Mr. Moar. We finally meet in person."

"Have we met before?" Ryan said, twisting his neck in an attempt to see him.

"We've spoken on the phone." He shone a flashlight in Ryan's face. "After you chased one of my men on a motorbike, you talked on his cell phone. My name is Rasul."

He burst out laughing.

"What's so amusing, Rasul?" Ryan asked.

"You are one sorry-looking *muzungu*. I told my boys to soften you up, but I never expected them to kick the shit out of you."

"Why am I a prisoner?"

"The police handed you over to me for questioning."

"What have you done with Bari Khan?"

"It is my job to ask questions, but I will answer this one. He is also being interrogated."

"Have you tortured him?"

"I ask the questions, remember?"

There was a sharp knock on the door, and a few murmured words in Swahili drifted into the hut followed by the sound of boots and angry shouts. A few seconds later, two men burst into the room. Their slurred voices sounded as if they were drunk. The men snickered as though sharing a dirty joke and pointed AK-47s at Ryan's head. They took aim and trigger fingers quivered. He squeezed his eyes shut in anticipation of oblivion. But he didn't hear shots or witness his soul rising to the smoke blackened thatched ceiling. His knees began to shake, waiting for bullets to riddle his chest. He wondered if his soul would look down on his blood-soaked body, before he drifted to some spirit world and find if it ever existed.

Still keeping his eyes shut, Ryan heard laughter. He felt little relief; the mock execution had terrified him. To his surprise, firing squad grabbed Rasul by the shoulder and shoved him out the door. Ryan was too preoccupied by his anticipated execution to fathom the reason for Rasul's arrest.

The grim hoax to shoot him stiffened his resolve to remain alive. Ryan gained some control of his shivers by being determined to show no fear of his captors. He calmed his mind by thinking about walks on the banks of the Red River accompanied by Joanne and the dogs. Ryan was in too much pain from the beating and the mosquito bites to doze, but he soon lost track of time. He had nagging doubts that he would ever leave Zanzibar alive.

Ryan guessed it was evening when he heard a key turn in the lock and the door opened. A low-slung ray of sunlight streamed into the hut. His tongue had turned to wood. Rasul gazed down at him. His intelligent dark eyes had an inordinate amount of white, and his boxer's flattened nose glistened from sweat.

"Why did those men drag you away?" Ryan asked.

Rasul grinned. "Sometimes we have dissention in the ranks. Those men wanted to use you for target practice. I persuaded them to lay off you for a while."

"Give me something to drink," Ryan said, his voice croaked.

"That depends on what you can tell me about your woman," he said, thrusting a facsimile photo in front of his face. Ryan stared at her picture in the slanted sunlight. The photo—grainy and shot using a telephoto lens—was of Aisling in a loose terry cloth robe. A pronounced V exposed her chest bone and extended to her belly button ring.

"I've never seen her before," Ryan said.

Rasul leaned forward. "She spent the night in your Serena hotel room."

"I've never had the pleasure of meeting this woman."

"The hotel's security tapes show you carrying her from the beach to the hotel."

"I've never stayed at the Serena. My pocketbook couldn't stand it. I'd like to remind you that the police ambushed me outside the Kaponda, not the Serena. You've mixed me up with someone else."

"Your friend Bari told us you hired a dhow to take your girlfriend to Dar."

"Well, he's mistaken. I hired a dhow to take a local girl on a romantic cruise. If you don't believe me, go ask the dhow's skipper."

Rasul pulled himself to his full height. "Humor me," he said, lighting two cigarettes, keeping one for himself and handing the other one to Ryan, who shook his head. Rasul crushed the cigarette's burning tip with his fingers and put it in his shirt pocket. "Is Aisling Quinn a good lay?"

"I wouldn't know."

He held her photo in front of him and used his forefinger and thumb to flick Aisling's picture. "You're lying."

A veil of smoke hung in the stale air between them. There was a sharp knock on the door and a few murmured words in Swahili. A bearded man in a floor-length robe put a tray of teacups and a metal pot on the floor. Rasul tore off the tape from Ryan's wrists and poured him a cup. Ryan sat up and drank the scalding liquid, not caring if the tea burned his throat.

Rasul observed him over the rim of his cup. "You Americans think we're a bunch of dumb natives who just climbed down from the trees."

Rasul put his cup on the tray and slapped Ryan's face.

"People on this island have been fighting pigheaded bastards like you for hundreds of years, and we've managed to get rid of them: Omanis, Portuguese, Germans, and British. They all wanted to conquer or enslave us."

"I know your history," Ryan said, rubbing his cheek.

"We have picked up a trick or two from these arrogant foreigners."

Ryan tilted his head. "What've you done with Bari?"

"My men are loosening his tongue."

Ryan paused to take a deep breath of stale air. "Keep me, but let Bari go. He knows nothing."

Rasul stretched his arms and took an intake of breath. "You can't make demands."

"It must be obvious to you now that Bari only acted as my guide and guarded my vehicle."

Rasul spun around with such a rush that his neck hanging over his collar jiggled.

"You stupid *muzungu*," he said, kicking Ryan in the stomach. "Don't tell me what to do."

Ryan doubled up in pain.

"Kwa heri, amekufa mwanaume," Rasul said. Goodbye, dead man.

He slammed the door shut and locked it.

CHAPTER 20

WHEN JOANNE STEPPED OUT ONTO the deck, the river was turbulent and swollen from spring floodwaters that often spilled over its banks to inundate the Red River Valley. She felt the cool evening air on her face as she watched a flock of pelicans skim low on the surface of the muddy water. It had been two weeks since Ryan had flown for Zanzibar. She missed him. Despite her advanced pregnancy, she continued to teach effective speaking and stage craft three days a week at Marsdon University. For two evenings, she also coached student actors at the university's theater school.

Joanne slumped into a padded chair and stared at a floatplane's final approach before landing on the river. Beside her, on a glass topped table, she had papers to mark and lecture notes to prepare, but she felt too uneasy and restless to tackle the work. The single engine Otter made a bumpy landing on the river, sending ripples fanning out across the Red's uneven surface. The floatplane then taxied to a dock on the opposite bank.

Joanne leaned back and closed her eyes. Why hadn't she heard from Ryan for three days? She knew he planned to fly to Dublin to continue his investigation, but he hadn't called from the Irish capital. Ever since his arrival in Zanzibar, he made a daily ritual to call her around noon Fargo time. She had tried calling him several times on his cell, but his iPhone was turned off. In desperation, she phoned the Kaponga. The receptionist told her Ryan had checked out and left no forwarding address.

Even more disturbing was her phone call to the American embassy in Dar es Salaam. She had spoken to Sylvia Bannerman, an assistant undersecretary. Sylvia told her that she was aware of Ryan's investigation of Dr. Willow's murder, but she added that the local police were annoyed by his unorthodox and disruptive investigative methods. For his own safety, she had warned Ryan to leave the island. When Joanne had asked Sylvia if the embassy could help verify whether Ryan was still on the island, she said the government didn't have the resources to carry out a search for him.

On the deck, the first stars that began to pinprick the deep blue sky failed to bring Joanne any clarity as to what she should do next. As it became too chilly to remain outside, Joanne went into the kitchen, feeling paralyzed by indecision.

Framed by the French door's glass windows, she glanced beyond her rose garden to the boathouse, where Ryan worked on solving cases. She went inside and sat at the kitchen table to mull over her options. She opened her laptop. On Google, she went to Ryan's Zanzibar private investigator's webpage. Although Ryan had told her that Amari had been murdered in the cathedral, she thought someone in the PI's office could help her. After jotting down the phone number, Joanne dialed Amari's phone.

The hoarse voice of a woman answered. She explained in pidgin English mixed with Swahili that her husband was dead and the office closed. Joanne asked her if she was aware that Ryan had been Amari's client. She replied that she knew Ryan, but she had no idea what had happened to him. A man had threatened her son with the same fate as his father, if he continued to look into Dr. Willow's death. The woman then disconnected the line.

Behind Joanne, she heard the soft padding of Charlene's slippers on the marble tiles. Ryan's daughter wore a silk robe, and her frizzy red hair smelled of shampoo.

"Any news from Dad?" she asked, joining her at the table.

"Nothing for three days, and no one knows where he is, not even the American embassy," Joanne said. "According to the local airline, they have no record of him leaving airport." She gripped the table. "According to a woman at the home of the local PI who helped your father, her son has been threatened with his life if he continues the investigation into Dr. Willow's death."

Charlene's forehead wrinkled with concern. "That's so awful. What's happened to Dad? He's always been so punctual about phoning, texting, and emailing." She groaned. "What time is it in Zanzibar?"

"Two thirty in the morning."

Charlene stared at Joanne's cell phone that she held cradled in her hands. "What if we wake him up?"

"I've already tried phoning him four times. His cell's switched off."

"What can we do?"

Joanne stared out at the Red, where dock lights reflected off the water. "I'm going to Zanzibar to find him."

"I want to come with you."

"That's out of question."

"What do you mean? Gary and I came with you and Dad to the Black Hills, and we were a great help."

Joanne smiled. "What you and Gary did in the Black Hills was extremely brave, although foolhardy. You nearly got yourself killed. But Zanzibar's different. It's a violent, unstable island off the coast of East Africa."

"What about you, Joanne? You're pregnant, and that tropical country isn't exactly healthy for either you or the baby."

Joanne glanced down at her swollen belly. "I'm still at the stage of pregnancy that allows me to do physical activity, including flying." She paused. "But this is one trip I do solo."

"Aren't you worried about catching one of those horrible diseases?"

"Of course I am, but I have to find your father."

"Can't you persuade Marleau to go?"

"He's impossible to reach in Canadian arctic, where he's trying to find that missing geologist."

Charlene started to tremble. Joanne got up and placed her hands on her shoulders.

"What do you think has happened to Dad?" Charlene blurted out.

"I sense he's in danger."

"Not dead?"

"I don't think so."

"Do you think he's injured?"

"I've done a search of Zanzibar's main hospitals on Google, phoned them, and there's no record of him having checked in as a patient."

Charlene narrowed her brow. "The PI he hired being shot in the church sounds as though something sinister has happened to Dad."

Joanne look down at her empty coffee cup and tried to sound casual."I have to go in person to find out what's happened to him—" Her voice trailed off.

Charlene made a clicking sound deep in her throat. "If you're determined to go, please don't suggest I stay with my mother and her obnoxious boyfriend."

"While I'm gone, I've asked Grandma Moar to look after you both."

Charlene straightened up. "Gary and I are old enough to look after ourselves."

"I know you think you are, but it would make me feel a whole lot better if she took care of you here at home."

The worry about Ryan roared back to Joanne in crippling waves. She knew worry would wear her down, exhaust her to past the point of caring. She needed a distraction, to keep moving.

"Something terrible has happened to him." Joanne picked up her cell phone. "I'm going to make arrangements for my flight, make appointments for my shots, and start packing."

The next day near dawn, the hut's rickety door opened. Ryan blinked at a flashlight shining on his face. Rasul hoisted Ryan upright. He cut off the tape around his swollen ankles. Ryan's legs wobbled after lying for so long. Rasul dragged him outside the hut, where he heard small animals skitter on dry leaves in the underbrush. He noticed an orange smudge in the sky, so he figured it must be close to daybreak. He stumbled in front of Rasul along a narrow track bordered by thick vegetation. A low mist clung to the uneven ground. Thick bushes and tangled vines grew on each side of the path. The air was cool. Ryan could smell salt in the wind, sweeping across the fields from the sea.

Ahead, he saw an abandoned grove of spindly pawpaw trees on the grounds of a ruined house. His thoughts focused on spring in Fargo, where crocuses bloomed in moist clay earth. He pined for Red River spring floods and long shadows beneath the elms. He paused to glance at an opening in the underbrush.

Rasul pointed his semiautomatic at his back. "If you try to run, you give me an excuse to shoot you."

At an iron gate, Rasul used a key to open the lock to a courtyard. Inside the walled compound stood a cement block shack without windows.

Ryan's eyes burned, his head throbbed, and his vision clouded. "Where are you taking me?" he said.

"I want to show you something," Rasul said. He hammered on the door and shouted in Swahili. Withdrawn bolts rattled. Rasul wrenched open the door and shoved Ryan inside a room lit by hurricane lamps. Inside, Ryan smelled wood smoke and stale vomit. When his eyes adjusted to the light, Ryan needed a moment to recognize Bari, naked, covered in a shiny layer of sweat, tied to a pole. His eyes were slits almost swollen shut. Blood flowed from his puffy lips, cuts in his cheek were deep enough to need stitches. Thin lacerations from whips crisscrossed his back, arms, and chest. Cigarettes had been ground into his shoulders, leaving rings of charred flesh like the craters of miniature volcanoes.

On either side of him, Bari's two tormentors stood as silent as altar boys, twin grinning hyenas eager to resume torturing him.

Wrapping his arm around Bari's shoulder, Rasul said, "Your assistant has told us everything we want to know about your investigation and your friendship with the whore, Aisling Quinn."

Rasul removed his arm from Bari's shoulder. He used a white handkerchief to wipe the boy's sweat and blood off his fingers. "Let this be a reminder to you, if you think you can treat us like bloody wogs, you're wrong. We will not hesitate to squash you like an annoying insect. By the time we have finished with you, you also will end up looking like this *watu*."

"Ryan?" Bari whispered, trying to see through tight eye slits.

"I'm here," Ryan said, stepping forward so Bari could see him.

Rasul yanked Ryan away from the prisoner.

"It's not your fault," Bari said in a hoarse voice out of the corner of his blood caked mouth. He twisted his neck as though trying to speak, the movement making him wince.

Ryan turned to Rasul, his fists clenched. "For God's sake, let him go."

Rasul went over to Bari and twisted his face so he could stare into his swollen eyes. "This cockroach is going straight to hell." Bari moaned, rounded his lips and spat out a mixture of blood and saliva into Rasul's face.

Rasul sprang back as though poisoned by the twin fangs of a puff adder. He kicked Bari hard in the stomach, and the boy cried out in pain. Ryan punched Rasul, a blow that landed on his nose. He stumbled back, hitting his head on the wall. One of the guards grabbed Ryan, pinning his hands behind his back, while his partner whacked him on the arms and abdomen using African clubs. After the beating, they dragged Ryan half conscious through a narrow door to a back road.

Beside a low wall topped by pointed battlements of an Arab cemetery, the men tossed Ryan into a deep drain half full of foul-smelling water. Ryan could feel his head about to explode with pain. He wanted to call for help, but his throat refused to obey him. Something heavy like a sack was tossed on top of him. He looked up into Bari's face, blood tricking from his hair to his swollen eyes and cheeks.

The beam of Rasul's flashlight played over the two bodies. "Mironko will know where to dump this trash," he said.

CHAPTER 21

"GRANDMA MOAR WILL BE HERE soon," Joanne said, straightening up from bending over a suitcase on her bed.

Charlene wasn't sure about this arrangement, but it was a better alternative than staying at her mother's condo. Her Mom's boyfriend, Josh Hardwick, was a toucher. Although Josh had never gone beyond placing his hand on her back and shoulder, she sensed that he wanted to boost these pats up a notch.

When she approached her mother on the subject of Josh's wandering hands, Audrey had dismissed her concerns. Her mother assured Charlene that Josh was only demonstrating fatherly affection and nothing else. She rolled her eyes at the thought of her mother's naivety.

In her father's North Fargo home, Charlene's problem was Gary. Despite her initial loathing of Joanne's son, her feelings for him had taken a dramatic swing. In the last few weeks, she had developed a vague yearning for Gary, a feeling that was hard to fathom. In unexpected moments, her head was full of him. The sight, smell, and image of him in her mind gave her a strange, hollow ache. She believed the attraction was mutual. One evening, while she was seated on a swing in the sun on the deck, he sat next to her. Gary pretended to read a *Fishing/Hunting North Dakota* magazine, while he took furtive, sideway glances at her. In the warmer April weather, Gary wore tank tops to emphasize his toned chest and abs. She also admired his tight jeans. Sometimes, when he bent over on the dock cleaning his sailboat, she spotted the logo of his Tommy Hilfiger undershorts.

Without Joanne's watchful eye, she wondered if she could summon the necessary self-control to resist Gary appeal. Even his mood swings and truculent attitude failed to lessen his attraction. They both loved horseback riding. She admired his daring and skill in the saddle, but she couldn't stomach his biting sarcasm that often left her feeling crushed.

Joanne looked up from her packing and must have noticed her wrinkled forehead.

"What's the matter?" Joanne said.

"I'm just worried about you in a mangrove swamp, eaten alive by mosquitoes, poisoned by snakes, and gobbled up by man-eating piranhas."

Charlene heard footsteps behind her.

"She going to East Africa, for heaven's sake, not the Amazon," Gary said, a sneer in his voice. "They don't have piranhas."

He leaned against the door frame, a quizzical look on his face, his chin speckled with black stubble. "I've checked out Zanzibar on the net, and it's a pretty cool, switched-on place."

Charlene groaned and glared at Joanne's son. "It's just that having both Joanne and Dad at the same time on that weird island—"

"Don't worry, the locals aren't going barbecue them and have them for supper," Gary interrupted.

"I'm more concerned about the region's political stability and lack of security. Look, pick up a newspaper and read the columns instead of the comics. You know the news, the print instead of cartoon frames. Try it sometime, and you'll soon realize that Africa is a dangerous place. Ever heard of Darfur, Somalian pirates, Ruanda genocide, and a particularly nasty former Ugandan president named Idi Amin?"

"Well, thanks for the lecture, Ms. Current Affairs."

"The only current affairs you're interested in are found in the *National Enquirer*, mister wise-ass."

Joanne held up her hands in a T. "Time out, you two."

"He started it," Charlene said.

"While I'm away, I want you both to cooperate with Grandma and always do what she tells you to do." She looked hard at Gary. "I hope I can trust you both. I can't say how long I'll be away, but I'll phone your cells every day. I expect you to continue with your film studies, Gary. Charlene, you're an A student, so keep it up."

Joanne zipped up her luggage, and she ushered them from the bedroom to the kitchen, where she had prepared a lunch buffet of salmon, shrimp, and an array of greens and fruit salads. Instead of grouping together at one end of the table, they sat several feet apart, isolated in their own space.

Gary attacked his food, his foul mood undiminished.

"You'll probably find out that the reason Ryan hasn't called is that he got himself into a Saturday night bar brawl at the good ol' Zanzibar saloon," he said.

Charlene's face flushed. "What do you mean?" she said from across the table. "My dad's a consummate professional, he hardly ever drinks, and he only goes to a bar if he's undercover."

"Excuse me, but I never understood in the first place why he had to go to Zanzibar to solve Dr. Willow's murder when he's plenty of work in the states," Gary said, a grin flickering across his face.

Charlene propped her elbows on the arms of her chair and rested her chin on her fists. She caught Joanne's eyes.

"Why did Renée hire Dad?" she said.

Joanne was studying her, and Charlene felt her scrutiny. It made her uncomfortable.

147

"He's helping out family. Renée is his first wife's sister," Joanne said. "Besides, if he plans to buy that floatplane, he'll need the extra cash."

"Isn't an amphib a bit out of his league?" Gary said.

"It's very much in his bailiwick," Charlene said.

"Maybe if he didn't charge so much, he'd get more local clients."

"I don't think it's for us to question his business practices or his motives for taking on this case."

"As it involves my very pregnant mother—on a dangerous rescue mission to darkest Africa—I have every right to question his motives." Gary sat back and laced his fingers around the crown of his head. "Mom, the truth is, you're in no condition to go to Africa. Crossing eight time zones in two days is no picnic. Once you get to this island, there's the heat and the tsetse flies. I think you're crazy to make this journey now."

"What if he's seriously injured?" Charlene said, pushing away her uneaten lunch.

"I've phoned the hospitals; they have no record of him," Joanne said.

"Don't put your life and the life of my half brother in jeopardy," Gary said.

"I'm catching my flight and nothing is going to stop me," Joanne said, her brow furrowed in resolution.

"That's it?" Gary threw his hands in the air. "How come I wasn't in on this decision? You obviously talked to Charlene about going to Africa. Why didn't you keep me in the loop?"

"I'm sorry, Gary, but there was so little time to arrange my trip."

He sat forward and pushed away his half-eaten salad. He poured more coffee in his cup. "What happens if this phantom menace that Ryan chasin' turns into just that?"

Charlene threw her napkin on the table and stood up. She glared at Gary. "I've heard just about enough of your BS."

Joanne leaned her knuckles on the table. "Stop this bickering now. Whatever's happened to Ryan, I have to focus on bringing him home safely."

CHAPTER 22

To Ryan, the mosquito net draped over his bed reminded him of a funeral shroud. Later, he would discuss with Bari how they survived after lying in the dark at the bottom of the drain beside the Arab cemetery. Ryan described the pain of being beaten up and then having Bari dumped on top of him in filthy water like a vulture's talons, ripping open his rib cage to get at his heart. He had almost suffocated from the weight of Bari's body sprawled on his chest. A sizeable portion of his terror stemmed from the nagging fear that he was responsible for the boy's death.

During the night, he had no recollection of being hauled out of the bottom of the drain and carried into the back of a van. Ryan's eye probed slits in the bandages wrapped around his head. Earlier, it had taken him a few minutes to fully realize that he hadn't died in the waterlogged ditch. After flinging Ryan and Bari hog-tied into the deep drain, he anticipated that their tormentors planned to bury them in an unmarked grave. If so, who had intervened to bring him to this sunlit room?

Wondering where he had ended up, he stared through the veil of netting at a ceiling fan's rotating wooden blades. Ryan tried to roll over on his side, but the pain in his chest pinned him down, forcing him to continue lying on his back. He closed his eyes to take an inventory of his injuries. His head hurt in a dozen different places. His mid-section ached. His hand probed his groin, which was tender and swollen. His tongue felt gritty and dry, as though he had opened his mouth during a sandstorm. A faint breeze came from an open window, full of the smell of sea salt and disinfectant. He tried to pull himself up, but he felt too weak and fell back on the pillow.

Ryan rested until he had enough strength to sweep the mosquito net aside. He spotted a table next to his bed piled with bandages and pill vials. On the opposite side of the room, Ryan could see the outline of Bari's motionless body. He had blood-stained bandages wrapped around his face, chest, and hands. An IV tube connected his wrist to a plastic pouch.

For clues, Ryan scanned mold streaked wallpaper and moisture stains on the ceiling. The room reminded him of a place unchanged by time, clinging to an era when slaves were traded in the marketplace and Omani sultans ruled the island. He squinted at sunbeams on the stone floor. The time could be early morning or evening. Some hours ago, during a moment of consciousness, he had heard an East-Indian man's voice give instructions to someone on how to apply antiseptic cream. Coming from the balcony, a car horn blared and then disappeared, leaving behind the gentle sound of surf washing the beach.

After about half an hour, he managed to heave his body to a sitting position. He felt his head spin. He hoped it wasn't his heart. Once on his feet, pain ripped through his legs with the force of jackhammer. On the wall, he noticed photos in gilded frames of sultans and the crowned heads of British royalty. He soon realized that he had seen these faded pictures before in Zoe Singh's living room.

He gritted his teeth and stumbled until he had a grip on Bari's bedpost. He saw no movement in the boy's chest. A muffled noise came from outside the door, and he waited for it to open.

150

When the door swung wide, Zoe entered with the quick movements of a bird as she carried a tray of bandages.

"It's good to see you on your feet, Ryan," she said.

"Zoe, Zoe, is it really you?"

"You should be lying down. Let me help you back to bed."

She guided him to the bed.

"How's Bari doing?" he asked, sitting down and feeling exhausted by his few steps.

She went to lean over the boy. "He's barely alive."

Her words hit home. Zoe came and stood beside his bed and leaned over until her lips were close to his ear. "Although the doctor has doubts, I think he'll pull through." She turned to Ryan with a grieving smile. "Ready to eat something solid?"

His stomach rumbled like a cement mixer. "You bet."

"Khaled will bring you some soup."

Zoe examined his bandages. "When we first brought you here, you looked so battered, I thought it was time to find a padre to take your confession."

Ryan stared at his face reflected in mirror on the wall. He didn't like what he saw. "How did you find us?"

"As is his custom, before sunrise, Khaled visits the old cemetery on the outskirts of Stone Town to pay his respects to his first wife. While at her grave, he heard a weak sound coming from the nearby drain. At first, he thought it was a kitten. In the light from his torch, he saw your bodies, which he suspected had been dumped there for burial. When he recognized you, he contacted a friend who owns a van. He and this friend pulled you out and drove you here. As soon as you arrived, I phoned my physician, Dr. Patel. He spent hours patching you both up."

"We owe our lives to Khaled and to the good doctor."

"Dr. Patel will drop in to see you after supper."

"What's his diagnosis of my condition?"

"You have cracked ribs, head wounds, and numerous cuts, burns, and bruises. You'll be on your feet in a day or two, but you'll need long-term care."

"What did Patel say about Bari?"

Zoe glanced over at his bed, a look of concern on her wrinkled face. "Dr. Patel has done as much as he can to treat his multiple lacerations. If he doesn't improve, he'll need to be treated in hospital."

"His wounds will attract the attention of the authorities."

"That's true, but Dr. Patel is worried about knife cuts to his scalp and the extensive whipping he received to his back, chest, and abdomen."

"Does Dr. Patel think he'll make it?"

"Dr. Patel gave him a powerful drug to make him sleep. The next twenty-four hours are critical. He's lost a lot of blood, and his wounds will take a long time to heal."

Ryan tried to straighten up, but the pain and the restrictions imposed on him by his bandages made him collapse back on his pillows. After a supper of chicken soup and shepherd's pie, he played back in his mind the conversation he and Rasul had in the compound, where Bari was tortured. Shark's penetration of the island was far-reaching.

"Having me in your house puts you at risk," he said to Zoe, who placed a candle beside his bed.

"Lay still, Ryan," she said. "I understand the nature of your investigation. I've told Dr. Patel not to breathe a word of your presence here and he's agreed. You can trust him. The servants have been asked to keep secrets in my house before. Their lips are sealed." She paused before continuing. "Now you must go to sleep."

"I need to call Joanne," he said in a weak voice.

Zoe stopped at the door, turned around, and placed her hands on her hips. "I should've mentioned this sooner, but I didn't want to upset you."

"What is it?"

"Joanne phoned me from Nairobi. She plans to fly to Zanzibar tomorrow morning," she said. Her voice turned as frosty as a midwinter night. "It's a good thing you got rid of that conniving Irish minx."

CHAPTER 23

THE NEXT MORNING, IT OCCURRED to Charlene that her father was dead. As she faced the river from her second-floor bedroom window, the weak sunlight made pale shadows on the blue rose-covered wallpaper above her bed. Her mouth felt dry from lack of sleep.

Even though she knew that he wasn't coming home, she wanted to believe he was alive. If the police had arrested him, was he languishing in prison cell? She imagined guards, rifle butts resting on their hips, watching her father and the other prisoners. She imagined the eyes of his cellmates, full of menace as they milled around him. Was this too much to hope for?

She wished her father would ask a prison guard to allow him to make one phone call. When the phone did ring in the kitchen, Charlene resisted the urge to race downstairs. She waited for a few minutes, too afraid to move. She heard Gary talk on the phone. When she went downstairs, she could see from the grim expression on Gary's face that something had gone terribly wrong.

Charlene remained rooted at the foot of the stairs, the bank of halogen ceiling lights staring at her like a row of evil eyes.

Gary swung around to face Charlene, her eyes wet, glistening. "I've news of Ryan."

"What is it?"

"He's alive, but he's severely injured."

At first, the pieces didn't come together in her mind. Charlene wanted to scream, and then she felt hot tears pour down her cheeks.

"I spoke to my mother at the Norfolk Hotel in Nairobi," he said.

Charlene raised her hand to her mouth to smother her crying. "So he isn't going to die."

"She doesn't think so. A doctor is treating him."

"Is he in hospital?"

"He's in a Zoe Singh's house. She doesn't know the circumstances of how he received these wounds that she described as multiple head injuries, cracked ribs, and severe cuts and lacerations to his face, back, and abdomen. It was just by chance, one of Zoe's helpers found him and a Zanzibar boy half dead in a drain."

There was a brief silence. Charlene felt as though her world had come unhinged. She was well aware of the dangers of her father's profession, but to learn that he was seriously injured made her want to scream. But more than anything else, she was driven by an overwhelming desire to see those who had hurt her father punished.

"Charlene, I'm really sorry," Gary said. When Gary held her for a moment, Charlene could feel his chest press against her.

"Is your mom all right?" Charlene asked.

"The pregnancy, you mean?" Gary said, releasing her. "She's okay, but she insists on taking the next flight to Zanzibar to be with your dad."

"That's a relief." Her mind looped back to her father's plight. "What if Dad's too sick to come home?"

Nursing a coffee cup, Gary said, "She'll find a way to bring him back." His voice sounded brittle and angry. "My mom warned him not to go to that part of the world without some sort of backup plan, but he wouldn't listen. He flew to East Africa without assessing the situation on the ground."

Charlene's lower lip trembled. "Maybe this beating has nothing to do with Dr. Willow's murder."

Gary hesitated, as if taking time to frame the right words. "Despite her condition, we didn't try hard enough to stop her from going to rescue him in this shitty place."

At sunset, Dr. Patel changed Ryan's dressings and handed him antibiotics and painkillers. The doctor observed Ryan through rimless glasses perched on the end of his beaked nose as he drank water to wash down the capsules. Dr. Patel's eyes were dark brown, the size of dimes, and they stayed riveted on Ryan. His facial skin was soft, almost translucent except for nests of blue veins at the temples. He breathed through hairy, thin nostrils that twitched as though the air contained an offensive smell.

"When I first started treatment, both you and the boy appeared close to death," he said in an accent that had a distinct East Indian lilt.

"Thank you for saving our lives," Ryan said.

"Zoe told me that I can't treat you both in a hospital for security reasons, but to satisfy my professional curiosity, who beat you and the boy in such a brutal manner?"

"It's complicated."

"Enlighten me."

"For your own safety, I can't tell you the identities of the men who tortured us. But the man who gave the orders is a criminal who heads a cartel of rogue enterprises. His corrupting influence has already penetrated many aspects of life on this island, including the police."

"Is there anything you can do to stop him?"

"I have a plan, but for it to succeed, I need to get back in top physical shape."

"You will." Dr. Patel stood legs astride, arms folded over his chest.

"Where will you go after this is all over?"

"North Dakota," Ryan said. "It's where I am from."

"Tell me about this place," Dr. Patel said, passing his hand over the dark stubble on his cheek. "I need something to distract me before I attend to Bari's terrible wounds."

"My home is near Fargo, North Dakota's largest city. It's close to North America's midpoint. I live in a small bedroom community north of the city beside the Red River. It is surrounded by flatlands, we call prairies."

"What do you do when you're not working?"

"In the morning, my wife and I go horseback riding when the dew is still on the grass. In the afternoon, we sail downstream to a secluded island, where we have a picnic lunch, sip white wine, and listen to the birds and the wind in the poplar trees."

"It sounds idyllic. If you ever need a *mkulima*, a gardener, or an *imara mkono*, a stable hand, let me know."

"You would not like our cold winters, but snow and ice have their own special magic."

"You sound anxious to get back."

"When I was half submerged in the murky water at the bottom of the drain, I imagined I was back home in North Dakota. These images helped me survive."

"You are both lucky to be alive."

Ryan smiled. "If it weren't for you and Khaled—"

"Don't mention it," he interrupted. "Please remember that Bari's life still hangs by a slender thread, and you're not out of danger from infections."

Dr. Patel went to Bari's bed. He made a series of clicking sounds as he used surgical scissors to snip the boy's bandages. Ryan lay back on his pillow, his mind and body aching.

He shuddered at thought of Joanne ever finding out about his fling with Aisling Quinn. When Dr. Patel returned to Ryan's bed, he rested his cool hand on his forehead.

"I sense something is bothering you," the doctor said.

156

"I'm okay."

After using a thermometer to take his temperature, Dr. Patel said, "This man who gave the orders to have you tortured intrigues me. I would like to meet him."

"You wouldn't, Dr. Patel. Given the chance, he would even make the ovens in a Nazi concentration camp sing."

An hour later, Ryan's pain eased, and he felt famished. Zoe's cook made him a mild fish curry, rice, and chopped mango. For dessert, he had pawpaw squares and ice cream.

After supper, Khaled pushed in a portable TV for Zoe and Ryan to watch the evening news. The lead story, the aftermath of the Air Tanzania air crash. Over a video of the airliner's charred fuselage and twisted metal, surrounded by grassland and thorn trees, the BBC correspondent described the crash as one of the worst disasters in the country's history. Meanwhile, a massive manhunt was underway by the Tanzanian police and an international security force to track down those responsible for sabotaging the airliner. After the news, Ryan asked Zoe if he could use her phone to call Joanne at the Norfolk Hotel.

She picked up the phone on the first ring. "How are you doing sweetheart?"

"I'm on the mend," he said. "I hear background chatter. Where are you?"

"Eating Italian salad in the Norfolk's dining room. I'm catching tomorrow's noon flight to Zanzibar, so I'll see you in the afternoon."

"Don't come."

"Your voice sounds distant."

He could hear her breathing, and his heart longed for her.

"There's no need for you to come. Dr. Patel says I'll walk well in a few days," he said, speaking louder. "You shouldn't be doing all this flying, if you can possibly help it."

"I'm fine. It's you I'm worried about."

"Did you get in touch with Marleau?"

"He's in a remote area somewhere northwest of Churchill."

"Stay in Nairobi, where you are close to a modern hospital."

She laughed. "I've been in far tighter spots before."

"Don't be flippant. It's too dangerous for you to come here. You'd think differently if you could see what these bastards did to me and Bari."

"Speak up, Ryan, you're beginning to fade again."

Behind him, he heard Bari moan in his sleep.

"I'm safe at Zoe's, but the men responsible for beating us have a long reach. Your ties to me will put you in terrible danger."

Ryan could feel his voice getting weaker. Fatigue took over and he ended the call. A fresh fear of what Shark could to do to Joanne gripped him. Before falling asleep, he was thrust into a prolonged wakefulness.

After breakfast the next day, Khaled hoisted Ryan to his feet. He held his arm at the elbow to steer him a few steps away from the bed. After he felt more confident, he asked Khaled to take him to the beach. He agreed on one condition: that they walk *pole, pole,* slowly, slowly.

The boiling heat and exertion from walking in a shuffling motion made beads of sweat pop up on Ryan's forehead. The street was empty except for a grizzled woman who stood watching them from a door front. His sandals crunched on the uneven shale leading to the beach. Khaled tightened his grip to prevent him from losing his balance. He dragged his feet along the sand, feeling strength build in his legs. The morning was windless, the ocean flat and calm.

Coming from the southwest, he spotted a sleek ferry speedboat. Above him, he heard tits chirping in a mango tree like the squeak of a treadmill that needed oiling. As Ryan cooled his feet in the gentle surf, he began to worry about Joanne, arriving in Zanzibar this afternoon. She had made it clear to him during a morning phone call that there was nothing he could do to convince her to change her mind. He wriggled his toes around a seashell, but knew it would be too painful to lean down and pick it up. Ryan needed to buy another cell phone and to recover his laptop taped to the back of the toilet tank in the Hotel Kaponga. Without Aisling, he wondered how he would track down the files she had transmitted to Ireland. If he decided to fly to Dublin, the first thing to do was to contact Aisling's widowed mother, who lived on an estate outside the capital. The files held the key to the identity of the assassin who shot Jomo. Carrying on with the investigation in Ireland could be risky. What if Aisling had told her sister about him and the affair could bubble to the surface, a liaison he wanted to remain buried?

He closed his eyes, feeling the sun burn his facial cuts and bruises. In the east, a bank of thunderheads had moved in from the Indian Ocean. He stared back at Stone Town, gleaming white in the heat. The city showed the beginnings of restoration from the storm's ravages. Workers were repairing roofs. Rain had washed dust out of palm fronds, cleaned narrow streets, rinsed the pollutants out of swamps, thickened maize stalks in the *shambas*, and given new life to bougainvillea flowers.

Khaled stood beside him in the surf, watching a dhow's crew rotate the sail to harness the wind.

"What are you thinking about, *bwana*?" he asked.

"The Chinese say that if you save a life that life belongs to you," Ryan said. "I am yours forever."

Khaled came to stand next to him and stretched his scrawny neck so he could whisper directly into his ear. "There's a police car parked in front of Mama's house."

Ryan spotted a squad car and two uniformed *askaris* were walking along the path, leading to the front door.

"You cannot go back," Khaled said.

Ryan's legs wobbled as though he was on board a boat in rough seas. "Where can I go?"

Khaled grabbed his arm. "My taxi driver friend—the man who pulled you out of the drain—has a flat you can rent."

"Take me there," Ryan said, wishing he had been forceful in persuading Joanne to remain in Nairobi.

CHAPTER 24

SOUTH OF STONE TOWN, NEAR a lazy bend in the coastline, there is an untidy little square where tourists rarely venture. On the north side, there is an ancient mosque with a cracked dome that draws few worshippers. The few who attend leave well-worn shoes in tidy rows outside the main entrance. Across the square from the mosque is a small bakery that makes white bread. Early in the morning, the smell of flour and yeast mingles in among the salty odor of dried seaweed. Beside the bakery stands a large concrete house, surrounded by a high wall. A former palace of a rich Omani trader, the van owner converted the building into flats. On the top floor is a small apartment, where it is possible to see the twin spires of St. Joseph's Cathedral.

As the tenement contained no elevator, Joanne had to walk up four flights of stairs. By the time she reached the landing, she started puffing. She noticed that there was a panel of cracked glass in the door with stained curtain to prevent anyone from seeing inside. She unlocked the door and removed her sunglasses to take a close look at sunlight streaming through a skylight in the ceiling. She put the grocery bags on the kitchen table and loaded perishables into a rusty fridge.

She glanced around the flat's plastic kitchen suite and a sagging living room sofa. The flat was hot and smelled damp and reeked of sour cabbage. The cement floors were bare except for a few reed scatter rugs. Geckos clung to the watermarks on the walls and black grease stains congregated around the gas stove.

When she entered the bedroom, Ryan was asleep, sprawled on his back on the steel bed's thin mattress. The signs of his recent beatings were still visible on his face, arms, legs, and chest, but the scars had begun to fade. Despite the bruises, he was still the handsome man she had learned to love. His sunburned face had lost some of its tan, replaced by gray hospital skin. His long unkempt hair made him appear more youthful, but his features looked gaunt, and he needed extra bulk in his hollow cheeks.

Joanne opened the living room window. The sultry midday air washed over her face, as if she stood close to a hair dryer. Directly across the street, she saw a school's weed infested playground. On the sidewalk, a woman wearing a black head scarf circled around potholes. Something made the woman look up. Seeing Joanne's face, she smiled before crossing the street.

Joanne heard Ryan stir in the next room. He climbed out of bed and shuffled toward her. He gave her a baleful look and a forced smile. Despite the stubble and scars, the swelling had gone down and his features had regained symmetry.

"Good morning, sweetheart," he said in a husky whisper.

As if unable to move, he remained still. Without a word, she put her arms around him.

"Joanne—" he said.

"You still look battered and bruised," she interrupted.

"Don't worry, I'm like a Mazda—fuel-efficient, reliable, but not so strong on the resale value."

"Never mind, I'm here to look after you and get you road ready."

He released her and gazed at her round belly. "How's junior?"

"He's fine." She guided him to the bed, sat beside him and stroked his hair. "You are getting stronger every day. That's all that matters."

She examined his sweat-stained shorts. "I've bought you new underwear, but before you change, I'm giving you a sponge bath."

While cleaning his body with soap and bottled water, she took care to avoid touching his wounds. "Dr. Patel showed me how to change your dressings. He has also given me the meds you need."

She placed tubes and vials of medication and fresh bandages on a chest beside the bed. Joanne applied an antiseptic cream to the whip welts and knife cuts. After attending to his wounds, she went to the bathroom and washed her hands in a small basin. The reflection of her pale face was obscured by smudges and a network of fissures embedded in the mirror.

When Joanne returned to the bedroom, she used a damp towel to dab his forehead. She hated the thought of him spending another night on the cramped cot's thin mattress. She imagined the brown marks on the mattress could be anything—urine, semen, blood, or worse.

"Shouldn't we be thinking of moving you somewhere else?" she said.

"Not yet."

For a while, neither of them spoke. Apart from his wounds, she sensed something was wrong. Zoe had mentioned that Ryan had rescued a woman from drowning, but she remained tight-lipped about the incident.

"Talk to me," she said, wiping sweat off her forehead.

He stared out the window at a palm tree that swayed in the breeze. "About what?"

"Well, you seem so distant."

"Joanne, I've gone through the worst beating I've ever experienced in my life. Not only the pain, but can you imagine what it was like to be forced to watch them peel the skin off Bari's scalp in thin strips? His life still hangs by the slimmest of threads."

"Dr. Patel thinks he's going to live." She leaned over to kiss him. "I know it's been hell. I just thought it might be helpful to talk. Apart from your wounds, what's troubling you?"

He gulped down some water. "Don't pay any attention to my gripes. Guys like me always do okay."

"I've never seen you so down."

She saw in his eyes that he was holding something back from her. Ryan must have felt her scrutiny, for he turned his head away from the window to gaze at her. His blue eyes registered hurt. She felt sorry for him. As if to mask his thoughts, he gave her a lopsided grin.

"Well, I admit I did screw up," he said.

He looked at her for a long time, and she saw the pain in his eyes and some new emotion forming that she couldn't decipher.

"Cheer up!" she said, massaging his shoulders. "What did Bari do for you?"

"Apart from being my guide, he also became a good friend and companion. If any further harm ever comes to him at the hands of these bastards, I'd never forgive myself."

Joanne swallowed the dregs of the coffee she had made on the stove and placed the cup on the chipped kitchen table covered in a kaleidoscope of food stains. "How do you plan to deal with the man you think is responsible for Jomo's murder, shooting Amari, and beating you?"

Ryan's face darkened. "I'm quitting this case."

"If you bow out of the investigation now, doesn't this man still pose a threat to you and Bari?"

Ryan sat up, as if he strained to hear some distant answer to her question. He held his back in a stiff, regimental stillness. He lapsed into a long silence. Through the window, she could hear morning rain smacking against the stained walls and the paving stones in the narrow street. Joanne interlaced her fingers as if in prayer, eyes fixed on a gray mold growing on the floor. The despondent room reminded her of an out-of-season, rundown resort.

"Zoe told me you plan to continue your investigation in Dublin?" she said.

"I did consider that an option." He grinned. "At the moment, I have one thing working to my advantage; the man who gave the orders thinks I'm dead."

Later that afternoon, Zoe threaded her hand through Joanne's arm as they strolled along the sand. Joanne had accepted Zoe's offer to stay in her decaying palace. She rather enjoyed living in the old place's faded decadence. She admired Zoe's chutzpah for persuading the police that she wasn't hiding fugitives in her home, but Staff Sergeant Lipumba had insisted in searching every room. Seconds before his officers combed the building, Khaled managed to hide Bari on the roof.

The afternoon air was thick and warm on the sand, the sky overcast and unsettled. As if lying at anchor, Joanne paused to watch a fleet of birds bobbing on the outgoing tide.

Neither Zoe nor Joanne talked for a few minutes, and she didn't find the silence between them awkward. In fact, it was rather pleasant and peaceful not to talk. She had enjoyed Zoe's company at lunch, when they had chatted about Joanne's family over glasses of sherry.

During the walk, Joanne allowed her gaze to settle on the older woman's face. Her pointed nose was a little too prominent for her face, her hollow cheeks made the bones stand out. Zoe noticed Joanne's stare and smiled, but the smile didn't extend to her eyes. Joanne recognized a distant sadness in their sky-blue color, as though she was grieving her lost loved ones.

Zoe was the first to break the silence. She squeezed Joanne's hand. "How is Ryan?"

Joanne blew out a heavy breath. "Ryan is *Ryan*," she said, as if no other explanation was necessary. "He's on his feet for a good part of the day now. At first, he wanted to quit the case and go home, but now he talks endlessly about how he plans to renew his investigation into Jomo's death in Dublin."

"After all he's gone through, I'm surprised he wants to go down that perilous path."

"I've told him it is mission impossible, but he won't listen."

"He's a stubborn one."

"Sometimes at night I think he climbs the walls along with the geckos." She laughed. "He does endless calisthenics to strengthen his legs and arms."

They walked to Shangani Point, to a spot where Joanne could see the white Arab battlements of the Serena Inn.

"Isn't that the hotel where he stayed when Ryan first came to the island?" Joanne said.

Instead of answering, Zoe's lined face turned as hard as granite. She pointed to a strip of beach, where children popped in and out of the surf in front of the hotel. "That's the spot where he rescued that Irish slut."

CHAPTER 25

The next morning, Ryan limped over to the window of his flat. The scab on his shin hurt like a burn. The morning shower had ended, leaving clouds soft and white against a blue sky. The palms along the boulevard were groomed and thick from new fronds. He expected any moment to hear Joanne chopping mangoes and pawpaw to make him fruit salad for breakfast.

He loved having Joanne look after him, but he needed his PI partner Marleau Belanger to help him decide what he should do next. He felt confident that his body would soon be strong enough to continue the investigation. Should he go home or fly to Dublin, where he would be on Shark's home turf? If he went to Ireland, how could he explain his reason to Joanne without mentioning Aisling and the files she transmitted from Shark's yacht?

When Ryan and Marleau were young police officers in Fargo, they were feared by gangs as well as pimps, street dips, and felons, who lived like worms in the city's underbelly. Above all, the criminals often dreaded Marleau more than they did Ryan. His temper was legendary. Not only among the felons, but also his superiors on the force. It had less to do with his cop partner's tilt to violence than his indifference to conventional investigative procedures. He was the trickster of Native American stories, the prankster who created mayhem wherever he went. He was the bane of his superiors, who established the protocols he broke with impunity. He often ignored his police bosses when they admonished him.

Despite Marleau's perchance for bedlam, Ryan longed to have his colleague extricate him from his conundrum.

In the morning sunlight, Joanne walked down the stairs from Zoe's house to the street. She passed a mosque facing a narrow, twisted road that led to the beach. The sky had clouded, and a warm breeze funneled through high walls covered in creepers. A waft of hot air carrying a faint scent of cloves brushed against her cheeks. A block before she reached Ryan's flat, she felt the baby's sharp kick.

When Joanne caught sight of the sea turned dark by clouds, flicked blue by muted lightning, she decided it was time to question Ryan about this Irish girl Zoe so disliked. What circumstances surrounded Ryan's rescue Aisling from drowning? Why did he feel compelled to smuggle her in a dhow off the island to the mainland?

She stopped beside a small *duka* beside an outdoor stall. She went inside the cramped store and bought bread, eggs, and spinach. While she climbed the stairs to Ryan's flat, she had to admit that she was shocked when she first saw Ryan lying on the stained mattress. But she soon found out his wounds weren't as serious as she first thought.

His swollen eyes were shut. His eyes were the first thing she noticed about Ryan when they met four years ago in Marsdon. They were still an intoxicating color. In Joanne's initial impression of Ryan, he had appeared stalwart and masculine, but she soon discovered that he could be vulnerable and sweet in the company of women.

After putting the groceries in the kitchen, she felt resentment rising. Why hadn't he mentioned anything about Aisling Quinn? Zoe had provided some details about this Irish beauty. What she heard made her suspicious. She rattled dishes in the sink to wake him.

When he rolled over to face her, she called out, "Zoe and I had a long chat."

"Oh, really."

"Don't worry, Ryan, we didn't spend all evening talking about you."

"That's a relief."

She placed her hands on her hips. Feeling nauseous, the weight of the baby pulled her down.

"While walking on the beach beside the Serena, she told me about the lovely red-haired colleen you hauled out of the sea, saving her from drowning." She paused. "Did you give her mouth-to-mouth resuscitation?"

She sensed Ryan was trying to stay calm, to control his thoughts.

"Why haven't you mentioned Aisling before?" Joanne continued, a note of bitterness creeping into her voice.

Ryan remained silent.

"Well?" she whispered, fingering the handle of the paring knife.

She gazed at his battered face. The skin on his lips was chapped and furrowed, but the scars had begun to blur and lose redness.

"Did she have a nice figure?" she asked, looking down at her distended stomach.

He laughed, a hollow sound.

Joanne leaned her aching back against the wall's cool stone. "Why did you have to smuggle her off the island?"

He came into the kitchen and reached out to touch her heart. "I only love the person who's inside here."

Ryan's face up close had the stark, hollow eyes of a prisoner trying to escape over a high wall, while all the searchlights focused on him. He held her loosely in his arms.

She spat out the words as though she were trying to expel from her mouth a foul taste. "Zoe described this young woman as ravishing, but troubled."

For a moment, he seemed to have lost his voice. She stared at him waiting for an answer, but he couldn't hold her scrutiny. "What happened between you two?"

"The man who owned the yacht threatened to throw Aisling overboard and feed her to the sharks. I pulled her half drowned out of the bay. I gave her CPR to save her life."

"How did it feel when your lips locked?" She pounded her fists on his chest. "After you revived this latter-day Isolde, did you take her to your bed? After saving her life, she must have been so eager, so grateful."

Ryan's unshaven face appeared to shrink and become hard and tight like the skin of an under ripe peach.

She pulled away from him. "I know you like beautiful women; they are attracted to you." She tried to sound casual. "Why didn't you mentioned her? She obviously plays an important role in your investigation."

When Ryan didn't answer, Joanne picked up the paring knife and started chopping mango slices. He sat down on a kitchen chair, propped his head on his elbow, and allowed his face to register discomfort. During a long spell of total silence, Joanne listened to a woman scolding a child and a bicycle bell ringing.

"If you want to tell me more about her, Ryan, you've got my full attention," she said, finally.

He stood up, shifting from one foot to the other.

"Aisling's dead," he said, a terrible imploring in his eyes. "She died in the Air Tanzanian jetliner crash."

"I saw the wreckage on the TV news in Nairobi. The police suspect terrorists planted a bomb on board."

He tried to put his hand out to touch her, but she moved away from him. She glanced at him, so wounded and broken. His shoulders sagged as he tried again to reach out to draw her to him. To her, his hangdog look said it all.

"No, Ryan, no. Don't tell me you shared the same bed," she said in a voice as fragile as a small child. "Your silence condemns you.

Did this affair happen during the night when the cyclone hit? Did her arms reach out to comfort you?" She stepped forward to place a finger across his dried lips. She avoided touching a thick scab at the corner of his mouth. "Hush, I don't want to hear about it."

She stiffened when she thought about another woman sharing his sex, even someone who had died a horrible death. She couldn't help imagining Aisling breathing in his smell and touching the familiar contours of his body that she had regarded as her own.

She shook her head and began to walk to the front door.

"Please don't go," he said.

She turned. His forlorn eyes and scarred face reminded her of a derelict homeless man she had once seen on Main Avenue. The sight of him made her feel a combination of loathing and pity.

Biting her lip, she gave him a sad smile. "I'm going back to Zoe's now," she said. "Your breakfast is on the table."

"Wait, please," he said.

Joanne's face hardened into a tight-lipped frown. "I know how unsettling severe storms are for you. Did her red hair remind you of Kathy? Did Aisling—"

His voice was soft, almost a whisper. "It had nothing—"

"Damn you, Ryan Moar. Damn you for saying that," she interrupted.

He stood up and limped to where she stood by the door. Her arms rested on her pregnant stomach, as she stared at the tops of palm trees waving in the wind.

"Well?" she asked, tapping her sandaled toes on the floor.

"Aisling Quinn was a guest on the yacht. She hacked into the owner's computer, downloaded files, and transmitted them to a terminal in Dublin." He lifted his head and watched her. "If I can get my hands on those files, I will know who hired the assassin who gunned down Jomo."

Joanne listened to a baby cry, a neighbor slammed a door, and a car horn being honked.

"The search for Jomo's killer threatens to tear us apart," she said.

Ryan had tears in his eyes, "Give me a chance to—"

Joanne's face flushed with anger. "You rotten bastard," she interrupted in a loud voice that scared a crow perched on the windowsill. She looked at him, overcome by such a wave of anger that she wanted to scream. "What makes you think I ever want to see you again?"

CHAPTER 26

AUDREY BRADT HAD ONE RIGID rule at dinner in her penthouse in the Al Mutlaq Hotel. None of the guests were allowed to discuss economics, particularly African economics. Economics had ruled Jomo Willow's life, and the professor had been a frequent guest at her dinner parties. He and his colleagues had heated debates on economics. Audrey was bored by the subject, almost as much as she loathed political discussions.

At her dinner parties, she indulged her guests when it came to food. For the couple at her candlelight supper, Ryan Moar and his pregnant wife, Joanne Sutter, she had gone to the kitchen to supervise her Mumbai chef, while he cooked chili chicken, artichoke frittala, garam masala, and for dessert, a coconut flan covered in a cream clove sauce. She had found an expensive twenty-year-old South African Charles Niehaus red sherry to wash down the meal.

Audrey worshipped East Indian cuisine and believed Europe would be a more civil place if it had been colonized by East Indians rather than the other way around. Her other passion was books, and she had an extensive library in her suite. She adored the classics. She also had a collection of rare books from the library of a former

Asian plantation owner, forced to flee Zanzibar after the Marxist revolution.

Throughout the meal in her antique filled penthouse, a waiter drifted in and out, carrying in each new course. Audrey guided the conversation to books, recent movies, and the description of a charming coastal villa she had bought on the south side of Pemba Island.

She smiled at Ryan to prompt him to join in the conversation, but he remained silent. The private investigator had cut his hair short and the scars on his face hadn't diminished his youthful appearance. Yet, his eyes, which she had found so attractive, were red rimmed and lackluster. In contrast, Joanne's pregnancy had given her a healthy glow that complemented her tanned cheeks and shoulders.

Ryan and Joanne had checked into separate bedrooms three days ago as Mr. and Mrs. Christopher Marlowe. Audrey didn't believe Joanne's explanation for the bruises and cuts on Ryan's face and scalp. She was sure these wounds were a direct result of his investigation into Jomo's murder. Audrey had become alarmed when she learned of Amari's assassination in the Anglican Cathedral, followed by Ryan's high-speed motorcycle chase to catch the killer. She had picked up gossip from her maid, who had a sister, a receptionist at the Serena Inn. She told Audrey about Ryan's rescue of a beautiful woman fleeing from one of the yachts in the harbor. She gossiped to Audrey about Ryan carrying the young woman from the beach to his suite, where she spent the night in his bed. Did Joanne's knowledge of this affair explain the awkward silences between them?

The waiter entered and poured Arusha coffee into tiny cups. After he left, they moved from the table to the soft cushions of Audrey's cream sofas. Audrey found it odd that Ryan had chosen Christopher Marlowe as an alias. She wondered if Ryan had given any thought before selecting the name of the famed British playwright, the author of *Doctor Faustus*, who had made a pact with the devil. She recalled the writer's motto: *Quod me nutrit me destruit.* That which feeds me destroys me.

When her guests were comfortably settled, she judged that the time was right to find out if Ryan still had the fight to continue looking into Jomo's death or had the thrashing persuaded him to quit.

"How much longer are Mr. and Mrs. Christopher Marlowe planning to remain at my hotel?" she asked, adjusting folds in her glittering yellow sari.

"Joanne is checking out of your hotel tomorrow morning, and I'm leaving three days later," Ryan said, rubbing his temples.

He shifted on the couch and complained of hearing a whirring noise in his ear that reminded him of someone blowing into a conch shell. Audrey wondered if the sound was related to his head injuries or from medication.

"Are you all right, Ryan?" Audrey asked.

"I'm fine," he said, sipping on passion fruit juice instead of alcohol.

"Ryan, are you planning to continue your investigation into Jomo's death," Audrey said.

"We'll see."

"Since we last spoke, have you made any further progress in finding his killer?"

His battered face brightened. "I'm getting closer to finding his identity."

Ryan rested his head in his palms, the heels pressing into his eyes.

He looked up when Joanne said, "He's continuing his investigation in Dublin."

Audrey leaned into him. "Are you really going to Ireland?"

His eyes appeared old and empty. "I expect I will."

She laughed. "Is there any chance I might know the suspect?"

"I don't think so. He's the head of a crime cartel, and I believe he is responsible for the recent airliner crash."

Audrey pulled on an earlobe. "The newspapers reported the disaster is the work of Al-Qaeda."

"They're wrong. This man is the mastermind behind the crash of the Air Tanzania passenger jet."

Audrey covered her mouth in surprise. "This crime lord sounds awfully dangerous."

"Ryan will carry on to the end," Joanne said. "He's such a fool."

"What can we do to dissuade him?"

"For the moment, a brief prayer of thanks to the Almighty that he is still alive is appropriate."

After coffee and liqueurs, Ryan and Joanne went for a walk on the beach. They were silent for a long time, until Ryan felt her grope for his hand. He could feel the sinews of her fingers strengthened by tennis games on the university's clay courts.

"I'm sorry I snapped at you during dinner," Joanne said.

"No need to apologize," Ryan said.

As he listened to the waves sweeping up on the sand, Ryan felt that the crisis in their relationship had reached a tipping point. He could only guess at what agonies of decisions were going on in her mind. Her quick flares of temper and sullen silences had turned her into a remote and isolated woman.

"I suppose, I knew deep down what I was getting into when we decided to share the same bath towels and tubes of toothpaste," she said.

"Would it do any good if I went into another profession?"

She shook her head. "I can't change what you do, but the strange part of it is I like nothing better than balancing teaching drama and solving mysteries." She glanced up at him, so he could see her face in the moonlight. "It came as no surprise to me when you said at dinner that you were flying to Dublin. I could see it in your eyes that you wanted to resolve this case, no matter how dangerous it would be."

"What special look did I have tonight?"

"Well, it is that hungry expression when you're in the home stretch of a case, closing in on the guilty party."

Ryan stopped to let the cool surf run over his feet.

Joanne continued, "I wonder if you still think of her, the woman whom you rescued and slept in your bed. What's her name?"

"Aisling Quinn."

She dug her toes into the wet sand. "Did you love her?" He licked his cracked lips. "Did you make love to her to give you some measure of comfort to ward off your phobia of storms?"

He didn't want to go back there, but what choice did he have? Joanne deserved a frank answer.

"It was such a strange night," he began. "After I swam out into the bay and hauled her to the beach, I never expected to take her to my suite. I anticipated she would rejoin her onboard cocktail party or whatever she was doing on the yacht. After bringing her back to life, she appeared so fragile, so helpless." He paused. He opened and closed his eyes as if he had sand in them or making an attempt to blink away the memory. "During that bizarre night, I was lonely. Above all, I wanted you by my side. Yes, I admit sex between us did blunt the panic I felt when the cyclone ploughed into the island, but the act itself meant nothing to me."

His honesty made her gasp. Ryan stared out at a pinprick of light from a night fishing dhow's hurricane lamp.

"I definitely never loved her," he added.

"You're a terrible liar."

"I speak the truth."

"Do you? Isn't deception the stock-in-trade of your profession?"

"I never lie to you." His throat felt raw and tasted of rust. "I've only kept things from you when knowing too much could put you in danger or our relationship in jeopardy."

The air was filled with the sound of a night wind and the pounding of the breakers on the rocks at a point jutting out into the sea.

"Do you still think about her?" she said, letting go his hand and leaning against a black coral outcrop. "Or the night you spent together?"

For a moment, he felt dumbstruck, as though the air had been knocked out of him.

"What happened to Aisling in that terrible air disaster is something that still haunts me, but other than that, I don't think about her at all," he said.

Tears in her eyes were caught for a moment in the beams of car headlights. "Your unfaithfulness hurt me. I still can't live with it."

Ryan threw her a look of exasperation. "My relationship with Aisling is over, sweetheart, gone for good." Ryan shook his head. "The whole incident means nothing to me. Why should you care?"

Enraged, she turned on him. "You made me feel rejected, despised. That's how your betrayal made me feel in my heart."

Joanne glanced toward the dhow harbor, his silence made her irritable.

Finally, she said, "You're in no condition to continue this investigation. Who is going to change your dressings? Ensure you take your meds?"

Ryan turned to face her. "I'm so relieved you are leaving tomorrow morning. I want you and the baby out of harm's way. The thought of dragging you deeper into this morass makes me want to puke my guts out."

She turned her back on him, and he spun her around.

Joanne looked up into his face. "I'm angry with you, but I'm having this child, and I don't want him to grow up without a father."

He pulled the back of her head until her cheek rested on his chest. As he often did, he stroked her hair. He heard her breathing, heavy and uneven.

He brushed grains of sand off her shoulders. "You're more important to me than anything in this universe."

Listening to the night wind rattle palm fronds, Ryan took her hand, and they strolled on the white sand toward the warm glow of the hotel's floodlights.

CHAPTER 27

I N A STREET TOO NARROW for cars, a vendor on his rounds
sold Ryan a small brass cup of coffee. To help blend into his
surroundings, Ryan wore a gray Swahili shirt reaching his upper
thighs, embroidered around the collar, over loose-fitting charcoal
sokoto pants and a red *fila* cap. He paused to drink his coffee.
Leaning against a wall, the pungent fragrance of a frangipani tree
reminded him Joanne.

He was so pleased to get her phone call last night. She was safe
at their home beside the Red River, north of Fargo. While Ryan
watched an old woman in black set up a street stall to sell maize,
mangos, and cassavas, he made a call on his new cell phone to Zoe's
house. He needed to find out if Bari's wounds continued to heal. Zoe
told him that Dr. Patel's prognosis was positive. Bari was expected
to recover without any lasting physical aftereffects from the torture.
Dr. Patel predicted that in three weeks, the boy should be strong
enough to walk on his own, but his mental condition remained a
question mark. Dr. Patel was worried about his depression. Ryan
ended the call by assuring the doctor that he had made provisions
for any additional medical treatment the boy might need.

Ryan continued to walk along Mnazi Street, breathing in the smell of spices and fried goat meat. The air was warm and still, and the sun drenched the shops and apartments on the west side of the street in white heat.

Ryan made his next call to the Irish embassy in Dar es Salaam. He introduced himself to a male receptionist as Donald Mason, a Zanzibar hotel owner. He told him he had in his hotel safe some personal effects belonging to Aisling Quinn. The receptionist said that he was sorry that Mr. Mason's former guest had died in the tragic Air Tanzania crash. Before Ms. Quinn's departing, Ryan explained, she had asked him to keep these items for her until she returned. Did he know her mother's address, so he could forward to her Aisling's Swiss watch, money, and camera? The receptionist transferred him to a protocol administrator named Eamonn Ballhack.

"So, Mr. Mason, you have Ms. Quinn's valuables," Eamonn said.

"That's correct," Ryan said.

"How much money did she leave behind?"

"She left five hundred euros. Aisling told me she had every intention of returning to my hotel after her visit to Dublin to see her mother. I hope you will be kind enough to give me her mother's name, address, and phone number, so I can send her the money and her daughter's other possessions by courier."

Ballhack cleared his throat. "I'm sorry, Mr. Mason, but I'm not at liberty to provide the name of Ms. Quinn's mother. I suggest you courier her things to my attention at the embassy, and I will make sure they are forwarded through diplomatic channels to her next of kin."

"That may prove difficult, Mr. Ballhack. You see, before Aisling left for Dublin, she gave me instructions that if she decided to remain in Ireland, I was to send her things to her at her mother's house. She neglected to give me the contact information."

"I'll be back in a minute."

While waiting, Ryan listened to pied crows squabble among the spiky cones of a spindly casuarina tree. When Ballhack came back on the line, he told Ryan that he had talked to his superior. They agreed not to provide him under any circumstances the name of Aisling's mother.

Feeling frustrated by bureaucrats, Ryan disconnected the call. Clouds blocked the sun, and the air had turned to wet cotton. Yellow lightning flared in the darkening skies. As he headed back to the hotel along the quay, he listened to the clink of chains connected to the dhow. A fish flopped in the water beside an outrigger boat laboring against the incoming tide.

An airliner on the horizon making a final approach to land at the airport reminded him to leave in plenty of time to catch the afternoon flight to Nairobi. Seeing the Air Tanzania 737 made him feel haunted by Aisling. Before her fiery death, she told him that she had descended from a long line of Irish witches. The ancient craft had been passed on to her from her mother. Was she prescient, or just superstitious about claiming to have the powers of her ancestors? Her body may have been incinerated to dust high above the sparse snows of Kilimanjaro, but could her restless spirit confront him when three days from now he would arrive at Dublin Airport?

A loud recording of the *Adhan*, the soulful Islamic call for prayer, interrupted Ryan's thoughts of Aisling's bewitching nature and made him think of his own mortality. He shivered as though suffering from malaria. If Khaled hadn't found him, his body would now be devoured by worms in the warm earth under a ripening crop of maize.

CHAPTER 28

T HE TAXI RIDE FROM THE Dublin airport to Ryan's hotel in
the city's center seemed to take almost as long as the Aer
Lingus flight from Heathrow to the Irish capital. It was a cool and
wet afternoon even for early May, and the heater in the Vauxhall
taxi only gave out a faint warmth. Ryan sat back in the well-worn
leather seat, his eyes closed, while the driver cursed the gridlock of
cars, buses, trucks, and cyclists.

A reed thin boy holding a squeegee darted in among the cars.
He tried to clean the taxi's windshield for change, but the driver
shouted at him to shove off. From the glowing tan of his face and his
new suit bought off the rack at London's Harrods department store,
Ryan assumed the taxi driver probably thought he was a Dubliner
back from a prolonged holiday in Florida, a favorite Irish winter
playground. Ryan's hunch proved right.

"Been in a hot spot, sir?" the cabbie asked, glaring at the muddle
of cars ahead.

"Yes, I have been in a warm country," Ryan said. "How are
things in your fair city?"

"The pits," the driver said. "The Irish economy is a bottomless sinkhole."

When they passed a bank of TVs in a store window, the taxi driver turned to stare at Prime Minister Brian Cowen's plump pink face. "He wouldn't be smilin' if he was down here stuck in this bog like the rest of us." He nodded at the city's skyline. "Those silent cranes you see all across this town are like bloody tombstones."

"They'll be working again."

The taxi driver shook his head. "Those cancelled building projects are empty holes in the ground, eyesores." The driver took a sip from a thermos. "Before the crash, Ireland was called a Celtic Tiger, but now we're just a shabby tabby. Unemployment is soaring, government spending is out of control, and the banks are oversaturated in toxic assets."

"That bad, huh?" Ryan said.

"You a Yank?" he said, examining him in the rear-view mirror. "Yeah."

"You started this financial crisis, but you're so big you'll soon be out of it." The driver jerked his thumb at a thickset man trying to elbow his way close to the front of a queue snaking around the corner of an employment office. "There's not much work now to be had in Dublin. It's worse in the countryside."

The driver swept back overgrown hair that he had brushed forward into his forehead. He wore a blue jacket over an open white shirt that displayed an elongated V down his hairless chest.

"If you ask me, the luck of the Irish has disappeared as fast as smoke from a stubbed fag," he said. "As for me, would you believe it if I told you I have a degree in computer science from Trinity College? I can't find a job anywhere in my field. I'm lucky to have work driving a taxi."

"Any sign of a turnaround?"

"Not bloody likely. After thirty-five years, my dad lost his job when Waterford Crystal went belly up. He told me I'd best think about emigrating to Canada or Australia." The driver made a sharp U-turn that startled a woman pushing a shopping cart of rags across the street. "Did yer know that since the start of this recession, over six hundred companies have gone belly up?"

The cab drove past Trinity College's iron gates. Ryan had a fleeting look of the university's architecture, a spellbinding mix of turrets, spires, and Doric columns. An overcast sky threatened rain and cast a blanket of gloom over the city's cobblestone streets.

"Couldn't resist showing off my alma mater," the young man said.

Ryan had never lived in Dublin, but during his tenure with the CIA, he had worked in London during the troubles in Northern Ireland. For a while, he was a control officer for an agent inside the Irish Intelligence Agency, G2. The agent provided valuable information on the movements of the IRA that Ryan passed to British Intelligence, MI5.

Ryan's hotel overlooked the narrow Grand Canal. Reeds and long grass choked the sides of the canal, interspersed with wood and iron locks, causing stagnant pools covered in green scum. Bordering the canal's footpaths were blackened row houses, broken up by empty steel-and-glass building constructed during the boom.

The driver pulled up to the Hilton's entrance. Ryan gave him a generous tip, wishing him luck. At the reception desk, he checked in to a third-floor suite. He took the precaution of giving his room a thorough search for bugs.

He left the hotel and to shake off anyone tailing him, he caught a double-decker bus and got off at the first stop, before doubling back to the Stephen's Green Shopping Centre, a replica of a Moorish palace. Inside the mall, he mingled among the shoppers and then went inside a tourist store to examine shamrock design jewelry and miniature statues of Saint Patrick. He found a payphone to speak to a receptionist at the Irish Intelligence Agency. He made a lunch appointment for the following day to meet his former G2 colleague, Sean Terenure. When he was sure he wasn't being followed, he strolled back to the Hilton.

At noon the next day, Ryan took a taxi to the Cork and Whistle pub near Trinity College to meet Sean Terenure for lunch. The pub's faded Georgian decor had the feel of old Dublin, rather like an elderly tart who putters around her flat in her tawdry working wardrobe. The pub's doorman wore a green raincoat trimmed in silver and a stovepipe hat. Ryan brushed past him and entered a salon, where men reclined in high-backed chairs accompanied by women in fashionable suits.

Ryan spotted Sean seated in a corner booth in a chair lined in red velvet. He glanced at Ryan as he approached and waved his hand. His head had the shape of a bullet, except for a fringe of black hair. Sean's cheeks were tanned like old leather, and his face had more deep lines than Ryan remembered. Ugly steel-framed glasses magnified green eyes that danced in the light of candelabra. Ryan recalled that his eyes and rich baritone voice were magnets for women.

"I hope you weren't followed," Sean said, getting up to shake his hand.

"I've taken precautions."

Sean stared at Ryan. "Ol' buddy, you look like you've been in a war zone. What happened to you?"

"It's a long story."

A smiling server came over to take their orders.

"I'll fill you in after the beer arrives," Ryan said, taking a seat in front of shelves of bound books.

They order pints of Guinness and plates of chicken wings, grilled bangers, and spareribs.

"You've come to Dublin at a miserable time," Sean said.

"You mean the recession."

"You'd better believe it."

"In the pub, you could've fooled me."

"As you can see, despite the appearance of a city in decline, Dublin still has this charming pub for the rich living the high life, while the majority of Dubliners suffer in one way or another." Sean lowered his slim frame back into his chair. "Why, only yesterday, a department store advertised a job opening on the shop's display window, and over five hundred applicants showed up."

"The decline happened so quickly."

Sean laughed without humor. "The end of the boom spelled the collapse of residential and commercial real estate. Property values and housing sales went to a severe slump. Companies here during the boom pulled up stakes and hundreds of high paying technical jobs disappeared."

"I noticed plenty of For Sale and Gone Out of Business signs."

"Let me give you an example of our misfortunes, lost dreams." He took a long pull at his Guinness glass. "Bono, the Irish singer and musician, the main vocalist for the U2 rock band, planned to build the city's tallest structure, a luxury hotel and recording studio. The scheme is now nothing more than a giant hole in the ground in an empty, boarded lot."

"You still have your pubs," Ryan said.

"You're right, pal. In good times and bad, there're no places on earth quite like an Irish pub for chat, grub, sing-along, and *craic*, the Irish word for good times."

While eating, they clinked glasses and chatted for twenty minutes about old times, when they were both in the spy game. Ryan finally got down to business by turning the conversation to his investigation of Jomo's murder and Aisling's death in the bomb explosion on board the Air Tanzania jetliner. He concluded by saying that he suspected Shark was behind both Jomo's murder and the bomb attack on the airline.

"If this is true, we've been looking in the wrong direction for the perpetrators of the Tanzanian airliner disaster. We all thought it was Al Qaeda's special brand of handiwork."

"Shark imitates Al Qaeda's attack methods," Ryan said.

He asked Sean if he knew Shark's real name was Darcy O'Connell.

"I've heard of this maggot's name linked to a Darcy O'Connell, a criminal mastermind, who heads a rogue organization" Sean said, lowering his voice.

Before Ryan signaled the server to bring them another round of Guinness, he told him how he had hacked into Shark's cosmetic surgeon's files.

When the server brought the drinks and left, Ryan said, "What can you tell me about Darcy O'Connell before he became Shark?"

"He was an orphaned Biafra baby adopted by a well-meaning Irish couple. Growing up, Darcy had a tough time at school. Being the only black fellow in class, he was often the butt of jokes. The girls teased him for his skin color and tight curls. They called him 'thick lips' and 'golliwog,' and that made him furious. From then on, he developed a special love-hate relationship for Irish colleens. We know the bastard even murdered a few, but he never faced a conviction."

"Before Aisling Quinn died in the air crash, he wanted to feed her to the sharks."

Sean scowled. "Did Aisling work for the Anglo Irish Bank?"

"That's what she told me."

"We've had her under suspicion for illegal hacking into bank computers."

"She's good. She even hacked into mine."

"I'm sure you're aware Anglo Irish is heavily exposed to property lending and ended up being taken over by the government."

"Is there a connection?"

"I'm sure there is." Sean raised his beer mug a few inches from the white Irish linen tablecloth and murmured, *"Mazel tov*, Ryan."

"I need to contact Aisling's mother."

He leaned forward. "It shouldn't be hard to track down Mrs. Quinn. I'll get back to you." Sean took a long pull on his Guinness. "You must realize, of course, the full extent of the powerful forces you're up against."

Ryan pointed to scabs on his face. "This is his thug's handiwork."

"I'm surprised you are still alive." Sean lowered his voice. "Shark has his tentacles in illegal enterprises worldwide. He controls a multibillion-dollar business through interlocking connections of

186

corporations, mostly involved in profitable criminal activities. He and the exclusive members of his cartel use bloody AK-47s and bombs to spread terror to keep his empire together."

"I know a way to put Shark out of business."

"Despite using some of our best operatives, his organization is so tight that we've never been able to penetrate it." Sean scratched the back of his neck. "You mean you can actually accomplish what most of the world's intelligence agencies and police forces have failed to do?"

Ryan nodded and drank his beer, which left foam on his upper lip.

"Well, my friend, you're full of surprises." Sean picked up a chicken wing and his perfect teeth stripped off the meat. "Tell me, what damning information or special insights do you possess on Shark to bring him to his knees?"

"Before Aisling boarded the doomed Air Tanzania flight, she told me she had downloaded Shark's files from his laptop and transmitted them to Dublin. If I can locate her mother, I have a chance of finding the terminal where she sent these files."

Sean pulled out a pipe and went through the ritual of tamping down the tobacco and then lighting the bowl. "G2 would love to get their hands on those files, but there's one problem in any attempt to shut down Shark's criminal activities. He knows every loophole in the law. He has judges on his payroll. Shark is a walking encyclopedia of criminal knowledge. It's rumored that he knows half the legislators in Leinster House by their first names, and many MPs are indebted to him for his donations to get them elected." Sean leaned back and puffed hard on his pipe while watching rain swirl across the street through a narrow window. "Let me give you an example of his clout. Shark was in involved in Irish construction and real estate as a major player. It ends up that he and his shysters were one of the main reasons for the industry's collapse."

Sean put down his smoldering pipe in an ashtray. His eyes scanned the other patrons until they came to rest on a woman seated alone near the entrance. An oversized handbag lay open on the carpet beside her.

"How do you know that the content of these files have anything of real value?" Sean asked.

"On board Shark's yacht, Aisling inadvertently told one of his colleagues about his involvement in real estate manipulations, information that could only have come from these files."

"Well, she's right. Shark and about a dozen other investors pulled out of the market before the real estate industry floundered. Days before the housing boom went bust, they ended up with theirs funds intact."

"Clever bastards."

Sean leaned forward. "One word of warning. Shark hires some of the world's best talent to carry out his assassinations. There's one to watch out for. His name is Talleyrand."

"How does he operate?"

"He prefers to works alone." Sean's eyes circled the room. "Time for us to go."

Ryan signaled the waiter for the bill.

Sean stretched his muscular arms. "One word of warning, if you think you're safe in Dublin, forget it. This is no longer the land of sweet singing ballads and smiling leprechauns. This country at the moment may seem resilient and dramatic, but the old bog is increasingly a violent place."

"Can you loan me piece?"

"You are going to need one." Sean suddenly stood up. "Leave the money to pay the bill on the table."

Sean saw the woman seated alone at the entrance reach down into her handbag. He sensed she had a loaded gun.

"We leave now and go out the back way," Sean whispered.

CHAPTER 29

THE CONVOY OF RANGE ROVERS drove through Laytown and rumbled along a cobblestone road beside the Irish Sea to a walled villa crowned by gold-painted spires. The convoy drew curious stares from shoppers pushing grocery carts and baby strollers along the village high street. The cars entered the villa through two steel gates that opened up to Japanese-style gardens and fountains interspersed with cameras and motion detectors.

Members of the Club seated in the backseats of the Range Rovers clinked champagne glasses behind bulletproof, one-way glass windows. They felt secure in the knowledge that the Club accepted no outside members except those selected by a vigorous screening process. Some members headed up rogue organizations involved in the lucrative drug and human smuggling operations. The Club's formal name—International Cooperation and Commerce Corporation—had a public persona of being a team of consultants assisting European and North American companies in investing and trading in the Arab world. Headquartered in Dublin, ICCC's unofficial motto was "Through chaos and upheaval there is profit and opportunity."

The men who climbed out of the Range Rovers were from Vienna, Damascus, Tehran, Geneva, Atlanta, Bogotá, Abu Dhabi, and the Isle of Man. An army of servants opened doors, carried luggage, and escorted guests through a towering lobby high enough to house an avenue of palm trees. Servants ushered guests to glass walled outside elevators that whisked them to suites overlooking Taibhse Beach, the Irish name for ghost. The beach's name originated during the Troubles when the bodies of several traitors washed up on the sand. Local fishermen still believed that the spirits of the turncoats haunted the beach at night.

Shark spent the evening relaxing around the Olympic-size indoor pool that overlooked the placid gray ocean. Waiters kept Shark's colleagues fed from trays of steaming curries and shrimp kebabs, while bartenders served the finest wines, fruit juices, and a variety of Caribbean and African cocktails.

Midway through the evening, Shark raised his hand to silence the chatter. For half an hour, he kept them enthralled. The Club had prospered even though the global recession had pushed economies into a worsening condition not experienced in decades. While Lehman Brothers went bankrupt and Wall Street teetered on the edge of oblivion, the Club had found ways to prosper.

To streamline its operations, Shark told them that the Club had upgraded its ability, through the installation of powerful new computers, to move money anywhere in the world to profit from national or regional fluctuations in stock markets, currency values, and real estate prices.

Shark reinforced the Club's fundamental strategy that political instability and economic turmoil presented members opportunities to make large profits by taking advantage of uncertainty. He cited how ICCC had sold properties in Ireland ahead of the crash. He now recommended members snatch up valuable Irish residential and commercial assets at bargain prices. Shark reminded them that well before the collapse of the Irish banking system, he had advised members to empty their portfolios of Anglo Irish Bank stock. The mass selling hastened the demise of the troubled bank now under the control of the Irish government.

Shark turned to Boris Kharkov, a Russian who spent last winter outside Cannes in a villa once owned by President Mobutu, the deposed president of Zaire, now the Democratic Republic of Congo.

"It sounds as though Boris made a killing, and I don't mean on the Cote d'Azur," he said.

The audience appreciated his in-house joke with subdued laughter.

"Surely, you mean the Congo arms deal?" Boris said, tossing back his vodka.

Shark chucked. "Before you had a chance to get in on the action, he financed arrangements through our bank and sold arms to both sides."

"Not everything's fair in love and war," the Russian oligarch said, his voice sounding like a rusty hinge.

Bernard Thames, a tall British arms dealer based in the Isle of Man, who limped on an artificial leg lost to a land mine, leaned forward as Shark spoke to him.

"You've rationed the guns you sell to the Forces Armée Congolaises and the Tutsis so you can prolong the conflict," Shark said.

"It's working out rather well," Bernard said, twisting the end of his mustache.

As the sun set, lights came on under the surface of the indoor pool, casting a blue hue on members standing at the edge.

"The time is ripe for us to consider taking control of the Somali pirates," Shark said.

Members in his immediate circle looked surprised. Shark regarded them playfully with his brown eyes.

"What do you think, Awaale?" he asked, turning to a tall man who wore a large gold pendant around his neck.

Awaale Madoowbe had iron-gray hair and the intense gaze of a revolutionary.

"If we want to employ these pirates, they'll be cheap," Awaale said, putting his hands in the pockets of his charcoal suit jacket. "There is widespread unemployment. The main occupation was fishing, until stocks ran low after Europeans and Asians illegally overfished in our waters."

"I'm not suggesting we hire them," Shark said. "These pirates are amateurs. Many of them are teenagers who go into action drugged or drunk on local brew. Even when they board and capture a vessel, they don't know what they're doing half the time." Shark smiled, displaying a perfect set of polished teeth. "In the beginning, I didn't pay much attention to these isolated attacks on shipping. I admired their *chutzpah*, but their operations are amateurish, too small, a minor irritant to wealthy shipping corporations. But now, gentlemen, these pirates rake in hundreds of millions of dollars a year in ransoms."

"Should we muscle in on the operations of these pirates and see what profits we can squeeze from their clumsy grasp?" Bernard asked.

"Perhaps we can reach out to their leaders and make them an offer," Awaale said.

"I think not," Shark said. "I want to take over the operations of these ragtag, disorganized scum."

"They won't give up without a fight," Awaale said.

"Should be easy. For most the part, these pirates are armed only with assault rifles and handheld rocket launchers." Shark rested his arm around the Somali's shoulder. "Don't worry, Awaale, I've taken care of Abukar al-Badri, who rejected my overtures to hammer out a shared arrangement—"

"Some captured vessels are loaded to the gunnels with weapons, and as you know, we're often short of arms," Boris Kharkov interjected. "We can siphon off these arms and smuggle them directly into our arsenals."

"With better vessels, we can attack more luxury craft and cruise ships. We can make a killing from ransom payments," the Somali said.

"Some ships are using armed guards and weapons to deter pirates," Bernard said. "Are you worried?"

"Not really," Shark said. "We've installed guided missiles on our new attack vessels. If they don't surrender, we blow them out of the water."

"Once we take over this operation, we may be forced to modify or close it down if the antipiracy forces become too powerful," Bernard said.

Shark held up his hand, the gesture of asserting his control. "I don't think the European or American navies are coordinated enough to really do much to a sophisticated operation such as our new fleet. We're equipped with the latest technology, including satellite tracking of vessels in the region." He turned and smiled at an American, Kim Daniels, whose bronzed face contrasted with his white shirt. "Kim's so-called rogue satellite has given us the edge to alert our vessels of any NATO warships in our area of operation."

A round of restrained applause followed. Shark turned to the delegate from Baghdad, Ibrahim al-Yussuf.

"Now that the American dogs are slinking back into their rat holes, are you taking advantage of the power vacuum?" he asked.

"Yes, Master," he said. He never referred to Shark by any other name. "Our last attack that killed thirty-five people helped us achieve several objectives at once. By hitting a semirural area, we are forcing the overextended Iraqi army into protecting even greater areas of the country. By doing so, we have eliminated confidence in the government's ability to maintain security."

"Are you continuing your successful ploy to bait ethnic communities to such an extent that they can't take any more attacks and thus retaliate, therefore sustaining the circle of violence?"

"We are indeed, Master, employing this tactic. However, we are reducing our focus on fermenting inter-fighting among the ethnic and religious communities. Our success in the Shia neighborhoods has been less than satisfactory as of late because of the resilience of the people, who, when we attack, are now saying, 'Turn the other cheek.' Some imams are even suggesting that bombing is a waste of their time and ours."

"What are you doing to counteract this complacency?"

Ibrahim hesitated, and the members waited in silence for his reply.

"We have been switching our attention to more fertile fields," he said. "The houses we bombed outside Mosul were under the protection of armed Kurdish fighters of the *peshmerga*."

"They have kept out of the sectarian fighting. How do you propose to bait them into the fray?"

"As you know, Master, the oil beneath the ground around Mosul is in dispute. Kurds and Sunnis both want it. This is where we can whip up civil war fever. A few hours after our truck exploded, Sunnis were demanding the expulsion of the ineffective *peshmerga*."

Shark pressed his fingertips together and smiled. "This festering dispute over oil may give us the *casus belli* we are searching for."

The Iraqi looked perplexed. "I am not familiar with the words *casus belli*. What do they mean, Master?"

"My friend, it's Latin for an event that provides us an excuse to provoke war. Any talk of civil war in your country ferments further unrest in the region. We all benefit from rising oil prices." Shark let his gaze wander around the patio. "How else can we take advantage of this conflict?"

"My master, a major war will create a flood of refugees."

Shark felt his head teeter and spin. "My God, Ibrahim, they will be seeking a safe haven in not only the adjoining countries in the Middle East, but also in Europe. It's a great opportunity for your people-smuggling business. I would like you to give us a chance to invest in your enterprise."

"Master, I welcome investment capital. I assure you, as the war in the region heats up, your profits, gentlemen, will be astronomical."

Shark rubbed his hands together. "Good, good, good." He smiled at Ibrahim, something he rarely did. "Enough from our brother from Iraq, what news have we from the Balkans?"

Before Shark could introduce his Albanian colleague, a servant in livery handed Shark a piece of paper.

"Excuse me a moment, gentlemen," Shark said, stepping back to read the hand written note: "The mosquito is alive and in the city. What do you want me to do?"

Shark recalled having described the American PI who rescued Aisling Quinn as nothing but a *mbu*, a mosquito. The servant hovered behind him.

"Do you have an answer?" the servant asked.

"Yes."

Shark scribbled on the bottom of the note: "Squash him."

CHAPTER 30

AFTER DINNER AT HIS HOTEL, Ryan jogged along the cobblestone quay bordering the Grand Canal. He inhaled the damp night air and the stench of stagnant water, duck droppings, and exhaust fumes. He longed for the smell of clean, prairie breezes.

Under the span of a wrought-iron bridge, Ryan spotted a derelict leaning against a brick wall. Dressed in a ragged suit, the man had a gin bottle in his mouth. He pulled on the neck as eagerly as a baby sucks a mother's teat. Suddenly, the man removed the bottle from his mouth. He puckered his lips to produce a low whistle.

Ryan gave the man a wide birth, and he jogged to a narrow walkway beside row houses of red brick blackened by a patina of grime. As he passed by the houses, the man ran by him. He jabbed his elbow into Ryan's side. The sharp blow almost made him lose his balance. Ryan stopped jogging. He reached inside his jacket, before he realized he was unarmed. When the man who had jostled him spun around, Ryan glanced at his wrestler's shoulders and thick waist. Ryan searched his face. He had a cruel smile that tugged at the corner of his mouth. Ryan waited until he met his eyes and held them.

"What do you want?" Ryan said, crouching in a defensive pose, his fists clenched.

The man swallowed, hardening his eyes.

"Stay the hell away from me," Ryan said. "Understood?"

The thickset man reached into his belt and pointed a knife at Ryan's stomach. "Gimme yer wallet."

"Come and get it."

The man lunged at Ryan. He dodged the blow, but the blade nicked his jacket. Before his attacker could regain his balance, Ryan drove his left foot into the man's kidney. The big man collapsed and lay writhing on the ground. When his attacker sprang back on his feet, he charged at Ryan, his knife pointed at his heart. The fingers of his other hand reached for Ryan's eyes. Ryan ducked and fastened his left hand under his attacker's chin. At the same time, he used his fist to punch the ridge of his nose. Ryan then pinned him against an embankment and banged the back of his head against the brick wall. When the man dropped to the cobble stones, he trembled from shock, his nose streaming blood. Ryan kicked the knife out of his hand.

Ryan left him surrounded by a knot of gawkers, who had stopped to watch the fight.

When Ryan returned to the Hilton, he climbed the fire stairs two at a time. In his room, he showered to wash away blood and sweat. He changed into jeans, a T-shirt, and a blue blazer. Ryan then called Sean on his cell phone. After describing his attacker as a stocky giant, Sean suggested that his assailant wasn't thief, but a hired assassin who wanted Ryan's murder to look like a robbery. His cover could be compromised. He suggested Ryan check out of the Hilton and into a safe house, an inconspicuous bed-and-breakfast. He gave him the name of the B&B used by G2 operatives named the Terrance O'Connor. He also gave him the address of the Quinn family's Dublin townhouse.

"For your protection, I've sent you an email in our prearranged code, where you can pick up a sidearm and ammo, as well as background on your girl." Sean paused. "Meanwhile, Ryan, try to stay out of trouble."

After a night in the safe house, it was a cool, wet dawn when Ryan took a taxi to the Quinn family's row house on Mullingar Street near the Victorian façade of the Pearse Railway Station. He rang the doorbell and no one answered, so he leaned over the railing and peered through the nearest window. White sheets covered chairs like ghostly apparitions.

Ryan returned to the Terrance O'Connor and examined his room for signs of intruders. The thread attached to the door was still intact, and his luggage showed no signs of tampering. His window overlooked a narrow alley and rows of cramped back gardens of vegetables and flowers hemmed in by brick walls. When the sun burned off heavy clouds blanketing the city, he pulled on a heavy sweater, jeans, and trainers. He strapped a knapsack to his back, left the safe house and went to a nearby pawnshop, where he bought a used bicycle. After pedaling around Trinity College, Ryan felt confident that he could blend in among the students. He locked the bicycle on a stand near BT Ireland telephone center and went inside. He found an empty workstation, plugged in his laptop, and tapped the keys for a few seconds. His email inbox revealed that he had new messages that appeared as a mass of jumbled letters. After typing in Sean's code, the message changed to clear text.

He read Sean's background on notes on Aisling Quinn. She was born September 12, 1988 in Drogheda, County Louth. She attended St. Mary's Academy, an exclusive Catholic girl's school. After graduation, she joined the Flair Modeling Agency, Basement Level, 329 O'Leary Street, for two years, where she appeared in catalogues, television commercials, jewelry ads, also worked as a film extra under the stage name of Nadia Ford. In 2006, she was employed by the Anglo Irish Bank, St. Stephen's Green, Dublin, where she worked as an analyst. Two years later, she transferred to the bank's international Middle East division. Her father Darragh

Quinn, a former managing director of Allied Holdings Limited, an arms dealership, died under suspicious circumstances in 2007. He left behind his widow Faye and daughters Aisling and Andrea. Faye Quinn now lived at the family estate, Caviston Court, on the outskirts of Monkstown." The message concluded with details of the Magnum .357 drop-off point downloaded to your computer. This was an encrypted file, and only a code name could decipher it. The note prompted him press escape to cancel this arrangement.

After deciphering the code, Ryan cycled to an Anglo Irish Bank in the Stephen's Green Shopping Center. He chained the bicycle to a railing and entered the branch. A young woman at a reception desk escorted him to the bank's basement to the safety deposit boxes. Ryan opened his assigned box and found the Magnum .357 and several ammunition clips. He slipped the Magnum into the waistband of his trousers at the small of his back. He quit the bank and at a car rental agency in the next block, he rented a white Mini.

Ryan drove the compact car south on his way to the Quinn family estate outside Monkstown. He checked the rear-view mirror several times to make sure that he wasn't being followed. When he was convinced there was no one on his tail, he took the M 111. On the outskirts of Dublin, he passed a patchwork of half-built housing estates, parks, golf courses, and quaint villages. On his left, he soon spotted the mist-shrouded Dublin Bay.

In half an hour, he parked in Monkstown's main square opposite the Anglican parish church, an unlikely hybrid of towers and turrets inspired by Gothic and Moorish architecture. He asked for directions to Caviston Court from a woman at a stall selling cheeses. She gave him the route to the manor house about ten miles south of the village square.

After following a twisting country road, Ryan drove through Caviston Court's open twin iron gates. Surrounded by a ring of Scotch pines and birches, the three-story Georgian house had rolling lawns spread out in front of the property, large enough to include a paddock and adjacent stables. Behind the house, he saw a small lake. The wind had died down, and the brown water's surface was like a sheet of tinted glass. Ryan parked the Mini in front of a pillared portico. The pebble stones on the drive were polished by the rain and reflected light from the windows of the house's ivory-painted façade. Above the mansion's slate roof, Ryan could see the cloud-shrouded rounded peaks of the distant Wicklow Mountains.

Ryan pressed the doorbell and heard chimes coming from behind the multicolored smoked glass embedded in the front door, where a faded black wreath was pinned to the oak. He rang again three times before a stout woman peered at him around the edge of the door. Her gray eyes set in skin the color of dough seethed hostility and stared at him in silence.

"Good afternoon, I'm Donald Mason," he said, using the same alias he had adopted when he spoke to the consular staff at the Dar es Salaam Irish embassy. "I phoned Mrs. Quinn earlier. She is expecting me."

"Before I let yer in, suppose you state yer business," she said, resting her hands on her wide hips.

"I'm a friend of Mrs. Quinn's daughter."

The woman swept back a shock of auburn hair from her freckled face. Her thick red fingers smoothed a rumpled tweed skirt, while she glanced at Ryan sideways. She wrinkled her snub nose as though the sight of him made her nervous.

"How do I know you're who you say you are and not some tinker?" she asked, a frown creasing her forehead. "Mrs. Quinn also don't talk to newspaper hacks or estate agents neither."

The gap she had opened started to close. Ryan stuck his foot in the door. "Didn't I make myself clear? I'm here to see Mrs. Quinn on a personal matter regarding her daughter, Aisling. I'm not here to sell her anything."

The heavy door creaked open and the scent of fresh cut flowers greeted Ryan in the hall. On the adjacent wall was a row of family portraits in gilded frames. The maid led him to a book lined library.

"Wait here," she said, the frost in her voice enough to penetrate the shelves of leather-bound books.

Ryan glanced through a window at a corral, where a pair of sorrels cropped green grass. Faye Quinn entered the library without a sound, and Ryan wasn't aware of her presence until she stood beside him at the window.

"Mr. Mason," she said in a cultured voice almost devoid of an Irish accent. Faye had a pale, unlined face, and she wore a black pantsuit, her gray hair tied in a fashionable chignon. "What is it you wanted to see me about?"

"I'll come right to the point, Mrs. Quinn. Your daughter Aisling left money in my hotel safe in Zanzibar. As I'm in Dublin on business, I thought I'd return the cash to you and send you her things later."

"Oh, yes, I remember your phone call now, Mr. Mason." She paused. "Did you find your way here without any difficulty?"

"The road trip was fine, but your maid was a bit reluctant to let me in."

"You'll have to forgive Orla. She's awkward with strangers, particularly pushy journalists, who will try any ruse to worm their way in." She smiled, stretching her generous lips. "Mr. Mason, please join me."

She ushered him to sit on one of two winged chairs, a glass-topped coffee table in between them. Her face turned solemn, filled by undisguised anguish.

"Why in God's name did Aisling go to Zanzibar of all places?" she said. "When I heard from the Dar es Salaam embassy that she had died in the Air Tanzania disaster, I was completely stunned. I was under the impression she had taken an extended holiday in Cannes." She pressed a lace handkerchief to her nose. "There's so much I need to know. Please be so good as to enlighten me."

Orla entered and removed a vase of flowers from a table and replaced it with a tray holding a teapot covered in a wool-knit cozy and a plate of scones and spicy fruit cake.

When Orla left, Faye stirred sugar into her tea. "Tell me, Mr. Mason, what exactly did Aisling tell you she was doing in East Africa?"

201

"She was a passenger on a yacht that anchored in Zanzibar's harbor."

Silence fell over the library, heavy and foreboding like the stillness that follows a bomb explosion in a crowded Belfast marketplace.

"Is that how she got there?" Faye whispered. "How did she end up at your hotel?"

"During the night, she attempted to swim from the yacht to my beachfront hotel. After one of my staff spotted her floundering in the sea, I rescued her," Ryan said, adopting a tone of clinical detachment. "Aisling stayed at my hotel until she took that fateful flight."

Faye's already pale face shed any remnant of color. "This is absolutely incredible." She shuddered. "Aisling has always been deadly afraid of open water."

While sipping his tea and nibbling on a scone, Ryan continued his made-up story about thinking it only proper to return the money she had deposited in his hotel safe.

He handed her an envelope. "That's the five hundred euros she left in my hotel safe."

Faye extended a slender hand with long purple nails to accept the money. "She must have been desperate to attempt to swim ashore."

"Being in the sea could have been accidental. The weather was rough. She could have been swept overboard."

Faye opened the envelope and looked at him in genuine surprise. "Thank you, Mr. Mason, for making this long journey from Africa to return her money." She appeared to shrivel, as though trying to suppress a painful memory. "I'm only sorry you weren't in Monkstown yesterday evening." She made a church steeple of her forefingers and pressed them against her lips. "We had a special memorial service for Aisling."

"I'd like to have paid my respects."

Faye ran her long spidery fingers around the rim of her Royal Doulton teacup.

"Whose yacht?" she asked, before being overcome by a fit of coughing.

When Faye recovered, Ryan said, "A Dublin playboy, who goes by the name of Shark. My understanding is that your daughter boarded his yacht in Cannes."

Faye lifted her hands to the molded ceiling, as if preparing to hear more tragic news. "Aisling must've experienced something traumatic on board that boat to force her to swim ashore. How did she manage it? She hates the water. Apart from the possibility of her being swept overboard, did she indicate exactly what happened?"

"She never told me the circumstances. I didn't want to pry." Ryan shifted in his chair. "She did mention she had transmitted some files from her host's computer to someone in Dublin. Those files may give us the yacht's owner's real name and help solve this mystery. Do you know anyone who could have received this transmission?"

She glanced at a diamond-encrusted watch. "Her younger sister, Andrea, could have been the recipient. She's a computer wizard. She'll be back from her ride soon." She patted the back of her hair, as if to straighten a wayward curl. "Would you like to join us for dinner, Mr. Mason?"

"Thank you, I'd like that."

"You have an interesting accent. I can't quite place it. Are you Australian, perhaps?"

"I'm a Canadian."

"In heaven's name, how did a Canadian find his way to owning a hotel in Zanzibar?"

Ryan laughed. "It's a long story."

"After you've freshened up before dinner, you must tell me more about yourself and what you and my daughter talked about during the time she stayed as a guest in your hotel."

CHAPTER 31

"A NDREA'S ALWAYS LATE," FAYE QUINN said, ushering Ryan into the dining room. The table seated twelve and was loaded down by crystal and fine china. As Ryan sat down next to Faye, a smell of spices drifted into the room.

"We may as well start dinner without her, or my temperamental cook will complain that the tom yum goong soup is overcooked and the spicy budoo has turned to mush." She rang a gold bell. "My new Thai chef considers Irish cuisine an abomination, barbaric. She insists on serving her specialty, anything Asian or North African."

Orla served the soup from a tureen under a gas heater on a sideboard groaning under the weight of family silver and a series of cups earned by Faye's husband for marksmanship. Recalling Orla's rudeness when he arrived at Caviston Court, Ryan studied her carefully. The maid's hair was an unruly mop, and her squat physique had gone to fat bulging out in rolls in a tightfitting uniform.

Ryan turned to his host. "I'm looking forward to meeting Andrea."

"Well, you're in for a shock," Faye said. "Years of expensive private schools in Switzerland and in the UK didn't do a thing for her. Andrea's enrolled at Trinity in dramatic arts or whatever that is. As far as I'm concerned, the only education she's getting is street marching and waving placards. She's obsessed by whatever is the latest *cause de jour*, whether it's saving the seals or breaking up the banks. Her latest craze is membership in a terrorist organization called the Irish Liberation Front." Faye twitched her nose, as though she smelled something bad. "At one time, Andrea even renounced her family and everything she considers we represent. For a while, she lived in a squalid east end flat above a Vietnamese takeaway. She wouldn't accept an allowance from me and tore up the checks I sent her. She broke my heart when last summer she joined a commune and survived on a diet of tofu and green tea, while she toiled during the day in sugar beet fields." Faye popped a small egg roll into her mouth. "It was only after her sister died that she finally came home for the memorial service. We've had a reconciliation of sorts. Thank God, we have come to some sort of understanding."

After a spoonful of soup, Ryan felt dampness form at the back of his neck from the spices.

"I expect she's going through a phrase," he said.

"I hope you're right. Her sister's death did have a sobering effect on her. She's different now. She used to be a bit on the plump side, but she's become lithe and athletic. She also appears to have grown a couple of inches." Faye rolled her eyes to the high ornamental ceiling. "Thank the saints, her abrasive manners have also smoothed out a wee bit."

To soften the effect of the spices, Ryan reached over to a plate of soda bread, buttered the crust, and pressed the slice into his mouth. Ryan choked on the bread as the door swung open and Andrea came in.

She wore a miniskirt, heavy and baggy black stockings, and a white silk blouse. Her hair was cropped short, spiked, and dyed black. She had several rings in her ears and an iron stud in her right nostril. When she spotted Ryan seated next to her mother, color flowed into her pale cheeks.

Ryan heard a dog barking and a collie bounded into the room.

"Be quiet, James Joyce," Faye said.

The dog's tail swished the polished floor and stuck a nose into Ryan's lap.

"Come here JJ and sit by me," Faye said.

JJ was slow to leave from sniffing Ryan's groin, before the collie settled at Faye's feet. She turned to her daughter, who lowered her eyes to avoid looking at Ryan. Andrea sat at the far end of the table, her face still flushed.

"Andrea, I want you to meet Donald Mason," Faye said, appearing unaware of her daughter's discomfort. "He has news about Aisling."

A faint smile formed on Andrea's black lips.

"Mr. Mason says she was a guest at his hotel in Zanzibar," Faye continued. "She apparently boarded a yacht in Cannes that took her to East Africa." Faye leaned down to scratch the dog's crown. "Mr. Mason has also returned Aisling's money that she left for safekeeping in his hotel."

"How did Aisling get the cash?" Andrea said, standing up to ladle soup on the sideboard into her plate. "She spent all her nicker on hairdos and party frocks."

After Andrea sat down, she spooned soup into her mouth without showing any signs of discomfort from the spices.

"Where did she get her dosh? She don't get nothin' from me father's estate until she's thirty," she continued in an accent that sounded as though she had mouth full of glass.

Faye turned to Ryan. "Mr. Mason, where do you think the money came from?"

Ryan ran his hand over the wiry stubble on the top of his head. "I honestly don't know."

"Aisling could've pinched it?" Andrea asked.

Faye fiddled with cat's eyes glasses hanging from a chain around her neck.

Andrea avoided her mother's sharp stare. "Me sister sent me an email from Zanzibar, but she never mentioned the yacht owner's name."

"How could you have not said a word about this to me?" Faye said.

Andrea remained silent.

"Aisling told me his name is Shark," Ryan said, narrowing his eyes.

"How are we going to find this Shark?" Faye said, while she gnawed at something inside her cheek. She turned to Ryan. "Any ideas?"

"I'll be driving back to the city this evening. I'll see what I can find out."

Andrea forced a smile as she caught Ryan's eye. "Gimme a ride to Trimmers?"

"She means Trinity College, Mr. Mason," Faye said.

His gaze wandered to Andrea's eyes, surrounded by mascara that made her look like racoon.

"Be glad to give you a lift," Ryan said.

She gave him an evasive smile, but remained silent.

The sun low on the horizon between broken clouds, reddened the pebbles on Caviston Court's tree lined drive. Before climbing into the Mini, Ryan unzipped his jacket, and Andrea opened her black leather coat to reveal her matching shiny black leather top and hot pants. After Andrea sat down in the bucket seat, she ground a cigarette on the toe of her thigh-high leather boot. Ryan grinned at her as she climbed in. On the way to Dublin, he wanted to question Andrea about Aisling's transmission of Shark's files.

Soon after they drove through the mansion's gates, they passed the small village of Monkstown, and then left behind a checkerboard of fields of new shoots of spring grain. At the M III highway intersection, Ryan drove north against the late evening rush of cars returning to the city at the close of the weekend. A layer of mist hung over the highway, and a gentle rain fell. The Irish Sea lay to their right, deep gray and covered in clouds.

Ryan glanced at Andrea, who had pulled up the collar of her leather jacket. Her gloved hands kept a firm grip on a knapsack wedged between her bare knees.

"What else did Aisling say in her email?" he asked.

She turned to him and opened her mouth as if to speak, but remained silent for a moment. In the dim light, Ryan thought her teeth looked too clean, even, and white for someone who had lived the life of a hippie.

"She was pissed off with Cannes," Andrea said. "If I know my sister, I bet she was shaggin' this bloke Shark."

"While your sister was on board, did she transmit some files to a terminal in Dublin?" he said, swinging the compact around a semitrailer.

"I ain't got the foggiest about her transmitting files from Zanzibar. We was never close." She sat up and drank what smelled like coffee from a thermos. "Yer didn't come all this way to return her cash, did you?" She sniffed, as if she smelled something nasty. "Did you rock 'n' roll with my sister, too?"

"If you're suggesting—"

In the glow of a streetlights, he saw a glint in Andrea's eye, like a sliver of flint. "Did you sleep with her?" she interrupted.

"You ask me that question, when our sister is barely buried?"

"Okay, don't bust a gasket."

Ryan kept his eyes on the lights of houses and shops in the city's outskirts, while her fingers stroked the inside of his thigh. Ryan appeared mesmerized by the wipers arcing across the windshield, sweeping away the rain.

"Don't do that," he whispered, tensing his leg muscles.

Her hand drifted over to the front of his shirt. "You're wearing a bulletproof vest?"

"Dublin is a crime ridden city. I felt it necessary to protect myself."

Before he could take his hand off the wheel and push her away, her fingers probed the back of his pants "My, my, what have we here? Since when does an innkeeper need to carry this kind of heat?"

"Dublin has one of the highest murder rates in the EU. The last thing I need is to end up floating in the Grand Canal."

"Don't get narky. How did you get a Magnum .357 through airport security?"

Ryan ignored her question. At a stoplight, he opened the window. The night wind had a dank smell coming from car exhaust fumes and stagnant water from the slow-moving Liffey River.

"Where can I drop you off?" he asked.

"I'm stayin' at 453 Mulligan Street." She touched the knuckles of his hands on the wheel. "Do yer take me for a git?"

"You're a good kid."

She chatted for a while about Dublin being shit and Ireland's economy in the toilet.

"So many of me mates lost jobs." Her voice turned soft, losing its hard Celtic edge. "When we get to Mulligan, come in fer a drink. Let's see if Aisling's laptop has those files yer lookin' for."

"That'll be great. Thanks."

They drove in silence to Mulligan Street.

"How did yer find Mulligan without me help?" she asked.

"I'm full of surprises."

Cars parked in a haphazard manner beside the Georgian row houses. Ryan was lucky to find a nearby empty spot, where he parked and switched off the engine. The night sky was the color of slate, the sidewalks lank and slick in the rain. Bowing heads to the wind, Ryan and Andrea scurried along the street to the three-story row house's front steps. Andrea allowed him to carry her knapsack, while she unlocked the door. They entered a dark, narrow hallway. Andrea led the way up a winding staircase to a second-floor living room. Inside the room, white sheets were draped over furniture like snow-covered hills. When Andrea opened the heavy curtains, he could see the lights from the steel-and-glass towers of the International Financial Services Center on the north side of the river. Andrea removed sheets from deep leather couches and chairs of the kind found in London's private clubs. Ryan settled into a wingback chair by a carved marble fireplace to listen to rain beating against the windows and the muffled grumble of night traffic.

"Me mother uses this house when she shops or goes to see a play," Andrea said, turning on table lamps before she headed for the door.

When she left the room, Ryan pictured her late father meeting in this room to haggle over the price of firearms, while his clients drank his whiskey and cigar smoke filled the air.

Andrea returned carrying a tray of bottles, shot glasses, and a bucket of ice. She had changed out of her leather outfit and into faded jeans and a tight sweater. Despite her garish makeup, spiky hair, and pale skin, Ryan noticed how much she resembled her dead sister. Even in stockinged feet, she had Aisling's lithe and feline walk.

"I raided me aul man's whiskey stash," she said.

Andrea put the tray on a table beside him, lit the gas fire, and sat cross-legged on the carpet in front of him. Ryan poured himself a scotch and added ice. While the scotch burned his throat, the whiskey loosened tension. Heat from the fire felt good on his thighs.

"Want another shot?" she said.

He examined his half full glass. "No, thanks."

She regarded him for a moment. "It's getting warm in here."

She yanked off her sweater and tossed it on the floor. She wore nothing underneath. Her milk-white breasts glowed red in the firelight. Ryan drained his glass and got to his feet. He tossed the discarded sweater at her.

"For God's sake, cover up," he said.

"What the firk is yer problem?" she said, using the sweater to cover her breasts.

210

"Wandering around half naked is not a good idea."

She switched off a Tiffany lamp, dropped her sweater on the carpet, and unzipped her jeans, kicking them away.

"Why?" she said, standing in her lace trimmed panties.

"Do you really think by showing off your nice pair of tits, I'd flop into your bed?"

"I know yer will."

She lowered her eyes, the color rushing up from her throat. She made his head spin. Without boots, she appeared small, her face and figure outrageously pretty, but not in a tidy way. He noticed something unkempt about her face. Her eyes were too far apart, lips so small they seemed out of place on a wide face with a square chin.

She threw back her head and laughed, her shiny colored hair catching the light of the fire. "Don't deny it, you firked my sister."

When her eyes widened in a flirtatious way, he spotted a speckle of copper in the right iris, and he felt shock hammer through him. He realized he'd seen that flaw before. But where? The sight of her firm body in the firelight and the sound of the steady pounding of rain on the window short-circuited his brain and drove any recollection of seeing this unusual eye coloring before right out of his mind.

"Well, darling," she said, her eyes roving over his face. She waited for him to respond. "Yer want me as you wanted her." He tried to resist loving her nakedness. "I can see a tent pole risin' in your pants."

Ryan looked over her shoulder at the reflection of his face in the gilt-framed mirror above the mantelpiece. It should have shown resolve to resist making love to the other sister, but instead his eyes had a hard light.

Andrea stroked his back. "She was so grateful to be saved by a good-lookin' bloke. Yer two gave each other comfort during the storm. I swear by everything that's holy, no power on earth could have kept yer apart." She took his hand and tugged him toward the rug in front of the fire, but he pushed her away. "Come to bed, gorgeous man."

"Tonight, I'm sleeping in your spare bedroom," he said.

Shark watched the late-night RTÉ TV business news on his iPod in the back of his Range Rover, as his chauffeur-driven bulletproof SUV crawled through the clogged traffic on a street in Ballsbridge. The Irish economic news was gloomy, so he turned off the iPod. Earlier in the evening, he had drinks accompanied by colleagues at Lillie's Bordello, a pricy private club on Grafton Street named after King Edward VII's lovely mistress, Lillie Langtry. The 1959 Château Latour had left a sour taste in his mouth that made him irritable and the Iranian osetra caviar on toast hadn't agreed with him either.

Despite his grumpy disposition, he chuckled out loud at the thought that some club members believed him to be a successful venture capitalist. To a degree, he considered them to be reasonably accurate. Shark sat back in the heated leather car seat and thought about his gorgeous new mistress, waiting for him is his penthouse.

His cell phone chimed, and he answered it. He heard the high-pitched voice of Pat Rafferty, his long-time lieutenant in Dublin.

"I've have a man keeping an eye on the Quinn residence near Monkstown," Pat said in a voice with a distinct Dublin lilt.

"What's going on?" Shark demanded, sitting upright.

"Well, Faye Quinn had a visitor. My man bribed the maid into giving him this bloke's name. He claims to be Donald Mason, who owns a hotel in Zanzibar. Apparently, Aisling Quinn left money in his hotel safe. And can you believe this? Mason returned the cash to Mrs. Quinn."

"He's the same bastard staying at the Hilton that your two clumsy oafs didn't wipe out. His real name is Ryan Moar, an American private investigator." Shark straightened up. "Where is he now?"

Pat cleared his throat. "Moar and Andrea Quinn left Caviston Court in a white Mini later this evening and drove to the city."

Shark could feel sweat break out on his forehead. His mind flashed back to Andrea's gorgeous sister sprawled out in his circular bed on board his yacht. Above all, he remembered the feel of her soft, warm skin. After he found out that Aisling somehow hacked into his laptop, he had longed to see the big fish attack her long legs and her blood stain the water. He considered guns and knives a clumsy and messy means to kill. Sharks had always been his execution of choice. He preferred the clean, efficient way sharks disposed of unwanted bodies. Following a minute or two of feeding frenzy, there was a moment of stillness on the ocean's surface as the stains of blood washed away in a restless sea.

In his study, he kept an original oil painting of Cuban President Gerardo Machado, known as the Butcher. Machado had a pool of hungry sharks in his palace, where anyone who opposed him soon disappeared without a trace.

"My man followed the Mini to an address on Mulligan Street, where they've settled in for the night," Pat continued.

"Keep an eye on them. Make sure Moar is dead this time."

"I'll handle it personally."

"That's my man." Shark ignited a cigar. "There's a big bonus for you if you do it clean. Otherwise, my friend, you may end up facedown in the Poddle."

"What about the girl?" Pat asked, a quaver entering his voice.

"Take her alive and then bring her to me."

Shark said nothing more. He was watching a boy on a motor scooter weave in and out of long shadows at the end of the street. When the boy disappeared, Shark stared through the skylight at the clouds.

Look at the rain, he thought, isn't it beautiful?

CHAPTER 32

ANDREA STARED AT RYAN ASLEEP in the guest room bed, his naked torso lying in the glow of a momentary burst of morning sunlight. Despite the scabs and scars on his body, she thought Ryan was one of the handsomest men she had ever met. Before going to bed, he had reminded her that he wanted to have a look at the contents of Aisling's laptop, a possible recipient of Shark's files. She had told him not to be so impatient; she would look for it in the morning.

Andrea ran her fingertips over the tight curls of black hair on his chest. When Ryan stirred, she laughed a little and withdrew her hand.

"I'm so white," she said, twisting her nipple through her pyjama top. She climbed into the four-poster mahogany bed beside him. "Yer's so brown. Does that mean I'm good and yer bad?"

"You're a naughty girl," he said.

Resting against the headboard, Andrea twisted a tuft of her hair. "You're a handsome devil."

"You look comfortable wrapped in these silk sheets," Ryan said. "Do you ever miss being a vagabond, a selfish flower child?"

She had a wistful look on her face, and some of her former finishing school accent crept into her voice. "I'm different now. I'm a little wiser, perhaps. The shock of Aisling's death sobered me up a bit."

"When you're at Trinity, is this the house where you live?" he asked, swinging his legs to the floor and sitting on edge of the bed.

She nodded.

"What do you plan to take at university?"

"Drama and theater arts."

Ryan stood up, and he stared out the window at the drizzle. "How will you pay for tuition, expenses?"

"An education fund set up by me capitalist father is more than enough to cover costs."

"Money you despise." Ryan rubbed his earlobe. "When I was growing up, I never had a trust fund to fall back on."

"Is that why you ended up an innkeeper on an island in the Indian Ocean?" She drew a series of rapid heavy breaths. "If you was so poor, how could yer afford to buy the bloomin' place?"

"I won the hotel in a poker game."

She leaned on her elbow so she could examine his face. "You a gambler? Yer pullin' me leg."

"I've never developed any marketable skills except for playing a mean hand."

She laughed. "Does your hotel make money?"

"The income allows me to live well and buy toys I want."

"You're a fat cat capitalist. All yer bloody care about is profit and pleasure."

His eyes scanned over original oil paintings hung on the walls beside a Queen Anne armoire and matching dresser. "You enjoy all this thanks to your father's toil and sweat in the dog-eat-dog world of arms trading. Let's face it, Andrea, if you can't beat the capitalists, you may as well join them. Look what they've done for you. You're free to drink your favorite latte at Starbucks or fly to France to visit Euro Disney. You know what?" He turned and poked her ribs. "You're nothing but an old hypocrite."

215

Close up, he noticed that the roots of her dyed hair were red. Outside, the rain dampened the street and umbrellas started to pop open.

"In my books, you're more of a realist," Ryan added. "I'm sure living here is better than working ankle-deep in beet field mud."

"I don't miss the stinkin' muck." Andrea yawned. "I want more zeds."

"Before you shut down," he said. "I'd need to take a look at Aisling's laptop."

She opened a drawer, handed him the laptop, and gave him the password. As soon as he heard her breathing deepen into the heavy pulse of sleep, he went to the living room, lit the gas fire, settled in a comfortable chair, and opened Aisling's laptop.

Ryan began by checking the dates of Aisling's few entries. She made them in the weeks before going to Cannes. In the first file, there was an entry from her boss at the bank, Frank Malone. He had suggested that while in Cannes, Aisling could find out about the owner of *Sundancer*, the yacht tied up in the harbor. *Sundancer* belonged to an Irish-Kenyan, a former major shareholder in the bank. Frank Malone explained how Shark had insider trading information that enabled him to sell his ten percent interest in Anglo Irish a few days before the bank's stock tanked. Frank Malone had also provided her with background information on Shark's parents, Jacob Osinga and Ariel O'Connell. The couple had met and married in London. After Ariel gave birth to a son, Darcy, the couple separated. Accompanied by the infant, Jacob flew to Nairobi, while Ariel went back to live in her native Dublin. Jacob and his son drifted to the capital's teeming Korogocho slum, where Darcy's father began illegally brewing *chang'aa*, a combination of embalming fluid pilfered from mortuaries and maize and sorghum added to the mix. When translated, this lethal brew was called "kill me quick." Ariel heard rumors about her husband raising their son in the notorious slum, so she flew to Nairobi. She found the shack where the pair lived and spirited the boy back to Dublin. Jacob followed his wife and son back to Ireland, where he got a job in a slaughterhouse.

Young Darcy, however, took his mother's last name. As a result of his mixed race, he was teased and bullied at school. According to Malone, this abuse from students left painful scars on his young mind. After leaving school, Darcy disappeared below the radar, while he amassed a fortune from illegal enterprises. Soon after he joined the roster of Dublin's hundred richest residents, he changed his name to Shark.

Ryan stopped reading to glance at rain beating on the windows. He couldn't help but admire the rapid rise of Darcy O'Connell to become a financial powerhouse. Ryan scanned the known list of criminal organizations Shark took over to expand his empire. According to the file, by manipulating stock markets, Shark had hastened the collapse of both the Irish housing market and the banks. The file also mentioned Shark's ties to Sean Fitzpatrick, the disgraced former Anglo Irish chairman. The onetime Celtic Tiger poster boy, Fitzpatrick lent billions to bankroll the property boom. He was later accused of using Anglo Irish as his personal piggy bank.

Apart from the Malone's notes on Shark, there was no trace of any files that related to his criminal empire. Ryan concluded that Aisling must have transmitted Shark's files elsewhere. Perhaps to Malone. He checked Malone on Google, only to discover that the bank executive had committed suicide.

Ryan rubbed his eyes; it wouldn't take long for Shark's assassins to track him down again. He turned off the laptop. In the silence of the room, he felt the sudden stillness of a crowded Baghdad market square, a quiet moment before a bomb exploded.

Later that same day, while having a breakfast in bed, Shark leafed through a pile of newspapers at his penthouse in the Clarence Hotel on Wellington Quay, overlooking the Liffey River. He lingered over tea, toast, and boiled eggs to flip through the pile

217

of world newspapers. A fast and prodigious reader, he predicted major upheavals to happen in the next six months throughout the Arab world. In his view, his friends, Egypt's Hosni Mubarak and Tunisia's Zine el-Abidine Ben Ali were vulnerable. Another colleague, Libya's Muammar Gaddafi, had the animal instincts for survival, but he couldn't outlive a full-scale revolt.

Shark paused, his brow furrowed. He didn't like what he was reading. The Israeli blockade of the Gaza Strip had eased, and this news would cripple his partner Abu Ghamdi's lucrative tunnel business into Egypt. Shark had provided the seed money for Abu to finance the construction of illegal tunnels. His tunnels had made Abu a millionaire. His huge profits had enabled Abu to build a palace in Gaza, where nearly half of adult men were unemployed. In a matter of weeks, Shark realized that Abu's operations would collapse; cheaper goods coming in from Israel would bankrupt him.

Shark munched a scone plastered with English marmalade. How much would Abu going out of business cost him in management fees? One hundred thousand euros a year at the most. What should be done about Abu's workforce of over two hundred skilled tunnel diggers? For God's sake, they had even smuggled through the tunnels a small armored car. Shark paused to think while he sipped Earl Grey tea garnished by a slice of lemon. He put down his cup and wrote a note on his iPad. He planned to fly these skilled workers to the Mexico-U. S. border, where he could put them to work to streamline the tunnels of his drug-smuggling operations.

He grinned when he read in the *Evening Herald* that the disgraced ex-Anglo Irish Bank chairman Sean Fitzpatrick had filed for bankruptcy. He chortled out loud when he scanned the news story that described his former friend as one of the smuggest and most arrogant Irish bankers, now publicly exposed as a charlatan and a fraud.

His cell phone chimed, and he answered it. Pat Rafferty wanted to speak to him. Shark spoke freely as his security staff had swept his suite for bugs and walls were impermeable to outside directional microphones.

"We've compared the photos of Mason with the ones you faxed over," Pat said. "They match up to Ryan Moar."

"Good work. Where is Moar now?"

"He's shagging Andrea Quinn at the family's house on Mullingar."

Better enjoy your last piece of ass before you die, Shark thought.

"No excuses, mistakes, or foul-ups," Shark said. "This time eliminate him."

"Will do."

"Apart from the Quinn's daughter, is he alone?"

"Andrea is the only person with him."

"Does she know anything?"

"I don't think so. Unlike her sister, she's more interested in being a radical, you know, save the badgers, ban Irish mutton."

Shark thought back to Andrea's stubborn father Darragh Quinn, and the ferocious and intense power struggle he had in a bid to wrest the arms dealer's business away from him. During the bitter negotiations for control of his lucrative weapons trading company, Shark had given the assignment to eliminate Darragh to his most experienced assassin, Pete Talleyrand.

A creative killer, Pete had managed to sneak behind Darragh's back at the Dublin Airport and wrapped a cloth coated in VX, a highly toxic nerve agent, around his face.

"After Moar's dead," Shark said, "Andrea's not to be wasted. Is that clear?"

"Yes, boss."

"It won't take garda long to connect dots between her murder and her sister's death on board the Air Tanzania jetliner. Andrea will simply disappear. Moar's death needs to be clean, surgical. No more of your so-called IRA expert killers on this job. The Irish police won't appreciate having a Yank murdered on their soil. It's bad for business."

"Garda don't make me terribly nervous."

"Don't be overconfident, my friend," Shark said, taking a deep breath. "Do you have Moar and Andrea under audio and visual surveillance?"

"I've two men I have watching the house haven't bugged the phones yet, but they're working on it."

"I want listening devices connected to their phones and electronic eavesdropping set up now." Shark paused to sip tea. "What's your recommendation for getting rid of Moar?"

"We need to hire an experienced shooter."

"Who do you have in mind?"

"Talleyrand's the best, but he's expensive."

"The stakes are high, don't you agree, Pat?" The line was silent as Shark waited for his reply. Then he added, "Moar's meddling represents a clear danger to our interests. Now is not the time to fudge about paying Talleyrand's two hundred thou fee."

"I agree." Pat coughed. "When to do you want Pete to do the hit?"

"Tonight. Do it tonight."

"I'll pull a sheet on Moar and send it via an encrypted message to Pete."

Shark turned his attention to his hardboiled egg. He tapped the teaspoon to the shell until it cracked.

"Does Pete still wear those outrageous rags?" he asked.

He heard Pat laugh. "I met him in a pub once. Pete is one flashy dude. He wore one of them powdered wigs, a lacy waistcoat, buckled shoes, silk stockings and all."

"Do you know what they called his French namesake, Charles Maurice de Talleyrand-Périgord?"

"Tell me, I can't wait."

"A piece of dung in a silk stocking."

"A good description of Pete, I'd say." He giggled. "Didn't realize, boss, you know your French history."

"I've studied Talleyrand, particularly his political instincts for survival."

"I'll let you know if Pete accepts our offer. If anyone knows how to wipe Moar's slate clean, without causing an international incident, he's the one."

Shark pushed the breakfast tray away and swung his bare feet to the carpet. The tight jeans he wore wrapped around him like a second skin.

"Pete has put his Lear on the market at a ridiculously low price," Shark said. "This tells me he has a cash flow problem. Instead of offering him his standard fee, start the bidding at half that amount. He'll be eager to bite."

"Will do, boss," Pat said, disconnecting the line.

Shark turned off his cell phone. He swiveled his head to stretch the tension out of his neck. As he did so, Shark felt a familiar, strong pair of hands on his shoulders and the sweet sensation of taut muscles being massaged through his T-shirt.

"That's lovely, petal," he said.

"Anything I can do for you this morning, Shark?" a woman's silky voice said as she began to knead his shoulders.

She was a slim woman of uncertain age. Her lacquered amber wig glistened under the halogen floodlights. Her tight white tank top and matching shorts accented her cocoa skin.

"Vikki, turn on the TV to the RTÉ news channel," Shark said.

After she turned on the set, he clapped at the lead news story about Sean Fitzpatrick publicly declaring bankruptcy in Dublin's high court. The news anchor woman explained that under the Irish legal system, Fitzpatrick would remain bankrupt for 12 years unless he could clear his debts. The court ruled that he couldn't borrow more than 650 euros without declaring he was bankrupt. In addition, all his assets and properties were to be controlled by a court-appointed official.

Shark slapped his thighs when he saw another news clip of Fitzgerald—his face in his hands to avoid camera flashes—escorted by police officers and surrounded by noisy reporters. The newswoman's voiceover described how Fitzgerald had nothing to live on except his wife's pension. Speaking in front of the courthouse, the reporter concluded, "Although Fitzgerald is not the most indebted of the Celtic Tiger highflyers, he is seen as symbolic of the rise and fall of the country's nouveau riche."

The newscast moved on to cover the Greek debt crisis.

Shark jotted a note on his iPad to look into the possibility of buying at a bargain Fitzgerald's palatial mansion and estate in Wicklow County. In a year or two, he could put the house back on the market and make a killing.

"You are tense," Vicki said. "Let me give you a full-body massage?"

"That would be lovely."

Vikki rolled in a folding table on wheels. He climbed on the table and lay on his stomach. Vikki stripped off her tank top, allowing her breasts to swing loose like overripe mangos. She removed his T-shirt and started rubbing his back. He sighed. Then, for a moment, he wasn't thinking about Vicki's fingers digging into his shoulder muscles. His mind focused on death. By bringing in Pete Talleyrand, Shark anticipated that the private investigator would meet a quick end. To him, Moar was the poisoned tip of an acacia tree thorn. When Shark was a boy living with his dad in the slums of Nairobi, he had stepped on a thorn that could have poisoned his foot if he hadn't had it treated at a neighborhood free clinic.

He thought a prick like Moar, if left untreated could cause a body to fester and eventually rot. A sudden fear made him swallow. He couldn't let his secrets be exposed to anyone. Shark rolled over on his back, and Vikki began to massage his thighs. He gazed up into her dark brown eyes; a look of concern flashed across her narrow face.

"You were gone from me for a while," she said. "Where did you go to, luv?"

CHAPTER 33

E VEN BEFORE THE SUN HAD reached its noon-hour zenith, Pete Talleyrand knew that the threat of a morning rain shower had proved illusory and that the temperature was going to reach twenty degrees centigrade by late afternoon. The unusual sun's heat had caused a blanket of humidity over his outdoor swimming pool. The light shimmering on the surface made his eyes water.

He turned away to admire Brugh na Boinne, one of several homes he owned in and around Dublin. The white Spanish mansion was patrolled by guards and a pack of Dobermans. Pete had acquired this faux-Spanish hacienda from a surgeon who wanted him to get rid of his wife. After Pete had shot the doctor's wife and disposed of her body far out in the Irish Sea, the physician neglected to pay him his full fee. Pete threatened the doctor by describing several ugly ways to die. To spare his life, he eventually forced the doctor to sign over Brugh na Boinne to him.

Beside the shamrock-shaped pool, the Irish tricolor fluttered in the warm breeze. Since moving to Dublin nine years ago, Pete had become one of the most sought-after assassins, equally at ease carrying out assignments anywhere in the world from Cape Town to Kabul.

Sitting in a high chair beside the pool, Pete wore a white silk robe and swallow-egg blue swimming trunks. A tall, fine-boned man, he projected a roguish, world-wise demeanor. Pete spoke four languages, possessed five passports, maintained a fleet of Mercedes sedans, and piloted a Lear passenger jet. The only thing to mar his chiseled features was a thin S-shaped scar under his eye, a red ribbon that looked as if it had been pasted on his cheek.

His cell phone chimed the opening bars of the Irish national anthem, *The Soldier's Song*. When he answered the phone, he recognized Pat Raffety's squeaky voice.

"What can I do for you, Pat, me darlin' boy?" he said, stretching out his hairy legs as he gazed up at the house's scrolled ironwork windows. "You have a job for me? This burned out economy is driving me nuts."

"We're all suffering, Pete."

"Knowing Shark, as I do, he is not only profiting from this financial tsunami, but also thriving in the carnage."

"Shark's a survivor."

"Haven't heard from you in a long time, mate," he said, glancing over at his plump wife, Esther, seated on a beach chair, and two of his six daughters, Sarah and Amelie, lying on air mattresses in the pool. Pete had always wanted sons, but Esther had produced only girls.

Pat lowered his voice. "We've a job for you."

"Local or international?"

"The hit is in Dublin. The name of the target is Ryan Moar. I've emailed you a coded file on this bastard. We have him under surveillance."

Pete's pulse quickened at the opportunity Pat presented to him.

"You know I appreciate the business." His attention was drawn to his daughter, Megan, in a bikini doing a swan dive from the springboard before slicing the water's surface without a ripple.

"I want you to tell Shark that I'm his friend and that I've always admired him, looked up to him as only a son can."

"Cut out the crap, Pete."

"What do you mean? I've always been loyal to him, no temptations, so to speak."

"We know you're a straight shooter, Pete." Pat laughed at his joke. "What's all this palsy talk leading up to?"

Pete held the phone pinned to his ear with his shoulder and propped his hands on his thighs. "To eliminate Moar, are you able to come across with my usual fee?"

The sun appeared between banks of clouds to warm the third-floor bedroom in the Georgian row house on Mulligan, once owned before the Troubles by Sir George Hathaway, a wealthy British tea merchant. Ryan pulled the drapes wide to let in the light. Andrea sat up, knees tucked under her chin, fidgeting with her negligee's lace drawstrings.

"Come into me bed," she said, glancing at a grandfather clock. "It's only just after noon."

Ryan continued to roam and pace, fingering a figurine on the dresser, glancing out at people walking on the sidewalks, and looking at cars parked in the street. His best chance of finding the elusive recipient of the files was to recruit Andrea to help him in the search.

Ryan sat on the edge of the bed. He told her that having escaped one attempt on his life beside the Grand Canal, he was sure Shark would dispatch other assassins to finish him off. He needed her help to find the recipient of Aisling's transmission from Shark's yacht so he could save his skin, hand over the files to Interpol, and bring down his corrupt empire.

"Were you aware that Aisling's boss at Anglo Irish, Frank Malone, committed suicide?" he asked.

"He croaked under a train at Malahide."

"From what I found on Google, the *Dublin Times* said that he took his own life as a result of pressure after the financial market's collapse and the banking meltdown."

225

"Frank never struck me as a quitter."

"You met him?"

"He came to the house for dinner once. The bugger's been murdered rather than take his own life."

"According to his bio, he was the father of five, who made over six hundred thousand euros a year. He allegedly wrote a suicide note to his wife saying that he didn't think he could carry on."

"Some bloke forged that note."

"You think so?" Ryan said, before going to the living room to tug on a shirt and slacks. "His wife, Thelma, said at the inquest that her husband had never been depressed or sought the services of a psychiatrist."

"Another of Shark's victims?"

"That's what I'm thinking."

He came close to her and cupped her face with his hands.

"There something I recognize in you," he said.

Her hands fluttered to her cheeks. "What do you mean?"

"You have that look."

Andrea's fingers pressed on her lips. "Are yer saying I look like me sister?"

"I can see Aisling in your eyes when she was worried."

She climbed out of bed and attempted to kiss him. He brushed her away with his hand. Andrea pouted. Ryan went to the adjoining bathroom to wash his face. In the mirror, scars around his nose and chin had almost faded away. When he returned, Andrea had covered her head with the bedsheet. He could see her body quivering and hear the sound of sobs.

"I miss my sister," she said.

"Why? I thought you and Aisling didn't get along."

"The catfights was nothin' but sibling rivalry. Underneath, we was soul mates."

He stood silently for a moment, gazing at her through narrow eyes.

"Get dressed," he said. "Together, we'll bring down those responsible for her death."

She dressed in a faded tartan skirt and a rose tank top. "You're a cautious man, and that's why you're still kicking." She stood in a pool of sunlight. "Jasus, I can't believe your bollocks. Aw g'wan yer only coddin me, yer no beach bum innkeeper from Zanzibar. Yer fooled me ma." She gazed at him, her cheeks burning. "Yer scars ain't no coral scratches."

"Shark's teeth are more convincing?"

"No more fibs, or I won't lift a finger to help you."

"All right, I'm a private investigator working on a murder case. Those scars are from a beating by Shark's men. I came within a hair's width of losing it."

The thought of his near-death experience hit him like an unexpected punch. He knew that he was embroiled in one of his most dangerous cases. Did he put too much faith in this flower child to find the files?

Andrea appeared suddenly animated; she sat up and stared through the open French doors leading to the living room with the bright eyes of a cat.

"You know everything about me," she said, "I know so little about you."

"It's for your protection. If we continue to hang out together, you'll be in the crosshairs of merciless killers."

"I'm not afraid."

"You should be. Considering they blew up a jetliner to make sure that your sister and Shark's files remain buried." Ryan regarded her seriously for a moment. "If we work together, it has to be on one condition. Sharing the same bed isn't going to happen."

She climbed out of bed, sat on a lace-bordered stool in front of a vanity, and balled her hands on her knees. She smiled at him in the mirror. "I'm sure me dear departed sister appreciated your yockers."

He walked to the vanity and rested his hands on her shoulders.

"Yer don't find me attractive?" she added.

"Like your sister, you're a knockout, but I'm committed to loving a woman in North Dakota. Who is expecting our child any day now." Ryan's eyes remained riveted on Andrea. "I feel ashamed at having betrayed her once. Trust me, I won't do it twice."

She stared at him, a grin on her face as she began applying lipstick. Her physicality seemed to exude sex, a whiff of estrogen, a tinge of lavender. Blood flushed his cheeks.

"Tell me yer real name."

"Ryan." He turned back to her, his gaze intense. "At the first hint that we're being threatened by Shark's men, you'll find a safe place to hide. Agreed?"

She lit a cigarette and breathed out smoke in two streams through her nostrils. He looked at her, his eyebrows raised.

He said, "You exhale smoke the same way Aisling did."

She laughed. "I don't usually puff, but I found these fags in the bedside table. I prefer weed, but there's none here, so I have to support big corporations providing slow poison to working class people."

"Big tobacco doesn't discriminate between the classes. They kill anyone foolish enough to smoke, whether they're rich or poor." He turned on Aisling's laptop and set the computer down on the vanity's glass top. "Let's take a look in your sister's files. I want you to look for any of the files related to Shark that I may have missed. Also, is there one close to her, who may have received her transmission?"

While she searched Aisling's computer files, he listened to the wind in the trees mingled in among the squawk of crows. After a few minutes, she tensed and pointed to the screen.

"She's the one," she said, bouncing on the balls of her feet. She went into Aisling's photo file and printed a portrait.

CHAPTER 34

BY LATE AFTERNOON, RYAN AND Andrea began the search for Ciara Redstone in the fashionable Dublin neighborhood of Ranelagh, stopping in front of a redbrick Edwardian row house on Mount Pleasant Square. Andrea seemed positive that Aisling's closest friend was the one who could have received the transmission.

A thin-boned woman, who wore a heavy black blouse and matching skirt, inappropriate for the sudden heat of the morning, answered the terrace house's doorbell. In broken English, she explained that Ciara Redstone no longer rented the apartment on the second floor. She provided Ryan with a new address in O'Devany Gardens.

"Why did she leave?" Andrea asked.

"No longer pay rent."

"Anglo Irish must've let her go," Andrea whispered.

After Ryan thanked Ciara's former landlady, he and Andrea walked back to the Mini. Meanwhile, the woman patted her chest so she could feel a wad of rolled-up cash tucked into her bra.

Half an hour later, Ryan drove down a narrow cobble street of grim-looking row houses.

Andrea switched from her finishing school accent to a harsh Irish brogue. "That O'Devany is a rough auld kip all right."

"Care to translate?" Ryan asked.

"O'Devany's one of the city's dodgiest districts. You wouldn't want to walk alone in its streets at night."

As he pulled into traffic, Andrea helped him navigate to the north end of the city's ring road. On the way, they passed dreary council housing projects, soulless and bleak, and an area of crumbling buildings covered in layers of graffiti.

"This is what the city calls renewal," Andrea said, staring at row houses, doors and windows boarded over like Band-Aids plastered haphazardly over bruises.

Ryan drove by several blocks of second-hand stores, church shelters for the homeless, and pubs. Ryan suspected the patrons lived like prisoners in time, measured not by the outside world, but by the first drink of the morning turned into a ritual and carried on throughout the remainder of the day.

The brick row house's front doors and windows were boarded up, every inch of plywood covered in rude words written in both English and Gaelic. He stared at blackened walls and listened to magpies chatter in a chestnut tree in a weed infested yard.

Across the street stood the Jeremiah O'Donovan Rossa pub. Made of sandstone, the public house seemed to rise like a forgotten reminder of Victorian elegance in the middle of twenty-first century urban decay. A pair of nuns in gray skirts passed them on the cracked sidewalk.

"We won't find Ciara here," Ryan said. "Are you sure she's the one?"

Andrea shrugged. "Aisling and Ciara were the best of pals, even worked together as models."

"Let's inquire in the pub. Maybe they know where she is."

"We're not having much luck, *bwana*," Andrea said as they entered the pub's lobby containing faded potted palms, a threadbare Persian carpet, and high-backed chairs.

"What did you just say?" Ryan asked, ducking to avoid hitting his head on the low oak-beamed ceiling.

"I was pulling yer leg," Andrea said.

"That's the name Aisling called me."

"Jasus, that's probably the saddest thing I've ever heard anybody say," she said, adopting her streetwise talk. "My sister must've got under your skin, laddie. Get over it, yer sad freak."

Defined by a long bar, the pub's main room had brass rails, a row of kegs, and spirit bottles on backlit shelves. Sandwiched in between beer barrels hung a gilt-framed portrait of a man in a wide-brimmed hat, who sported a white Buffalo Bill goatee. The plaque under the portrait read "Jeremiah O'Donovan Rossa, Fenian Leader and Member of the Irish Republican Brotherhood."

Ryan and Andrea sat on high stools and leaned on the counter's shiny surface. Ryan slid the photo of Ciara Redstone in front of the publican, a silver-haired woman whose gnarled fingers rotated a sodden tea towel to wipe the countertop.

"Excuse me, madam, have you ever seen this woman before?" he asked.

The publican examined the photo with one eye, the other being covered by an eye patch. A heavyset woman, she placed her thick forearms on the counter to squint at the photo held up to her good eye. Just above her wrist, she had a tattoo of a stylized emerald green shamrock.

She smiled. "Cain't say I've seen her around 'ere."

"You may have seen her friend," Ryan said, sliding a photo of Aisling across the polished counter wood.

"Aye, I've seen this one. She used to sit in the hall before going upstairs."

"Did you rent her a room?"

"She used to stay for one night, always wanting the same room, overlooking the street."

"Did you ever see anyone with her, a friend perhaps?"

"Come to think of it, she did have one."

231

"Do you remember if her name was Ciara Redstone? Take another look."

The woman stared at the photo. Ryan leaned forward, and when he came close to her, he could smell the sour odor she gave off, a combination of Guinness and sweat.

She shook her head. "Don't know any customer by that name." The publican was distracted by a young girl in a short skirt who hung around the foyer leading to the front entrance. Her one good eye widened, and she raised her hands in a shooing motion. "Be off with you! We don't allow chiselers in 'ere."

The young girl's doll-like face had a black beauty spot on her cheek in the shape of a crescent moon. She batted thick-coated eyelashes at Ryan.

"Be off with yer, yer tart."

The young woman gave the publican the finger before moving away from the door.

The woman wiped her hands on a checked apron. "I've seen some of them girls as young as ten, trying to peddle their arses inside and outside me pub." She puckered her lips. "What is this bloomin' world coming to? It's hard to keep me place open. The pub down the street closed on account of our economy disappearing into the bowl. I'm telling you, the Celtic Tiger is dead. I've 'ad to dish out for a couple of plasma TVs to keep customers comin' back." She fingered a gold crucifix hanging around her neck. "I used to be a good Catholic, go to mass every day, but since the church had them sex scandals, you don't find the likes of me goin' much." She paused to pull a pint of Guinness for an elderly man wearing a cloth cap. "If you ask me, the church should allow priests to marry to cut down on them abusin' children."

"Gimme a crapper?" another customer said.

"Sure, Tom," she said, pouring a half glass of whiskey into a mug of Guinness. Instead of ringing the sale on a cash register, she wrote the transaction on a scrap of paper by using a pencil attached to a string.

The man made a guttural sound that came from deep within his throat.

"Take care of that cough, Tom," she said.

The man's lined face crinkled into a smile, as he buried his mouth in the dark brown brew.

"Guinness and whiskey is me best medicine," Tom said, before wiping his mouth on his jacket sleeve.

When Tom went to sit by the fire, the publican straightened up. "Tom's got emphysema. The gang killed his best friend Mick. His wife died of a heart attack a week ago, so he's bereft of everything." She tapped her eye patch with her forefinger. "Lost me eye to cancer last year. You never know when sickness is going to strike."

"The woman we are looking for could have changed her appearance," Ryan said, snagging the publican's eye.

"What does she look like now?" she asked.

"Slim, early twenties, blond hair," Andrea said.

"Cain't say I can remember seein' her in the pub, although we get every bloody color here on Saturday night."

"Did you ever see a girl who had beautiful butterfly tattoos?"

The publican raised her bushy eyebrows. "Come to think of it, I do remember seeing her in the pub. She had red butterfly wings on her arms and legs. Thin as a whippet, that one. Could she be the lass you're looking for? She mostly comes in here on her own. Her friend, the one that used to stay here, she don't come to the pub no more." The publican shifted her weight and looked over at a few white-haired men sitting on chairs and sipping beer. "Why you lookin' her?"

"To get her back on her feet," Ryan said.

"Well, as long as you mean her no harm." The woman leaned forward. "If she'll be anywhere, she'll be at the Cleggan, a private club for men. It's only about a good spit from here. Go to the end of O'Neill Street and then turn left at MacBride." The publican played with a wafer-thin gold wedding band and lowered her voice. "Well, if the truth be known, the Cleggan is really an escort service.

I suspect the woman you're looking for is one of them sheilas." She glanced at her watch. "Well, it's nearly five o'clock, and we be close soon for supper."

As Ryan and Andrea walked out of the pub, he heard what sounded like a rifle shot. Ryan spun around and thrust Andrea behind him inside the pub's doorway. He pulled out the semiautomatic tucked in the back of his pants. When he saw black smoke pouring out of the truck's exhaust, he tried to smooth the tension from his face.

Andrea smiled at his discomfort. "It's only a bloody truck farting."

She glanced up at a plaque written in Gaelic script above the front door and translated it: "You may as well put your trust in the devil to get to heaven as to trust the English to free the Irish."

CHAPTER 35

RYAN BRAKED THE MINI AT a street corner and rolled down the car window to ask for further directions to the Cleggan from a craggy faced woman and a pigtailed girl. The woman was picking through trash in a bin, while the girl held open a plastic bag to put anything of value in. Above them, the sun was pale and watery behind a low layer of thin clouds.

"There's no place like that here 'bouts," the old woman said.

"Is there a building in the neighborhood that's a men's club?" Ryan said.

"No, mister, never heard of them either." The woman was large and straight-backed for her age, and her hands were calloused and covered in liver spots. She wore a yellow plastic coat over her plaid skirt, and a wool tam covered her frizzy gray hair. "It's hot as hell today, ain't it?"

Ryan showed her the photo of Ciara.

"If she lived around here, I ain't seen her. What did this lass do?"

"She's a sheila who frequents the Rossa," Andrea said.

"Oh, you don't say. I go there meself." She glanced again at Ciara's photo. "She looks young and innocent like. It's a bloody shame to see her take up the trade, but it's the young'uns what them men want. Leads me to think what happens to those who get older? Have to find another line of work, I suppose." She looked down at the girl. "Show her picture to me granddaughter. She knows these streets better than I do."

The girl's eyes slid across Ciara's face, the wind tousling her tattered coat, her face as placid as still canal water. She wiped her nose on the back of her hand. Ryan climbed out of the car and crouched on his haunches next to her.

"Have you seen her before?" Ryan asked, suppressing a twinge that flared up from the kicks to his knees that Shark's men had inflicted on him in Zanzibar.

"Maeve is a smart one," her grandmother said. "Not much gets by her."

The girl smiled, revealing a mouthful of stained brown teeth, but she remained silent.

"Maybe if you told her why you're looking for the lass, she might tell you what she knows," the grandmother said.

Ryan straightened up. "Maeve, this young woman has information that will put a bad guy who hurts people behind bars."

"You garda?" Maeve asked.

Andrea leaned out of the car window. "He's a private investigator trying to put a murderer in the pokey."

Maeve regarded Ryan with a solemn look on her freckled face and glanced at her grandmother.

"You can tell the man," she said.

Maeve touched the photo with the tips of her nails, encrusted in grime.

"I seen her outside our store yesterday," she said.

"We run a second-hand store the next street over," the grandmother said. "You might call it a rag-and-bone shop."

Ryan patted Maeve's shoulder. "Did you see where she went?"

She pointed to the tallest building on the block.

"You ain't the first person this mornin' to ask about the lass in the picture," the grandmother said, looking weary and fragile, her eyes askew as though pulled in separate ways. "I had nothin' to tell. I didn't have Maeve with me."

"Can you describe this man?"

"A tall geezer he was, a pink face full o' freckles he had. Drives a shiny black German car. He had a scar like a little red worm below his eye."

Ryan got back in the Mini, and they drove along the street, looking for a parking place, while keeping a lookout for a man defaced by a crooked scar. A low black rainstorm moved over the city and cast the street into permanent shadow.

The Cleggan stood at the end of a terrace of Edwardian houses on East MacBride Road. The sign above the building's double green doors was in a stylish, faded, gold-leaf script. The building's exterior was made of sooty pink coral brick accented by ocher sandstone in a Romanesque style, a forgotten reminder of musty elegance.

As Ryan climbed out of the Mini, Andrea reminded him that he should have no worries about any police visiting the Cleggan, as prostitution in Ireland was legal. She explained that masseuse parlors, pimping, and brothels were banned, while those involved in these trades were persecuted. Prostitution had shifted to escort services run out of private homes and clubs. These establishments attracted clients on the Internet without fear of arrest, drawing customers from all over the world.

"Dublin's a major sex tourist destination, more popular than Amsterdam or Bangkok," she said as they entered the Cleggan's dimly lit foyer.

They climbed a winding staircase to the second floor and stepped inside an expansive lobby, accented by potted ferns. A sweeping staircase led to a mezzanine. In the old days, Ryan imagined women in low-cut gowns peering down over lattice-wood railings to evaluate customers below. Behind an oak desk, a heavyset woman regarded them through horn-rimmed glasses, as if trying to determine whether Ryan was a customer or a curious tourist.

"This is a private club open to members only," she said.

"I'm not a member, but I'm willing to join," Ryan said.

"My name is Cecily. The fee is five hundred euros." She handed him a glossy brochure. "Here's a full list of our benefits. Our bar facilities, gym, spa, and billiard room are available for your use."

He gave Cecily the money, and she didn't seem surprised when he asked her for the services of one Ciara Redstone. The receptionist turned to her computer. After clicking keys, told him that Ms. Redstone was available, but he would have to wait in one of the bedrooms for about fifteen minutes. He offered the woman another hundred euros to make sure no one other than Ciara would disturb him. She slipped the money into her bra and promised Ryan's hour would be secure and private.

Cecily stared hard at Andrea for a moment. "We have a guest waiting room for your friend."

"No, she will join us," Ryan said.

"Oh, I see," she smiled knowingly.

Cecily escorted them upstairs and opened the door to a third-floor room. Furnished with an untidy double bed and a dust-covered vanity, the room smelled of loneliness and the previous user's cheap cologne. Cecily smiled and gave them a little wave before heading for the stairs. Closing the door behind him, Ryan checked out the back lane to make sure that he wasn't being watched. He then wedged a chair against the doorknob.

Ryan slumped down on a wicker chair, while Andrea tumbled onto the bed. Ryan leaned back and closed his eyes. He longed to return to his river property north of Fargo and reconcile with Joanne. When she gave birth to their son, he wanted to hold the infant close to him. He had not chosen this life. It had been chosen by others, particularly the killer who had raped his first wife, Kathy, and dumped her unconscious body in the Red River. He would never give up in his search to find her killer.

Ryan stood up and opened the heavy curtains a crack and peered out through the bedroom window's smeared glass, looking for signs of surveillance. The only movement in the alley below was a cat walking stiff-legged by a rusty sedan resting on two flat tires. The alley appeared quiet, but for how long?

Feeling the need to nap, Ryan stretched out on the chair while he listened to Andrea's snores from the sagging bed. Ryan laced his hands behind his head and stared at a crucifix on the opposite wall. Brought up a Catholic, he found strength in the cross, an ironic symbol in a room that catered to satisfy the natural, human lusts of so-called sinners.

To pass the time, Ryan checked mail on his cell phone. He put the phone on the dresser and tried to relax, but questions kept his mind in overdrive. How could Andrea be so certain that Aisling had transmitted the files to Ciara? Her younger sister claimed that she was estranged from Aisling, so why did she appear to know a surprising amount about her elder sibling? If indeed Ciara had the files, what terrible reversal of fortune had forced her to resort to becoming a call girl for the escort service? He glanced at his watch. Ciara was ten minutes overdue. How long would it take before Shark's assassins closed in. Had the man who had the wormlike scar on the lookout for a woman matching Ciara's description already intercepted her?

Where are you, Ciara? he thought. Where are you?

A sharp knock caused Ryan to jump out of the chair. He took the handgun out from the back of his belt and switched off the safety.

"Who is it?" he asked.

"Ciara Redstone."

He removed the chair jammed under the handle and opened the door a crack. He caught a glimpse of a freckle-faced woman, her hair cut in bangs in the front. Ciara's waifish figure in her photo had transformed into a chubby woman, but a surprisingly sexy one. The only makeup she wore was a brush of mascara. She had transformed from a model into a buxom young woman. Her severe tweed skirt, matching tan jacket, and sensible brogues gave her more of the look of a squire's daughter than a call girl.

"Ciara, come in," Ryan said.

She placed her hands on her wide hips and glanced at the bed. "She has to wait outside. I don't do peep shows or threesomes."

"I'm not here for the reason you think I am," Ryan said. "I've a mystery to resolve that has your name written all over it."

She glanced at the bed again. "What is Andrea Quinn doing here?"

"I don't have much time to explain," Ryan said. "Did her sister Aisling transmit files when she was in Zanzibar to your computer?"

"Aisling's dead, right?" Ciara said, looking stunned, shrunken, as though frozen inside. She straightened her back and walked into the room. "Before I answer your question, I'm entitled to an explanation."

Ryan told her how her friend had managed to download Shark's files and sent them to a computer in Ireland. After she died in the jetliner crash, he explained to Ciara that he had flown to Dublin and sought out Aisling's mother to help him find the files. Andrea had agreed to help him locate the files so he could both solve a murder case and expose Shark's criminal empire.

"I am surprised she agreed to help you," Ciara said, glaring at Andrea.

Andrea sat up and puckered her lips.

"What I find truly amazing is that her younger sister is taking an interest in her suster." Ciara trailed her fingers through her brown curls. "You two haven't spoken to each other for years."

"Aisling's death prompted Andrea to reconcile with her sister and her family," Ryan said.

Ciara turned to Ryan. "Don't believe that conniving bitch. She wouldn't do anything for anyone except if it satisfied her addictions and absolute devotion to her bizarre lifestyle. When she joined a commune, Andrea broke her mother's heart."

"What have you to say, Andrea?" Ryan asked.

"Malicious gossip."

"Andrea thinks Aisling transmitted these files to you," Ryan said, stepping closer to Ciara.

"Why did you, uh, switch to your current profession?" Andrea asked.

"My father lost a fortune in land speculation schemes; his debts forced him into bankruptcy." She let out a long exhalation of breath. "Working for the escort service is my only way of getting my hands on quick cash."

The wail of a police siren coming from the alley reached a high pitch and then receded.

"Having those files puts you in danger," Ryan said. "This guy will stop at nothing to protect his worldwide crime cartel."

Ciara closed her eyes, as if to collect her thoughts.

"We don't have much time, Ciara," Ryan continued. "There is a man looking for you. Fortunately, they have your model agency photo that doesn't exactly resemble how you look now. Believe me, it won't take him long to trace you to the Cleggan."

"I didn't say I have Shark's files—"

"How the Devil did you know his name is Shark?" Ryan clenched his fists. "This isn't the time to play games." He put his hand behind his back, his fingers wrapped around the comfortable feel of the Magnum's handle. "Where are the files?"

For a moment, she looked confused, but soon recovered her composure. Ryan grabbed her by the shoulders and shook her, a sudden edge creeping into his voice. "Tell me now."

"I don't have them," she cried, her eyes pleading.

"You know where they are, right? You've probably had a look at them." He pulled out the Magnum, locked the door, and pointed the gun at her knees. "I wouldn't be surprised—given your precarious financial position—if you haven't tried to shake down Shark, using the files as leverage." Ryan was silent for a moment. "If you attempt to negotiate the sale of these files to Shark, you've doomed yourself and your loved ones to the worst kind of torment followed by execution."

"Dear God," she said, covering her face in her hands.

"Don't try and deny it."

Ciara looked at the gun. "You aren't seriously thinking of using that thing on me?"

"Don't tempt me. I know all about your infamous IRA kneecapping. One well aimed bullet, and you'll never walk straight down a runway again." He stepped closer. "Where are the files?"

She didn't reply.

"I repeat, where are the files?" Ryan said.

"Wait, I'll cooperate if I'm rewarded. I need money, at least a quarter of a million euros."

"Are you out of your mind? How do you expect me to get my hands on a large sum of cash?"

"G2 wants to get their hands on the files. Surely, the secret service could persuade their political masters to provide the money."

"If your government is like any other, it will take months for such a request to work its way through the bureaucracy."

"I'm prepared to wait."

He stared at her ruefully. "By the time the bureaucrats approve your reward, we'll be dead."

Ryan peered through crack in the bedroom curtain, and he spotted a priest in the back lane running toward the Cleggan's back door. He held a bulky black case almost hidden under his black robe. Dark glasses covered his eyes and a fedora pulled down in front obscured his face.

Ryan gripped Ciara's arm so hard that she cried out. He heard the sound of footsteps in the corridor.

"We have to leave right now," he said, wedging the chair back against the door handle.

He helped Andrea and Ciara climb out of the window and onto a narrow ledge.

Before following them, Ryan paused to recover his iPhone. He was too late. The door quivered from the impact of multiple blows and bullets fired into the lock. Ryan climbed out the window and swung down to the ledge.

CHAPTER 36

J OANNE SAT IN THE WAITING room for almost half an hour and was starting to feel foolish. She wondered whether she needed to be at the Sanford Family Birth Center on Broadway North in Fargo. Across the sunlit, polished floor of the waiting room, a young nurse approached her, thin to the point of emaciation. Her cheeks were sunken, almost collapsed, and her red lips and pointed nose were as slim as the rest of her. She escorted Joanne to a hospital room to change into a gown.

"I'll be back in a minute," the nurse said, closing the door.

Joanne dug into her purse for her cell phone. She dialed Ryan's cell phone number and waited, listening to the clicks of the overseas connections. After two rings, a male voice with a pronounced Irish accent said, "Who is this?"

"I was going to ask you the same question," she said. "The cell phone you answered belongs to my husband. Where is he?" She could hear shouting voices over the line. "Is he there? I need to talk to him."

The thin nurse stuck her head around the door. "You're next, Ms. Sutter. We need to get you prepped."

The nurse spotted the cell phone clutched to her ear. "It's time to go, Joanne."

"I'm trying to call the baby's father."

"You're having a baby?" the man on Ryan's cell phone asked.

"Yes, I am, and I need to speak to Ryan."

Joanne heard a click as the line went dead.

"Now isn't the time for phone calls," the nurse said, her arms folded across her chest.

"This isn't a social call, it's an emergency."

"So is having a baby."

The nurse helped her onto the gurney and an orderly wheeled her down a long corridor to the operating theater.

Dr. Henderson pulled up his mask and came into the operating theater.

"You look a little agitated, Joanne," he said. "There's nothing to be concerned about."

"Dr. Henderson, my husband's in trouble in Dublin," Joanne said.

"Well, there isn't much we can do for him right now in the land of saints and scholars, is there?" the doctor said, nodding to his team. "Let's get started."

Ryan heard the first shots when they hid behind a chimney on the roof. On one knee, he aimed the Magnum at the man wearing the clerical collar. When he swung out of Ryan's view, answering fire came from an adjacent roof as bullets tore into the chimney, chipping off pieces of brick.

When the firing stopped, Ryan peered around the chimney and spotted a man take cover behind an air vent. He aimed at his exposed arm. He squeezed the trigger twice. The man cried out, dropped his weapon, slumped on the roof, and clutched his shattered arm.

Ryan took Ciara's hand and climbed down to the window ledge of a connected row house. They inched their way to an open window.

Ryan helped the two women crawl headfirst into an empty room. They crept past a bed and ran down a flight of stairs that led to a kitchen. The door leading to a walled garden was locked. Ryan used the Magnum to blast the lock. When the door opened, they raced for the back gate. They ran down a lane until they reached the street, where a double-decker bus had just pulled up at a stop. They climbed on board and blended in among the passengers. Ciara stood in the aisle and hung on the straps. Andrea reached out to Ryan and wrapped her arms around him. He could feel her trembling.

"Did you kill the man shooting at us?" she whispered.

"He'll live. If he's right-handed, he'll have to learn to shoot with his left."

The bus lurched to a stop and they got off. A gentle rain was falling when they stepped onto the sidewalk. Ryan seized Ciara's shoulders with both hands and shook her so hard that passersby paused to look at them.

"Ciara, for the last time, where are those files?" Ryan said, pushing her against the graffiti-spattered wall of a boarded-up storefront.

He struck her across the face with the flat of his hand.

"Answer me or I'll keep hitting you," he said.

"Please, stop," she said, putting her hands up to protect her face.

Ryan released her and stepped back. She leaned against the plywood boards and fought for breath.

She gasped, "The files are hidden at Caviston Court."

The failure to shoot Ryan Moar and capture the two women made Shark furious, although his face reflected none of his anger. A shootout on a high street roof was bound to attract unwanted garda and media attention. What the devil was Pete Talleyrand and Pat's men thinking when they opened fire on Moar, Andrea Quinn, and Ciara Redstone on the roof of the Cleggan, instead of executing him far removed from public scrutiny in a locked room. Having lived a lifetime in society's shadows, he knew the importance of maintaining a tranquil outward appearance, projecting nothing more than bored insouciance.

He took the unprecedented step to go out on the penthouse balcony to watch the njght traffic swoop past. He looked at the Ha'penny Bridge, an arched single span with iron railings and decorative lamps. Vikki popped her head around the sliding doors, her cheeks glowing.

"Pat's on the line, baby," she said.

He closed the door, went into the living room, and punched the light on a multiline telephone. Vikki remained behind him, her hands folded in front of her white Toledo pants. The thick hair of her ocher wig lay about her weight lifter's shoulders.

"What went crooked, Pat?" Shark asked.

"He's damn good, boss. We had them surrounded. Talleyrand and Terry were on the roof, and me and the boys in the bedroom. On the roof, Moar's fire pinned us down. He made a clean getaway."

"You lost him?"

"We'll find him." He heard Pat's hard intake of breath. "Talleyrand will follow the radio beacon tracking device attached to the Mini."

Shark knew Pat Rafferty to be charming and intelligent. He was also a liar, a thief, and a sexual deviant—a man devoid of morals. For some reason, Shark had now started to suspect his loyalty.

"I'm thinking this guy's a top marksman. Terry's right arm is shattered," Pat rambled on. "He's evaded experienced tails—"

"Whenever you start thinking, Pat, it means that it's time for me to watch my back," Shark interrupted.

Pat was silent for a moment.

"We have Moar's cell phone he left behind at the Cleggan," he said. "His wife's having a baby."

Shark paused and took a deep breath. "Track down his woman's hospital. It's useful to have a baby in the mix to put the squeeze on Moar."

Shark disconnected the line. He heard Vikki's stiletto heels squeak on the polished parquet floor. She rubbed his tense shoulders.

"Anything I can do for you, big guy?" she whispered in his ear.

"Not now, Vikki, I've got work to do."

Shark went inside his living room. He was tired of chasing phantoms. He phoned Joseph Lipumba at home. On the phone, the staff sergeant sounded either drunk or he had just woken from a deep sleep. Lipumba told him in a thick voice that after the police had issued a warrant for his arrest for dangerous driving and damage to private property, he had handed Ryan Moar over to Rasul. Shark examined a grainy photo of Mason getting out of a Mini. He gave Lipumba his description. The police officer told him that Mason matched Moar's over six feet in height and curly black hair.

The next phone call was to his lieutenant in Zanzibar, Rasul Bendera. Rasul was confident Ryan Moar was dead, buried in a vegetable plot. Shark ordered him to dig up the grave to make sure that Moar was indeed fertilizing maize. Shark added, "If Moar isn't there, you had better start digging your own burial plot." Shark disconnected the line and turned on the TV for the six o'clock BBC news. The lead story impacted his drug operations and could make it more difficult to smuggle marijuana from Mexico to the US. According to the report, the Mexican federal police force had sacked over ten percent of its officers for corruption, incompetence, or links to criminals. He turned off the set, undressed, and slipped into a terry cotton robe. He went to the bedroom, where Vikki lay naked, her dark skin in sharp contrast to the white silk sheets.

Men in his wealth bracket often bought racehorses or gambled at upper-class casinos in London's Mayfair or on the Côte d'Azur, but Shark's overreaching passion remained a variety of nubile young women. He stretched out on the bed beside Vikki, but even her stunning figure couldn't prevent his mind from looping back to Ryan Moar.

From what he had discovered of Moar's background, he was a skilled private investigator, who had once worked for the CIA. The thought of Rasul's failure to eliminate Moar in Zanzibar filled him with rage. He had him a prisoner. How could he let him escape? Then he thought about how the attempt by Pat's hired assassin to kill the private investigator beside the Grand Canal went pear-shaped.

What if Moar managed to get his files into the hands of Interpol? The outcome could be catastrophic. What if Talleyrand failed to eliminate Moar? He didn't even want to contemplate the worst case scenario of the contents of his files becoming media fodder. He stared at the erotic fresco on the ceiling of cavorting gods and goddesses of Greek mythology before his gaze returned to Vikki's dark eyes fixed on him.

"Where did you go, lover?" she said, cupping his face in her hands. "For a moment, I thought you'd gone to some other place."

Shark's cell phone chimed and he answer it. Pat was on the line.

"We have him cornered," he said. "Talleyrand's tracking device attached to his new rental led him right to the Quinn estate."

CHAPTER 37

TALLEYRAND CRAWLED ONTO THE BLUFF overlooking Caviston Court to take a look at the layout of the grounds and the main house. The mansion's stout oak double doors faced well-cut lawns, a sprinkle of birch trees, and a gravel drive leading to the main gate. The back door looked out at a garden of wildflowers and bean rows. Set in a horseshoe of higher ground, the house looked as though it was nestled in the center of two cupped hands.

Talleyrand decided to use the stables as a base of operations even though he noted that the stalls were about 50 yards from the main house. Apart from a few shrubs in between, there wasn't much cover. The only other structures were a toolshed at one corner of the vegetable patch and a redbrick guest cottage beside a duck pond. Talleyrand shivered in his tight-fitting black tracksuit. He blew on his thin gloves and wrapped his hands around his chest in an attempt to keep warm in the cool evening air.

While he waited for the sun to set, he spotted a stout man with a shotgun resting on his shoulder striding across the lawn. He headed toward the copse of pines where Talleyrand hid. The man wore a tweed cap, raincoat, rubber boots, and he held a dog in check. The border collie's mouth was open, a tongue lolling over its lips as it strained on the leash.

Talleyrand backed away from the edge of the wood and knelt behind the trunk of a pine tree. He removed the Beretta Cx4 Storm semiautomatic combine from his combat gun case. He checked to make sure that the magazine was loaded. The dog's ears picked up at the slight noise of snapping dry pine needles and twigs made by Talleyrand's knees on the forest floor. The dog barked and dragged the man closer to the trees. The dog leapt on his hind legs and twisted his head in a frantic bid to break loose, his breath coalescing white clouds in the cool air.

Talleyrand heard the man trying to calm the black-and-white by telling the dog not to be distracted by what was probably a rabbit. The assassin braced his elbow against the tree trunk and aimed at the man, who had looped the leash on his wrist and leveled the shotgun's barrel in Talleyrand's direction.

Talleyrand realized the dog's barking would attract attention of those in the main house. He had better end it now or he would lose the element of surprise. He fired a burst of bullets into the base of the man's throat. His hands flew to the wound as blood gushed from his shattered arteries. He let go of the dog's leash. The collie raced toward the assassin, lips stretched back in an attack snarl. Talleyrand fired at the dog's chest and skull. When the bullets hit, the black-and-white gave a muted yelp before collapsing in the tall grass.

Despite massive wounds to his throat, the man somehow managed to crawl to his shotgun and pull the trigger. The pellets splintered pine needles that showered down on Talleyrand's head. The assassin cursed for not making a clean kill.

He crept up on the fallen man and fired into his back. The man lay sprawled out, a series of bullet holes stitched into his raincoat. In the grass, the dog's back leg twitched, lips bunched up into a snarl. He aimed his weapon at the dog's silky furred head, but didn't pull the trigger. Even though the silencer dampened the sound of firing to a dull thud, he decided not to risk attracting any further attention.

As the last light began to shrink in the west, Talleyrand crept along the edge of the property. He kept close to the ring of pines until he reached the open ground surrounding the stables. When the sunlight faded, lights went on in the main house. It started to drizzle, and Talleyrand used the light rain and the gathering darkness as cover. He streak across the open area between the pines and the stables.

After shaking the rain off his waterproof tracksuit, he scanned the stalls, empty except two horses at the far end, where a draught mare and a gelding were chewing on pieces of straw. From the window, he had a clear view of the east side of the house, but what he saw disturbed him.

Tucked in beside a hedge, Talleyrand spotted the outline of a sedan. Using night vision goggles, he brought the vehicle into sharp focus. The car was a BMW. He could make out the outline of a man seated on the driver's side. He was sure that he wasn't garda, as the police didn't drive expensive cars. He determined that he must be either private security or G2. Rainwater streaked the BMW's windows, making it hard for the occupant to see out and easier for Talleyrand to kill him if he came at him from the rear.

Later that night, the chauffeured bulletproof Range Rover bearing Shark returned to the Clarence Hotel, owned by the singer and musician Bono. Shark wanted to forget a tedious, frustrating evening, much of it spent coordinating the search to track down Ryan Moar. He was beginning to tire of Dublin. A few years ago, the city was listed as the fifth richest in the world, a global financial hub. Crushed by the recession, the once highflyer had slipped into a backwater. He couldn't avoid seeing closed stores, workers on strike, dole queues, and placard waving protest marchers outside the banks and government buildings. Despite the setbacks, Dublin still maintained its magical charm. Pubs overflowed with laughter, modern buildings were sandwiched in between Georgian townhouses, and the roar of motorcycles mingled with the sound of cheerful chatter on the sidewalks, competing with the squawk of ravens.

Shark took the private elevator to his penthouse. On the way up, his mind settled on leaving the damp, crippled city and returning to the Mediterranean. Splashed in warm sunshine, *Sundancer* awaited him, berthed at the Old Harbor of Saint-Tropez. The elevator stopped on the sixth floor. Shark stepped out and went through his penthouse's hall furnished by a pair of Louis XIV Aubusson tapestry upholstered chairs. In the library, he poured himself a large glass of Bushmills whiskey. Sipping his drink, he went into the bedroom.

Floor-to-ceiling silk draperies blocked one the best views of the river, but Shark didn't care, as long as he was protected from snipers. The adjoining bathroom door opened, and Vikki came out naked except for a towel she was using to dry her short-cropped black hair, damp from the shower.

"Sugar, you look tired," she said, discarding the towel and getting into bed. "Come and join me."

Shark tossed his dark blue Savile Row suit and his striped raspberry shirt on the carpet. He stretched beside her on the bed in his underwear. Vikki sat up, propped her head on her elbow, and with her other hand, stroked his pockmarked face that had the texture of an avocado's skin.

"Hello, baby, tell me about your day," she said, massaging his forehead to stretch out the furrows.

"Pat's underestimated the man I'm after, and he's made a fatal mistake. He lost him. But the good news is, a more reliable man will soon have him in his sights." Shark took another pull at the whiskey glass he had set on a bedside table. When he settled again beside her, Vikki ran her fingers through the shag rug tufts of hair on Shark's chest.

"Pete thinks he's so superior to me," she said. "He looks down on me as though I'm dirt."

"Next time I talk to him, I'll tell him to treat you like a queen," he said, gazing up at the painting of Leda being raped by a swan on the high ceiling, while still thinking about leaving Dublin, a city that had been the scene of some of his greatest financial coups. In the early nineties, Shark and his colleagues had invested nearly a billion euros in the country's property and financial markets. Without fanfare, a few months prior to the market meltdown, he and his associates sold their real estate holdings and bank stock. These withdrawals helped accelerated the country's economic decline. While markets tumble on his BlackBerry, Shark had leaned back in any easy chair on the deck of his yacht under an azure Mediterranean sky.

This economic coup was now overshadowed by his inability to eradicate Ryan Moar that even one of Europe's most talented assassins had failed to meet his deadline. Had Talleyrand lost his edge? Was it time to bring in additional support?

In the halls and offices of Leinster House, the gray stone Georgian National Parliament Building, Shark's lobbyists had bribed MPs to ensure favorable legislation that would benefit his forays into real estate and banking. He had spent millions of euros around Leinster House. At one time, half the senators owed him favors. In case Moar's death resulted in an international inquiry, he might need to apply pressure on these politicians.

When he thought about Aisling Quinn somehow managing to hack into his impenetrable laptop, it made him queasy. He didn't want to throw up the superb veal and Pétrus red wine that he had enjoyed at Lillie's Bordello, at a dinner where he had invited a few of his closest political friends. They appeared frightened by the country's economic collapse and feared a backlash from the electorate.

"You're so restless," Vikki said.

Shark turned his face away from her. "I'm planning to leave Dublin soon for the Med."

"Will you take me to Saint-Tropez?" Vikki whispered, attempting to kiss unresponsive lips.

"Don't pester me," he said, leaning against the quilted headboard.

"I'll do anything you want if you take me on the yacht, honey. Of course, you know that."

He took in a deep breath and blew it out in a long, slow sigh. Thoughts of Moar continued to plague him. Vikki appeared to read his mind.

"It's this man you're trying to find that's bothering you, isn't it?" she said, making lazy circles with the flat of her hand around his belly button. "Has he found out about your game?"

"You've been eavesdropping."

"Do you mind?"

Shark took in her sensual curves. "He's only an annoying mosquito."

"I'm surprised Pat hasn't yet let you know he's dead," she said. "This mosquito is obviously still buzzing and has the ability to suck blood."

"I'm willing to bet, Vikki, that I will squash him tonight."

"How can you be sure?"

He shifted his position so he could see the flawless complexion of her brown face. "I have someone close to him who is tracking his movements."

He pulled her hand away from his groin and swung his feet on a Tabriz carpet. Heat began to race to his head.

"Let me give you a piece of advice, Vikki." He leaned back to tweak her cheek in a hard pinch. "Stop taking so much of an interest in my game, as you call it." He dug his nails into her flesh, and she tried to pull away from him. "Trust me when I say that finding out too much about what I do isn't exactly good for your health."

It was after midnight by the time Ryan parked the sedan in front of the Doric columns of the Quinn's family seat. Having switched rental cars, he climbed out of the Subaru. Aisling and Ciara hurried inside the mansion. Before joining them, Ryan headed across the

255

lawn to the BMW parked under an oak tree at the side of the house, facing the pond. The position gave the hired security man a view of the drive and anyone approaching the back and front doors.

When Ryan came near the car, the security specialist provided by G2 opened the window.

"Good evening, Mr. Moar," Damien McGuiness said.

Damien was over six feet tall and broad through the back and shoulders. He wore a leather jacket. When he grasped Ryan's hand, it felt has though it was chiseled from concrete.

"Any sign of the killer?" Ryan said.

"All is quiet," Damien said, cradling a revolver on his lap. "If he comes near the house, I'll shoot him."

"Be sure to recognize the bad guy."

"Men who are killers by trade recognize each other and often form an unbroken bond."

"Is that an Irish proverb?"

"Our proverbs are sacred. We Irish have a long history of knowing ways to kill our enemies by stealth and cunning."

"What if he sees you first?"

"The Irish believe our fate is written at birth."

"What would you say is my fate?"

Damien's dark eyes narrowed. "You are destined to be forever solving the problems of others."

"There are worse ways to make a living."

"Saint Patrick said that the good Lord helps those who help themselves."

"He's being charitable."

"Charity is for saints, priests, and idiots." Damien handed him a portable radio. "You can reach me on this."

"Thanks," Ryan said, pocketing the radio.

Damien glanced at the lights inside the house dim and switch off. He whispered, "It's best you go inside."

Ryan turned on a portable flashlight and headed up the stone stairs to the green doors. Ryan banged on the door until he heard bolts being drawn. The door opened a crack. Orla glared at him, her eyes blazing.

"Where's your bloody patience?" she blurted out. "You banged so loud you will wake the dead."

Orla tugged at the buttons of her smock. Ryan stepped around her and headed for the living room.

"Wipe the muck off yer boots," Olga called after him.

Faye Quinn paced in front of the fire, the living room drapes drawn. In the lights from the fireplace, her face was gaunter than Ryan remembered.

"If the phones weren't dead, I'd call garda and have you arrested." She smiled unpleasantly. "You can imagine how shocked I am when Ciara told me you're not Donald Mason. You are Ryan Moar, an American private investigator."

"I'm sorry I deceived you, Faye."

"You are nothing but a fake and phony."

Andrea enter the room holding a hurricane lamp.

"He needed a cover," Andrea said, standing beside Ryan.

"We need reinforcements," Ryan said.

"What are you talking about?" Faye demanded.

Ryan had left his phone at the escort agency, so he borrowed Andrea's phone to contact Sean, but he couldn't reach the G2 operative on her mobile.

"Where is Ciara?" he asked.

Andrea ran her fingers through her cropped hair. "She upstairs sleeping in my mother's bedroom."

"I need to talk to her."

"No you don't," Faye said. "The poor dear is exhausted and terrified. She told me how you abused her."

"He had a job to do," Andrea said.

"Don't try to defend him, Andrea. Why did you let him drag you into this quagmire?" Faye's eyes were fixed on her daughter, her back to the blazing fire. "Whatever you are doing, I want you to leave Ciara and my daughter out of it." Faye tugged on a strand of pearls. "You've involved them in enough danger." Her lower lip trembled. "Before I gave her a sleeping pill, Ciara talked about a shooting. I don't want to lose my other daughter as well."

"He's armed and here to protect you," Andrea said.

"May the good Lord save us," Faye said, wringing her hands.

"There is a security guard in a car outside." Ryan stepped forward. "I must talk to Ciara."

"I've a pistol upstairs and if you try to break into my room, I'll use it."

"When can I see her?"

"In the morning."

Faye poured herself a tumbler of whiskey from a bottle on a lamp table without offering them a drink. "I wish you had never come into my house, You've caused me nothing but grief and mayhem." She paused to take a sip of whiskey and wrinkled her nose, as if the smell made her nauseated. "I saw on the evening TV news a story about a rooftop shooting garda thinks is gang related. I presume it has your foul stench all over it."

"What else was in the TV news report?" Ryan asked.

"Garda is treating the shooting as an exchange between drug gangs. The police are searching for two young Irish women and a man believed to be an American. They were seen near the site of the shooting on the roof of a men's social club. Gard blame this violent crime on gangs of unemployed and recent arrivals from Eastern Europe." Faye picked up a rolled up newspaper and shook it in his face. "Are we to expect this kind of shocking carnage in my house, Ryan? Who was shooting at you?"

"Killers for hire."

"Have they followed you here?"

"I am expecting one killer; he prefers to work alone."

Faye held the tumbler up to the light from the chandelier. "Apart from you and this guard, all we have to protect us is my groundskeeper Hugh Beresford and James Joyce. And they are both missing."

CHAPTER 38

AFTER FAYE AND ANDREA WENT to bed, Ryan heard James Joyce whining and scratching outside the back door. He took the Magnum out of his belt and switched off the safety. He put the latch on the door, and through the crack, he scanned a low stone wall surrounding a vegetable patch. He opened it wide enough for the dog to limp inside. James Joyce's hind leg was bloody and a bullet had made a hole in his side.

After locking the door, he used the portable radio to contact Damien. "This is Ryan. Are you there, Damien?" he said. There was no reply.

The border collie allowed Ryan to carry him upstairs, and he eased James Joyce down in dog basket in the hall. The dog gazed at him with his sad eyes and then turned himself into a tight ball, burying his nose in his hindquarters.

He needed to call Sean's emergency number for reinforcements and contact the local police, but Andrea had taken her phone to her bedroom. He found her sitting beside a dying fire, her eyes half closed.

"I need your phone. James Joyce has been shot, but he's alive. This means the killer is outside and will attack the house anytime now."

She bolted upright in the chair, her sleepy eyes blazing.

"Give me your phone," he said.

She switched on a flashlight and searched the mantelpiece. Her face twisted in frustration. "Who snitched my phone?"

"Are there any other people inside this house apart from us, Ciara, Faye, and Orla?"

"No one else."

"You stay put, and I'll warn your mother and Ciara. I'll also alert Orla."

Ryan rapped on Faye's bedroom door. When she didn't answer, he opened the door. In the flashlight's beam, he saw Andrea's mother propped by pillows, a mask over her eyes. She was snoring, making a slight whistling sound like the wind that blows across the crags of a lonely moor. Ciara was sound asleep on a couch.

He stepped to the side of the bed and shook Faye's shoulders. She stared at him, her eyes glassed over from sleep. She swung her feet over the bed to the carpet. Her thin red face reminded Ryan of a well wrinkled pixie. Under her pajamas, her physique was hard and lean; the skin on her bare legs and arms were stretched tight over the bones.

"The killer is here," Ryan said. "We need to prepare for an attack. Your dog is wounded."

"The blessed saints save us."

She thrust her feet into a pair of slippers and went into the hall. She called the dog's name. The black-and-white gave strangled yelps when he heard her voice.

"I'll attend to his wounds," Faye said.

"Be quick about it."

"If James Joyce has been hit, does this mean Hugh is in trouble?"

"Afraid so."

"Where's your security guard?"

"I called him on the portable radio; he's not picking up."

Her hands flew to her face. "What are we going to do?"

"Barricade yourselves and the others inside your bedroom. Pile as much furniture as you can in front of the door."

"How can you protect us?"

"I will fend him off from coming upstairs with my semiautomatic." He showed her the Magnum. "Where is Orla's room?"

"Third floor, second door to your right."

Ryan raced up to the third floor. On the landing, he knocked on the maid's door. "Orla, are you there? Wake up."

There was no reply. The door was locked, so he kicked it open. Inside the tiny bedroom, not much bigger than a broom closet, Orla's bed was made and her night clothes folded on a chair. Where had Orla gone and why wasn't she in bed? Could she have taken Andrea's phone to prevent them from calling for help?

He ran down to the second floor.

"Where's Orla?" Faye asked, applying a bandage to James Joyce's wounded side.

"She isn't in her room," he said. "I suspect her disappearance has something to do with Andrea's missing cell phone."

Faye stared at him, disbelief flooding her smooth face. "You really think my maid would steal it?"

"Orla is also a likely candidate to have told the killer of our presence at Caviston Court."

Ryan heard James Joyce's low growl. He again checked the Magnum's magazine to make sure it was loaded. "He is here."

Faye clutched at her heart. "The killer?"

Ryan nodded. "Roundup Andrea and Ciara. Then start piling furniture against your bedroom door."

"I have an antique revolver."

"Keep it primed in case you have to use it."

"What do you think happened to Hugh?" she said, pulling on slacks and a blouse over her pajamas.

"He's more than likely met the same fate as the security guard."

She squeezed her eyes shut for a moment. "You mean dead."

He nodded. She headed to the bathroom, where he could hear her retch.

"Without the landlines and Andrea's cell phone, we're cut off, on our own," he said.

Ryan heard the dog's growl grow in intensity.

"James Joyce is telling us he is coming," he said.

Talleyrand preferred to work alone, but as events at Caviston Court unfolded, the assignment had become more complicated. He was creating way more collateral damage than he had anticipated. He wondered if he should call in reinforcements, but he decided against contacting Pat Rafferty. Shark's right hand man had hinted that after he killed Moar and recovered the files, to expect a large bonus, which he didn't want to split.

He knew that the element of surprise was his best weapon. He never expected to run into the groundskeeper armed with a shotgun, or to find the security guard. He had easily killed the man in the BMW by creeping up behind the car and killing him with a bullet fired through the rear window.

By having Orla disable the only cell phone in the house and by cutting both phone and power lines, there was no way now for Moar or the women to contact the local garda. From behind the low wall surrounding the vegetable plot, he crept to the back door and crouched down to work his lock pick inside the keyhole. In two minutes, the lock mechanism snapped and he eased the door open.

As soon as Talleyrand crept inside, he took cover behind the kitchen's central island. Above him, a floorboard creaked. Somewhere on the second floor, he heard a throaty growl full of menace. Talleyrand gritted his teeth and swore without making a sound. The dog had ruined the element of surprise. Why hadn't he snuffed out the collie when he had the chance? As soon as Moar and the women were taken care of, he wouldn't hesitate to shoot the dog.

CHAPTER 39

FROM THE LANDING, RYAN COULD hear the soft pad of footsteps below. He knew the assassin would soon realize they were upstairs and prepared for him. To outsmart him, Ryan would have to come up with a plan. A key advantage he had over the killer was that he knew the layout of the house, while the assassin operated in unknown territory. When he heard the killer move to the bottom of the stairs, Ryan tensed and leveled the semiautomatic at the winding staircase. Looking up, he saw a skylight that let in light from thin clouds crossing in front of the moon.

"Moar, listen to me very carefully," a voice called out. "Your pissy peashooter is no match for my high-tech arsenal. I know Faye Quinn, Andrea Quinn, and Ciara Redstone are upstairs with you. If you come down with your hand above your head, no harm will come to any of you. But if I have to hunt you down like a fox trapped in a hole, I swear I'll kill yer all."

Ryan remained silent, listening to James Joyce grow. He heard trainers advance on the stairs.

The best thing to do, he thought, is try to keep him talking.

"I hear you, Talleyrand," he said.

"How did you know my name?"

"You're a worldwide celebrity from Zanzibar to Dublin."

"You escaped from me once, Moar, but you'll never do that again. There are no fire escapes or rooftop exits in this house. Don't even think of jumping out of the upstairs window, unless you want to break your legs. If you persist on being pigheaded, I have no qualms about killing you and the women."

The upstairs hall turned bone chilling cold, and he heard faint footfalls behind him. Ryan spun around and aimed the Magnum at a figure looming at him out of the dark. In the dim light of his pencil flashlight, he recognized Andrea brandishing a golf iron aimed at his head.

"What the hell are you doing?" he said, his hand shaking at the thought that he could have shot her. "Never creep up on me again."

"Sorry if I startled you, but I thought you might need reinforcements," Andrea said, lowering the golf club.

"Why aren't you in your mother's bedroom?"

"I wanted so desperately to help you," she whispered.

"Go back and lock the door. We're about to be rudely interrupted."

When she closed the bedroom door, Ryan wondered why Andrea had appeared behind him as if she wanted to use a number five iron to knock him out. Was she planning something sinister? He didn't have time to sort out that question.

The assassin began mounting the stairs again.

"Stay where you are," Ryan said, fingers tightening on the trigger.

"You've been a busy bastard between the sheets here and in the States." He laughed. "Thanks to your cell phone, it's been easy to trace Joanne to Fargo. Unless you want her and the baby harmed, give up now."

"Did you say baby?"

"Yeah, Joanne gave birth to a boy."

The news of his son's birth made him want to dance a jig on the landing, but the threat to Joanne and the baby caused his sudden burst of pride and pleasure to be replaced by rage, rising in his throat with the force of a riptide. He knew that if he allowed the killer to inflame his emotions, he would think irrationally and make mistakes.

How could he have been so careless as to leave his cell phone behind in his rush to exit the Cleggan? He had put the lives of the ones he loved in terrible danger. As long as he held the high ground, the assassin was vulnerable, but for how long? The Magnum was no match for the killer's arsenal of automatic weapons.

"As you pointed out, I am used to operating internationally. I have a roster of successful hits in America. It will be easy for me to waste your woman and her newborn brat," the assassin said.

"You bastard," Ryan said. "If you touch them, I swear I'll track you down and kill you."

Talleyrand laughed, a raspy sound like a dry desert wind blowing sand over the worn surface of an ancient tomb.

"Tough words, but killing is something I am awfully good at," he said. "It's the way I make my living."

"Does Shark pay you by the body count, or does your fee only cover my termination?"

"Come on, Moar, we're wasting time."

"Is collateral damage a nonmonetary bonus to satisfy your fucking lust for blood?"

"Give yourself up and the women upstairs and your woman and child live."

"I don't trust you."

"It's your choice."

Ryan recalled what Sean had told him about Pete Talleyrand's family.

"If anything happens to me, how do you know that I haven't hired a hit man to eliminate Esther and your six beautiful daughters?" Ryan said.

The killer was quiet for a moment. Ryan listened to the night sounds, a loose shutter banging in the wind and furniture being moved in Faye's bedroom.

"It will be easy to wipe out your family now that you've cut back on your guard detail at home to reduce expenses," Ryan said, his voice becoming almost seductive. "I know you're hurting financially. Your Lear at Dublin International is for sale. You're having a hard time finding a buyer. I bet the demand for your services is way down."

Ryan waited to Talleyrand's next move. He listened to the *tick-tock* of the grandfather clock at the end of the corridor and the muffled ping of raindrops landing on the domed skylight.

"Come on up, I'd like nothing better than a square fight." Ryan tensed as he listened to the creak of the assassin's footsteps on the stairs. "How do you know there isn't a well armed security guard detail upstairs with a lot more firepower than you have?"

"You're bluffing, Moar."

"They are standing right here on the landing, and they can't wait to take a shot at you, particularly after you wasted one of their own."

"You're so full of shit, Moar, you're choking on your dung," he said. "If there was someone else up there, Orla would've told me."

"So you roped another innocent victim into your infernal web."

Ryan heard the scraping of furniture coming from Faye's bedroom. Ryan knew he couldn't hold Talleyrand off much longer. He hoped the women were putting his escape plan into effect.

"You and the women are on your own, trapped like stinking sewer rats," the assassin said.

Ryan exhaled heavily. "How did you persuade Orla to inform you of our movements?"

He heard footsteps once more ascending the staircase.

"You and the three bitches will never get out of here alive," Talleyrand shouted.

CHAPTER 40

WHEN TALLEYRAND REACHED THE EMPTY landing, he saw a slight movement in the light of the narrow beam of his flashlight. He fired several rounds, smashing the pendulum of the grandfather clock. He flung open the nearest bedroom door and the dull thump of his silenced weapon fired into the darkness. Window glass shattered and wooden paneling splintered. He opened the next door, and he sprayed bullets that stitched a row of holes in a four-poster and shattered a table lamp. He ejected the empty cartridge and rammed a new one in place.

He seized the handle of the third bedroom and found it locked. He fired several rounds into the lock. At first, he couldn't push the heavy pieces of furniture away from the door. While Talleyrand put his shoulder to the door, Moar's question, harsh and metallic, ran through his head liked a looped announcement at an airport. How do you know I won't play your game and hire a hit man to eliminate Esther and your six daughters?

How did Moar find out about his family? Their very existence was kept so secret that only a handful of people knew where he lived. How did the private investigator know not only about Esther and his daughters, but also his cutbacks in home security.

The background provided him by Pat Rafferty on Moar was sketchy, but he made the point that the PI was searching for sensitive information that could jeopardize Shark's operations. The report mentioned that Moar had contacts within the Irish Intelligence Service. G2 had to be aware of his existence. Pat's information sheet also mentioned Moar had been beaten up by Shark's African guards. Yet, despite severe injuries, he had escaped from one of Rafferty's most experienced executioners, a former IRA hit man.

Talleyrand pushed on the door until he heard a creak as the barrier shifted. He sprayed rounds through the crack into the bedroom door and crouched down, expecting a return of fire. Instead, the room remained quiet. Where was Moar? He took a run at the door, using his body as a battering ram. When the bookcase and chiffonier crashed to the floor, he peered into the bedroom, the flashlight picking up details of a four-poster bed, a vanity, and a bullet-smashed mirror. The room was empty. He made a quick search of the closets and under the bed. At the windowsill, he discovered the sheets tied together into a rope leading to the lawn below.

Talleyrand cursed for being fooled by one of the oldest and simplest escape tricks. He climbed over the windowsill and slid down the sheet rope. As he streaked across the rain soaked lawn, he tripped over stones in a rock garden. He felt sharp pain shoot up his left leg from a twisted ankle. He limped forward and paused to fire at distant shadows of Ryan and the three women, running for the line of pines.

Ryan plunged for cover among the trees when he heard Faye cry out as her foot tripped on Hugh Beresford's body. Andrea helped her mother to her feet and they stumbled for protection behind the pines. On the other side of the trees, Ryan saw a group of farm buildings. He turned to Andrea.

"I'll keep him occupied while you run to the neighbor's house," he said. "Wake the occupants and call garda."

Faye bent over, her breathing labored.

Ryan turned to Ciara. "Where did you hide the laptop?"

"In the stables, behind some loose bricks in the tack room wall," Ciara said.

Ryan glanced back at the pines, expecting to see the killer burst through the underbrush. Andrea wrapped her arm around her mother's shoulder, while Ciara ran toward the farmhouse.

"I can't hold him for long." Ryan paused for breath. "If I don't make it, Andrea, make sure you give the laptop to G2."

Andrea stretched on her toes to give him a quick kiss on the stubble of his cheek. "Good hunting," she whispered.

Ryan took cover behind trees and waited. Lights from nearby Monkstown reflected off dark clouds that had blotted out the stars.

Although hard to spot, he saw an outline of Talleyrand, limping across the clearing. Before he reached the edge of the trees, Ryan aimed and fired. The assassin crouched and pivoted in the direction of Ryan's fire. Ryan fired several times, but his shots sailed over his head. Talleyrand fired back in the direction of Ryan's muzzle flashes. A shower of bark rained down on Ryan as bullets gouged chunks out of the tree trunk.

It started to drizzle, and a few water drops trickled down Ryan's face. Tree branches twisted in the wind, reminding him of the flap of eagle wings.

Keeping his gun leveled, Ryan waited for the killer's next move. He glanced back at the farm house and spotted lights going on, so he knew the women were safe inside. Ryan's fire kept Talleyrand pinned down, but he was almost out of ammunition. He knew he would be dead if he didn't keep firing. Having only one bullet left, he waited for the end. Then the wail of sirens gave him a jolt of adrenalin. Ryan gauged by the sound that garda had reached Caviston Court's front gate.

"Drop your weapon. It's over," Ryan yelled, before diving behind some underbrush. The assassin's trainers crunched wet twigs about fifty feet from where he hid. Ryan saw muzzle flashes as bullets whizzed over his head. He spotted a slight movement among the trees and fired back. He heard Talleyrand cry out.

Sirens screamed louder and garda flashlights like laser beams probed the open area between the house and the pines.

"You're boxed in. The police are at your back, and you won't get past me," Ryan said.

"I can never be cornered," he said in a weakened voice.

"You're wounded. I'd say the game's over."

"Hell no. In this game, the king has one last move."

Ryan heard burst of gunfire as the killer sprayed bullets at the oncoming garda crossing the open area.

A police officer screamed in pain.

A man's voice shouted, "Over here. On the double."

A stiff wind drove rain across the field, as the police officers took cover in the tall grass and crawled to assist the wounded officer.

Dawn was not far off. Ryan heard Talleyrand scramble through bushes in a bid to escape. In the faint light, he could see him trying to reach the road behind the pines. He had discarded the combine. Before reaching the road, he stumbled and fell.

Ryan took his flashlight from his pocket and picked his way across the uneven ground. The flashlight's beam caught the figure of the tall man sprawled in the mud. His right hand hung loose by his side, oozing blood. The beam played back and forth for a few seconds before finding his face. He was at least forty, and his smooth features were twisted in pain. He recognized Pete Talleyrand's cold, penetrating eyes from the photo Sean had sent him.

He nudged the toe of his shoe into Talleyrand's side and he groaned.

"How does it feel to be on the receiving end?" he asked.

Talleyrand squinted up at him. "I warned Shark that you were a tough customer, but he thought you amounted to nothing."

"Nothing?" Ryan answered.

"I made it clear to Shark that you were a stubborn bastard. After you survived his torture squad, you would come back to haunt him."

"I'll not only haunt him, but I'll also see that scumbag locked up for the rest of his miserable life."

"Don't write him off yet."

"Once Interpol has his files, there's no court on earth that won't convict him."

Talleyrand laughed. "Don't be so sure, my man. As I said before, the black Irish king always finds a way to make the last move, but in this case it's the queen."

Ryan could hear the squish of footfalls behind him.

"Checkmate," Ryan said, dropping his gun and raising his hands above his head.

For an instant, a police flashlight shone on Talleyrand's rain-streaked face, and his uninjured hand protected his eyes from the fierce light.

"Hands above your head, or we shoot!" a voice yelled.

Three men wearing black waterproof jackets with garda printed on the back pointed firearms at Talleyrand's head. One of them searched his body and disarmed him of a tiny revolver attached to his leg, while the other two hoisted him on his feet. They hauled him toward revolving blue-and-white lights on cruisers parked on the drive.

A police officer called out. He had found Hugh Beresford. Two men with a stretcher removed the groundskeeper's body. A few minutes later, a policewoman found Orla, facedown in the pond. After police officers questioned Ryan, they released him. He jogged across the sodden field to the neighbor's farm house, where warm yellow lights were on and the first sign of dawn light reflected off ivy-covered walls.

CHAPTER 41

A FTER A POLICEWOMAN TOOK THEIR statements and then left, it was quiet in the dining room at Caviston Court. A blazing fire warmed the chill in the room. Ryan and Andrea flanked Ciara, seated at the head of the dining room table engrossed in the laptop's screen.

Faye carried in a coffee pot and a plate of warm scones.

"Are you having any luck, dear?" she asked, placing the tray on the table.

"I'm having a hard time remembering the password," Ciara said.

"Mommy, don't worry, G2's computer geeks will crack it in no time," Andrea said.

Faye looked puzzled. "That is so sweet of you, Andrea. You've never called me mommy for ages."

Andrea smiled at her mother and went to the fireplace to pile on more logs.

"Please, Andrea, enough." Ciara eyes were glued to the computer screen. "My back's roasting."

Andrea ignored her and jabbed a poker in the hot embers to stoke logs, resting on massive twin andirons.

Faye yawned. "Now if you'll excuse me, I'm going to go upstairs, take a pill, lie down, and have a long, peaceful, and uninterrupted sleep."

"You've earned it, Faye," Ryan said.

"Sweet dreams," Andrea said as her mother left the room.

Ryan removed his jacket and tugged at his shirt collar, shifting his position away from the heat of the roaring fire. The room was quiet except for a bluebottle fly bouncing off the window's mullioned glass. Beyond the window, the Wicklow Range was shrouded in mist.

To pass the time before Sean arrived for the laptop, Ryan and Ciara continued to try a long list of words and combinations of words to find the laptop's password.

"Try Cavistoncourt, but capitalize the second 'C' this time," Ryan suggested.

Ciara tensed as her fingers raced across the keys. Harp strings sounded in a short symphony of welcome. Her eyes widened as she opened a file and a series of flowcharts appeared on the screen.

Ciara opened another file. Ryan read memos from Shark to his business partners. The messages contained a tantalizing glimpse into how Shark ran his criminal empire.

"We've hit the jackpot," Ryan said, squeezing Ciara's shoulder.

He skimmed the data as she scrolled the contents of another file. The operational details of the Club spilled out on the screen; company profiles, membership rolls, and names of front organizations in North America.

"Good God, look at Silvara Enterprises, NYTBS, and Farogram Technologies. These legitimate corporations are members of the Club." He let out a long burst of air. He glanced at his watch. "Sean's helicopter should be here anytime now."

Andrea had left the room, so he turned to Ciara.

"Remember, no one talks to the media about what happened here," he said.

Ciara stood up and went to the credenza and poured coffee into a mug. "After last night, I could sleep for a month."

The room was quiet except for the roar of the fire and James Joyce's snores. Behind him, Ryan heard a mechanical click, the sound of a handgun safety being released. He spun around. Ciara dropped her coffee, and the Royal Doulton mug shattered on the parquet floor.

"It's not over," Andrea said, holding an automatic pointed at Ryan's chest.

She had removed the barrettes and gel from her exotic hairdo, allowing her hair to fall around her shoulders. She had wiped off her crimson lipstick and replaced her black stockings, ill-fitting miniskirt, and bulky sweater for a checkered shirt, jeans, and hiking boots.

"Put the gun down before anyone gets hurt," Ryan said, sweat building up on his forehead.

"Raise your hands above your head, Ryan, and then turn to face the wall," she said.

Ryan swore under his breath. Andrea's voice had changed to become a doppelgänger of Aisling's manner of speaking. He could feel the heat and moisture trapped between his palms.

"You're not Andrea, you're Aisling," he said.

"Yeah."

Aisling picked up an andiron beside the fireplace and hit Ryan on the back of the head, hard enough for him to see a burst of stars. He staggered and almost fell to the floor. She pulled out his Magnum from the back of his pants and tossed the handgun in the fire.

"I bet hitting me made you feel good," Ryan said.

"You don't know how easy it is going to be to terminate your life," Aisling said.

Ryan rested his palms on the uneven surface of the antique wallpaper. Aisling had somehow survived the plane crash and then changed places with her sister.

"Aisling?" Ciara gasped. "You died in the Air Tanzania crash. I attended your funeral."

"Make a move, and you're both dead," Aisling said.

"It's been a long night, and we're all tired," Ryan said. "Let's stop playing stupid games. Just tell us what you want . . . Aisling."

"Ciara, throw the laptop into the fire," she snapped. "Do it now."

"If you're Aisling, what did you do with your sister?" Ryan asked.

She laughed, a cruel sound without any trace of humor. "Wouldn't you like to know?"

"Let me guess," Ryan said. "After you managed to take a later flight to Dublin, you went to stay at your sister's place. You knew that if Shark found out you had survived, he would kill you. Is that why you assumed Andrea's identity down to every last detail, including her nose rings?"

"Right so far, Mr. PI."

"What did you do to get rid of Andrea?"

"I strangled her, locked her body in a trunk. I persuaded a homeless man to help me throw her into the bay."

Ryan reached for the bump on his head.

"You bitch," he said, feeling the sharp pain behind his ear.

"I had to assume her identity or die," Aisling said.

"Why do you do want to destroy the evidence that will bring this bastard to justice?" Ciara asked, clutching the laptop to her chest.

"I made a bargain with the devil," Aisling said.

"What did Shark offer you?" Ryan said.

"He'd transfer five million euros to my Caymans account."

"You're insane if you think you can trust him," Ryan said.

She flexed her mouth, as if to remove a piece of food in her gums. "I'm finished with Ireland."

They stood for a long moment and none of them spoke, like three figures beside an open grave.

Aisling tightened her grip on the handgun. "Ciara, throw the laptop into the fire or Ryan's head opens up like an overripe tomato."

Shark heard the news of Pete Talleyrand's capture from Pat Rafferty, who didn't have the backbone to deliver the bad news in person. His terse message left on Shark's answering machine made him livid. He was tempted to phone Pat back and fire him. He opened the heavy drapes a crack to stare out the window at the river dimpled by raindrops. The quays shone with rain and lights from the redbrick facades of the Georgian terraces.

When does the rain stop in this cursed country? Even a brief respite of sun between the heavy clouds could bring some relief to his dark mood.

If Talleyrand weren't so good at handling assassinations, Shark would be less inclined to regret his capture by the police. What could have gone sour? Talleyrand was one of the world's best, much in demand on every continent. It was the first time Talleyrand had botched a job for him. Shark also realized that he had always given the killer for hire work in other countries, rather than on his home turf.

Had this assignment in Ireland been his downfall?

In Talleyrand's words, his work was brutal, surgical, and effective. Shark felt his heart beat faster. He slammed his fist against his cupped hand. It was Ryan Moar's initial rescue of Aisling Quinn that had set this series of disasters in motion. Moar believed Aisling's story that she had hacked into his computer aboard the *Sundancer* and transmitted top secret files to Dublin. In the wrong hands, those files were lethal.

When he had pressed Lipumba for information on Moar, the staff sergeant described him as a bumbling, amateur sleuth. It was too late for Shark to realize that Moar was a seasoned private investigator, a former Fargo police officer and CIA operative.

Had the agency's training helped him survive the torture administered by his death squad? Moar had disarmed Pat Rafferty's top former IRA assassin. During an ambush near the PI's hotel, the American had injured the hit man so severely that he would never walk again without a cane. When Shark found out that he had contacted a G2 agent, he knew that it had been a serious miscalculation to mistake him for a lightweight.

What if his last hope to keep his files out of Interpol's hands failed? The consequences were too painful to contemplate.

For the time being, Shark needed to slip out of Dublin unnoticed.

He went into the bedroom where Vikki lay asleep; her impeccable complexion reminded him of an expensive chocolate bonbon nestled in delicate white lace paper. She stirred. He leaned over to kiss her cheek.

"What is it, lover?" she said in a husky voice, while she stretched her thin arms peppered with exquisite tattoos.

"Get dressed, Petal, we're leaving," Shark said.

"Where are we going?"

"Saint-Tropez."

"Oh, goodie."

She gazed up at him. Her love brimmed out of her eyes until she noticed the scowl on his unshaven face.

"Get dressed," he said in a low whisper. "Time to go."

"Are we taking the Lear?"

"Not on this trip."

She looked at him nonplussed. "What do I pack?"

"One small suitcase."

"The Pierre Cardin outfits you bought me in Paris will never fit—"

"We're travelling light," he interrupted, removing a Van Gogh of sunflowers to reveal a wall safe. He punched in a security code and the safe's door swung open.

"Hurry up," Shark said.

She was startled by the harshness of his voice.

"How will we travel to Saint-Tropez?" she asked, crossing her arms on top of her breasts.

"We'll take the ferry to Liverpool," he said, stuffing euros and American dollars from the safe into a briefcase.

CHAPTER 42

THE HEAT FROM THE FIRE had turned the dining room into a sauna. A sudden gale-force wind rattled the mullioned windows at Caviston Court.

"I'm saying this for the last time," Aisling snapped. "Ciara, throw the laptop into the fire."

Ciara stood at the fireplace, the glow of embers reflecting off the computer's underbelly.

"Do it now," Aisling said.

Ciara paused as she held the laptop over the hot coals. She turned her head away to avoid the heat.

"I hate you because you deceived me, your best friend," Ciara said, her face drenched in sweat.

"I had no choice," Aisling said.

The embers stirred and filled the room with a new blast of heat.

"Garda will be after you." Ciara inched closer to the fire. "Where will you go?"

"As soon as it's safe for me to leave, I'll go anywhere in the world I want." Aisling smiled at her. "Why don't you come with me? You can't imagine how warm the ocean is in St. Vincent at this time of year."

Ciara leaned forward and stared into the fire. "Are you making me a genuine offer, or is this another of your lies?"

"You might find this hard to believe, but I'm telling you the truth." Aisling's voice softened. "I've enough money to pay your family's debts. Instead of the demeaning life of a call girl, you and I will live in absolute luxury."

"Your offer does sound tempting," Ciara said, edging closer to the fire.

"Even if you destroy the evidence, Shark and his colleagues will now be under constant surveillance by Irish intelligence, not to mention Interpol and the CIA," Ryan said.

Ryan detected a slight movement behind him. Faye Quinn had entered the room in a nightgown. She pointed the dueling pistol at Aisling. Ciara held the laptop close to the flames.

"Ciara, for God's sake, don't," Faye said.

Aisling didn't look at her mother, but kept the semiautomatic trained on Ryan. Ciara pulled the laptop away from the fire.

"I don't think you'll use that ancient relic to shoot me," Aisling said, flicking her eyes toward her mother of a moment.

"I wouldn't be so sure about that, Aisling," Faye said, staring at her daughter as though regarding something rotten that James Joyce had dragged into the house. Her voice was choked with anguish. "Damn you, Aisling. I suspected something was wrong when you couldn't keep up that dreadful accent. Your voice began to slip back into your natural way of speaking. At first, I thought perhaps Andrea had reverted to how she spoke after finishing school, before she adopted that awful common way of talking."

Faye stepped closer and aimed the pistol at Aisling's chest.

"For God's sake, mommy, don't shoot," Aisling said. "You've never fired a gun in your life."

"You're wrong. Your father took me to his range and taught me how to use this thing."

"You're bluffing."

"Unless you put that gun down, I have no recourse but to shoot you." When Aisling made no move to lower the semiautomatic, Faye added, "After what you did to Andrea, I won't hesitate to kill you."

"If you pull the trigger that relic is likely to do you more harm than it could possibly do to me."

"Would you like to make a last confession?" Faye said, her lower lip quivering.

"You know I don't believe in all that mumbo jumbo." Aisling shifted her weight from one foot to the other. "Surely, you don't want to kill me."

Faye narrowed her eyes. "May the fires of hell consume your soul."

Faye pulled the trigger and the pistol enveloped her in black smoke. Aisling dropped the gun and staggered, clutching her stomach. Blood from her abdomen stained her blouse. She toppled against Ryan, who caught her and eased her to the carpet.

Faye wiped soot off her forehead and nose with the back of her hand.

"Oh, Mary, mother of God, what have I done?" she whispered, her lower jaw quivering. Still clutching the smoking pistol, she gathered the hem of her silk robe. Holding her head high, she swept out of the room like an actor's dramatic exit from the stage.

Ryan heard the distant thump of a helicopter.

Ryan read the *Irish Times* headline over breakfast at another safe house close to Trinity College. Much of the front page was devoted to Pete Talleyrand's arrest on three counts of murder. Talleyrand's victims included security guard Damien McGuiness, groundskeeper Hugh Beresford, and kitchen maid Orla Maloney. Also under investigation was the death of Aisling Quinn, the daughter of the estate's owner, Faye Quinn, whose husband, the late arms dealer Darragh Quinn, died under mysterious circumstances a year ago at the Dublin Airport. The story implied that an unnamed Irish investment dealer had hired Talleyrand to kill Ryan Moar, an American private investigator. Talleyrand's killing spree was described by a garda spokesperson as a massacre unprecedented in recent times. The news report concluded that the police were on the lookout for Pat Rafferty, a South Dublin businessman, believed to be the mastermind behind the shootings.

Inside the chauffeur driven Mercedes, Shark twisted on his middle finger a gold ring's enormous blood diamond from Sierra Leone, while he waited for the unexpected traffic tie-up to untangle. Beside him, Vikki craned her neck to see what was going on. Shark's hooded eyes widened when he heard the sharp wail of a police cruiser's siren. Through the tinted bulletproof window, he saw gendarmes climb out of police vehicles topped by pulsating blue lights. In front of his limousine, police officers swarmed over the line of vehicles to question occupants.

When the Mercedes started to inch forward through the narrow street of outdoor cafes, tacky tourist shops, and aged apartments, he caught a glimpse of *Sundancer* anchored in the Old Harbor of Saint-Tropez. Sunlight bathed the yacht's sleek lines in a golden light.

"That's her, isn't it?" Vikki whispered, her eyes sparkling.

A uniformed gendarme rapped hard on the driver's window, and the limousine pulled to a stop a block away from the harbor.

"Identifactions s'il vous plait," the police officer said.

Shark handed the false passports to the chauffeur, who gave them to the gendarme.

He ground his teeth in frustration as the policeman took his time to turn the pages. Then he stepped back to speak into a mobile phone. While Shark waited for someone to pick up the phone in a call to his Paris office, he speculated on how his life would have been if he hadn't hired Talleyrand to assassinate the professor and his two colleagues outside the pub in Stone Town. Shark stopped trying to reach Paris and placed his fingertips on his temples to try and ease the throbbing pain. Why had he been so stupid to recruit Jomo Willow and his mistress Audrey Brandt to manage his operations in Zanzibar? At first, the professor covered his tracks well, while he embezzled over two million dollars from Shark's businesses. It was only by chance, after Shark ordered an unexpected audit, that he uncovered Jomo's money skimming scheme.

The thieving bastard deserved to die.

On the surface, the unexpected arrival on the island of a private investigator from an obscure Midwestern city in the vast American heartland—hired by Jomo's widow to look into his death—didn't appear to be a threat. He had regarded Moar as a minor irritant, nothing more. But the PI's was determined to find the professor's killer. He never dreamed Moar would be just as determined to find the stolen files on the secret inner workings of his empire. As a resulted, the international police and security services had breached the protective walls he had taken decades to build. Interpol's systematic dragnet was sucking the lifeblood out of his world.

Shark glanced at Vikki, who adjusted the bow on her silk bodice. She had a vacant look on her face, as if she didn't realize that the gendarmes posed a threat to them. He closed his eyes and shouted in rage, a sound that bounced off the limousine's hand-tooled padded interior.

"What's got into you?" Vikki said, her hand tugging on the sleeve of his jacket.

"This place is swarming with cops," Shark bellowed.

"You told me we'd be safe in France."

Vikki narrowed her eyes to retain her tears. Shark stared at a thickset gendarme in front of the limousine. He stopped questioning the driver of a Porsche. He strode toward the Mercedes, a determined look on his narrow face. Shark made another phone call to the unlisted number of the Saint-Tropez police chief. After he listened to a busy signal, Shark threw the cell phone on the floor and stomped on it.

Through a gap in the buildings, Shark could make out his yacht's sleek bow in the crowded harbor. After rain clouds blocked out the sun, the yacht's glossy paint had turned a dull and gray.

So close, yet so far.

"We're in for a rough ride, petal," Shark said.

He leaned over and tried to kiss Vikki's cheek, but she winced, as if she thought he was going to hit her. She straightened up and pushed him away. He left her alone, and he could see in her eyes the disappointment of an unfulfilled dream to cruise aboard *Sundancer* on a moonlit ocean. She longed to smell the mingled scent of cloves and sea salt conveyed by a gentle tropical breeze.

Two weeks after Shark's arrest, Ryan dangled his feet in the Red River at the end of the dock, where the glare from the light on the water's surface made his eyes water. He held his infant son close to his bare chest. Beyond St. Olaf's church, the river was shrouded by a summer haze, a careless smudge hung above the fast flowing current. The sun felt hot on Ryan's skin, while whining mosquitoes swarmed above his head.

Ryan felt fit and relaxed, but drenched in sweat after a rigorous Krav Maga workout developed by his trainer, Daniel Strieber. Ryan had always wanted to master this elite brand of the Israeli Defense Forces hand-to-hand combat. During the hour-long training he did every week, he had gone beyond the basic fighting stances and moved to honing his punch and kick skills, using pads and bags. At the next training session, Daniel would begin to teach him direct strikes to vulnerable body parts: groin, throat, eyes, and knees. He wanted to be smart and strong to protect his family.

Gulls squawked overhead and clumps of reeds clung to the dock. Some nights, Ryan would dream of Talleyrand's rain-streaked baby face just before his capture by the Irish police. At other times, he would dream that Aisling shot her mother instead of the other way around.

Ryan swiped a mosquito zeroing in on Michael's cheek, and his son stirred in his sleep.

When he heard her cairn's bark, he turned away from the river and saw Joanne shading her eyes as she studied him from the edge of the rose garden. He thought about calling out to her, but there was something fragile in the air, almost like being in a bubble. He stood up without waking the baby. He stared at her profile, the swan neck, the powerful shoulders, and the way her hair moved in the slight breeze.

He felt a stir hold him spellbound. The feeling made his stomach flutter. He felt that their relationship was on the cusp of something richer and deeper. He had been in love before with Kathy, his true soul mate. But that was a long time ago. When Kathy was murdered, her death blew a cannonball-sized missile into his heart. For months, he never thought he would recover. He thought he might be destined to settle for second best or remain alone.

He thought about when he saw Joanne for the first time in Marsdon, and he recalled his immediate physical attraction to her, so powerful and all-consuming. At the sight of her face, his heart had done a wild dance, as if filled by the fluttering wings of sparrows.

"Hey there," he called out.

She turned a little, and he saw tears running down her cheeks, sparkling in the sunlight. She didn't wipe them away. He resisted a sudden urge to run toward her and gather her and the baby into his arms.

Ryan took a few tentative steps toward Joanne, while he held the sleeping baby close to him, his head on Ryan's shoulder, his tiny mouth open and twisted out of shape.

"I'm so sorry," Joanne said.

"You've nothing to be sorry about," he said.

His heart swelled when she faced him and gave him a great-to-be-alive-and-in-love smile.

THE END

FREEFALL

Michael D. Hartley

A Ryan Moar Mystery

Turn the page for a preview of *Freefall* the next
novel in the Ryan Moar Series . . .

CHAPTER 1

Berlin, November 11, 1943

H IGH EXPLOSIVES AND INCENDIARIES DROPPED from British
Lancaster bombers fell during the night on Potsdamerstrasse
not far from Karl Bremen's art deco row house. Karl ignored the
bombs even when the blasts made walls quake, window glass rattle,
and cracks zigzag across his molded ceiling. Even though cold night
air streamed through cracked windows, he neglected to stoke the
dying coal fire, his attention instead glued to three heavy carpet
bags beside his wing chair.

Karl's fingertips probed the nearest bag's coarse canvas fabric.
The rough edges felt like tiny stones. He wondered if these pebbles
could be ore samples. Before the war, His brother Waldheim
had often reminded Karl about how they could make a fortune
prospecting for nickel. He also suspected the contents of the carpet
bags were somehow connected to Waldheim's close ties to the
Gestapo hierarchy.

Karl turned off the Tiffany lamp and opened the blackout
curtains to gaze at the hostile glow of low-lying clouds, reflections

off raging fires in the city's southern sector. Slender needles of light from crisscrossing searchlights cut through the night sky.

Karl closed the curtains, turned the lamp back on, and he put rimless reading glasses on his youthful face. He grunted when he tried to pick up one of the scuffed bags by twin leather handles. Mining engineers before the German assault on Poland, Karl and Waldheim often planned to prospect for nickel, a scarce metal in high demand during wartime. As a military intelligence operative, Karl and his Abwehr colleagues had researched the availability of the strategic metal to meet the demands of German industry, in short supply until Finland fell into the Third Reich's orbit.

Karl rubbed his deep-set eyes as a feeling of desolation swept over him. Prior to his brother's departure for the Russian front, Waldheim had asked Karl to store the three bags in his safe. He worried about his brother's chances of surviving the war in the east. Following the surrender at Stalingrad, the Sixth Army had ceased to exist. Even massive reinforcements from the west failed to restore the balance of power in his country's favor.

He ran nicotine stained fingers through his premature gray hair. During the afternoon briefing, spies in England had reported seeing increased troops on the move to the southern counties. This could only mean invasion. He and his Abwehr colleagues had estimated Allied landings could take place in the next eight months and bring war to Germany's throat.

When the drone of bombers and the intermittent bursts of anti-aircraft fire died down, the sudden silence unnerved him and Karl's hands picked up an unexpected tremor. When he heard the all clear siren signal the end of the raid, Karl stood up and went to the wall to remove a full-length portrait of Adolf Hitler. Behind the Fuhrer's oil painting, he spun the dials of a massive wall safe's combination lock. The door swung open and he heaved the bags inside the steel lined safe.

On the mantelpiece, the Kieninger clock chimed two and Karl pulled the curtain open for one last look at the city. Apart from the fires, the blackout had left the capital in a darkness the city hadn't witnessed since the Middle Ages. Karl drained the dregs of a brandy snifter and tugged off his polished jackboots. In his bedroom, he hung up his captain's uniform and crawled under a four poster bed's quilt.

Before the sun brightened the city's smoldering ruins, he needed to squeeze in a few hours of sleep before rising early to say goodbye to Waldheim in the Tiergarten. As his bloodshot eyes closed, a sinking feeling clawed at his gut—this could be the last time to see his elder brother alive.

While Karl waited in the morning twilight for Waldheim, a biting Siberian wind cut through his military coat and a thick layer of smoke muddied the low fog hanging over the park, the city's lungs clogged by the acrid smell of war. Karl sat on a bench beside a ragged man digging potatoes out of a frozen flowerbed. In front of him, two Gestapo officers riding thoroughbreds galloped by a row of linden trees with charred upper branches.

Coming through the smoky fog, Karl recognized Waldheim's muscular shoulders and slight limp. He wore a major's uniform, an iron cross attached to his jacket pocket. Karl noticed his unshaven face's wartime pallor and hoarse breathing. Waldheim slouched down on the bench, while his gloved hands fiddled on the stem of a smoldering pipe.

"Good day, brother," Karl said, leaned forward on the one remain bench's back board.

"Not for me or the Fatherland," Waldheim said in a weary voice. "I'm barely walking and General Berger ordered me on tonight's troop train." His brother stared at scattered bomb craters, altering the Tiergarten's natural symmetry into grotesque and twisted shapes. "How's mother?"

"The air raids are drive her crazy."

Waldheim removed his cap to reveal his thick blond coppery hair. "Ship her to the country estate."

"She would rather die than leave the city."

"If she stays in Berlin, she'll be die sooner or later. If you think last night's bombing was bad, believe me, it will get far worse, spinning out of control until the whole city is reduced to rubble."

"You make it sound as though we are falling into abys."

"Under Hitler, we are spiraling ever faster into total ruin."

Karl glanced at his brother. "Be careful what you say."

Waldheim made a smacking sound as he sucked in on his pipe and blew out blue smoke. "It won't be long before you follow me east,"

Well aware of the horrors of the crumbling eastern front, Karl dreaded the thought of being transferred to face the Russian winter and the Soviet artillery's ferocious reputation of ripping bodies to shreds. Karl's attention was riveted to the two riders wearing black Waffen-SS uniforms and distinctive red swastika arm bands. When the officers trotted closer to avoid bomb craters, Karl recognized the younger man, a blond poster boy for the Third Reich. Two days ago, Abelard Freudenberg's sudden appearance in Karl's office rocked him on his heels, as if the major had slapped his cheeks. A month ago, Freudenberg had enticed Karl's wife Sonya to leave him.

"The Gestapo top brass will soon decide your sharp analytical mind is no longer needed and off you go to the Russian front," his brother continued, unaware of Karl's discomfort at seeing Sonya's seducer.

Waldheim looked up when Freudenberg's mount neighed and bucked when the major pulled tight on the reins and dug his spurs into the white's horse flank.

"Isn't that Major Freudenberg?" Waldheim said.

Karl tugged at his coat's lapel to shield his face from a gust of cold sting his aristocratic cheeks. He used the heel of his gloved hand to massage his forehead to relieve a familiar headache, the pain spreading from his sinuses to the back of his eyes. These headaches became more frequent ever since Sonya had left his bed to live in her SS lover's luxury flat.

"Have you met him?" Waldheim asked, trying to snag his brother's eyes.

Karl shook his head. "I haven't had the pleasure," he whispered.

They both looked up at the roar of Messerschmitt 109Es flying in formation in the direction of Tempelhof airport.

"What's in your bags?" Karl said, anxious to get off the topic of Major Freudenberg. "Ore samples, perhaps?"

"Still obsessed with nickel mining?"

"Yes, after the war, we could-"

"Talk about nickel," his brother interrupted, "what ever happened to your Abwehr's plan to cut off the flow of nickel to the Allies by sabotaging Canadian nickel mines?"

"The Fuhrer ordered the funds diverted to develop secret weapons."

"Oh, God, please don't tell me you believe in the myth that Hitler's secret rockets will somehow reverse the rot in our fortunes." Waldheim extinguished his pipe, narrowed his blue eyes, and hauled his muscular frame from the bench. He punched his brother's shoulder. "I want to pick up those bags immediately."

"What?" Karl glanced at his watch. "If we go home, I'll be late for the morning briefing."

"Don't be fool." His brother waved a cane in Karl's face, his eyes acquiring a glint of life. "Those ore samples are a means for us to escape this hell on earth."

Waldheim strode ahead of his brother on a gravel path leading to the ruined city.

When the brothers arrived at Karl's row house, he unlocked the front door and led the way up a winding staircase, leading to his third floor study, where the Fuehrer's painting dominated the book lined room. Dust from cracks in the ceiling covered Hitler's cheeks like layers of face powder. Karl removed the portrait and opened the safe. He reached inside and hauled out his brother's carpet bags. He staggered to carry the bags to the desk.

"Aren't you going to tell me what's inside, Wally?" Karl asked, using his nickname for his brother.

Waldheim ignored the question with one of his own, "Has anyone else seen them?"

"Anna helped me carry the bags up the stairs."

"I don't trust that woman."

"Why? Anna's a harmless housekeeper who has served our family since we were boys."

"The Gestapo recruit servants to report on officers who waiver in their support of the Reich."

"Anna would never betray us."

"What time does she get here?"

"Shortly after nine."

"Well, there's no time to waste."

He unlocked one of the bags and spilled a handful of small pieces on the desk.

"These ore samples as you call them are both our salvation and our curse," Waldheim said.

Karl stared at the gold fragments scattered on the desk blotter, his mouth hanging open. He drew a couple of deep breaths as he ran the tiny pieces through his fingers.

"Where in the name of God did you get these terrible things?" he stammered, his voice a hoarse whisper. Revulsion came and went in waves. "I want no part of this." His faced clouded. "These pieces look like gold teeth from the mouths of concentration camp corpses."

Karl was so shaken he sat down at his desk and stared in horror at the mound of gold, winking at him in a shaft of light. He took off his cap and used a handkerchief to blot sweat off the rim.

"What's the point in staying in Berlin?" Waldheim said. "I've heard gossip at the officer's club that Sonya has traded you in for a dashing SS major."

Humiliation burned Karl's cheeks. He was shocked his brother knew all along about Sonya leaving him. In the beginning, he had loved his wife, a pretty woman who adored French champagne and expensive jewelry.

"Believe me, you'll never get her back," Waldheim continued.

"I have a duty to remain in the city," Karl said. "My job is important to the Reich."

"You're deluding yourself if you think the admiral is going to survive much longer." Waldheim's voice seemed to originate from a well of night. "Any day now, you'll have a new boss, Heinrich Himmler."

Karl had heard the same rumor swirl along his office's corridors like the Black Death.

"You'll soon find out your friendship with Admiral Wilhelm Canaris makes you vulnerable in the next purge," Waldheim added.

His scenario had certain logic and a wave of pessimism swept over Karl, leaving him paralyzed by fear, as if icy hands were closing in around his heart.

"Under the new order, the only choice left for you is the eastern front," his brother said in a low voice. "Try to resist and Himmler's thugs will be all over your miserable hide and turn you into a vegetable."

The thought of being interrogated and tortured by Himmler's Schutzstaffel throbbed in his head, as though hot needles were already stabbing the sensitive flesh under his finger nails.

"Where are you taking the gold teeth?" Karl asked.

"To Zurich."

Karl stood up and put on his captain's cap. "How will you get out of Berlin to reach the Swiss border?"

"I have access to a high level staff car. I've forged papers to identify us as German businessmen travelling to Zurich on a special mission for the Reich."

"How did you know I'd come with you? Betray my country."

"Underneath your civil servant's polished veneer, you will always be a realist."

Karl's tried to sift through the consequences of Waldheim's plan and grasp the idea of what an escape all meant. Karl heard footsteps on the landing outside the door and then silence. He suspected Anna had arrived to clean and cook.

"You have to go, Anna's here."

Waldheim leaned on his cane, vaulted to the door and flung it open.

Karl's housekeeper Anna Kolb stepped into the shaft of light from the window, her beefy arms folded across her chest, her blue eyes burning suspicion. She glanced at the pile of gold.

"What are you doing, Herr Bremen?" she said to Karl through pursed lips. "Why aren't you at the office?"

Waldheim grabbed Anna from behind and twisted her arm.

"Let me go," she said through gritted teeth, trying to tug free from his grip.

When Waldheim twisted her arm further, he forced her head down, arching her back, Anna lashed out at him, kicking his ankles with the back of her brogues.

"For heaven's sake, let her go," Karl said.

"If she betrays us to the Gestapo, she'll ruin everything."

Waldheim released the pressure on her arm, so she could straighten.

"Anna, Waldheim is leaving us," Karl said, resting his hands on her shoulders.

"Filthy swine, you are both betraying the Fuhrer," she said, flexing her neck back so she could spit in Karl's face.

Karl stepped back and wiped her spit off his face.

"You will never get away with treason," Anna said, elbowing Waldheim's chest with her free hand. The jab caught Waldheim by surprise and Anna broke loose. She swung around and punched him in the face. Waldheim staggered to the wall, blood streaming from his nose. Anna turned to face Karl.

"I will report you traitors to the Gestapo," she said, picking up an andiron from the fireplace a swinging it at Karl.

He ducked, but the blow swept off his cap. Behind her, Waldheim gripped his Luger with both hands and fired three shots at close range into the back of her head. The bullets shattered the roof her skull. Karl stood too petrified to move, staring at blood forming beads on his shiny boots.

"Time to go, little brother," Waldheim said, using bloody fingers to sweep the gold teeth on the desk into the open bag.

CHAPTER TWO

Bremen Nickel Mine, Northern Manitoba, Canada

O N THE EVENING OF THE miner's funeral, the shadows of the stunted pines stretched long over the graves and a chill gripped the mourners grouped around mounds of new earth. While the cool glow of the sun faded toward cold and silence, the air became still, and an absolute pitiless hush fell upon the gathering. Ravens circled above the clearing, having flown in from feeding at a garbage dump. A layer of mist off the river clung to the graveyard and the sunlight's yellow glow stained the pines.

When a single-engine float plane droned overhead, Ryan Moar read the inscription Northwing Air painted in red italics on the Beaver's fuselage. The private investigator had flown north from Fargo, North Dakota, a prairie land basking in a balmy August sun to face chilly northern winds, sweeping unimpeded from the arctic. As Ryan drove the five miles from the mining town's core to the tiny cemetery, he had watched wind blow the last leaves from the short skinny birch and poplar trees in a battle of the seasons whose outcome was now without question.

At the end of the service, a stooped bald-headed priest in a white robe and Roman collar shook the hands of the men grouped around the grave. Ryan waited until the mourners drifted away before approaching a local reporter Joel Kinnerman, who sported a thick mop of brown hair that tumbled over his forehead.

CPSIA information can be obtained
at www.ICGtesting.com
Printed in the USA
LVOW03s2114180417
531289LV00001B/1/P

9 781524 591823